Coastal del Rey

Billie L. Stephens

Domhan Books

ISBN: 1-58345-915-4 hardcover
1-58345-916-2 paperback

Published by Domhan Books
9511 Shore Road, Suite 514
Brooklyn New York 11209
www.domhanbooks.com

Printed by Lightning Source
Distributed by Ingram Book Group

Contents

CHAPTER ONE

As the sun began to set behind the Coastal Del Rey mountain range, a rider could be seen silhouetted against the skyline. Spence could not tell whether the rider was approaching his camp, or riding back over the mountain. Being a cautious man, he moved out away from the fire he had built and squatted down behind some thick undergrowth and watched.

By now Spence could tell that the rider was coming down off the mountain and was riding directly toward his camp, the fire being the guiding light for the stranger. From a distance, he could see that the man was dressed all in rough black range clothing, and had his rifle lying across his legs. About three hundred yards from the camp, the rider cocked the rifle, loading a shell into the chamber.

Spence now wished that he had thought to bring his own rifle into the brush with him, but there it lay, right across his bedroll where he had put it when he first made camp. All he had with him was his twin Colt .45 caliber pistols. But he knew that as the rider approached the camp the pistols would be more accurate if it came to a gunfight.

Having just crossed the Coastal Del Rey Mountains himself, Spence did not have any idea why the rider would be so interested in his camp. Maybe there was another range war here, or some big, rich rancher figured all this open range belonged to him and he was trespassing. If a gunfight did not take place, and if he did not have to kill the approaching rider, maybe he would find out.

The rider was now only about one hundred yards away and Spence could tell that he was a rough looking man in his early thirties, with a five-day growth of beard. Spence figured that he was most likely a range rider for some ranch.

About that time the rider yelled out, "Hello, the camp." The rider stopped and was looking around like he didn't want to just ride in without a welcome. Spence debated whether to answer or not when the rider yelled out again, "Hello, the camp, I'm John Restless from the Triple Y ranch. I saw your fire and figured that a hot cup of coffee would really be good for a tired rider."

"Come on in then, rider. I was just putting on the pot," Spence replied, and stepped out from behind the brush.

John looked Spence up and down, decided that he liked what he saw and started his horse slowly toward the camp. Spence was watching Restless closely. If the rifle even started an upward motion, he was ready to pull his .45s. But the rider kept the rifle lowered and just had one hand on it to keep it steady as the horse walked in.

The rider pulled up just short of the camp, slid his rifle into the scabbard and tied his horse to the brush. Turning around he took off his hat and pounded some of the dust from his clothing before he started into the camp. Meanwhile Spence was filling the coffeepot with water, poured some coffee grounds into the water and set it on two rocks in the fire. He had never taken his eyes from the rider, and had watched him as he came on into the camp. Although the rider's clothes were rough and dirty, his pistol was well oiled and maintained. It looked like it was the rider's prize possession, as the horse and saddle were old and beaten up. The pistol was a Smith & Wesson Model No. 2 used by a lot of lawmen and some U.S. Army officers.

"How far is the Triple Y's main headquarters?" Spence asked. He didn't really want to know, but figured that it would be good to leanr how far he would have to ride to bypass the ranch.

"Just over three days ride due west from here. I didn't get your name by the way," the rider replied. Spence could tell that the rider was not entirely at ease and he had noticed that he had loosened his gun before he came into the camp.

"I guess I didn't say it," Spence answered. "They call me Spence. I didn't see any cattle out this way. Why are you riding a barren range?"

"Have to ride to mark the outer edges of the ranch or those dang sod busters will keep trying to homestead the place. We only use this range in the winter after the upper pastures get snowed under. You not trying to claim any land, are you?"

"Don't reckon so. In fact, I haven't seen anybody for over a week now," Spence stated. He thought to himself that all the land he had ridden across the last three days wasn't worth a plugged nickel, and any farmer in his right mind would have just kept on riding through here. It sure wasn't worth the effort to even unload a plow in this rough, dry, barren land.

The coffee had started to boil, and Spence reached into his saddle-bag and withdrew two tin cups. He filled one and handed it to John before filling other for himself. The rider smiled his appreciation and took a couple of short swallows of the hot coffee.

"I've got a range cabin about a good hour' ride on up the trail. Got some beefsteak and beans there if you want to ride on up. I ran out of coffee about three days ago and the re-supply wagon hasn't made its rounds yet. Been looking for it the past day or so. They try to feed us pretty good out here so a rider doesn't tend to wander off his post looking for food. The Colonel don't like you leaving your post until your relief rider shows up," the rider rambled. He seemed like he wanted the company more than the coffee, Spence thought.

"Been out here long?" Spence asked.

He had noticed that the scabbard the rider wore had a large U.S. stamped on it. His pistol belt and boots also looked like they had belonged to the US Army Cavalry, and the rider's short stubby spurs were definitely cavalry spurs.

"Bout three weeks this time. I should have been relieved this week, but haven't seen anyone yet. Maybe he will be with the sup-ply wagon when it comes. The Colonel is usually pretty good about making sure the relief is on time. Makes me wonder what's going on at headquarters," the rider replied.

"Who's this colonel you're talking about? You recently from the army, or just like the Army's leather goods?" Spence asked, as his curiosity had gotten the better of him.

"We all followed the Colonel when he left Fort Davis and came out this way. The Indian wars were over and the army was muster-ing us all out. Hell, there wasn't anything to do around there, so we all just followed the Colonel out here. As long as he pays us our wages we'll stay with him and the work ain't so hard," the rider stated as he reached over and filled his cup with more coffee.

That had not answered Spence's question, but he let it go for now. Having served in the cavalry during the war and fought along side Jeb Stuart, he knew how a bond could grow between good leaders and their men. He had been glad the fighting had ended, but he had been sad to leave the men he had lived with for over two years of hard times, rough rides and intense fighting. That group of soldiers was the only family he had ever really known, as he had been or-phaned when he was three and passed around kinfolk until he had run away from his uncle's farm in Tennessee.

"What are you doing out this way? We don't see many drifters coming across the mountains this time of year. Just seen a bunch of those damn sod busters and their children, chickens and livestock coming looking for the easy life. You ain't here for hiring that gun out, are you?" the rider asked as he stood up and placed his hand on his gun butt.

"Just relax there, partner," Spence said, "I'm just here because the pass through the mountain over there was easier than riding across over to Los Cruleto. I was figuring on getting a grub stake and looking around a little for some of that gold they say was found around there. Here, finish this coffee."

The rider squatted back down and was noticeably more relaxed. Spence poured the last of the coffee into the rider's cup and threw the coffee grounds back into the brush. He didn't figure that he would get a chance to use them in another pot of coffee.

"That offer for a beefsteak still hold?" Spence asked after a time.

The rider, surprised at the question, sputtered a little on the coffee and blurted, "Yea, if you don't mind my cooking." With that he took a big swig of the coffee and flick the rest back into a bush. "It'll take us a little while to get there, but it'll make the steak and beans taste that much better."

Spence began to pick up his bedding, and said over his shoulder to the rider "You can unload that shell in your rifle chamber now, I guess."

The rider once again looked surprised and pumped the shell out of his Winchester Model 1886 and put it back into the magazine. "Durn near forgot I'd loaded that when I rode up here," he said.

As he pulled the cartridge Spence noticed that the rifle was chambered for a .45-70 cartridge.

Mounting up they rode up the trail heading for the range cabin, speaking only when necessary. It was dark now and the moon had not risen yet. The stars were bright enough to silhouette the brush and the starlight reflecting on the snow helped keep them on the shallow trail that the rider had led them to. It took them about two hours to make the trip to the cabin, and the full moon had begun to rise over the mountains, making it almost as light as day. As they approached the cabin, the rider reined in quickly and motioned Spence to stay quiet. Spence could see three horses tethered close to the cabin. He figured that this was unexpected after what the rider had told him earlier. They dismounted and tied their horses to some undergrowth. The rider motioned to split up and approach the cabin from two angles.

Now Spence was uncertain as to what was expected of him since he didn't know a Triple Y rider from the typical outlaw in this part of the country. He figured to just sort of hold back and see what developed and to take his queue from the rider's action. He pulled each Colt .45 out and rotated the magazine one hole so the first trigger pull would fall on a live round.

John Restless was also unsure of what he would find. He didn't recognize any of the horses as belonging to riders from the Triple Y, but the Colonel was always hiring new riders. Except for the soldiers that had followed the Colonel out here, the others were just drifters. They would stay around long enough to get some hot meals under their belt, their clothes mended some and maybe their boots patched, then one morning they would be gone. Every time he made it back to headquarters there were always three or four new faces and a couple of the old ones would be gone.

As he eased up closer to the cabin, he pulled his pistol from his holster and cocked the trigger. He did not know what he would find, but he wanted to be prepared. As he got closer he could hear the men inside laughing and talking. It didn't sound like they were trying to hide in ambush for anyone, and he could smell meat cooking on the fireplace. It sure seems like they had made themselves at home. John motioned for Spence to come in closer to the door. He was going to stomp around and scrape his boots and see how the men inside reacted.

When Spence got up to the door John whispered to him to stay back a little so when the door was opened he wouldn't be in the light. Spence pulled both .45s and motioned that he was ready. John began to stomp and scrap on the doorsill. It got quiet inside the cabins and then a man yelled out, "That you John? Come on inside, I've got your relief riders here with me."

John smiled real big and told Spence, "Come on in, that is Hess Fester, the range boss."

He holstered his pistol and then opened the door and started inside the cabin. John was already tasting that slab of meat and beans with maybe some hard-tack biscuits. Spence continued to stand outside the light of the door, waiting to see exactly what was going down. Years of the unknown had made him a cautious man, and a friendly voice could not dispel years of experience.

About that time two shots rang out, and John Restless fell back outside the cabin. He didn't even have his gun pulled, and now had two holes in his chest. Spence jumped back a couple more steps from the light and waited.

A man stepped up to the door, looked around and said "Looks like he's by himself." He squatted down to get a closer look at the dead rider. Spence then saw the other man lower his guns. He didn't know what was going on but he did know that a friendly range rider had just been shot in cold blood. He raised both .45s and aimed one at each of the two men he could see. Pulling the triggers at the same time he watched both men fall with a hole through their hearts. Sometimes justice had to be quick out here where there wasn't any law.

"You, the other man. Throw your guns out the door or face the same fate as your partners did!" Spence shouted out. He could hear scraping on the floor and a man shouted, "I'm not armed. I'm tied up to a chair here. Those two hooligans ambushed me as I came up to the cabin."

"You'd better be tied so tight you can't squiggle or I'm going bust you good," Spence shouted back. He slowly approached the cabin to a crack in the logs and looked in. He couldn't see the whole room, but he could see a pair of legs tied to a chair. He moved closer to the door and cautiously looked into the room. There he could see the man tied securely to a chair and no one else. He holstered one gun and then pulled John into the cabin. There wasn't anything else he could do for the dead rider except give him a decent burial.

"Now who are you and why did you call this man in to his death?" Spence asked.

The other man looked at the dead rider mournfully and stated, "He was a good friend, soldier and rider. I rode with him for over four years now and goin' to miss him bad. Those two there had a gun to my head and said they was just goin' to tie him up like they did me. I sure didn't know they was goin' to kill him, mister."

"And who are you. Why did Restless trust you to put his gun away and walked into a couple of bullets?" Spence continued to question the man.

"I'm Hess Fester. I'm the range boss for the Triple Y. I came out here to pull John back to headquarters. The Colonel is needing as many men as possible right now, and we're pulling all the range riders back in."

Spence reached down and grabbed John Restless and pulled him back outside the cabin. He then dragged the other two men outside. No use smelling up a perfectly good cabin with the reek of death.

Anyway the cold night air and snow would help preserve the bodies until they could be buried. Spence then went and brought in the two horses, tying them to some brush opposite the side of the cabin from the other horses.

Coming back into the cabin he looked hard at the other man. "There's no Triple Y brand on your horse. If you were the range boss then you should be riding a Triple Y horse." Spence said.

"We just got that horse a few days back with a herd the Colonel bought off some Mexicans. We've been too busy to try to burn their hides and didn't think it should matter on our own range," the man stated indignantly. If it hadn't been a serious matter Spence would have laughed at the man's face and tone. As it was, he believed the man.

"I'm gonna untie you, but don't go reaching for a firearm. I think you can finish burning that meat there and dish up some of those beans. You got any coffee you can boil to wash them down with?" Spence asked as he started to feel the hunger pangs of being on the trail without a good meal in his belly.

"I ain't much of a cook, but I can burn some beefsteaks. That pot over there on the fire should be about ready to boil. Those hooligans had just put it on when you boys rode up. I had just brought enough for two pots, as we were going to ride out in the morning."

Pouring out some coffee Spence, looked the man over. He was in his late thirties and looked like his life had been mostly astride a horse. He would have been fairly tall if his legs hadn't been bowed so much. He was dressed in store-bought pants, shirt and vest. He had a holster still strapped on, but his gun was nowhere to be seen. The holster was well-worn but maintained and oiled down. His boots were fairly new and looked hand-stitched from a good cobbler. They had recently been polished and still had a shine on them that told Spence that this range boss didn't spend much time in the saddle any more.

"What type of pistol did you carry there in that holster?" he asked the range boss. From the indention in the leather, Spence figured that it must have been a Colt 44.

"It was an old Colt 44 that I liberated from a Apache war chief. No telling who he had killed and scalped to get it. I figured I could use it a lot more than he could as he didn't even have a bullet for it at the time." Hess said. "That was during the decline of the Indian battles and he was one of the renegades that was hiding out in the hills. Him and a few old squaws and children. Those two threw it out the door earlier, and I hope I can find it in the morning."

Spence knew how the man felt. A good horse and a dependable gun were all most men had out here. It would be hard to part with either one.

The range boss pulled two metal plates down from a shelf and slapped a piece of sizzling meat and some beans on each plate. He handed Spence one of them along with a wooden spoon. "Eat up and now tell me how you happened to be with my rider tonight," he said.

"This here slab of meat's the reason. I gave him a cup of coffee and he offered a beefsteak. Seemed he thought more of having company then keeping his rations."

"Yea, John always was a sociable man. Going to make him not being around all the more harder to take." The man looked at the door and sort of winced. Spence could tell that the man had lost a good friend. That was third in his priorities behind a good horse and gun.

"Who were those two men, and why did they have it in for you and John? Seems like they weren't taking any chances pulling down on John without giving him a chance."

"Those two were hired guns from the Bar S ranch on down the valley. It's owned by Maxwell Wardlow, and he runs it with an iron fist. Wardlow has been trying to expand his holdings, and the only way he can is to push out onto the Triple Y. Wardlow came out here and staked out a claim in a box canyon. He's got more cows now than land, and the only pass across the Coastal Del Rey Mountains is here on the Triple Y. He's been pushing the Colonel for a couple years now, and recently he's hired some guns and been driving his cows out onto our range. It's even rumored that he's had some sod busters murdered and burnt out.

"John was pretty good with his gun. That's why he had this part of the range by himself. The Colonel figured John could handle anything that came his way. We just didn't figure on the low-down dirty trick those two came up with. They must have been afraid to face John fair and square," the range boss rambled.

Spence just let the man talk, as he needed to square the death of his friend with himself. It is bad enough to see a friend killed, but to have been part of the reason was hard for a man to take.

Having finished his beans and meat Spence reached into his bags and brought out a small bag of tobacco. He didn't smoke much, but this seemed like a good time. He offered the range boss the bag, and watched as Hess rolled himself a smoke also. Getting a smoking ember from the fire, Spence lit both cigarettes. It was quiet in the cabin as both men smoked and reflected on the night's happenings.

"You handled those .45s pretty well. Much experience with them?" asked the range boss.

Spence took a few minutes to reflect on the question before he answered. "Some, I guess. They are more for comfort than for use. I would just as soon never have to pull them from their holsters. But they've done their share of killing."

"Want to ride down with me to headquarters and meet the Colonel?" asked Hess. "I think the Colonel would want to hear your side of John's death. John was always one of his favorites, and his death will be hard to tell."

"Well, I was planning on riding around this range, but I guess I owe it to John to tell his side of the story to this here Colonel fellow," Spence answered.

CHAPTER TWO

The next morning dawned bright and clear. The sun shining off the snow glared right through the holes in the walls of the cabin. Spence hadn't slept until sun-up in quite a while. As he lay on the rough log bed he could smell fresh coffee boiling. He jumped up and looked around for the range boss, but he was not in the cabin.

Stepping outside in the fresh air, Spence saw the range boss digging a shallow grave in the rocky soil. He stepped back inside, filled two tin cups with coffee, put the pot on the edge of the fire and walked out to where the range boss was busy shoveling dirt. Handing one cup to Hess he said, "Don't seem like much of a place to bury a friend."

The range boss looked at him saying, "No, it don't. John should have been buried in one of those city cemeteries with people all around him. That way he could cut up and joke as much as he wanted."

They finished their coffee and then dug John's grave a little deeper. After laying John to rest, they scoop out two shallow graves and tossed the two hired guns' bodies in and pitched some dirt and rocks on top of them. Murderers didn't deserve much of a burial.

Mounting up, they tied the other horses together and began the trip down the valley to the headquarters of the ranch. As they traveled, clouds began to form and gather above the mountains. It looked like they were in for some more snow before the afternoon was over. The range boss prodded his horse to a faster gait, as he wasn't use to being caught out in bad weather. During the last four years Hess had created a cozy position for himself at the ranch supervising the range riders and drifters. The Colonel had left handling the crew to him, and he was good at handing out chores and keeping track of the progress of each man's work. Fifteen years as a sergeant in the Army had trained Hess very well for his job. Having served under the Colonel for six years had created a bond between the two men. They knew the strengths and weaknesses of each other and knew that they could trust each other.

Spence was left along with his thoughts as the distance between the two men and the blowing wind made conversation difficult. Spence did not like what he was learning about this valley, and certainly knew that he did not want to get involved in someone else's fight. As he rode along he remembered the last fight he had been involved in. His thought drifted back to how he had ended up coming out west.

Spence had worked around various farms, stables and assorted jobs until the war had broken out. When Jeb Stuart's cavalry had passed through Chambersburg, the owner of the stable where he had been working had volunteered him a horse so he could join up. It hadn't been much of a horse but it could stay up with the band and Spence had figured that they wouldn't have to do much running. Some of the guys in the band had given him enough clothing and gear to make him look like a soldier until they could get some regular supplies. The war was still new, and women were still sewing uniforms, while farmers were offering stock and supplies to the newly-formed regiments.

After some of the regular volunteers had got new horses, Spence had been able to trade his old mare to a farmer for a young black gelding that was barely broken. He had to stay alert every morning when he mounted, as the gelding would try to throw him. He didn't try to break the horse of this habit as he figured that it was a sign of a spirited horse and he liked the excitement of a few minutes of crow-hopping. Because of this he named the horse Black Crow.

As battles had been fought, and men lost to wounds and death, Spence had been slowly hardened to life on the back of a horse with little food and less rest. The regiment was in constant movement trying to stay ahead of the enemy as they moved across Virginia, setting up ambushes and skirmishing with patrols and small groups of enemy cavalry units. Rumor of a major battle in Pennsylvania was heard, and then finally confirmed when they began a forced march to a little town named Gettysburg.

The battle at Gettysburg had been the beginning of the end for Spence's life as a cavalryman. During the charge against Four Corners, he had been hit three times, and had ended up in a Union hospital. Recovery from his wounds had taken him through the end of the war and the final dissolving of the Southern resistance. After leaving the hospital Spence went back to the Gettysburg area to try to understand the reason of the charge that almost took his life.

Walking over the battleground, Spence had resolved to himself never to get involved in another conflict based on someone else's reasons. He had not owned land or slaves, and did not have crops being taxed by the government. He had only joined the war for the glory of being a cavalryman and winning the favors of the young ladies around Chambersburg. Staying out of wars started by other men would be the foundation of the rest of his life.

As he had approached the barns at the far edge of the open field, he was startled to see a black horse that looked very familiar. He could not believe that Black Crow had survived the rain of musket balls and cannon balls that had fallen on them. But there he was, looking like he had never seen anything more terrifying than a moody cow. Spence whistled his short double notes, and the horse looked up, snorted and then started trotting toward him. About that time a farmer walked out of the barn carrying a pail full of foamy warm milk.

Spence waved at the farmer and then whistled again. Black Crow broke into a run and came right up to Spence, nuzzling him with his nose. As Spence was rubbing the horse's nose the farmer put down the milk pail and started walking over.

"That beats anything I've ever seen. That horse acts like he has known you all of his life. He has never been this friendly to me or my boys. In fact, they can hardly get a saddle on him and sure can't get him into a plow harness. He's broken the harness, turned over a wagon and run through a fence. I've been trying to trade him to my neighbors but they won't take him," the farmer stated.

"Where did you get him?" asked Spence.

"Why, when that battle was over, there were men, horses, cannons and wagons all over the place. With men crying out in pain, animals screaming from wounds, it was like hell on earth. I helped pull men off the battleground and get them into the hospital and people's houses. I helped dig graves to bury bodies and then clean up the mess some. Never did get that cannon ball out of my barn wall over there. I found this old guy over in the trees by the creek, and figured it was good pay for my efforts," the farmer said to Spence.

"What would you take for him?" asked Spence.

"Why I'd almost give him away for all the trouble he's caused me. But I'll tell you what, you work around here for seven days and he's all yours," the farmer replied.

After seven days of labor, Spence talked the farmer into giving him an old beat-up saddle. Mounting up, he rode away hoping to leave all his memories of this place here with the dead.

For the next few years he had drifted from one job to another, always moving further west. He knew that there was nothing to keep him in the East, and it was rumored that the West offered many new opportunities. He would work a few days for various small farmers for just enough food to get him a few days further on down the road. Then he took a job as a hunter and scout for a wagon train trying to get to Oregon. He had left the wagon train in Nebraska after they had stopped and wanted to settle there. The farmers had thought this was God's country, and could not be talked into continuing on. Spence had wished them good luck and rode off. They did not know what they were going to face when the first winter fell, and would not believe anyone telling them how tough it would be.

Spence had drifted south into New Mexico and worked on a ranch for a few weeks. There wasn't any other type of work around Mesa Lorde, so he turned west again. Winter had found him in Colorado, and he had worked for the railroad until spring came and the snow melted. He made his way to Denver, a little town on the mud flat at the foothills of the Rockies. There wasn't anything there to keep him, so he had decided to take his small stake he had saved and held across to the gold finds in the Coastal Del Rey Mountains. He figured he wouldn't get rich, but he might find enough to buy a small spread somewhere and stock it with a few head of cattle and a couple of horses.

Drifting over the mountains had now put him in a spot he was becoming more and more uncomfortable with. He figured the Colonel would try to entice him to stay and throw in with the Triple Y. He would eat a few good meals, sleep in a warm bunkhouse for a couple of nights, and then mount up and ride on out. But he didn't have to make that decision for a couple of more days. He remembered that John Restless had said the ranch headquarters was a couple days ride on up the valley.

As they rode along the storm clouds continued to build. The afternoon grew darker, and Spence figured they wouldn't get much farther before the snow started to fall. He kicked his horse in the withers and pulled up beside Fester. "Reckon we'd better pull in and gather some wood and build some type of shelter before that blizzard comes on down the mountain," Spence said.

If he had been by himself he would have just dropped his horse and thrown his poncho over the two of them and curled up in his blankets beside the horse. But there being two of them he figured they needed to build some type of shelter and keep a small fire burning until the storm blew itself out. This time of year, it could snow three inches or three feet. You never knew what to expect.

They rode a little farther, and then Fester spotted a gully running off to the side. They rode over to it and went down into the dry streambed. They followed it a while, until a turn in the gully showed a cut into the bank where the water had washed out the soil, and was conducive to building a shelter that would help protect them. It was on the opposite side from which the wind would probably blow. Fester started gathering wood to build a fire and also brought in some logs that would burn for a long while. Since they didn't know how long they would have to weather the storm, he put a pretty large pile gathered next to the shelter. He tethered the horses close to the bank and brought all the saddlebags over to the shelter. Going through the bags from the hired guns' horses he discovered some jerky and hard tack, tobacco, coffee and a small bag of sugar. There were also some boxes of shells for their pistols and Winchester rifles they had both carried. The rifles were fairly new, and Fester figured that they had been given them when they had been hired on at the Bar S. Most drifters and cowpunchers couldn't afford a rifle of that caliber.

The snow had started falling before the chores were finished. It was snowing quite heavy before Fester had the fire going. Spence emptied the last of his water from his canteen into his coffeepot and threw in a handful of grounds. If they were going to be here for a while they might as well be comfortable, and a good cup of coffee and a cigarette would help.

"Did you bring any of that beefsteak with you from John's cabin?" Spence asked the range boss as he looked at the jerky and hard tack. A piece of juicy steak would help the hard biscuits go down easier.

"Didn't think of it. Burying John just took my mind off what I was doing," replied the range boss. He handed Spence a big piece of hard tack and a handful of jerky. "I guess this will have to do for a while."

"At least we have some coffee to wash it down. Otherwise it would be a rough meal."

"Here, put some of this sugar in your coffee. Those ol' boys were better equipped than we were," Fester said as he took the bag and poured a good deal into his cup.

"Naw, I figure I'll save it for dessert. Don't want to get used to taking sugar in my coffee. Don't hardly get any, so I'll save mine as a treat," Spence replied.

By then the wind had picked up and had begun whipping the edges of their ponchos around. Spence finished his hard tack and coffee, went out into the storm, and brought in some large rocks to try to stake the edges down. The storm would be bad enough without the ponchos blowing down and everything getting snow-covered. By the time he got enough rocks around the bottom of the shelter his hands, nose and ears were almost freezing. He went back inside and threw a couple more sticks on the fire.

He looked over at the range boss. Fester had curled up and was snoring away. Well, not much bothers that guy, thought Spence. He poured himself another cup of coffee and sat there listening to the wind blow. It sounded like this storm was going to drop closer to three feet rather than three inches. It looked like it was already about six inches deep. He could hear the horses moving around, stomping their feet and snorting some. He was glad they had found this gully. It would sure have been messy if they had been caught out in the open when the storm hit. He put a heavy log on the fire, reached over for his blankets, curled up and tried to sleep.

CHAPTER THREE

Dawn arrived with the stillness of a cold wintry day after a major storm. Spence woke and looked around him. The wind had shifted during the night and the inside of the shelter had about four inches of snow covering everything. Fester was just a lump under the snow, and the fire had long since gone out. He put his boots on and crawled out of the blankets and started a fire. He wasn't about to start a long cold ride without something hot in his belly.

As he was out checking on the horses to ensure they had not wandered away during the storm, Fester got up and filled the coffeepot with snow and put it on the fire. Normally he would have shaved, as he liked to be clean and close shaven but he decided to skip it this morning. A shave in ice water was just not very appealing. He brought out some more jerky and hardtack. He placed the jerky on a rock close to the fire to warm it up some, and then threw in a little more coffee grounds into the coffeepot. He sliced open a couple of biscuits and put a little lard on them and sugar, and put them alongside the jerky. He figured that as the lard melted it might soften the biscuits a little.

By this time Spence had saddled the horses and made a wide circle around the camp. Being a cautious man, he wanted to know if anything had approached the camp after the storm, be it man or animal. There wasn't sign of any kind, so he went back to the camp and the fire feeling more at ease.

He squatted by the fire and rubbed his hands, thinking that he really should get some good gloves next chance that he got. His gloves were left over from his railroad days and were worn and the stitching had started coming undone, leaving holes in them. He filled his cup with the steaming coffee, and decided to put some sugar in it this morning. It might help keep him a little warmer on the ride. The lard had softened the biscuits some, and the sugar killed most the of the lard taste. It wasn't like a nice hot biscuit straight from the oven, but you had to make the most of what you had.

The ride started out just like the day before, with Fester taking the lead pulling two of the extra horses. The snow made the going rough and slow, and the horses kept balking at having to push through some of the chest high drifts of snow. Spence hoped that Fester knew the trail, as he didn't want to have to pull a horse out of a hole after plunging in over its head. Worse yet, he didn't want to be on that horse when it fell into a hole.

As the sun progressed across the morning sky, the temperature began to rise and the snow began to get soggy. This just made the going rougher as it became slippery and Spence could feel his horse slip and slide occasionally. As they got farther into the valley the snow become less deep. This only lead to it melting faster, and small rivulets began to form along side the trail. The mud was becoming deeper, and the horses were starting to have more trouble as the mud built up under their shoes. It got so bad that every half-hour they would have to stop and clean the clay and mud from the horses' hooves. This ground would be good for building adobe huts but weren't much for farming, Spence thought to himself. Rough cattle range was all it was good for, but Spence noticed that there was more vegetation in this part of the valley.

Rounding a bend in the trail, Fester suddenly came to a stop. Spence hesitated and then rode on up so he could take a look. "Well, I'll be damned!" he said.

There in the trail was a beat-up covered wagon sitting side-angled and one wheel off. A small campfire was going and a woman was stirring a big pot hanging over the fire. A man was bent over the wheel working on the hub with a young teenaged boy looking over his shoulder.

"Now that sure weren't there when I came through here yesterday," Fester said. "I wonder where they came from?"

"We didn't see any tracks from that wagon, so they must've come through here yesterday or during the night in that storm," Spence declared.

They slowly approached the wagon and Fester yelled out, "Hello the camp!"

The man jerked up and suddenly had a rifle in his hands. The woman also had reached over and picked up a rifle she had leaning close to the fire. It always paid to be prepared, and it showed they had probably encountered trouble before somewhere back on the trail.

Fester stopped his horse and yelled out, "I'm Hess Fester and

I'm the range boss for the Triple Y ranch, this spread you are travel-ing across. I see you've had some trouble. Maybe we can help."

"Come on in, but do it slowly and keep your hands up so I can see them!" the man yelled back.

Spence could appreciate the man's caution. He lifted his hands with the reins in them up about ten inches over the horse's neck and started forward. As he approached he looked around to see if there was anyone else around. He noted that the wagon was well-used and the mules looked on their last legs. This farmer wouldn't get much plowing out of them whenever they reached their new home. They had a milk cow, but it looked dry. A couple of chickens in a make-shift coop and a yearling pig were all under the wagon. The boy looked about fourteen years old, and was dressed in clean, mended clothes that looked like they had more patches on them than regular cloth.

The woman reached over and added some water to whatever she had in the pot. Looked like she figured there would be a couple more mouths to feed. Spence noticed that she also had a covered Dutch oven in the coals of the fire. That probably meant some freshly-baked corn bread to go with her stew.

Fester rode on over to where the man was standing. He looked at the wheel and said, "I think you're gonna need more than that pole to fix your wheel. Looks like you're gonna need a good black-smith. You got any spare parts with you?"

"Nothing but what you see," the man replied, "Used them all up just trying to get this far. Name's Will Harris by the way. You say you're from the Triple Y Ranch? Heard about it some, didn't figure we was close to it yet. Trying to stay clear of the Bar S. Heard some bad things about it. You boys light down and have some soup. Ma! You got that food ready yet?"

When the man started talking it was like a dam breaking; words just kept flowing. Spence and Fester got down and tied the horses to the broken wheel. The man talked the whole time, all the way over to the fire. Spence and Fester just sorta grunted answers, as they couldn't get a reply started before the farmer was asking the next question.

They found out that the farmer and his family had left Pennsyl-vania in early spring and had been trying to get over the mountains before winter hit. They had run into a series of broken wheels, lost a mule, been robbed twice, and had a lot of bad weather. The trip had taken them out of their way while trying to find a replacement mule to make up the two-mule team. The cow had been used to help pull the wagon, and she had dried up before she could get her calf strong enough to make the trip. The farmer had hidden what little money they had, and the robbers had taken just about everything but his seed corn and wheat. All of their possessions that could be carried off on horseback had been taken. He was hoping to purchase more supplies come springtime.

He stated that they had been coming through the pass when the storm had come up behind them. They had kept moving during the storm until it got so heavy he couldn't see his team. He had just been ready to stop and try to make camp when the wagon had hit a gully and broke the wheel. He stated that he wasn't surprised, as it was just like his luck for something else to happen.

"No use fretting about it though or you would worry yourself sick. Worrying don't fix no wheel or get you farther down the trail. Why if'n I worried and fretted about what happens, I'd still be in Nebraska somewhere. No, just hunch your shoulders and get to work, that's what I say," rambled the farmer.

"You don't talk much, do you, son? Why I haven't heard you say two words since you rode up. Why, my boy talks more than you do. Here, have another piece of cornbread. Need some more stew in that bowl? You part of the Triple Y also? Why you got so many extra horses, been riding the range? Is that why there weren't any livestock that we saw? Just rounding up strays?"

Spence tried to keep up with all the questions but just answered, "No, I'm going the same direction you are. Just passing across this here spread." He couldn't keep up with the questions but he did take the cornbread and some more stew. The farmer's woman sure could cook, even if it was just simple fare.

"You folks just make your camp here. The ranch is about another day and a half ride from here. When we get back I'll send a couple of the boys back out here with our smithy and they'll have you put back together in no time," Fester stated.

Spence looked at him and asked, "What about those Bar S boys? Figure any more of them are hanging around?"

"Reckon I don't rightly know. Don't know how far they been ranging. Don't figure they are that bold yet," the range boss replied.

Considering the circumstances Spence replied, "Then I reckon I'll just hang around here until your boys show up, that is if Will here don't mind. I figure a little extra safeguard and a couple of days won't matter none."

Will broke in, asking a dozen questions about the Bar S boys and why Spence figured he needed some extra safeguards, and what they thought might happen. Fester motioned the farmer and Spence to walk with him, and said something about a smoke so the woman wouldn't get alarmed.

"Reckon you need to know what's been happening lately around this valley. You've already heard rumors of the Bar S bunch and them rumors are all probably true. We had a run in with a couple of them day before yesterday. I lost my good friend to those cold blooded murderers and would have probably lost my own life if'n this young feller hadn't been there."

The farmer looked at Spence and then at the twin .45s. He took a step backwards out of sudden fear. "You a hired gun? I don't think I need a hired gun staying around my family, especially out here alone on this range."

Spence broke in. "I'm not a hired gun. I was just lucky to get the first shots off after they plowed Fester's friend. That young rider didn't stand a chance, and didn't even have his gun drawn when they both shot him in the chest. If you don't want me to stay, I'll just mosey on into the ranch then."

The farmer looked hard at Spence before he answered, "I guess I was hasty. If that bunch is as bad as that, then I think you should stay around."

After taking another look at the wheel and making note of what was broken, Fester mounted up and rode off toward the ranch. He left the extra horses with Spence, as they would have just slowed him down. Spence unsaddled all of them, and put ankle tethers on them so they could graze but still not get too far from the camp. Coming back to camp, Spence tossed his poncho and blankets on the outside edge of the fire. He hadn't wanted to go into the Triple Y ranch and meet the Colonel anyway. The longer he postponed the meeting the better, he figured.

The farmer came back over to the fire and rolled himself a cigarette. He didn't offer Spence the tobacco bag, but did pour some more coffee for him. The farmer finished the cigarette and then looked over to the wagon. His wife had moved over close to the tailgate and was doing some mending. She had seemed to be talking with herself, speaking quietly but constantly as if she was answering someone.

About that time the boy came running back into camp, jumped

up on the wagon's tailgate and shouted, "Look at this, Sis. You ever seen a rat this big?"

A shriek came from the wagon and a young woman came barreling out the front side, hitting the ground on both feet running. She came running over to the fire and stopped beside the farmer.

"Guess you might as well meet my daughter, Emily" the farmer said. He didn't look too pleased to have to introduce her to a stranger.

The woman was in her early twenties with long chestnut colored hair and blue eyes. Her hair glowed and looked like she had been brushing it when she had to take flight. Her blue eyes twinkled at her father's discomfort, but she bowed her head when she saw Spence starring at her. He had not seen a woman in a while, and suddenly to be presented with a woman of her beauty staggered him. He couldn't get a word out, just some stutters that made the woman burst out laughing.

"I've never had this effect on a man before," she laughed. This only added to Spence's embarrassment and also to her father's discomfort.

"I'm sorry. I've got better manners than to stare, but I sure weren't expecting something like you to come barreling out of that wagon," Spence stuttered.

Now it was the woman's time to be embarrassed. She muttered something and quickly ran back over to where her mother was sitting, picked up some cloth, and pretended to be sewing. She would glance over to the fire and quickly look back down at her sewing.

Spence turned to the farmer saying, "I'm sorry. But your daughter caught me by surprise. I sure didn't know she was in there."

Will Harris looked over at his daughter and said, "I can see why you're surprised. She is quite a gal and she's a handful at times. Raised like a boy but still kept her mother's ways also. Can rope a cow and mend a sock. Sure don't know what I'm going to do with her. But she has been a great help on this trip."

Spence pulled out his tobacco bag and started rolling a cigarette. He didn't really want a smoke, but it broke up the conversation as he offered the bag to the farmer. Seems he saw the need for a unneeded smoke also.

"Better that I gather some more firewood, since we're going to be here a few more days, "Spence said.

With that the farmer yelled to his boy to help Spence gather wood and the boy walked off with Spence out into the brush.

CHAPTER FOUR

"What did you say your name was, son?" Spence asked the boy. Might as well get to know them some if he was going to keep tabs on them until the blacksmith could make it back here.

"Names David Elliot Harris. Most folks call me Davie though, just like Davie Crockett. Ever hear of him? I ain't killed a bear yet, but that's just cause I ain't seen one yet, but just wait. First one I see, I gonna get me a bear skin," the boy rambled. Seems like he sure took after his Pa.

Spence didn't know whether to ask another question, or just appreciate the quiet. He attempted another question anyway. "How old are you?"

"I'll be fifteen this coming February and almost a man now. Why, I can do any work a man can do now, and more than some. I've been plowing fields ever since I was eight, and can handle those mules better than my Pa. Mom says I'm quite the man now, and Emily keeps asking when am I going to hit the road for myself. It's just my Pa that don't think I'm big enough yet. Why look at Emily. She's twenty-two and Pa's still got her at home."

Spence endured the rambling as he had got the answer to the question he had really wanted to ask. They continued to gather wood and some large logs and carried it all into the camp. The weather had started getting bad again, and it looked like they might have to weather another storm before the blacksmith could make it back out here.

Spence had been looking at the wagon, and after they had gathered a pile of wood he went over to the farmer. "Seems like we could level out that wagon there, make it a little easier for your women folks to sleep in," he stated.

Will Harris looked over at the tilted wagon, thought about it a couple of minutes and said, "Reckon you're right. Hadn't thought about it myself and the women don't complain none. How you think we can do it without any thing to lodge under the axle?"

"We brought in a couple of large logs. Just hitch a mule up and put one log under the down side with the mule on the up side and the boy can slip that wheel back on the axle when the wagon lifts. As long as they don't get to rocking too much inside, that wheel will hold."

"Then you got to take it back off when that smithy get here. Seems like a lot of work just to give a woman a level place to sleep," stated the farmer, just being logical.

"With another storm fixin' to hit here it would keep more snow off your belongings as it'll start gathering on this side and then seep into the wagon. It'll also be easier to fix a shelter under the wagon for us to sleep in. I'm not looking forward to another night sleeping in the wind and snow," Spence pointed out.

"Didn't think of that. Me and the boy had just rolled up in blankets and ponchos and like to froze our tails last night. Got up early and built that fire before daylight just to get warm. Davie, drag one of those big logs on over here then go get Molly," the farmer shouted to his boy.

It didn't work quite as easily as Spence had figured but eventually they got the wagon lifted enough for the boy to slip the wheel back on the axle. Then Spence took the log and braced the wagon to keep it from rocking back toward the broken wheel. Taking their ponchos and rocks they were able to tie the ponchos to the sides of the wagon, creating a cozy shelter under it. It would be better than what he had built the night before.

Finishing the shelter, Spence and the boy went and brought the horses and mules back in closer to the camp. They took a rope and made a makeshift corral, so when the wind started blowing the horses wouldn't wander away seeking shelter from the storm. They brought the cow up and tied it to the wagon on what Spence figured would be the downwind side of the storm. Luckily it was opposite the broken wheel.

"Pa! Look over there. Looks like we got company coming in," Spence heard Davie yell out.

Looking to where the boy was pointing he saw three riders sitting on a small rise looking at the camp. He reached under the wagon and pulled out his rifle, noticing the farmer had done the same. He saw a barrel poke out the canvas on the tent and knew the woman had heard the boy also.

The riders just sat on the rise. It looked like they were discussing whether to ride into the camp or not. One kept turning and pointing to the storm brewing like he didn't want to waste anymore time, and they needed to get somewhere before it blew in. He must have convinced the other two, as they suddenly reined their horses around and took off in the general direction of the Bar S Ranch. Spence figured they must be hired riders for the Bar S and they were up to no good. He was glad that they had decided to ride on, but he didn't put his rifle away. They might have seen the two men with guns, and decided to circle around and come in from some other direction.

He told Will to stay alert and to keep his rifle handy. Then he walked out into the brush and made a wide circle around the camp. Finally he walked out the where the riders had been sitting and followed the tracks for a ways to ensure that they had indeed ridden off.

Coming back to camp, he told Will what he had found. The woman got out of the wagon and went back to the fire and started cooking. Even though it was early afternoon, she said she had better get something cooked now before it started snowing again. Emily got down from the wagon and went to help her Ma. It looked like she knew her way around a cook fire as well as her Ma. In just a short time they had the stew, some cornbread fritters and a dried apple cobbler cooking on the fire.

Spence never let himself relax, and kept watching the horizon around the camp. He didn't want to be caught unaware of any more incoming riders. It had startled him earlier when the boy had seen the riders before he had. And it looked like they had sat a few minutes before the boy saw them. Being caught unaware like that again could prove disastrous to this family and to himself. He swore to himself that he would not let his guard down again like that. Just being around this family a few hours had made him seem like part of the group. They were quick to make a man feel at home.

When the food was done the woman heaped two big plates and brought them over to her husband and Spence. "Better eat up now," she said, "And there is plenty to eat, so don't be bashful."

Spence had never had cornbread fritters cooked like these. They were light and fluffy and just melted in your mouth. That woman could really cook. Having finished two plates of fritters and stew, he went back for some apple cobbler and a cup of coffee. He thought that he would like to sit down to one of her meals when she had a real fireplace to cook on and a cupboard of food to cook with.

After eating he told the farmer he wanted to take another look around the camp and started out. The boy quickly finished his food and came running after him.

"Oughtn't you be helping your Ma back there?" he asked the boy.

"Naw, that's woman's work. Besides she has Emily to help and there's not that much to do anyway. We done brought in the wood."

"All right then, but try to keep quiet. If there's anything out here we don't want to give notice we're coming," Spence told the boy. He didn't figure the boy could be quiet more than a few minutes but he didn't expect to find anything anyway. This walk was just for his own sense of being aware of what was there and also to get away from camp where the young woman was. He had caught himself staring at her as he was eating and it unsettled him to think that someone could have that effect on him. He especially didn't want to stir up her Pa, as he was beginning to like this family.

Before they could make a circle of the camp it had started snowing on them. The ground still had snow left from the previous storm and the snow started accumulating quickly. By the time they started back to camp the snow had covered any possible tracks there might have been. The boy had done very well and had only spoken when required. Spence thought that he might turn out to be a good hunter or range man after all, as he was quick to pick out animal tracks and identify them. Seems he had spent quite a bit of time in the woods and on the prairie tracking small game for their meals. That had probably explained the meat in the stew his Ma had cooked.

When they got back to cam,p Spence threw a couple of logs on the fire so it would burn through the storm. Even if it went out later there would be hot coals to start the next fire with. The boy had already crawled under the wagon with his Pa, and Spence could hear them making up their beds. With the snow falling like it was there wasn't much else to do. Spence didn't feel comfortable going inside the shelter while it was still light outside, so he hunkered down close to the fire. He didn't figure anyone in their right mind would be trying to travel in this storm, but he felt he should still keep watch.

He took out his tobacco bag and rolled himself a smoke. It wouldn't be much longer before his tobacco would be gone. He only had enough for a couple more cigarettes. Being so generous with his tobacco the last few days had depleted his small supply pretty quickly. But he figured that the companionship of the men he had let smoke his tobacco was worth running out. He wasn't a heavy smoker, and just considered it a luxury, like having a bag of sugar.

Throwing the last small butt of the cigarette into the fire, he stroked the fire some, put the logs more into the center, took one last look around the circumference of the camp and then climbed into the shelter as the storm continued to build in intensity.

CHAPTER FIVE

The storm had blown all night, and when Spence rose the next morning the snow was still falling. With three of them, a pig and the chickens in the shelter, they had stayed fairly warm during the night. He rolled out of his blankets, pulled on his boots, and taking care not to disturb the other two, he opened a flap and looked outside.

The snow was waist-high and still falling. He pushed on outside and went over to where he thought the fire used to be. It had gone out under the fall of the snow, and Spence had to clean powder away from the circle of rocks. Digging down through the top layers of wet ash, he finally found some live embers. Taking some kindling from the bottom of the wood pile, he finally got a small fire started again. Nursing it along, he added some larger sticks and finally got it large enough to take a log.

By this time Will had got up, and was stomping a path around the wagon. His wife Francis had stuck her head out, but the farmer had told her to go back inside, they didn't need anything right now. She looked glad to hear that, and quickly disappeared back into the wagon. As Spence went to check on the livestock, the farmer continued to stomp a path in the snow between the wagon and the fire. He then got a bucket out, filled it with some oats, and took it to the cow. He was hoping that maybe he could get her breeding by a bull on one of these ranches he had to cross. She should have been bred this past fall, but the farmer didn't want her carrying a calf over the mountains and while on the trail. A late calf would be as good as a spring calf, and then his family would have milk up into the next winter.

The boy had got up, left a yellow hole in the snow out away from the camp, and then gone back into the shelter. He began feeding the chickens and the piglet, talking to them the whole time. He had had a dog when they had started this trip, but the first group of thieves had shot the dog when they had attacked them. Davie sure did miss him, and was going to ask his Pa for a pup first chance he got. In the meanwhile, he had adopted the piglet and was trying to teach it some tricks.

Spence came back into camp and said the horses had pulled through the rope corral, but he had found them in a gully not too far away. That had helped them weather the storm better, so he had just left them there. He would bring them back to camp when the storm finally broke. Since there were four horses, and two mules they didn't try to take enough oats down to them. They could graze on the dry prairie grass for now.

Amazing Grace suddenly burst forth from the wagon. Both women's voices lifted in the hymn familiar to most. It filled Spence's heart to hear the singing as both women had beautiful voices, and they were in perfect harmony with each other. They sang four hymns, with each trying to out-sing the other, and the voices rang out over the snowy countryside. Afterwards Francis stuck her head out of the wagon and yelled to her husband, "Will, get those last few eggs that chickens laid. This being Sunday, we should give thanks to the Lord and have a decent breakfast. Get some of that smoked ham out too. Mr. Spence, when was the last time you had a good Sunday breakfast?"

Spence had not even known this was Sunday morning. Being off by himself most of the time, he didn't bother to keep track of days. He barely knew what month it was. "Been a while, Ma'am, " he replied. "That sure was pretty singing. You two make a great match. Haven't heard those hymns in quite a while," Spence rambled. It seemed the longer he was around this family, the more talkative he was becoming.

Both women climbed out of the wagon and started cooking. Emily had brought some flour out with her and had started making biscuits. Francis sent the boy up into the wagon and he brought out a small crock pot. Opening it, he dipped his finger inside, and brought out a honey-covered finger. He popped it into his mouth just as his Ma whacked him upside the head with her dishtowel. He grinned at her, put the top back on the crock pot and moved back out of range of her towel.

"We robbed a bee's hive back the other side of the mountain," he said, and grinned at Spence. "Just fired up some smoky branches to keep those bees away and got two jars of honey. That's the last jar, and Ma only brings it out for special occasions. I guess that means you're special, Mr. Spence."

Sitting around the fire in the snow eating hot vittles, Spence could see why a man might want to settle and raise a family. He hadn't realized just how lonely a man could be off by himself. Most of the time he just didn't think about it, and could make do with his own company. He had been by himself most of his life, and had learned to live with it. This pleasant family, though, showed how life could be.

Watching Emily help her Ma clean up and put things away, Spence had a few thoughts of how this young woman would make a man a pretty fair wife. He couldn't help but glance in her direction quite often. He was trying not to keep looking at her, but she just drew his eye. He tried to make conversation with the farmer to help keep his mind off of what it would be like to have her in his life.

"Whereabouts did you say you were trying to get to?" Spence asked Will. He found that he was actually interested in the older man's plans now.

"I had reckon that if'n there were ranchers out this way, then a farmer would have a good market for his grain crops. Even if there is plenty of range grass, they still need some corn, oats and wheat. I was going to look for a place close enough to haul the grain, but still with some decent farming land. With winter storms like this one, the rancher's cows can't get to the grass and they need something to eat. I had thought of raising and cutting hay on the side also. I figure there is plenty of opportunity, as cowpunchers don't want to cut hay and raise crops. They just wanna sit on that there horse and move those cows around," the farmer stated matter-of-factly. It seems he had put some thought into his plans after all.

"I hadn't thought of it that way, but I reckon you're right. I sure wouldn't want to have to spend all day on my feet behind a plow. Did that when I was a boy, and didn't ever care for it," Spence voiced his thoughts. "Have you got enough seed grain left to make a start?"

"Yea, those thieves weren't interested in big bags of seed. If it wasn't light enough to carry on their horse they didn't want it. The biggest problem was trying to keep it dry and not beginning to rot. I figure the boy and I could have a good start on a spring plowing if we can get on down this valley some. Surely the ranchers don't have it all claimed."

Spence didn't want to say it, but he was afraid the farmer had quite a ways to go before he would find some unclaimed land. And if he did, it probably wouldn't be worth the effort to lay a plow to it. Most was like the land they was sitting on, dry, barren and full of rocks.

Spence let the farmer ramble on about his plans for the future. That gave him time to watch the young woman as she went about her chores. The snow had begun to taper off, and the sky was beginning to lighten up. Spence figured it had just about blown itself out, and by mid-afternoon they would have some sunshine. This storm and the depth of the snow would probably delay the blacksmith from making it back in just the couple of days the range boss had figured. Spence was beginning to get itchy just sitting around. He always liked to be on the move unless he had taken a job to build his money reserve back up. And then he just stayed long enough to get his finances situated again.

Wanting to be moving around, he went and got his rifle. Turning to the farmer, he told him that he was going out to scout the layout some and see if he could catch a deer or elk moving around as the snow stopped. Fresh meat was always welcomed in a camp. Spence figured that the elk might have moved on down into the valley with the storm covering all the grass with snow. He was partial to elk meat, as it tasted more like beef than the other antlered animals. One elk would last this family most of the rest of the winter.

The boy started out after him, but Spence waved him back into camp. The boy had turned out to be quiet enough but Spence wanted the solitude to think about the happenings of the last few days. He hadn't expected to be tied up with a family, and also to have the obligation of meeting a ranch owner. Life was funny in its unexpected happenings, and Spence had learned to just accept things as they came. All the same, it took a bit of thinking about.

He circled the camp on the low side, so when he hit the high side of camp he could continue on out into the brush in the area most likely to have elk. He checked the horses as he passed them, and they seemed content to stay in the protected gully. Continuing on, he didn't see any signs of anything having moved around since the storm. Most animals were holed up keeping warm until some of the snow melted off.

Spence reached the high side of the camp and scanned the horizon. He looked back down on the camp, and it looked like the family had all moved into shelter as there wasn't much they could do outside. He figured the farmer thought no one or nothing would be moving around today, and he didn't need to stand watch. Spence thought the farmer was probably right on that matter, but he continued on anyway. He tried to move keeping brush between himself and the direction he was traveling. That way if there were any elk down here in this part of the valley he would stand a better chance of getting close enough for a shot.

He got to a ridge and moved up it a ways. This would give him a better view of the valley and also keep him out of sight of anything down below. He slowly walked along for about forty minutes scanning the ridge ahead of him and the valley below. Suddenly he heard a gunshot ring out. It was just in front of him and he dropped into the snow. He hadn't seen anything and he figured it wasn't a shot at him, but he was just being cautious. Slowly he continued on going from brush to brush. Rounding a large rock he looked down across the valley.

Then he heard talking. At least two men were discussing a downed animal. It was a young bull elk, and they were bleeding it after cutting its throat. Then two more men rode up, leading the horses for the two on foot and a pack mule loaded with bundles. They dismounted and reached into bags and brought out some skinning knives. These looked like the knives used by the buffalo hunters out on the mid-west prairies. They were designed to enable a man to skin a large animal in just a few minutes, and these men looked like they had experience with them. It only took them a little while to gut, skin and quarter the young bull elk. They split the meat up between themselves, wrapped it in pieces of the hide and mounted up again. As they started out, they were moving in the direction of the farmer's camp.

Spence had moved in a little closer as the men were busy with the elk. Seeing their direction of travel he broke into a run. He might not make the camp before the men did, but maybe he would get there in time to stop any trouble. It was tough going through the heavy snow, but the horses laden down with a rider and a quarter of an elk wasn't moving much better.

Spence hoped that the farmer had heard the shot and was on alert. He continued to plow through the snow, falling often and gagging on the snow as it filled his mouth. He was gasping for breath, and every time he fell he would fill his mouth again with snow. He was wet with perspiration and from melted snow by now, and that only weighed him down more but he kept struggling. Since he has on the high side the snow was not as deep here as the drifts in the valley where the riders were. It seemed like maybe he had got the lead on the rider,s and if he could keep up the pace he would make the camp first.

Finally he broke his trail that he had made on the trip out and travel was a little easier. He slowed his pace just a bit so he could get his breath back. Rounding the last bend he came to the camp. The farmer was standing by the fire with his rifle in his hands. He had heard the shot and was watching in the direction it had come from. Hearing Spence come stumbling in, he turned raising his rifle.

"Hold it, it's just me," Spence shouted out. "But I'm not alone, there's four riders coming this way." As Spence talked he noticed two barrels poke out of the wagon canvas. He knew now that everyone was alerted to the incoming riders.

"Move back out from the fire. You don't want to give anyone a clear shot," he said to Will. They both moved back into the edge of the brush some and waited. By now they could hear the horses thrashing through the snow. It sounded like they were having a hard time breaking through the snowdrifts. They could hear the men talking amongst themselves also. Spence thought that they weren't trying to sneak up on the camp. Either they didn't know there was a camp up here ahead of them, or they knew and wasn't up to no good. Spence had thoughts that this might be the Triple Y men, but he didn't move out of the brush. Best to know for sure before you exposed yourself.

About ten minutes passed before the riders came into sight. They continued to talk, laugh and joke among themselves. They pulled up about fifty yards out and yelled out to the camp.

"We're from the Triple Y and Fester sent us out here to help you folks. I'm Hank Moore, the blacksmith, and these boys are with me. Hello the camp, anyone around?"

Spence and Will stepped out of the brush and walked in toward camp. "You boys come on in," he shouted, relieved that they were from the Triple Y. His duties as a guard was about over and he figured he could get about his travel in a couple of more days.

The farmer made a motion to the wagon and the gun barrels disappeared inside, but no one moved from in there.

The range riders and the smithy rode on in toward the camp, still joking with each other. They seemed in pretty good spirits after having spent the night out in the storm.

As the riders came into camp they rode over to the wagon. The rider that had shouted out took the mule and tied him to the rear wagon wheel, gave the reins of his horse to another rider and then went to the bundles on the mule. The other riders took their horses out of camp a ways and tied them to some bushes. One stayed with the horses and started unsaddling them and stacking the gear. The other two came on back into camp carrying one of the rear headquarters off the elk.

They looked over to see what the blacksmith was doing, and then went into the packs on the mule, drug out some iron skillets and pots, a coffee pot and some bags of grub. One stoked up the fire while the other started cutting strips of steak off the elk. It looked like they were very familiar with a cook fire.

Spence and the farmer walked on over to the blacksmith to introduce themselves and to see what they could do to help.

"You must be that rider that Fester was talking about, the one that was with John when he got it in the chest," the smithy stated. "I'm Hank Moore and as you can tell, I'm the blacksmith for the Triple Y."

"Yea, unfortunately I was with John. Iwas too late to keep him from getting shot. Looks like you boys came to stay for a while," Spence replied.

"Well, you never know exactly what you're gonna need, and Fester's explanations are usually wrong. He's a good pusher but when it comes to fixing things he's totally lost," the smithy stated.

"This here is Will Harris. The wagon belongs to him. It sure surprised me some when Fester volunteered your services and supplies."

"Well, there's probably a logical reason he did so. Fester usually has a sound reason behind most things he does. Always looking out for people and the ranch," the smithy stated, smiling. "How you doing, Will? Looks like this wheel has seen its share of hard times. Won't take but a couple hours to get it into shape though."

"That's good to know. It was beyond my limited knowledge this time. I reckon I was going to have to whittle a new hub or something for it. If'n you got some type of grease, the others could probably use some also. What you want us to do for you now?" The farmer sounded more than pleased to help. After all, getting a repair done on a wagon and not costing anything didn't happen very often.

"Nothing right now. I'm just going to lay out what I'm going to need. We'll take that wheel off later and then with some measurements and a good fire I'll start shaping a new hub for it. But before I get too involved, I think I'll partake of that there supper those boys are finishing. We didn't get too much last night or this morning because of the storm and trying to get here as soon as we could," the blacksmith replied.

With that he laid out a couple of iron working tools, then started over to the cook fire. "You boys come on and let's see what the cooks came up with. Those elk steaks should be pretty tender off that young bull. Might as well call your boy and womenfolks out. Those two boys will take care of everything."

The farmer was startled with the word 'womenfolk'. He knew that Emily hadn't been out of the wagon when Fester had been here, nor since these riders had come into camp. "What do you mean womenfolk?" he asked.

"Why I told you, Fester was on the ball. He told us of your wife and daughter. He sees things most men just overlook. I sure wouldn't have known you even had a wife unless Fester told me."

With that the farmer gestured toward the wagon, and his wife and daughter jumped down and came over to the fire after getting the boy from underneath the wagon. They tried to help with the vittles, but the two cowboys told them to sit and just enjoy, that they had it all in hand. The wife seemed uneasy, but Emily was enjoying being waited on.

The cowboys had cooked up some cornpone, the elk steaks, beans and even some pan-fried potatoes. It was a meal fit for a rich man, and they all ate their fill. There were some left-over beans and potatoes and the boy filled his plate and headed for the shelter.

"Don't go feeding that good food to that pig," the farmer yelled at him.

The boy stopped until one of the cooks told him, "Go ahead. We got enough supplies for this trip and it'll be good for the pig. We don't waste food, but once or twice won't hurt us too much."

The farmer nodded and the boy took off with his plate. He didn't like it, but it wasn't his place to say anything about another man's food.

The blacksmith went back to work while the cowboys cleaned up around the cook fire. Spence and Will didn't know what to do, so they went on over to the smithy. He had his supplies laid out and was looking the broken wheel over. He took some measurements of the hub and the wood spokes on each side.

"This wheel wobbled a little while rolling," he said to the farmer. "The spokes on this side are a little bit shorter than the opposite side."

"That's right, it sure did. Just sort of rocked along. Didn't notice it after I bought the wagon until we were out on the trail. Just thought it was ruts in the road at first. Then just got used to the rock after a while."

"You want to even it out or leave it as it is?" the smithy asked looking at the farmer.

"Naw, that's too much work just to get us on down the trail," the farmer said not wanting to get too deep in an obligation to this man and his boss.

"Actually it will be easier to even it out, as we have to take the hub out anyway."

"Well, if you think it'll be easier. I know my wife will appreciate an even ride, as she made mention of that wheel off and on all the way across to here."

"O.K. then, I guess we're about ready to take that wheel off. Better get that boy and his pig out from under there. Boys, get some heavy logs and we'll cross hitch them over some forked logs and it'll brace the wagon level," the blacksmith yelled to his helpers.

Spence thought to himself that that was such a simple solution, why hadn't he thought of that himself. He helped bring over some logs, and with the six of them working and the boy they didn't need the mule to help lift the wagon. They got it braced on the crossed logs, and the smithy lifted off the wheel. He looked around and told the others that was all they could do tonight and to go ahead and lay out their bedding. He continued to take measurements, and then went to the packs that had been on the mule and got out some iron-work. He took it over and placed it in the fire, poured himself a cup of coffee and then settled down close to the heat.

"Seen anyone else out this way?" he asked Spence.

"Seen three riders yesterday just before the storm hit. They watched the camp a few minutes and then rode on up the valley," Spence said.

"I guess we'll set some guards tonight then. If we could make it on in here, then other riders could make it. Best we not get caught unawares. Don't expect no trouble with six of us now, but you never know what to expect," Moore replied.

Spence was beginning to like this man. He seemed like a solid man you could trust and had a lot of common sense about him. Spence volunteered to take the first shift and to let the riders get some sleep, and the farmer volunteered for the second shift. He figured they had slept better last night than the riders and weren't as tired. No one disputed that logic, and the camp got quiet as the men rolled up in their blankets and ponchos.

Spence walked out of camp a ways and then went and checked on the horses and mules. The riders had put their mounts in with the others and had built a brush corral to keep the animals in the gully. Unless spooked, it didn't take much to keep a horse where you wanted him to stay.

CHAPTER SIX

The morning broke crystal clear and cold. It would still be a couple of hours before the sun broke over the mountains but the moon was still hanging over the morning sky. The last cowboy on guard had built up the fire and had started a pot of coffee. The others got up and picked up their bedding, and then wandered over to the fire. One went out to check the livestock.

Suddenly a shot rang out over the morning sky. It had come from the direction of the horses. It didn't take but seconds for guns to appear in the hands of all the cowboys, and Spence had his .45s out. He took off out in the direction of the horses, but angled out into the brush. He had noticed that another rider had done the same on the other side.

Approaching the horse gully slowly, he couldn't see or hear anything out of the ordinary. He saw the other cowboy come out of the brush on the other side and Moore and Will approached from the front. He suddenly had a bad feeling and broke back for the camp.

As he took off running he heard the first shot from the camp. Then two more shots rang out in quick succession. Then he heard the different sound of a pistol firing rapidly. He knew that the first shot out here had just been a ruse to get the men out of the camp. He ran harder, feeling that he had let the family down by being fooled this way.

Approaching the camp, he circled a little to the side. He looked and couldn't see anything, and the firing had stopped. Then he saw the cook lying out by the woodpile. He looked hurt, but was looking back down the trail that they had ridden in on yesterday. Spence started through the brush and circled out that way. Maybe he could catch the ambushers off guard.

As he slowly worked his way through the brush he could see four men. Three of them were talking and pointed to different directions around the camp. The other was sitting on the ground and looked like he had taken a round. It looked like they had been caught

by surprise at the number of guns in the camp, and were now planning new tactics. Spence turned around and made his way back to
the camp. Seeing Moore and the others, he told them what he had
seen.

Moore took over and laid out a counteroffensive. He knew the
number of attackers, but they didn't know how many more were in
the camp. They dispersed to their positions and waited. It wasn't
but a couple of minutes before Spence could see two men approaching his position. As they came within range he cocked both .45s,
aimed and fired simultaneously. The two men fell but one got up
quickly, jumped into a nearby ravine, and Spence could hear him
running hard. He went over to see if there was any blood, but could
not find any. He finally found his round lodged in a small tree right
in front of where the man had been when Spence fired.

Within seconds more gunfire rang out. It was a short battle, with
the firing coming from the Triple Y men. The ambushers were totally out-maneuvered and had lost the element of surprise. Spence
cautiously came back into camp. When the Triple Y men took count,
there were three dead ambushers and the other two had taken off
running across the countryside. The woman came down from the
wagon and told of the initial assault on the camp. After the first
gunshot, she and Emily had climbed into the wagon and taken up
their rifles. The cook had moved over into the brush and the boy
had his father's rifle in the shelter with him. They had heard the
ambushers coming and waited until they were almost in camp and
had fired. The first round fired had hit the cook in the shoulder and
then the women and boy had fired, taking down one man and they
thought wounding another. The others had backed up very quickly
out of range of the camp. That was when Spence and the Triple Y
men had come back in.

Spence suggested they ride out after the two men before they
could get to their horses, but then the smithy came back into camp
with both hands full of reins. He had located the horses and had
brought them into camp. The other cowboy said he was going to
watch their horses and went out to the gully where their mounts
were corralled. It was going to be a long walk for those two
ambushers.

Looking at the brand on the horses, it was clear that all of them
were from the Bar S, pretty clear evidence of wrong doings if there
had been a lawman in these parts. As it was, it looked like the working horse herd of the Triple Y had just gained some new additions.

The women took the cook aside, cleaned and patched his wounds. The bullet had passed clear through the meaty part of the shoulder, missing the shoulder bones. He was in pain, but it would heal cleanly.

The smithy went to check his hubs he had placed in the ashes the night before. They looked hot enough to work onto the wheel and work the spokes into. The woman said to him, "Don't pull those out yet, I'll have some grub finished and you need a good meal before you start hammering on that wheel."

They ate their breakfast, and then the men gathered around the smithy responding to his directions as he finished up the wheel. With the trouble from the Bar S riders, he wanted to finish this wheel up and get started back toward the ranch headquarters. They had been lucky the first encounter, having taken the riders by surprise. The next time it might be them that were surprised.

The blacksmith worked the wheel on the hub and beat it into shape. He then worked the spokes of the wheel into the hub and then put the retaining ring on the hub holding the spokes in place. They put the wheel back on the wagon and he put the holding ring on the axle that held the wheel onto the axle. Lowering the wagon back down, the wheel held and they started loading the farmer's belongings back onto the wagon.

Meanwhile, the other cowboy brought in the mules and the other horses and they hitched up the teams, loaded the pack mule and saddle the men's horses. They did not have room to carry the extra saddles, so they just saddled the extra horses. The boy claimed one horse and mounted up. Emily looked at her father, hoping to ride also, but with all the men around he shook his head no and she climbed up on the wagon with her Ma.

They started out and Spence rode out on the side and slightly to the back, and one of the cowboys took the other side. They did not want any surprise visitors. The blacksmith took the lead pulling his pack mule behind him. The wounded cook and the other cowboy herded the horses along behind the wagon.

The ground was fairly level along this part of the valley, and they made good time during the afternoon. The smithy kept the group traveling, and he meant to travel up until well after nightfall. Late afternoon, the woman gave the farmer some jerky beef and biscuits to pass out to the riders so they could keep moving.

Night fell, and the blackness enclosed the group. The moon wouldn't rise until after midnight, and it was only a quarter moon. They had to depend on starlight to maneuver the wagon and the horse herd. The cowboys had linked the extra horses together using the reins and some rope so that they would have to move en masse. It was easier to see the whole herd start to wander than to keep track of individual animals.

Moore decided to stop and let the people rest about midnight. He told them to keep the team hitched and the horses tied together, and to throw their beds close to the wagon. He posted a guard and had the others turn in. The animals didn't need to forage for food tonight, and the people didn't need any warm food. They would pull out early in the morning and everyone could eat and rest after they got to the ranch.

Spence had the last watch, with Moore waking him about an hour before first light. He got up and walked out from the camp a ways so the noise of the animals and the cowboys snoring would not interfere with his hearing other sounds. It was very quiet this time of morning. Spence enjoyed the quiet, as it gave him time to think over the happenings of the last few days. He had come over the mountains alone, and now he had a family and a bunch of riders as company. Things sure could change in just a few days.

As it began to grow light he moved into the camp and started waking everyone. After a little while of stretching, scratching and yawning, they got around, mounted up and started on down the valley. The cowboys were used to waking, mounting and riding. All of these men had been part of the Colonel's cavalry unit. Will didn't mount up this morning but took the reins of the wagon. Francis and Emily stayed inside, and Spence figured they were trying to sleep a little longer. The boy, though, was first to mount and ready to ride on down the trail.

Moore kept them moving until noon. He pulled up and told the cowboy cooks to hustle up some quick grub and a pot of coffee. Spence and the boy gathered some quick wood for the fire while the cooks started preparing some dough for flat bread. Spence and the other rider then moved out a ways from camp to stand watch. They rotated with the two cooks after the quick meal was prepared so everyone could get a hot cup of coffee. Then Spence and the rider cleaned up the camp and when the fire was out, called the two cooks into camp. They mounted up and continued the ride.

The trip was uneventful and they reached the ranch headquarters mid-afternoon. The mules had pulled like they knew a warm barn and hay was waiting for them. Riding over the last ridge, a group of riders from the ranch met them and rode on in with the group, exchanging jokes and kidding the cook about his wound. It was all good-natured kidding, and Spence could tell that they had ridden together for a while. Kinship like this comes from sharing the same hardships and dangers.

The ranch hands took all the horses as Moore led the wagon over to the protection of the main barn. The hands unhitched the mules and led them away to the barn. Moore told Spence to find himself a empty bunk in the and make himself comfortable. He told the family that they could use his quarters while they were here. It was a small cabin attached to the barn and it would give the family some privacy while they were at the ranch. He pointed out the mess hall to everyone and told them the times the meals were normally served, and then he went off to report the trip and events to the Colonel.

CHAPTER SEVEN

As Spence was sitting around the breakfast table the next morning in the mess hall, Hess Fester came in and looked around. Seeing Spence he went and got a cup of coffee and then came and sit down opposite him. "A little more excitement I hear," he said. "You sure are a helpful man to have around."

"More so than I would hope to be. I'm just a peaceful man trying to get through this valley," Spence replied.

"Well, the Colonel wants you to join him at his supper table tonight. It's in the main ranch house and he eats promptly at six. You got a time piece so you won't be late?"

"No, never had need to know the exact time of the day. Here lately I don't even track the day of the week. I reckon someone around here has a timepiece though," Spence stated.

"See me mid-afternoon, and I'll have one for you to use for this evening. Make use of the tub in that little room off the kitchen and tell the cook I said to heat some water for you. Otherwise, make yourself at home around here and look around. I think you will find the boys here pretty friendly and always looking for a fresh face to kid around with," Fester replied as he got up to go.

Spence watched him walk out of the mess hall. He might not make a good range rider, but he sure looked comfortable in his role here as range boss.

After he finished the coffee, he looked in the little room and saw that they had fixed it up to be a bathroom, with a tub and a rack with worn but clean towels on it. It had a small stool and some buckets with water sitting in them, and some rough home-made soap on a small stand close to the tub. The cook yelled to him to give him about thirty minutes notice if he wanted hot water for the tub.

Spence yelled back that he would try it this afternoon as he wanted to look around the ranch a little first. He then walked out and started towards the corral where a bunch of the riders were sitting on the top railing yelling at someone inside the corral. As he got closer he could see that they had a range pony with a sack over its head and were trying to put a saddle on the pony.

He joined the riders on the top rail. They glanced at him and one spoke up, "You the one that helped John?"

When Spence had bedded down last night, these same riders had let him have his peace but now they were ready to find out the details. They had all been good friends with John Restless. They hated to see anyone killed, and more so when the person was shot down in cold blood without even being given a chance.

Spence replied, "Yea, I was with John. He heard Fester in the cabin and just busted through the door. Didn't even have a gun out. He was just too trusting, and they took advantage of that fact. Had him shot before John even knew they were in there."

This information quieted the riders a bit as they thought that over. Just then, one of the men with the pony climbed up and the other yanked the sack from the pony's head. It just stood there a few seconds quivering and then went head down, tail up and three feet in the air, all in the same movement. The rider wasn't so quick to adjust, and he went head over tail and landed in the dirt as the pony jumped around the corral and came to a stop on the opposite side.

With all the yelling and shouting and action, the riders had forgot about Spence for the time being. They roped the pony and got him still long enough for the rider to start to mount again. He had one leg in the stirrups and one almost over the horse when it jumped again. The rider went tumbling again and the cowboy with the rope had a little ride across the corral until the pony stopped.

"Get that dang sack on him again," the rider shouted.

They roped the pony again and with two cowboys holding the ropes on opposite sides, they were able to hold him still while a third cowboy got the sack back over the pony's head.

Climbing back on, the rider settled himself and they pulled the sack off again. The pony didn't hesitate this time, but took off bucking. He was hell-bent to get the rider off his back, and after about twenty seconds of straight bucking he went up into the air with all four feet off the ground and did a turning motion to the right, and when he hit the ground he jerked to the left leaving the rider where the pony had been. The crowd on the fence got to laughing so hard a couple of them fell off the top rail.

Spence was chuckling himself. He knew how hard it was to break a horse, and this pony was going to be a handful for anyone. The rider picked himself up off the ground, brushing the dirt off his clothes and then gathered his hat, whacking it across his legs.

"O.K. Thomas, it's your go at this pony," he said to one of the cowboys on the fence. Thomas climbed down and said to put the sack back on the pony. He didn't want a spill before he could even get into the saddle.

The rider settled into the saddle and the pony started quivering. They pulled the sack off and the pony went to the left in a side hop. The rider went to the ground in a crumpled bundle. The cowboys on the fence tumbled with laughter. This was the best entertainment they had had in a long while.

Thomas got up holding his hip and saying, "Anyone else want a go at this pony?"

"What? You giving up after just one fall?" one of the cowboys yelled out.

"You think it's so funny, you get out here," Thomas yelled back. But he was gathering himself for another ride. Climbing on he said to the cowboys holding the ropes to tighten up from the sides so the pony would only be able to move forward. They pulled the sack again and the pony took off, bucking straightforward as the rider knew he would.

After about fifteen seconds the pony's jumps became less high and with less force. He was tiring and could not put as much into his hops. After about ten more seconds he took to just running around the corral and then he stopped. Thinking the pony was about done, the rider relaxed a little and then the pony made his last attempt, jumping up and dropping his head at the same time. That was too much motion and took Thomas by surprise. He once again landed in a bundle on the ground.

The boys on the fence rolled again with laughter. They all knew it was hard work to break a pony, and a hard ground to land on, but that just made it funnier to watch.

The cowboys pulled the ropes off the pony. They didn't want to over-tire the pony. It might take longer to break a horse than just totally wearing the horse down, but they wanted a little spirit left in the pony. Spence respected these cowboys more as he watched them bring in buckets of water and some grain for the horse.

With the show over, the cowboys drifted back to the work they had been doing. Fester never bothered his men when they got to watch a show like this. The cowboys knew when serious work was required and never hesitated to work hard. In the wintertime there wasn't much work to do and the mending of harnesses, rebraiding lariats and such could wait until the cowboy got back to it.

The farmer came out of the blacksmith's cabin and looked around. Seeing Spence he started over digging out his tobacco pouch as he came. He rolled himself a cigarette and offered the pouch to Spence.

"How'd your night go?" Spence asked.

Will had got back his rambling speech again.

"Right comfortable. That's a cozy little cabin. Warmest night I've had in a while, and the wife did wonders with breakfast this morning as their cook brought all kinds of vittles over. I thought that boy was never gonna get full. I've never seen such a friendly group of cowboys in my life. I'd just about forgot how sociable people can be."

"You're right about being friendly. It don't take long to feel at home around here," Spence replied.

"The Colonel has me and the wife coming over for supper. Been told to be prompt, as the Colonel likes to start right at six. Had to dig the clock out of the wagon and then find someone with a time-piece so I could set it. That sure pleased the wife to see some famil-iar furniture around her."

"Yea, I'm supposed to be over there too. I think he wants our view of what happened out there on the range. Getting two or three stories and sorting through them, a man gets an idea of what really occurred," Spence said. "Looked around any this morning?"

"Naw, just relaxing after stuffing myself on breakfast this morn-ing. Heard some doings around the corral but didn't get over there until it had broke up. Wanna walk around some?"

They walked around the ranch headquarters taking in the con-struction of the buildings and the layout of the ranch facilities. The main building faced out over the valley and the rest were built to-ward the rear. A lot of work had been taken to ensure the walls were straight and all the gaps had been filled in the log walls. A three-sided porch had been built around the main house and the bunkhouse had a big porch out front. There was a separate mess hall, animal barn, hay barn and blacksmith shop. There were three smaller cabins built around and they figured that there had once been riders with families living on the ranch. Now Moore, Fester and the head cook had cabins by themselves.

Everywhere they encountered cowboys, they got a nod and friendly greeting. They stuck their head in most of the buildings, and found a well-stocked and maintained ranch. Leather goods were mended and oiled, hay stacked tight, food goods up on shelves and protected from animals and the weather and the bunkhouse clean and warm. They went on into the mess hall, where the cook kept a pot of coffee warming on a wood stove and poured themselves a cup.

"A man could get used to this in a hurry," the farmer stated. "This is the type of place that says the men working here are as important as the animals, the land and any money being made here."

Spence nodded his agreement. He thought that the Colonel must have been a good commander in the Army and took care of his men well. He had often heard it said 'take care of your men and the men will take care of you'. It showed here with the care the men took of the buildings, the gear and the animals.

"You boys the first in line for grub? Don't serve much for dinner but soup and biscuits but you get all of that that you want," the cook yelled over to them.

Spence and the farmer looked at each other, then walked over and filled a bowl with soup and grabbed a hot biscuit. They had just sat down when the door opened and there was a rush on the food. The room filled with the good-natured talk of cowboys pleased with themselves, their work and their surroundings. Spence finished eating, but sat there enjoying the banter of the cowboys as the ones watching the bronco busting this morning related the rides to the ones working out mending fences or tending the cattle. The farmer was laughing as hard as the other cowboys at the tales told.

Having eaten, the cowboys wandered back to their jobs, leaving Spence and the farmer sitting by themselves. "Wanna another smoke?"

Spence took Will up on the offer and they went outside, rolled themselves a cigarette and lit up. They walked over to the wagon and Spence looked at the wheel that had been broken. It looked in better shape probably than when the wagon had been bought by the farmer. That blacksmith knew exactly what had needed to be done to the hub. He could have built himself a good business in any town across the country.

Spence made an excuse to the farmer then went back to the mess hall to have that bath. He wanted to finish it before the cowboys started coming back in for the evening. Public bathing wasn't something he particular cared for. The cook already had water heating, so Spence was able to start his bath right away. The soap wasn't the best but since it was the only available he used it to shave with also. He had pulled his other pair of pants and a clean shirt out of his gear and having dressed, he washed some of the dirt out of his clothes. There was a little tub of grease with wood ash coloring mixed in to use on boots so he applied it and worked it into his boots giving them a nice shine. He walked back out and the cook looked twice at him saying "You sure you're the same cowboy that went into that room a while back?"

Spence just grinned at him and went on back to the bunkhouse. He hung his wet clothes on some rope strung around the corners of the room and then went off to find Fester to get the timepiece. He had heard that as good as the food was in the mess hall, that the Colonel's cook was even better. He had even gone to San Francisco and bought a regular cook stove for his kitchen.

Finding Fester, he got the pocket watch and then went back to the bunkhouse to sort through his gear and start mending some items he had been putting off. He wasn't much good at sewing, but he did keep his socks mended and repaired a couple small holes in his other shirt and replaced a button. The cowboys were beginning to drift back in by the time he finished. Watching the time he listened to the stories of the day; which cow had wandered off, how the harness was pulled loose on which gear, which saddle had the leather rubbing thin, and so on.

About ten to six he got up and started over to the main house. He figured to be a little early in case the watch was off. As he rounded the main barn, Will and his wife were just coming out of the cabin with the farmer yelling back inside, "You two kids stay inside now. I don't want you wandering around outside and if'n I catch you outside, I'll whup your backsides good when I get back."

He grinned at Spence and then the three of them continued to the main house. They could smell the supper being prepared, and knew they were in for a treat.

Approaching the door it swung open, and Fester told them to come inside. He led them through the foyer, through a room with stuffed chairs and a large roaring fireplace and into the dining room. The Colonel, a tall, distinguished-looking middle-aged man was at one end fixing himself a drink from a bar made of finished cedar. It not only looked good, but it still had the sweet cedar smell. He looked up and asked, "What can I get you folks to drink? I'm low on liqueur but I do have some Kentucky bourbon and some whiskey that the Lord only knows where it came from."

Spence and the farmer took bourbon. Meanwhile Fester had seated the woman at the table and poured her glass with water. The

Colonel exchanged pleasantries with the two men asking them what they had seen today and their impressions of his ranch. He kept the conversation light and on the daily happenings of the ranch until dinner was announced as the cook started bringing in the first course.

The meal centered on roasted pheasant with a berry pie for dessert. It was simple fare but well-seasoned and cooked and there was plenty of it. The visitors politely refused seconds but when asked again, they each accepted another large portion of pheasant, sweet potatoes and corn. After the berry pie and coffee, the Colonel moved them all into the den, where he offered the men some small cigars and some home-brewed brandy. The cook let his helpers clear the dishes, and he also came into the den where he uncovered a piano in the corner and started to play some old favorites. Francis moved over and sat next to him picking up the chorus.

The Colonel now got to the reason that he had invited the men over for dinner. First he asked about the details of the trip into the ranch and the fight at the camp. He questioned each man about different details as they had seen the fight. He had a few questions to ask Will about his trip over the mountain range and through the valley and then he turned to Spence.

"Now I want to hear your version of the killing of John Restless, and don't leave anything out," the Colonel told Spence.

Telling the complete story took a little time, but the Colonel was intent and listened to every word, asking a short question every now and then. After Spence finished his explanation of events, the Colonel seemed to think through the story. He asked Spence about the twin .45s as Spence had left them in the bunkhouse instead of wearing them for dinner. The Colonel then asked Spence about his background and a few questions of his experience in the war.

Having heard all he needed, the Colonel poured them another brandy and raised his glass. "Here's to good men cut down in their prime," he toasted.

Spence and Will raised their glasses and sipped of the brandy. It might have been home-brewed but it was still pretty stout. A couple glasses of this would warm a man on even the coldest day.

The Colonel seemed contented with the stories that Spence and Will had told him. After a while he told Spence to come see him in the morning after breakfast. Turning to Will, he told him to come over after lunch because he had a proposition for him. Will and Spence looked at each other. The farmer smiled broadly, but Spence wondering what else the Colonel wanted from him.

They left shortly thereafter with the farmer talking to his wife about all kinds of possible offers the Colonel might make him. He acted like he had found his gold mine right here on the Triple Y ranch. The woman kept telling him to keep his foolish thoughts to himself, and that the brandy had gone to his head. Spence tended to agree with her.

Getting back to the bunkhouse Spence found that most of the cowboys had already bedded down. There were three playing cards over in the far corner so they wouldn't disturb the others. Spence went over and watched for a few minutes. When invited to join the game, he declined and went to his bunk. He laid awake for a while thinking of ways to decline the job offer the Colonel was going to make him. He figured that the Colonel was looking for a man with gun skills, and Spence did not want to be that man.

CHAPTER EIGHT

As the sun rose the next morning, Spence was sitting on the corral fence smoking a cigarette. He had not slept well, and was beginning to get anxious about riding on. He had located his horse and moved it over to a small corral next to the barn. He had watched the cowboys open the large corral gates, and let the horses wander out to the pastures to feed on the winter grass growing there, and he did not want his horse too far away this morning.

As the cowboys started drifting to the mess hall for breakfast, Spence joined them. Might as well start out on the trail with a full stomach, he thought. He got his food and sat next to Fester and listened while the range boss gave out the morning jobs as the cowboys wandered past him. Hank Moore came in, and getting his food, he also sat next to Fester. He had need of a couple of hands today to help shoe a couple of the new horses. Fester yelled over to two of the cowboys and let them know their new assignment for that day.

After Fester had finished eating and had refilled his coffee cup, he turned to Spence. "Saw where you had separated your horse. Planning on riding out today?"

"Don't rightly know. I have to talk with the Colonel this morning, but been getting itchy to be riding on down the trail. Appreciate the bed and food here, but don't like to take advantage of a man's hospitality," Spence replied.

It surprised him that Fester didn't mention anything about maybe staying on at the ranch. He had thought that the range boss might have said something about the Colonel's plans, but Fester just nodded and went back to sipping his coffee and checking his job list. The range boss got up and made a motion to the cowboys, and the mess hall began to empty out. Fester turned to Spence saying something about seeing him before he rode out, and then went out of the mess hall himself.

Spence was soon left alone drinking his coffee. It wasn't much longer before the farmer came in. Will took a tin cup, filled it and came over.

"You really think I was all that wrong last night?" Will asked.

"About what?" Spence wasn't going to encourage the farmer any about possible offers from the Colonel.

"Why about what he might have to offer me. I don't have anything he could possible want except the cow and the pig, but it looks like he don't have need for either of those," the farmer rambled talking as he was thinking. "My grain seed isn't worth anything to a rancher, my boy is too young to work, and he has more chickens that I brought with me."

Spence turned to him saying, "Man, you're going to worry yourself sick thinking about that offer. All you gotta do is just wait and you'll know for sure in just a couple of hours. No wonder your wife ran you out of the cabin. You probably talked her ear off all night."

The farmer looked at him and turned a shade of pink. Spence knew that he had hit the mark. The farmer was quiet for a while, and Spence stood up to leave.

"Let me know what you're going to do when you come back," the farmer said to Spence. After what they had been through, he felt a kinship to Spence and was really beginning to like the man.

Spence nodded and walked out. Going over to the ranch house, he wiped some of the dust off his boots and ran his fingers through his hair. Putting his hat back on, he saw the Colonel was sitting on the porch talking with Fester. He hung back until he saw the Colonel wave for him to come on over.

Fester continued to explain some of the jobs he had the cowboys working on this morning. It seemed that he had full control of handling the work around the place, and just kept the Colonel informed of the progress on major projects. Finishing his report they both turned and looked at Spence.

"Got an offer you might like. I've got a big place here and don't have enough hands to take care of all of it," the Colonel started. "I have an agreement with each of my hands that if they stay with me for five years then I will give each of them five hundred acres of land. The only price I put on it is that if they don't want to settle on it, then, I will buy it back. They can't offer it to anyone else."

Spence looked at the rancher wondering what this had to do with him. He had never figured on working for anyone for five years even if there was a plot of land offered.

The Colonel continued, "Some of these boys are approaching that five year mark and I'm preparing to make good my offer. A couple of them have wives they are going to bring out and some have children. This valley will be a good place for a man to raise a family and it is time for a real community to be established."

Spence glanced over at Fester who was nodding his agreement. It looked like the two men had discussed this idea quite often.

"What I'm going to offer that farmer is a piece of ground back up the valley a ways where the ground is better for farming. There is a range cabin already built up there so he can move his family in out of the winter. I'm going to buy his crops from him and encourage his wife to start a school after more families move in."

Spence was glad to hear Will Harris and his family had been taken under the rancher's wing. This sounded like what the farmer had been thinking about. However, Spence could not see where he fit into this grand plan of the Colonel.

"Now this land is back toward the river that runs down the valley and I own both sides of it. The Bar S owner has been trying to claim parts of this land so he will have complete access to the water for his cows. There is more than enough water even in the summer, but some people always want more than their share. My offer to you is the same amount of land up the other side of what I'm going to offer to Harris. This will put you in-between the Bar S and my first endeavor with a farm."

"Now if you accept the offer I will give you an option on some cows come spring after the first roundup and count. The land will be fully yours after five years but you will have full rights to it now. The work I expect in return is the safety of the Harris family and any others that settle in that area of the valley. I don't expect you to take on the entire Bar S, as I will have riders in the range cabins as before. They will be ready to respond to your call when needed. I have been thinking about this for a while, and you seem to be the answer."

This offer had taken Spence totally by surprise. He had figured he would be offered a straight job as a gun hand, and he had been prepared to turn the Colonel down on his offer. He knew that he was good with his guns and could usually spot trouble coming, but he did not like dealing with it. This was the reason he had come across the Coastal Del Rey Mountains though, to acquire some land and cattle.

Before he could say anything the Colonel continued, "I know that this is a surprise to you. I pride myself on being able to read a man's character and I liked what I've seen with you. I also noticed that you and Harris seemed to get along and you've already had some history together. I thought that you two would make good partners, and would take care of each other. Plus you might be tempted to settle down with his daughter, ensuring that I had a good neighbor protecting my flanks out on the river. Don't even think about giving me an answer yet. Make yourself at home here, think about it and give me your answer in a few days."

Spence nodded his agreement and walked off in a daze. Here a man that he had just met was offering him what he had dreamed of for a long time. The Colonel had seemed to know his feelings about the young woman better than he knew himself. He had not dared to even think about being with a woman and starting a family. Land, cattle, wife, family, settled; all these thoughts were flying through his mind. He wander over to the corral, saddled his horse, while taking care not to run into the farmer. He didn't want to discuss this until he had thought it through. He rode out onto the open range and let his horse go where it wanted.

Will Harris went on up to the ranch house after lunch. He heard the offer from the Colonel, and did not hesitate to accept. He only wanted to know when he could take possession of the cabin and if he could get some help loading his wagon back up. The Colonel had even thrown in two saddle horses and breeding for his cow. The farmer went back to tell his wife and he felt like he was floating on air. Will Harris was a practical man and knew a good deal when he heard it.

Will's wife was also pleased with the offer. She had been dreading living in the open while their first cabin was being built. Now she would not have to endure that hardship and they would not have to spend any of their money trying to buy land. Also, their travel was ending, and the valley seemed like a good place to settle. She was more pleased when Will told her of the other families being brought out to this area.

Emily listened to the offer, and what the Colonel envisioned for the future. She knew that her Ma would not be able to teach the children and saw an opportunity for herself. She had finished school in Pennsylvania and had started attending a teacher's college also. Although she had not finished, she had her own thoughts of how children should be taught. She had practiced on her brother, and knew that if she could get him to learn to read and write then she would do well with other children.

David Elliot Harris also had listened and his feelings of anticipation grew with his Pa's explanation. Finally they would have a farm of their own with good soil. Having a ready-made market for their grain and whatever else they grew ensured their well-being for the future. He knew that they could expand their crops and sell or trade with the families that would be moving in. His father might be a great farmer, but David had more of a marketing sense about him. Crops with no one to buy them did not help a man very much. He was already thinking of riding out to the surrounding ranches to survey expanding their market.

The family discussed the move out to the cabin and started preparing their wagon and belongings for the move. The wife suggested that the two men take a ride out and actually see the cabin and the land before they left the comfort of the ranch. The farmer had to be strongly urged to take this precaution, as he wanted to get everything moved and a start at getting settled. With winter still being here and more snow expected, the woman wanted to ensure they had a snug cabin in which to finish the winter. The farmer reluctantly agreed and he started to make plans to ride out the next day with the boy.

The Colonel had not mentioned to the farmer the dangers from the Bar S nor of his offer to Spence. If Spence refused him, he would add to the offer. If Spence still refused him, then he would station more riders in that part of the area. He did not want the farmer and his family to be placed in any danger. Since his own men would be moving their families into that area, he wanted to ensure a safe environment and a ready food supply. He was going to encourage the farmer to grow a large variety of vegetables along with his grain crops.

Spence rode all afternoon not even noticing the lack of a noon meal. Even though he had got used to eating at noon lately, it had been his practice not to stop while on the trail. Old habits were hard to break. Toward mid-afternoon he stopped his horse and looked around. He had not paid any attention to where he was going, and was surprised to find himself on the small river that flowed down the middle of the valley. It was about twenty feet across at this point and looked fairly deep, as the water was still and dark. He could hear some rapids at the lower end of this pool and started that way. He startled some antelopes and watched as they ran off across the fertile plain. As he approached the water again a flock of quail took flight with a swoosh of their wings. The birds spooked his horse and he had to grab the saddle horn for a couple of jumps until the horse settled back down.

Watching the ground he saw a trail where deer, elk and the antelopes came down to the water. If this was the area that the rancher was giving to his men and the farmer, it would provide for their families with wild game until they could get their first harvest. Just seeing the land made Spence think about accepting the offer. The danger that he might be facing in trying to keep peace between the new settlers and the Bar S might be worth owning part of this valley.

Turning his horse he settled into a slow trot. It would be well after dark when he got back to the ranch, and he did not want to have to spend a night on the trail without even having his poncho with him. He had not even thrown a saddlebag on his horse when he had started out. Reaching down to his side he realized that he did not even have a pistol with him. He had been in such a daze he had not thought about anything at the time.

Realizing that he did not have a gun, he stopped and took a long look around. Starting out again he kept to the low land and ravines so he would not silhouette himself against the horizon. Being a cautious man was different from being a foolish man and he felt very foolish at the moment.

Spence was glad when darkness finally fell. He had not encountered any other riders nor seen sign of anyone having been in that area since the snowstorm. He knew that he had been lucky not to run into anyone that day. He also knew he would not tell of riding off without a firearm on him. He did not want others to know of his foolishness.

Riding back into the ranch area, he put his horse into the corral after unsaddling it and brushing it down with some loose straw. He gave it some grain from the barn then he started over to the mess hall to see if anything was left from the evening meal. The cook was still in the kitchen laying out supplies for the morning meal. Looking over at Spence, he reached for a tin plate and filled it with fried meat, beans and a couple of biscuits. Handing it to Spence he stated, "I always fry up extra, as you never know when riders will come in from the range. You're not the last that will come in here tonight, as Fester had them hitting some of the areas in the foothills today."

Spence nodded his pleasure at having a warm meal, smiled and took his plate over to the table after filling a tin cup with coffee on the way. Settling in, he started on the biscuits and beans. Fester walked in saying, "Thought I heard someone ride in. Been out at the river? Saw you was headed that way."

"Yea, but didn't realize that was where I was going until I got there. That's some pretty good land down that way. Is that part of what the Colonel is offering you and the boys?" Spence asked.

"Part of it. He wants to spread the boys around but still give them land worth having. That is where he's offering Harris and the other side and up a ways is the land he's offering you. It will feed more cows than you can raise for quite a few years."

"I've been thinking about that. It seems the price of that land can get to be pretty high. I don't know the history of this valley but if the Colonel is willing to give away a spread and some cattle just to a have a neutral barrier between the Triple Y and the Bar S, then I need to know more about it. How long has this been going on, how many has been killed so far, the reasons behind it and why the Bar S is harassing farmers?"

Fester thought about these questions for a while and then said to Spence, "I'll pass those questions on to the Colonel. I'm sure that he would not want you to make a decision without having the background information."

They then talked of the farmer giving his decision to the Colonel before he ever left the ranch house. Talking about what this would mean to Harris and his family helped Spence some in his thinking. When Fester told Spence that the farmer and his boy were going to ride out to look at their new home tomorrow, Spence was a little startled. He asked Fester if anyone would be riding out with them, and said that he thought he might make the trip again. He got up and walked over to the cabin to talk with the farmer but finding all the lights out and the cabin quiet, he went back over to the mess hall.

Fester had left but the cook was still there. Spence asked the cook, "Who gets up the earliest around here?"

The cook looked over at him and replied, "Well usually my two helpers are up and about before anyone. After they have the fires started, coffee on and biscuits raising then they get the hands up and moving."

"Tell them to make sure that the farmer and his boy don't get out of here before I'm up and ready. I don't want them out riding toward the Bar S by themselves," Spence told him.

"Don't worry about that. Harris was in here and asked if he and the boy could get breakfast with us so his woman wouldn't have to be cooking so early in the morning. Johnson is going to be riding with them to show them the range cabin they are taking over, then you'll be woke up when they get Johnson moving also," the cook sort of chuckled as he told Spence. "Fester came by early this afternoon and said that you would probably be wanting to ride out with the farmer in the morning."

Spence nodded his thanks to the cook and went out into the dark night. His respect for Fester was growing daily. It seems that the range boss was always one step ahead of most everyone else.

He continued over to the bunkhouse and prepared his stuff for the ride tomorrow and then prepared to turn in. He blew out the fire in the kerosene lamp and rolled into his bunk. The cowboys must have had a rough day, as they were all asleep already.

Lying in the dark Spence found that he had too many thoughts rolling around in his head to fall asleep. Finally he forced himself to block his thoughts, rolled over and went to sleep.

CHAPTER NINE

The next thing he knew was the cook shaking his shoulder, telling him to get up. Spence got up, dressed, grabbed his saddlebag and walked over to the mess hall. Getting a cup of coffee, he saw the farmer and his boy already eating breakfast. He walked over and sat down at the table saying to the farmer, "I thought I would ride with you today and look your land over." Spence did not want the farmer to know that he was riding along to protect him and the boy in case there was trouble.

The cook's helper filled a tin plate with potatoes, a slab of meat, and some hot biscuits. As he gave it to Spence, he stated that Johnson would be in shortly. The two men talked about the trip as they finish their breakfast. As they were filling their cups with more coffee, Johnson walked in the door ,muttering his apology for being late. The farmer told him that he wasn't late, they were just eager to hit the trail and they had come in early.

As Johnson was eating his breakfast, Will sent Davie out to saddle the horses. The farmer had ten thousand questions to ask Johnson about the trail, the range cabin, the land around the cabin, the river that ran through the valley, and if there were any game in the area.

Before they could leave the mess hall, Fester and the rest of the cowboys had begun to file in for breakfast. Fester just got a tin cup of coffee and came over to the table. "Johnson, you know the range cabin that the Colonel is giving Harris? After you get to the cabin, ride due west for about twenty minutes and mark that spot. From that point, turn due north and ride for another twenty minutes, marking that point. Then go due south for twenty minutes and also mark that point. That will be a rough layout of the one section of land or 640 acres for Harris."

Turning to Spence, Fester said, "All the land north and west of these points, up to the start of the foot hills is the land the Colonel is offering you."

Will looked at Spence with a puzzled look. Spence knew that the farmer had a lot of questions to ask but for once he held his tongue. About that time the boy stuck his head in the door, and told his Pa that the horses were ready.

They said their thanks to Fester and turned to go out the door. Before they got to the door, the cook came out of the kitchen with a leather bag. He said, "There's some biscuits with meat in them here in this bag. That should hold you boys until you can make it back in tonight."

Out at the horses Spence took out his gun belt and strapped the twin .45s on. Just that simple act made him feel better about starting out on the trail. He had noticed that Johnson had also strapped on an old Colt pistol and sheathed a rifle into his saddle scabbard. The farmer looked at the other two men, walked over to his wagon and brought out two rifles. He gave one to his son and sheathed the other on his own horse.

The day had dawned bright but quite chilly. It felt good to the riders to get the horses moving. They moved out four abreast, and Will started his questions again to Johnson. Spence just rode and halfway listened to the questions and answers. The boy was too excited to ride with the others and kept spurring his horse to investigate gullies and rock formations, then would come running back to the group. Johnson must have thought this amusing as he smiled at the boy each time he came riding back.

They made better time than Spence had yesterday. Johnson had ridden this part of the range quite often and was taking the most direct route to the cabin. They reached the range cabin about mid afternoon and dismounted so the farmer could look at the cabin to determine the amount of work it would take to reach his wife's expectations. The cabin was small but well-made and maintained. There was a small corral in the back with a two-sided lean-to.

While Harris was assessing the shape of the cabin, Johnson had thrust a stick in the ground. He kept looking at it, and finally looked at Spence and asked if they were ready to start laying out the farm's sides. Spence nodded, and yelled for the farmer and the boy to mount up. They still had two hours of riding to mark the farm and then the ride back to the ranch.

As they started riding the farmer was looking at the soil. He was already planning the fields and which crops would be planted in which areas; high land for the grains, lower lands for vegetables and the area around the river for grasses. He told the rider to keep riding, but he would get down occasionally and poke the soil, letting it run through his fingers. He would come riding back into the group smiling as wide as the boy had been earlier. Johnson would smile at him much like he had the boy. He thought the farmer's actions quite amusing also. Spence enjoyed Will's enthusiasm and plans for the future.

At the end of each twenty minutes of riding they would dismount and collect rocks to make a large pile that could be seen for quite a distance. Then the rider would poke a stick in the ground to take another reading of the sun and head out in the new direction. As they rode the west and north legs of the square, Spence kept watching the land. If he was going to accept the Colonel's offer, he wanted an idea of the land he would be getting. It was as abundant with grass as the land the farmer was getting. The only problem with the land was the lack of running water, but he was sure Will would allow him a passageway through his land.

Riding back on the last leg, they passed within sight of the range cabin. Spence was impressed with Johnson's sense of direction. Coming back so close to the cabin showed great skill in land navigation. They came to the river and went along the bank until they came to some shallows where they crossed. They were just upstream from the cabin. Coming up the bank on the other side they startled five deer, two does and three first year fawns. They all looked in good health, showing that they had wintered well here in the valley.

Johnson took out his rifle and took sight on the largest fawn. It would be tender and would give the cowboys a change of meat from the beef they had been eating lately. The cowboys would bring in a deer, elk or antelope occasionally to help keep meat on the table. Often one of them would take out a shotgun and bring in a turkey, a mess of quail or prairie hens. The birds were a good break from beef, and the cook would stuff them with corn pone and herbs.

One shot and the deer fell. They walked out to where it lay, and it only took a little time to have it cleaned and ready for carrying back to the ranch.

They started back on the trail to the ranch. The boy stayed with the group this time. He wasn't used to riding horseback, and the trip was beginning to tell on him. He was sitting pretty tender in the saddle. The rest of the trip back was uneventful. They did see a pack of wolves running in the distance, and heard a mountain lion squalling in the foothills, but did not see it.

They got back to the ranch well after dark. Will was pleased with the day's ride and Spence was also content. They both had decided that the Colonel's offer was more than generous and they both were going to make the best of the offers. And they were glad that they were to be neighbors.

The farmer and the boy unsaddled their horses and turned them loose in the corral. Then they went to the cabin, where the woman was waiting in the doorway. She was anxious to find out what their new home was like, and she had cooked a special supper for her men.

Spence and Johnson unsaddled and went over to the mess hall. They knew that the cook had kept supper warm for them, even if it was a slab of beef and some beans. After just the cold biscuits for dinner they could have eaten almost anything. Johnson had given the deer to the cook's helpers and they had started skinning it out and cutting up the meat. They were planning on deer liver and scrambled eggs for breakfast in the morning.

The next morning Spence found Fester and told him that he needed to talk with the Colonel. Fester smiled at him and already knew what his answer was going to be. He told Spence that he would arrange a meeting mid-morning with the Colonel. He asked if Spence wanted to help with the new horses this morning. They still had six that weren't broken and needed more working. Spence agreed to help and wandered over to the corral.

There weren't any spectators this morning, as Fester had the cowboys riding the near ranges preparing for the spring roundup. It was a time of hard work and long hours, and all the advance preparation would pay off later. There were only three riders in the corral, and they had one horse roped and were preparing to saddle it.

Spence offered to take the first ride on the horse. It had been a while since he had tried to break a horse. The other cowboys did not hesitate to agree. They had been working at these six for a couple of weeks and had just about reached the conclusion that the horses were going to break them first. They finished saddling the horse and put the sack over its head.

Spence climbed on the horse and nodded to the cowboys. They pulled the sack off the horse, and he started his bucking and jumping. Spence was feeling good about his ride, and he tightened up and hung on. The horse bucked himself down, and started running around the corral trying to rub the rider off his back. Spence lifted his outside leg and waited for the run to stop and the horse to start his jumps again. After two and half rounds of the corral with the horse rubbing against the rails and hitting the posts, he suddenly jerked to his left and hopped four times and then stumbled and fell. Spence rolled with the horse and was back in the saddle as the horse got back on his feet. The horse was too tired now to do anything else but just stand on trembling legs.

Spence spurred him a little under the rib cage and caused him to start walking around the corral. The other cowboys took the horse's reins and Spence dismounted. They asked him if he was ready for the next one. Spence replied that he would try another one.

The next horse took four leaps after the sack came off, and Spence took a flying ride over the horse's head. This horse wasn't going to be as easy. He remounted the horse and tried another ride. It only took two hops and a sideward leap and Spence was on the ground again. This wasn't fun anymore. Picking himself up, he told the cowboys he would try it one more time.

Will and Davie had walked up during his last ride. They were smiling at him and he knew that they had been laughing at his dump off the horse. He didn't mind, as he knew riders going head over heels was funny. He waved and smiled back at them and turned back to the horse.

One more ride, one more dump, and he told the cowboys that it was time for one of them climb on board. He grabbed one of the ropes and helped hold the horse still. The broncobuster climbed on and was able to ride the horse to a stand still. Riding the horse around the corral, he said that Spence had ridden the horse down for him and he had just got the glory ride. Spence knew that the man was just talking, as he had watched the ride and knew the horse had a lot of energy left in him.

They tried each of the other four horses, but didn't have any other horses willing to give up their freedom. They gave up finally and left the horses in the corral. They wouldn't turn them loose on the range until after they were broken and trained to respond to the riders' knee action and reins.

Walking over to the mess hall, Will walked next to Spence. "When you thinking of moving out to your land?"

"I've not even given the Colonel my acceptance yet," Spence replied. "What are your thoughts on moving out there?"

"I've been thinking, and although I'm ready to move on out there, my wife wants to wait a while. She thinks the winter hasn't blown itself out yet, and she's heard talk about the Bar S riders. She wants me and the boy to go whenever you do, so there will be help available in case something happens. She's been through quite a bit of trouble on this trip, and I don't want to put her through any more. If'n the Colonel don't mind us staying a while longer in the cabin, then I think we'll just do a few trips out there for a couple days at a time until spring."

Spence nodded his agreement. "I'll let you know when I'm ready. Did you hear anyone mention anything about a range cabin on my land? I never thought to ask on the trip yesterday."

"Nope, never heard mention of one. If there isn't one, though you can put up with us whenever we go out. We can start you a cabin and work on it until spring. Might be too busy after that for a while until the plowing and planting is finished," Will told him.

Before they could get inside Fester came riding up and asked Spence if he was ready to talk. Spence nodded and started up to the ranch house with Fester. The farmer and his boy turned and went back toward their cabin. For once they were both quiet.

CHAPTER TEN

Life went on as usual at the ranch. There were two more storms that kept the cowboys snowed in at the ranch. In between storms they rode the close ranges beginning to gather the cattle into large groups. The larger groups would be easier to herd together in the spring. They also worked preparing the range corrals that would be used later for the horses.

Moore, the blacksmith gathered all the branding irons and repaired the broken ones. The YYY was a little difficult to make on the brand and it took the smithy quite a bit of time hammering the iron. Moore didn't mind the work, though, as it took more skill than just pounding out horseshoes.

Spence, Harris and the boy had ridden out to the range cabin a few times, but the weather kept them from doing very much work. Spence had found out that there was a cabin on his land, and they had cleaned it up and repaired the roof. It didn't have a chimney or fireplace, just a wide fire pit under a hole in the wall. The first thing Spence was going to do was to get the blacksmith to help design and show him how to build a fireplace for his cabin.

The rest of the winter passed quick enough. Then after a couple of days of warm weather, Will came to Spence and told him that it was time to go back out and check to see if the fields were ready to start clearing for plowing. Spence agreed, as he was feeling restless and the ride would do wonders for his spirits.

The next morning the farmer and his boy were ready to ride before Spence finished his breakfast, so he grabbed a couple biscuits and some meat thinking he would eat it on the trail. The morning was brisk and the air crisp. The horses were feeling frisky, and the morning passed quickly. It was as if the animals were feeling the excitement of the men at being on the trail again.

They had the trail memorized by now after having made the trip four times during the past couple of months. As they got nearer to the cabin, the boy took off riding ahead of the others. He was out of sight for a while, and then he suddenly popped up over a hill yelling at them and waving them on. The distance was too far to hear what he was saying, but he seemed excited about something.

Spence and the farmer spurred their horses and took off at a gallop. As they approached, the boy turned and took off in the direction of the cabin. Whatever he was excited about seemed to be close to the cabin. They continued after the boy and the horses picked up the urgency and continued to gallop after the other horse.

Crossing the river and coming up the opposite bank put them in view of the cabin. There seemed to be something different about the cabin, but from this angle they could not tell what it was. As they got closer and the angle on the cabin changed they then saw what the boy was yelling about.

The cabin had been burnt-out since their last visit. The only thing left was the chimney, and the stone walls. The roof and everything inside the cabin had been burnt to ashes. Pulling up in front of the cabin along side the boy they just sat and stared at the farmer's dreams lying in ruins.

"Now who would have done something like this?" the farmer asked. "This is a crazy act by some vandal. This is just the worst thing I think could have happened."

Will couldn't even think straight. To see his dreams burnt and knowing that he wouldn't be able to move out here with his family had him speechless. Davie and Spence were both affected the same way. They couldn't even think how a person could burn a range cabin down like that. These outlying cabins had saved many a rider's life, protecting him from the weather, and no telling how many others had used them as they traveled down this trail.

The boy finally dismounted and walked into the ruins. It had been a while since the fire, as everything was cold. He moved burnt logs around looking for anything they could salvage, but there was nothing left. The bunks, table, chairs and storage shelves were all gone. He looked around for the coffeepot, iron skillet and pots but there weren't any around. He called out to his Pa and told him. Spence and Harris looked at each other. This was definitely not an accident. It seems someone had looted the cabin before they set fire to it.

"No use spending any more time here right now. Maybe we better ride on out to my cabin and see if it's still standing," Spence said to the other two.

They mounted up and took off for Spence's cabin. It was a hard hour's ride out to it and they didn't waste any time. As they approached the ridge just before the cabin the boy took off again. He hit the top of the ridge and stopped. Spence was watching the boy and saw him sort of slump as he looked over the ridge. As they approached the top of the ridge and saw that this cabin had been burnt down, it confirmed what Spence had read in the boy's posture. All that hard work on the roof had just made it burn better.

"No use going on down there. At least I didn't have anything in the cabin to loot or burn," Spence said.

"Well, that tells me that my cabin wasn't an isolated case or an accident. Someone burnt both of these down intentionally. I would think someone didn't want us moving out here. What do you think?" the farmer asked Spence.

"Yea, I think you're right. Whoever it was at least wanted to delay our move. Maybe they thought that this was a warning and that it was all it was going to take to scare us off. I figure it might slow us down a bit, but it sure isn't going to scare us off," Spence stated.

They turned and started back to the farmer's cabin. He still wanted to check the condition of the land and mark some fields he wanted to start plowing first. He figured to burn off some of the brush and just plow under most of the grass. The weather was clear and they could sleep out under the stars that night.

Getting back to the cabin, Will told his boy to start trying to clean out the inside of the cabin. They would have to lay the floors and build back the bunks and shelves after laying a new roof on the walls. Harris figured that they would do without a wood floor for a while and lay it back in after the fields were plowed and planted. The wife could sweep out the loose dirt and they would pack the rest down with a clay base.

He rode on out to where he wanted the first field, dismounted and started walking out his field. The boy started trying to clean the trash from inside the walls of the cabin.

Spence got off his horse and walked a wide circle around the cabin. He didn't notice anything close up as their horses had trampled any signs there might have been. As he circled in a wider sphere he came upon the tracks of four horses. They had approached the cabin from the direction of the Bar S ranch. It looked like they had known exactly where they were headed.

He widened his circle, and eventually came upon the same set of four horses' tracks leaving this cabin and moving in the direction of his cabin. Whoever these riders were, they knew where each cabin was located.

Returning to the cabin he dismounted and then went to bring in some firewood. The boy had enough space around the fireplace cleared so the three of them could bed down inside the walls. Spence started a fire and went to his saddlebag, pull out his pot and went down to the river to bring back some water. He had just pulled the pot out full of water when a gunshot rang out over the countryside. Spence threw the pot up on the bank and took off running. As he neared the top of the bank he pulled a .45 from his holster. At the top of the bank he veered to the side staying in the brush. If there was anyone out there he didn't want to just run into the trouble.

Looking out over the area around the cabin he couldn't see anything moving. He checked Will's direction but couldn't see him either. Being down in the riverbed he had not been able to tell where the gunshot had come from. He continued moving in the brush until he could see the front of the cabin. Still no movement was detected from anywhere.

If the boy and the farmer had heard the shot, they were being as cautious as he was. Spence scanned the horizon but did not see anything. Finally he broke and ran for the cabin. Before he ran twenty feet another shot rang out and dirt spurted up right in front of Spence. He jumped and rolled back to his feet and then ran zig-zag toward the cabin. Two more shots were fired but neither was close to him as he hit the doorway of the cabin.

The boy was peering over the edge of the window-opening trying to locate the source of the shots.

"I sure can't see where they are coming from, and here I sat without any gun at all," he said to Spence.

"Any idea where the first shot was placed?" Spence asked. He was afraid the first shot might have been at the farmer and took him by surprise.

"They hit the wall about three inches from my head," the boy replied. "Whoever is out there, they wouldn't win any prizes at a turkey shoot."

"Well at least we're lucky they're poor shots. Judging from the spacing of the shots though, I would say that it was only one shooter. If there had been more then I would have been lying out there behind something instead of running on in here," Spence said.

He looked out the door opening and tried to peer inside the brush. If the shooter would fire again he might be able to see a puff of smoke or movement. As it was he couldn't see anything.

"Did you see anything when he was shooting at me?" Spence asked.

"No, the first shot I thought was at me. It wasn't until the second shot didn't hit anything in here that I thought he might have been shooting at something else. At the third shot I was looking to see who he was shooting at. I didn't get a chance to look for signs of smoke or anything," the boy rambled. Now that Spence was in here with him he was feeling better. He knew that the man shooting wouldn't stand a chance of getting close to the cabin.

Spence looked around for something to try to make a target out of so they could try to fool the shooter into giving his position away. "When you clean up you sure do a good job. I don't see anything I can use in here."

The boy reached behind him and pulled out a stick with some prairie grass tied to it. He had been using it as a make shift broom. "Will this do?" he asked Spence.

"Sure will," Spence said taking the broom. He took off his coat, then his vest. He put his coat back on and then wrapped the vest around the broomstick. He sure hated to put his hat on the target but finally took his hat off and stuck it on the grass.

"Now watch very closely at the brush in front of the cabin. I'm just going to stick this up for a short while like a person was getting ready to run. Maybe it will fool him into firing again."

He moved the stick around with just the top of the hat sticking out the edge of the door. He then moved it up some like a man was trying to stand up. Then he moved the hat and vest out the doorway. As he was starting to move it back inside a shot rang out and the hat flew off the broom.

Spence had been looking out the bottom of the door and the shot knocked the stick from his hands. Jerking back inside he turned to the boy who said, "Got him now. Look over at that bush next to the third fir tree. He's lying at the bottom in the bush. If you look close you can see just a bit of red from his bandanna."

Spence looked and could just make out the outline of the ambusher. It would be a long shot with his .45, but it was the only gun he had with him. He didn't want to risk running out and around the cabin to where his horse and rifle were. It seems the shooter had finally got the range and had his aim down now. Spence took aim on the outline and raised his aim just over the shape. The first couple of shots would be trusting to Kentucky windage as he didn't know where they would hit. He squeezed off the first shot and saw dirt kick up ten feet in front of the man. He raised his aim about an half an inch and fired again and watched dirt kick up three feet in front of the man. As he was taking aim again he heard a whack in the rock right in front of his face just as he heard the rifle fire.

Jerking back, another shot hit inside the cabin and ricocheted off the back wall and whined out the open roof. He was right about the shooter having the range now. The second shot was where his face would have been if he hadn't jerked back. He glanced over at the boy and saw that he was staying down. The boy had noticed the increase in the shooter's accuracy also. The boy shrugged his shoulders and grinned at Spence.

Moving over to the window Spence prepared to try to take another shot. He told the boy to take the broom and just stick an edge of the vest out close to the bottom of the doorway. He figured that would draw the shooter's attention while he took aim and fired another shot. He nodded, the boy moved the broom over to the door, a rifle shot sounded and the broom stick flew into two pieces, but it was long enough for Spence to take aim and fire again. He didn't see any dirt kick up this time but a branch right in front of the shooter fell down on him. Spence saw him scoot down behind the brush some. He didn't have a shot at all now.

He stood up to try to get a better angle on the shooter. As he was figuring if he had a shot, the shooter suddenly moved up and fired again. Spence felt his coat shift on his shoulder, and saw a hole where the bullet had barely ripped through his jacket. He moved back before the shooter could fire again.

Suddenly the air was filled with shots and then all was quiet. Spence had recognized the shooter's rifle firing twice but a different gun sounded the last shots.

"That sure sounded like my Pa's rifle," the boy yelled and started to get up. Spence pulled him back down and told him to wait and just watch. If it was his Pa then his had been the last shots.

They waited and watched the edge of the brush. Finally, not seeing any movement from the shooter's position or anywhere else Spence moved over to the door. The boy stood up also.

"Be careful and move off to the left. Circle around keeping as much brush as possible between you and the shooter. Here, you know how to handle this," Spence asked as he gave his other .45 to the boy.

"Yea, sure do," Davie replied as he skipped out the door quickly and move off to the left of the cabin. Spence moved rapidly to the right to the first bushes. He approached the shooter's position with his .45 cocked and ready. Nearing the man Spence could tell they didn't have anything to fear from him any longer. He was starring up to the heavens and the holes in his chest plainly said this man would not be doing anymore shooting.

Spence then yelled out for Will. He figured the farmer had heard the shots and worked himself around and came up from behind the ambusher. Spence heard some commotion about thirty feet away behind some thick undergrowth and thorny bushes. Moving around them he saw the farmer leaning up against a tree with one arm hanging at his side. The boy was already working to stop the flow of blood from a hole in the upper arm.

"That ol' boy sure was fast. I yelled at him to drop his rifle and before I knew it he had plugged me good. If I hadn't already had my rifle in the fork of this tree and lined up on him, he might have got me again. My first shot though took most of the fight out of him but he still got another shot off. I plugged him a couple more times just to be sure he wouldn't try another one," the farmer told the two.

He then sat down hard on the ground. The excitement of the firefight had worn off and the shock of being hit himself took hold. The boy had the bleeding stopped and was tying his handkerchief over the wound.

"Looks like that ol' boy was left to keep an eye on the cabin. He must of thought he could take care of things here and had visions of returning a hero. Must not have been able to count or figured I was in the cabin," Will mumbled.

"Well, he sure figured wrong. He had us pinned down pretty good. We couldn't even stick our head up without him shaving it," Spence told him showing him the rip in his coat. "Lucky you were on the back side and could work yourself around behind him."

"Well, I hope he was the one that burnt the cabin. Makes me feel better just to think that he was," Harris said as he tried to get up. The boy reached down and help him up, then put his shoulder under the farmer's good arm and put an arm around his Pa.

"Well, appears supper is up to you two. Don't think I can handle that iron skillet tonight," the farmer joked. He might have been shot but he still had a sense of humor.

Spence and the boy helped the farmer make it to the cabin. The boy got the bedding from the horses and made his Pa's bed close to the fire while Spence started cooking some supper. They ate supper and then Spence unwrapped the arm and cleaned it with hot water and then took a clean shirt and made some bandages with it. With a clean dressing on his arm, Harris lay down and went to sleep. The boy also turned in and it didn't take long for him to fall asleep.

Spence got up and taking another cup of coffee walked out from the cabin into the night. He made a wide circle of the cabin and listened to the night. If there were any more riders out there, then they were quieter than the grave. As he walked back to the cabin he heard coyotes howling in the distance.

CHAPTER ELEVEN

The morning dawned cold, with a layer of frost over everything including the sleeping men inside the cabin. It was deathly quiet without a thing moving. The boy was the first to stick his head out of his bedding. He looked around, surprised that Spence was still sleeping. He had never seen the cowboy sleep past dawn.

Looking over at the fireplace, he noticed a fire still burning. Now he knew that Spence hadn't been in bed very long. He figured the cowboy had stayed on watch until it had begun to lighten the sky, took another walk around and then turned in.

The boy went over and felt his Pa's forehead and neck. There wasn't any fever, so he hoped that his Pa would heal up quickly. It sure would have been bad luck if a bone had been broken or the bullet had hit anywhere else.

He bundled up, and taking the cooking pot, headed off to the river. He reached down and picked up his slingshot as he went past his bedding. Walking along he picked up a stone whenever he spotted a nice round one that would fit inside his slingshot pouch.

Approaching the riverbed he slowed down and tried to walk a little more quietly. He might spot a rabbit or squirrel and could make a pot of stew for breakfast. He didn't see anything so he filled the pot with water and sat it up on a rock. Then he washed his face and hands in the cold water. If he hadn't been awake already, the cold water sure would have done the trick. Using the sleeves of his jacket he dried his face and turned to get the pot of water.

As he grabbed the handle of the pot and looked up the bank he stared right into the face of a puma. The big cat was ready to spring at the boy and just as it started, the boy flung the pot full of water into the cat's face. The puma was not expecting to be doused, and it jumped sideways instead of at the boy. Davie grabbed a rock and pounding on the bottom of the pot, and ran at the puma. Not having ever seen a creature like this one that could throw cold water and make a dreadful noise, the cat ran off up the riverbank.

The boy watched the puma run and then broke out in laughter. He didn't know if he was laughing from the sight of the cat when the water had hit it or just laughing from fright. Then he suddenly had to sit down before his knees buckled. He sat there for a few minutes gathering his wits and then refilled the pot with water and started back to the cabin.

When he got to the cabin and went inside, his Pa rolled over in his blankets. With a little moan he sit up and asked the boy what that noise had been down at the creek. It surprised the boy that he had been loud enough that his Pa had heard the banging. No wonder the puma had been scared off.

Telling the tale, his Pa got to laughing so hard that he rolled over onto his back. The laughter caused Spence to lift the edge of his blanket, "What's so dang funny out here that a man can't even get a little shut eye?" he asked.

Then the boy had to tell the tale again and then both men got to laughing. "It sure wasn't that funny to me," the boy said. "I was almost ate up out there and all you two can do is laugh?"

This started them laughing again. The farmer got up and took the pot and filled the coffeepot and put it on the fire. "You should have brought that ol' cat into camp and we'd have had some lion stew," he said to the boy.

"Well I guess you'll have to settle for some corn mush and fried meat then. I didn't have nothing with me but my sling shot and that pot, and the pot seemed to be the better weapon at the time," the boy replied.

That started all three chuckling again. Will got up and started rolling up the bedrolls and the boy went to bring the horses up to the cabin as Spence cooked breakfast. After eating, they mounted up and started the ride back to the ranch. With the two cabins burnt there wasn't much else they could do here, especially with Will having his arm wounded and tied up in a sling.

Crossing the river, Spence did stop to look at the puma's tracks. He was curious as to how large the cat had been. Looking at the cat prints he realized that the boy had been lucky he had had the cold water and the pot to bang on. That cat could have brought down a full-grown deer or antelope.

Riding into the ranch mid-afternoon, Spence helped Harris get settled into his cabin, and then left him with his wife Francis fretting over him. That would do more to cure him than anything else.

Spence went out to find Fester to report the situation on the north-west range and the cabins. He was sure Fester would be most interested in the actions of their northern neighbors. The burning of the cabins had been a direct action against the Triple Y ranch and not just on passing settlers.

Spence found Fester over in the blacksmith's shop. He had been giving the smithy some new designs for door hinges that the Colonel wanted installed up at the ranch house. As Spence begin to tell him what had occurred out at the cabins, he told him to save it and come on up to the ranch house. He said that it was best just to tell it to him and the Colonel at one time so they could both hear the same story.

As they went into the side door of the main house, Fester motioned to the cook to bring some coffee into the main room. He told Spence to take a seat and then went on into the back to get the Colonel. Coming into the room, the Colonel grinned broadly at Spence and said, "I hear you've got a tale to tell. Hope it's got a happy ending."

"Depends on what you consider happy," Spence said and then went on to tell the two men of what had occurred out at the cabins and of the death of the Bar S rider.

"Well, the rider part is happy. I sorta figured this was coming. They have slowly been building up to a confrontation with their dirty deeds getting a little bigger and meaner each time. I guess it is time we take action and not just sit and wait for the next deed. Those two cabins were built well back onto my land, and there could be no mistaking it was Triple Y range cabins that they were burning," the Colonel stated.

"Fester, go bring in Hank, Joey, Carl and Bob. We need to lay some plans before we take off half-cocked. Spence, you're welcome to stay and put in your two cents, since you've been involved in a couple of actions with these boys from the Bar S already," the Colonel continued.

As Fester left the room the Colonel turned to the cook and told him to bring in something for the boys to chew on while they discussed these doings. He told Spence to make himself comfortable until the others could make it up to the ranch house, then he walked back to his study and closed the door.

Spence poured himself some coffee and then walked back to the kitchen with the cook. The kitchen was a lot more comfortable than the main drawing room. He watched the cook cut up some meat and bread and put them together. There was a pie left from supper the night before and the cook dished up a big piece for Spence. They filled the time with small talk until they heard the front door open and boots come trampling inside.

Going back into the main room Spence saw some of the cowboys from the bunkhouse. He hadn't really paid them any attention, but it was apparent that the Colonel respected their opinions.

The Colonel asked Spence to repeat his story and then he presented some options that he had been working on. The men discussed the actions that might be needed for each option and the possible outcomes. They pointed out the negative reactions that might occur also if they took some of the actions. It was well into the evening before the cook brought in some more food so they could continue with their planning. Spence was impressed with the thought these men were giving to each plan the Colonel presented.

It was almost midnight before the Colonel stood up and told them that it was time to turn in. They would gather again after breakfast and finalize their plans. The group had narrowed the proposed plans down to two and would continue to finish them in the morning.

Walking back to the bunkhouse with the others Spence listened to them as they continued their discussion. These men were used to planning campaigns and were probably part of the Colonel's staff officers and senior non-commissioned officers of his unit. This confrontation was just another campaign to them and it didn't matter who the enemy was this time.

They quieted down as they got to the bunkhouse and silently went inside to their bunks. They didn't want to disturb the sleep of the hard working cowboys. It wasn't but a few minutes until the bunkhouse was quiet except for the normal sounds of the sleeping men.

Spence had thoughts of his own about what was going to take place. No matter which action was selected by the Colonel, he figured that he would be a center player in it. It seemed to be time to start paying for that land the Colonel was giving to him.

Boots dropping, men coughing and beds screeching woke Spence the next morning. It seemed just minutes to him since he had been thinking of the meeting. He rolled over, not wanting to get up yet. Two nights of missing sleep was rough, and a couple more minutes of sleep would do wonders for him.

Suddenly he sat up. The bunkhouse was totally quiet and no one was about. Spence didn't know how much longer he had slept or what time it was. He quickly dressed and rushed over to the mess hall. It was still full of cowboys eating, and Spence relaxed a little then. He wasn't as late as he thought he might have been. Fester did give him a look as he came in the door, and then grinned at him.

Fester sent the cowboys out on their daily tasks as if nothing was up, and did not discuss anything about the Colonel planning a counter-action to the cabins being burnt. The cowboys knew something was up, but they just discussed it among themselves and didn't ask Fester what was going on.

Mid-morning the Colonel called the planners back up to the ranch house and they continued their discussion on the various plans. Spence found himself getting more involved in the discussions as he began to feel more comfortable with the men and in the planning of the action. He had always had his own views of how cavalry should be deployed and used on a battleground.

Mid afternoon saw the finalization of the plans, and the Colonel told Fester to prepare the men for an early morning departure. He wanted a full allotment of ammunition issued to the men, and the cook was to prepare enough food to last them for five days on the trail. This was to be a quick and decisive campaign, but the Colonel wanted to be prepared in case it did last more than one skirmish.

As the men went back down the hill they were fairly quiet, with only a couple of comments being made. Fester went to send some riders out to bring all the cowboys back to the ranch and then went to talk with the cook. He sent Spence to inform Hank to prepare rifle ammunition to be issued to the men as they came through. All the spare ammunition for rifles and pistols was kept in the blacksmith's supply shop.

As the out-riders began to come in off the range Fester would meet each group and briefly inform them of why they had been pulled from the range duties. Then they were sent to the bunkhouse to start preparing their gear.

At supper and later in the bunkhouse the cowboys discussed what they had been told and gave their own thoughts to anyone that would listen. There were a few of the cowboys that stayed quiet, having never been in the war or in the Army. They just listened to the past experiences of the other cowboys.

Rain was falling the next morning. Spence had looked out the bunkhouse door as soon as he had awakened and heard the rain on the roof. He could barely make out the barn and the mess hall. He went back to his bunk and starting digging his poncho out of his bags. After getting his rain gear, he took out his pistols and applied a coat of oil on them, and then on his rifle. This would help keep them from rusting up as much from the weather.

The other cowboys had seen him dig out his poncho, and they did the same. They didn't need to be told to lay a sheet of oil on their firearms; it was second nature to them to protect their gear.

As they finished preparing for the trip, they moved over to the mess hall to get a hot meal before they departed. If the rain kept up then it would be a while before they got another hot meal. The cooks had fixed a corn mush with butter and syrup to go in it, fried meat, eggs and hot biscuits. Spence ensured that he filled up and then had a second cup of hot coffee. They were waiting for Fester to show up to give directions for the departure.

Most of the cowboys had finished breakfast and were nursing another cup of coffee when Fester finally walked through the door. He stopped at the doorway and looked around like he was taking a head count. Then he walked over to the coffeepot, took a tin cup, filled it with coffee and took a couple of sips before he turned to the group.

Everyone had put down their cups and watched Fester. He knew how to get everyone's attention without saying anything. He walked over to the first table and put his cup down.

"I guess everyone has heard a little bit of what we are going to start today. The Colonel asked me to tell you that since none of you hired on to be a gun hand, then none of you are obligated to ride out with us today. There's plenty of work to do around here to keep you busy until we get back."

The room was quiet. They all waited for Fester to continue with his comments.

"We are going to try to settle up with the Bar S ranch on this continuing harassment they have started, and range encroachment. The Colonel has decided that the cabin burnings were the last straw, and it is time for us to show the Bar S that we are not going to tolerate any more acts of violence from them. There are some hired guns over there, but most of you are seasoned soldiers and have been under fire before.

"The Colonel doesn't want anyone to participate unless they want to do this. Each of you have a stake in the outcome though. If you want to settle your land and bring families out here, then we need to be able to provide a safe place for you to raise your children. No one will be required to ride, and no one else will say a word against you if you don't. This is a decision for each man to make on his own, and for the ones that do ride, I had better not hear anything said against those that decide not to. I will mount up in fifteen minutes out by the corral."

With those comments he turned and walked out of the room. It was quiet for about five seconds, and then the tables cleared as the cowboys went to fetch their gear, guns and saddle their mounts. Spence was the last to get up. Looking around, there were only two men left sitting; one old man with a limp left arm and one new drifter that had only been hired the previous week. Spence nodded to each and then went to get his gear.

As Spence got to the corral to get his horse, he found that the farmer's boy had already saddled him and had the horse waiting for Spence. Will was mounted and was waiting to ride.

"I don't think anyone expects you to come on this trip," Spence told Harris. "They all realize that you are a farmer and that you have your family here. I myself would feel better if you stayed here and looked after your family and let us finish this business."

"I have a stake in this business also. That was my cabin they burnt down and my land they rode over to do it. I'm not helpless, and you already know I can handle myself," the farmer stated.

Spence nodded his agreement and saw that the farmer was going regardless of what anyone said, so he dropped the matter. He sheathed his rifle and mounted. Fester then came out of the barn already on his horse. He looked over the final preparations of the cowboys. Seeing Will already mounted he grinned at him. He had halfway expected to see the farmer here.

As the cowboys finished saddling their horses, they mounted. When the last cowboy was ready Fester reined his horse around and started out of the ranch yard. As they were riding past the main house the Colonel came outside and saluted the group of riders. He was in trail clothes, and his horse was waiting for him. Fester turned and told two men to drop off and come on when the Colonel was ready to ride.

Johnson and his partner dropped out of the formation and ride up to the ranch house. Spence didn't know it at the time, but these two had been the Colonel's aides-de-camp when they had still been in the Army and were used to escorting the Colonel.

It wasn't very long before everyone was wet. The ponchos would turn the water for a while, but they were soon soaked and started seeping. After that they were just good for turning some of the water off the riders. They rode in quietness, each with his own thoughts. Occasionally a cowboy would get his hat turned wrong and the rainwater would roll down between the poncho and his neck. A couple of good curses would split the air and the others would sympathize a couple of seconds with the victim, and then all would be quiet again except for the creaking of saddles and the plodding of the horses' hooves through the mud.

The Colonel caught up with the group around mid morning. He was as wet as they were. As he came through the group he spoke to each man. He was the type of leader that knew his men and appreciated their different skills. He knew the background of each man and had talked with them of their future plans. Each man spoke back, and by the time the Colonel was at the front of the group, Spence had noticed a difference in the attitude of the entire group. Just the presence of the Colonel had lifted the spirits of the wet men.

Around mid-afternoon the rain began to let up some. Fester stopped the group and the cook brought up his supply mule. Reaching into his bags, the cook handed out handfuls of jerky and hardtack. The men munched on the chewy grub and washed it down with water. Food like this was designed to just keep a man going. There wasn't any pleasure in eating it, but these men had eaten food that tasted worse than this and so there were no complaints.

Fester was planning on making the burnt out cabin on the outer range of the Triple Y and stop for the night. They would have a hot meal and try to dry out some now that the rain had stopped. Looking at the sky he could tell the clouds were beginning to break up and would soon be a clear sky. That meant a chilly morning tomorrow.

Stopping for the night, they gathered wood for a couple of fires and as the cook started supper, the cowboys laid out their bedding. Some of them cut small brush and gathered grass to make a bed up out of the mud while others just laid out their poncho and made up their bed on top of it. Johnson pulled a dry poncho from the cook's bags for the Colonel. He laid the bed out close to the wall of the cabin next to one of the fires. Since this was higher ground than most of the valley, the rainwater had ran off or seeped into the ground fairly fast so there wasn't as much mud.

They ate their supper, and Fester posted a guard while the others turned in. Tomorrow had the promise of a busy day and the cowboys were going to get their sleep tonight. Spence didn't draw any guard duty, so he got another cup of coffee and rolled himself a smoke. Fester had checked in with the Colonel and came over and got Spence and the others that had planned this action.

They walked up to the cabin where the Colonel was squatting by the fire. The cook had started another smaller coffeepot up here and the Colonel motioned for them to fill their cups. After everyone had their coffee and settled, he stated that he wanted to go over the plans real fast before they turned in. This would be the last time to make changes before the action started tomorrow.

The Colonel ran back over the plans and no one could think of any changes that needed to be made. The only thing left was to split the men up into the groups under each leader. Spence figured that they would discuss this matter, but no one mentioned it. He didn't figure it was his place to bring it up, but he still wondered about it.

They finished their coffee and small talk and drifted back to their beds. As Spence started down to his bedroll he fell in beside Fester. "How they going to decide which man goes with which group to-morrow?"

"Don't have to worry about that. They have a natural grouping amongst themselves. As the leaders split up you'll see certain men just naturally follow the man they're used to following. I'll just have to break off a few to go with you," Fester replied.

Spence nodded and was satisfied with the answer.

CHAPTER TWELVE

As the night sky began to lighten the last guard woke Hess Fester first. As he stuck his head out from under the blankets he looked around. There was frost over everything just as he expected there to be. The sky was clear, and this time of morning always seemed to be the coldest. He put on his boots while still wrapped in his bedroll, and then reached inside and brought out his coat. He put it on and buttoned it up while walking over to the fire.

The other cowboys were beginning to stir. They were all slow getting out of the warmth of their bedrolls. Fester thought to himself that he was letting them get soft. He would have to start getting them out on the range more often. He failed to see his own actions in those of his men.

As the riders dressed they cleaned up the bedrolls and packed everything back on their horses. As they finished they came over to the fire where the cook was finishing the morning grub. He already had a big iron pot full of coffee boiled and sitting on the edge of the coals. Each cowboy dipped his tin cup in the brew and moved back from the cooking area. They didn't need the cook jumping on them for being in his way. They probably all had at one time or another a tongue lashing from the cook.

Fried bread and fried meat was the menu for the morning, with some corn mush on the side. It wasn't much, but the pots were emptied out by the time the cowboys had finished eating. The cook never had to deal with leftovers when he was cooking out on the range. Either the exercise or the fresh air increased a man's appetite.

When everyone was finished Fester had them mount up and then turning to the cook he said, "We'll be back before dark, one way or the other. Just have a fire and hot food waiting for us."

Then turning his horse around, he rode off with the rest of the men following. The Colonel was already waiting for them on the trail and he took the lead as the group approached him. There were no comments this morning, as it was time for action.

Fester figured that it would be about a four-hour ride to the Bar S ranch house. He had never been up to it himself, but a couple of the men in the group had been there in the past. They had had to request the return of some cattle that the Bar S claimed had strayed onto their range and had somehow got included in their herds during the spring roundup. It had not been a confrontation, but no one from the Bar S had helped them cut the cows out of the herd or keep them from rejoining the herd while the cowboys were busy getting other cows. A thirty minutes job had turned into a six-hour effort.

One of those cowboys had been Charlie Simson, who was now riding up with Fester and the Colonel to help guide the way. He had been with the Colonel for only three years, but he had made a great hand and was not afraid of anything, man or beast.

After about three hours of riding, Fester turned on his horse and waved a hand. The three leaders spurred their horses and joined the men at the head of the group. After a brief discussion they fell back a little from the head of the column, turned around and made a hand gesture. They then slowly started drifting out from the main group, and different men moved to join the three leaders. Spence was left by himself in the center, but was joined by three men. He had not seen anyone speak to these three or make any motions to them. It seemed they naturally knew to fall in with him.

Spence looked them over and was pleased with what he saw. They were all mature men with well-maintained firearms. He knew that neither of these men would jump into action until they were told. He relaxed some and rode on behind the main leaders.

As they rode on, the other groups continued to spread out away from the main group. The two outer groups kept their horses at a slightly faster pace so they would be on the sides of the ranch when they got there. It was almost a V formation. Spence kept the four of them about one hundred yards behind the leaders and spaced out from each other. If there were any ambushers, then they would not have a bunch to shoot into. He could barely make out the other groups beginning to space themselves and form their battle lines.

Topping the last ridge above the Bar S ranch, the Colonel brought his group to a halt. He waited until the other three groups had reached their positions. As the last group came to a halt he started his horse down the ridge. Spence brought his group in a little closer and followed. The other three groups maintained their positions on the ridge.

It surprised Spence that the ranch had not been alerted yet. It was well up in the morning and the Bar S riders should have been about their chores already. He kept a close watch on the bunkhouse which also had the mess hall attached to it. The accommodations here at the Bar S were more like a poor dirt farmer rather than a ranch with lots of cattle and ranch hands. The barn was also the blacksmith shop, and the main ranch house wasn't much better built than the bunkhouse.

As they got within ninety yards of the ranch area, a cowboy came out of the mess hall scratching himself and trying to roll a smoke. As he lit the cigarette he looked up and saw the riders approaching. He turned suddenly and ran back inside and within a couple of seconds the yard was full of cowboys in various states of dress. A couple of them turned back inside and came out with their pistol belts and rifles. The others just stood there and watched as the riders came into the ranch area.

The Colonel continued and when he got to the group he moved his horse slightly and rode on around them. At the edge of the group a big man moved out from the group and said, "Hey, where do you think you're going?"

The Colonel ignored him and continued on. The man reached out as if he was going to take a hold of the Colonel's horse reins. Fester cocked his rifle and the sound caused the man to stop in his tracks. Fester said to him, "We have business with your boss, not with anyone in this mob. Now if you are not the Bar S owner, I suggest you step aside."

The man stammered a couple of syllables, but stepped back and let the riders continue. As they went past they were followed by the entire mob of men. About that time Spence and the other three came up and he pushed his horse on into the mob. A path quickly cleared, but there were a lot of remarks directed at these four riders and one man reached out to grab Spence's leg. A quick draw of his .4,5 and the hand loosened its grip very fast. Spence continued on with the group around and behind his band of four.

Coming up to the ranch house the Colonel called out to the house. "Max Wardlow, come on out here. We need to talk."

The big man walked up close to the Colonel and said, "The boss and the gun hands rode out yesterday. There's no one here but us cow punchers right now."

"What are you saying? There's no one here but you boys?"

"Yea, they rode out to take care of something the boss wanted done. He took all the gun hands with him. I was sorta giving the boys here a break this morning. It gets sorta rough and tumble with those gun hands always trying to pick a fight. These boys don't have nothing to do with what the boss gets involved in. We just herd a few cows around," the big man said.

The Colonel reined around and faced the mob of cowboys. "I don't have any fight with you boys. Our business is with your boss and his gun hands. But rest assured that the first one of you to pick up a gun will get our full attention. Anyone here have any quarrels with that?"

No one said anything. The few that had a rifle slid it down along their legs. There wasn't any fight in these boys.

"O.K. now, you boys just go on about your chores." He rode his horse back through the crowd and started to wave the outlying cowboys into the ranch yard.

As he raised his arm gunfire sounded out close to the far group. He saw his men come over the ridge and then rein their horses in and dismount quickly. A couple reined their horses to the ground and got down behind them. They were shooting back toward their rear. He saw a couple of his men go down before they could reach shelter.

Turning he yelled to Spence to bring his men and follow him. Spurring his horse he took out for the ridge. The other Triple Y men were right behind him.

As they were riding toward the ridge Spence saw that the other two groups had also turned and were riding to reinforce the group under fire.

Suddenly riders broke over the ridge and were rushing into the downed Triple Y cowboys. The small group of Triple Y cowboys were outnumbered but putting up a good fight. They were used to being the underdog in fights and were holding their own. The Bar S gun hands were used to sod busters that didn't fighting back, or shooting from the darkness. This wasn't the type of battle they had any experience fighting.

The center Triple Y group broke out of the trees and was quickly in the fight. The numbers were almost even now and the tide of the battle quickly turned. There were Bar S riders falling now, and they turned and were beginning to retreat to regroup. As they pulled up the other side of the ridge a big man dressed in black started yelling at them. He then took out a riding crop and began hitting some of them across the back and head.

The riders began another assault on the group on the ground. As they were in full gallop, the Colonel and his group soon reached the battle area. He dropped his horse, and sliding his rifle out he yelled encouragement to his men. Spence rode up close to the Colonel and told the other three to take up positions to protect the Colonel. He remained on his horse and he took out both .45s.

Gunfire started again before the riders were within range. As they approached, the Triple Y cowboys took aim with their rifles. The first round of fire took down six riders. The others hesitated and the man in black started yelling and hitting again. The gun hands didn't know whom they feared most, this man or the gunfire.

The riders continued on toward the Triple Y cowboys. The second round of fire took all the fight out of the group, and they broke ranks and started splitting up. The last group of Triple Y riders rode out of the trees behind the retreating riders. Seeing this last group of Triple Y cowboys, the gun hands reined in their horses and dropped their guns, holding their arms up in the air.

The man in black had not stopped. Galloping into the group of cowboys on the ground he raised his pistol and took aim at the first man. Spence had seen him coming and maneuvered his horse around close to where he would hit the group. Seeing him take aim on the Triple Y man, Spence fired two shots, the first going through the hand of the man in black and the second hitting him in his other arm. The momentum of the two shots knocked the man off his horse.

Coming up to the man, Spence aimed both guns on him. "I suggest you stand up and keep your arms away from your other gun," Spence told him.

"You stupid fool," the man in black blasted back at Spence. "I got holes in both arms and you think I can lift a gun? Get down off that damn horse and help me up. You shot me, you can at least patch me up."

Spence couldn't believe the gall of this man. Just who did he think he was? Spence just sat on his horse and watched as the man struggled to get to his feet.

"Just wait 'til I get up, and I'll knock you off that damn horse!" the man shouted at Spence.

"You get up and I'll kick your ass back down and just might put a slug through a leg to keep you down," Spence replied back to this obnoxious man who had managed to finally get to his feet.

About that time the Colonel walked up and kicked the legs out from under the man. As the man fell he set up a string of curses at both the Colonel and Spence.

"I reckon you're Wardlow?" the Colonel asked.

"Yes, I am and what the hell are you doing on my ranch and shooting up my boys? I have a good mind to stretch your whole bunch up from the nearest trees. I haven't seen such low down ambushing skunks since I left Georgia."

The Colonel laughed out loud at the man. Spence hadn't ever seen anyone with more outrageous behavior. How this man thought he could hang forty riders when he was shot in both arms Spence didn't know.

"I think I should just go ahead and string you and what's left of your hired guns up right here on this ridge. You and your back shooting ambushers took down some of my best men," the Colonel told the man.

The Colonel had his men round up all the hired guns and place them in a circle. They collected all the firearms from the gunmen and also all their knives. They were tied with their arms behind their backs and then each was mounted on a horse and tied to the man in front of him. After this was done the gunmen were like a pack train being tied to the rider in front and in back of himself.

All the firearms were gathered and distributed among the Triple Y riders. The Colonel was not about to leave the weapons on the Bar S ranch as they might be used against him later.

Having patched up Max Wardlow, the Colonel pitched him over a horse's back and with a group of five of his own riders he lead the horse back down to the main ranch bunk house. Pulling up in front of the bunkhouse the ranch foreman and his men spilled outside.

"Here's your boss back," the Colonel said. "He's going to be laid up for a while until he heals up some. I'm going to take those hired guns with me and send them back over the pass with a warning not to come back over this way. Any objections to that?"

A shout of hurrah sounded from the cowboys. They might catch hell from their boss later, but they were all glad to see the gunmen being taken off the ranch. Their life could get back to normal without being afraid of getting gunned down in an argument started by a hired gun.

The Colonel tossed the reins of the horse carrying Wardlow to the range boss and then turned and led his men back up the hill. Getting to the main bunch of men he led them back towards the Triple Y ranch. Fester had Jess McCoy leading the string of gunmen and had guards on both sides and in back. He didn't figure that the gunmen could make a break for it, but he was going to be carful anyway.

After crossing onto the Triple Y ranch boundaries they came to a Y in the road. One way lead back to the burnt cabin where the cook was preparing their supper and the other way lead to the pass over the Coastal Del Rey Mountains.

The Colonel called Spence up to where he had stopped the group and said, "I want you to take your four men and lead these gunmen back over the pass and set them on their way with a warning not to come back over to this side of the mountains."

With a few final instructions he turned and rode to the string of hired guns.

"I'm going to set you boys free once you are on the other side of the mountains. We were pretty lenient with you, as you should have been lynched back at the Bar S. I don't want to see any of you back on this side of the mountains. I won't be so easy next time, as you'll just fill a hole in the ground if I ever see you again."

With those comments he rode down the string of men looking each one in the face. It was as if he was memorizing each man's face for future reference. Most of the men looked down at the ground, but some stared defiantly back into the Colonel's face. With these he just grinned back at them with a look of promised death.

Getting to the last man in the string he turned and rode back up to Spence "Better be on your guard the whole time, as I sure wouldn't trust anyone of those riders. Might watch your back trail a couple of days before you come back to the ranch."

Spence nodded his agreement then he motioned for Jess to follow him as he turned down the trail heading to the pass. Jess pulled the lead gunman's horse behind him and the other three men assigned to Spence followed with one on each side and one bringing up the tail.

The Colonel watched them for a minute and then turned and led the remainder of the group toward the cook's hot supper.

CHAPTER THIRTEEN

It took Spence and his group two days to get through the pass over the mountains. It was a couple of rough days, as they weren't prepared for the ride. They just had some jerky and hard tack with them. At the first camp Spence had his boys go through the saddle-bags of the other riders and they didn't come up with much else, as these riders had been coming back from their ride.

Spence divided up the food and then sent one of his men to try to kill a deer or antelope to help augment these sparse supplies. The man came back into camp with a Bighorn Sheep that he had killed. Spence didn't really like the taste of sheep, but fresh meat was better than just hardtack.

They didn't get much sleep either, as Spence wanted two men on guard at all time. The Triple Y men were all glad when they finally got over the mountains. As they came down the last foothill Spence turned his horse around.

"I'm going to turn you loose here. I'll put one knife here in this man's belt. I want you to ride an hour before you stop and try any-thing. If you stop in rifle range I'll put a bullet in you. Remember the Colonel's warning. I'd find myself another way of making a living before I'd come back over these mountains if I was you."

With that he took an old knife and put it in the lead man's belt. It was old, bent and not very sharp. It would take them a while to hack through the ropes. He then hit the lead horse with his hat and shouted at it. The horse took out over the valley pulling the others with it. Spence and the four others sat for a while watching the string of riders until they were out of sight.

"Well, that's that. How far back up the pass do you think we need to go to make camp?" he asked the others.

It was mutually agreed to go back up the trail until the point where the trail wound back on itself and they could make a camp and watch back down over the trail. It was going to be a lazy couple of days and they could catch back up on their rest. They had taken the rest of the food and the fresh meat with them so they weren't going to have to hunt again until they started back over the mountain.

Making camp Spence sat up a guard schedule and then while the first man took a post that allowed him to watch the trail, the others made a fire and started gathering branches for beds and a lean-to.

It was a nice, easy two days. They hadn't seen anything on the trail or any dust in the distance. It seems the riders had taken the Colonel's words to heart. The second day Spence saddled up and rode back down the trail to the valley. He wanted to ensure that the riders hadn't just made camp and was waiting until they thought he and his boys had left. He made a wide circle and couldn't see any fresh signs of anyone being in the area. He knew that the closest settlement had been about five days ride from the pass and he figured that is where the riders had gone. He hadn't given them a gun and the only thing they had with them had been the old knife. He figured that it was a bunch of hungry riders when they finally got to the town.

He rode back up the trail to the camp and told the other men that they would ride out in the morning. The man on guard started down from his perch, but Spence stopped him and said that they would continue their watch until they left though. Best to be sure and to stay cautious than to be caught with everyone asleep.

The others nodded their agreement. Long experience had taught them all the same lessons. One more night of guard duty wouldn't hurt them any, and with five of them the hours weren't so long.

They had finished the jerky and hard tack, and just had the remains of the sheep to eat. Spence took the last hindquarters and staked it over the fire to start a slow roast. He would go over and turn it every little bit so it wouldn't burn on one side. Roasting over a small fire would take a couple of hours. but the meat would be juicier and more tender than trying to just pan fry it. He had found some wild onions down by the small stream and he was going to insert them inside the meat as it got closer to being cooked. This would give it a little more flavor. Out here there wasn't much of anything else growing wild that could be used to season a meal.

After a few hours Spence took his knife and cut into the meat. The fire started sputtering and flared up as the juice from the meat dripped into it. He cut around the onions and divided the meat between the five men. They sat and ate it and licked their fingers as the meat juice ran down over their hands. Sometimes meat alone could make a meal.

They finished eating and then the men started to turn in. That would be the last meal they would have until they came to the first range cabin back on the Triple Y. Spence took the first watch and let the others bed down. He moved out on an outcropping of rock so he could watch back down the trail. Anyone moving through the pass at night would have to be using some type of light to see by as it was a moonless night and the pass was very dark. A traveler would need a kerosene lamp or a torch and those lights could be seen for a long distance.

Spence sat on the rock and listened to the night. He could hear an occasional owl hooting, the rustling of leaves from small animals and a wolf howl in the distance. He sat and thought about what his next plans would be until the stars had rotated a third way around the night sky. He got up and went to wake the next man to take watch.

Walking back to camp he saw a raccoon prowling around the fire looking for scraps. Another one was going through his saddlebag. He ran over to scare the raccoon off but it saw him coming and ran out into the brush with something in its mouth. Spence couldn't tell what the raccoon had so he followed a ways but it didn't drop the object. He went back and ran the other raccoon out of camp then woke up the next guard.

Sitting down on his bedding he went through his saddlebag and tried to determine what was missing. It turned out to be the locket he had had with his mother's picture in it. That was the only thing he had left of his parents and it was only a picture of his mother painted right after his parents had married. It saddened him to think that he had lost his only possession that linked him to his family. He hoped that the raccoon had a good use for the locket and wouldn't just drop it in the woods somewhere.

He packed up his belongings and tucked the bag under his bedding so he could use it as a pillow. If the raccoon came back it would wake him if it tried to get back into the bag. He turned over away from the fire and closed his eyes to sleep.

Splat, splat, splitter splat was the next thing Spence knew as he woke to rain falling in his face. It wasn't morning yet so he pulled his poncho up over his face and tried to sleep just a little longer. The rain falling on the poncho over his face though kept him from falling back to sleep. He finally looked out from under the poncho toward the other cowboys. They were all covered with their rain gear.

"Any of you boys actually asleep or you just trying to stay dry?" he asked.

Getting a reply from each of them Spence said, "Well we're going to get wet anyway today, so we might as well get an early start."

"Maybe if we stay here a little longer it will quit and then we can start out dry anyway," George Cress said. George was not one to volunteer for anything he didn't have to and he didn't like being in the weather unless he had to be.

The man on guard, Jess McCoy then walked up and said, "This is going to last for a while. It's been misting for the last hour or so and it's just going to get harder. Might as well get up and about before it really starts to rain."

Seeing that there wasn't going to be any reprieve from the rain, the others started to get up. The guard had walked off and he came back into camp with the horses. Each man took his own mount and started saddling and stowing his gear. There wasn't much for the men to pack except their bedding.

Spence finished and then decided to walk out in the direction the raccoon had taken. It was a slim chance that the animal had dropped the locket instead of carrying it off. He walked out and made some wide half circles but didn't see anything. Giving up and deciding the locket was lost forever, he went back to camp.

As he got back to his horse and started to mount Jess gave a little chuckle. "You out there looking for gold or something?"

Spence looked over at him and saw a large grin on his face. "No, just something I lost to a coon last night."

Jess grinned again and chuckled, "Got robbed right here in camp, huh? Came in with a mask on his face and just robbed you in the middle of the night, huh?"

Spence grinned back at him, "Yea, had a black mask on and everything. Dadburn thief came prepared."

Jess then moved out from behind his horse a little ways and Spence could see him twirling something around on a string. Jess was grinning even more broadly.

"Found something this morning as I was getting the horses, I did. Couldn't figure how something like this could have gotten out in the woods so far from the trail. Right pretty it is too."

Spence looked closer at the object being twirled by Jess. Yes, it was his locket. He looked at Jess and grinned again saying, "Why I bet there's a picture in that there locket of a very pretty young woman. The only flaw is that some water has seeped in and ruined her dress."

"Yep, she could have been quite nice except for that there water stain." And with that comment he pitched the locket to Spence.

Catching it in mid-air Spence said, "Thanks. I sure thought that coon had robbed me blind."

Jess grinned and nodded saying, "I thought someone might be looking for this, but was going to wait to see who strolled out in the woods for a look 'fore I said anything. Knew right away what he was looking for and saw the disappointment in your face when you came back in. Always glad to help." And with that he swung up into his saddle and turned his horse for the trail.

The others had been watching, and as Jess headed out they too mounted and followed. Little items like this helped bind people together. They all appreciated the little act of kindness that had just occurred.

Spence was the last to mount, and he stowed the locket before he swung up onto his horse. He rocked the saddle around a little to make sure it was belted tight and then followed the others.

It was still misting as they started out. This area of the country was known for the rainfall it received. Most days during the spring were like today, it would never break out into a full rain but would just mist all day. Spence thought that if it would just rain full out then maybe it would get it over with and the sun would come out like it did in the South.

Jess led the group on down the mountain keeping his horse at a steady pace. The quicker they were out of the mountains, then the quicker they would reach the range cabin. A strong pot of coffee would go down good right now and maybe they would run across an antelope or young deer on the way. Jess figured there would be beans and corn meal in the cabin to cook up for supper.

The men stayed fairly dry under their ponchos, as the mist wasn't heavy enough to soak through. It would just sort of gather on the poncho and then roll off. This made the ride a little better and after they reached the valley floor they pushed the horses into a faster gait. After being out in the weather for eight days the modest comfort of the cabin was calling them.

As they were nearing the range cabin Spence told George that the two of them should ride out to try to find some fresh meat. Orders were to shoot anything but another sheep. Spence had all the sheep meat he wanted for a while. They broke out from the group and went off in different directions. One of them was sure to see some game and they listened for a shot from the other. There wasn't any use for both of them to bring in meat when one deer would last the rest of the trip.

After only fifteen minutes Spence heard a shot coming from the direction that George had taken. He headed back in the direction of the trail at an angle that would bring him back into the group. It took him about thirty minutes to break the trail, and looking both ways he could not see any riders. He looked for tracks on the trail and not seeing any, he turned and went back up it.

After only five minutes he rounded a bend in the trail and saw the others sitting on their horses looking out over the brush. Riding up he asked, "What's up? George coming back in?"

"Not yet. He should have had time to butcher that deer and been in by now. I reckon one of us better ride out over there and see what's up. Blame fool probably cut his arm off trying to gut that deer. He never was known to be very handy with a knife."

"I'll ride out and see. Could you tell about where the shot came from?" Spence replied.

"Bout where that tall fir is looking over those rocks. Sounded like somewhere at the base of the rocks."

Spence heeled his horse out in the direction of the fir tree. He expected to have to find George's trail and follow it a ways to where the deer fell. If it wasn't a clean shot then the deer might have ran a ways before it dropped. Spence figured that was most likely what had happened.

As he approached the area he started looking for horse tracks. If he continued straight up the hill he was bound to cross George's trail somewhere along the way. He got to the base of the fir and kept going up past the rocks. As he rounded a ledge he came upon a set of three horse tracks. They were unshod tracks. Spence was beginning to get a feeling that he didn't want to continue on this mission.

Bracing himself and drawing a pistol, he continued down the path the three horses had taken. He kept his horse to a slow walk and scanned the area as he moved. He came to a point that looked like the riders had stopped and watched something. He could tell, as there were lots of horse prints in the same area like the horses had been moving side to side. Then he saw the brass cartridge.

Whoever had fired the shot had not taken time to pick up the spent shell. He took a long look in the direction the horses had been facing and then started out that way. He was looking for a downed man and was hoping that was not what he was going to find. About sixty yards out he ran upon George's trail and he turned and followed it. Coming to a gully he looked down into the leading hole of a rifle barrel.

Falling backward off his horse he yelled out, "Don't fire that thing, it's me George!"

"Hell Spence I saw it was you, just making sure no one else was with you," George said. "Come on down here and help patch this hole up. Some coyote shot me though the leg and probably into my horse. I fell off into this here gully. Luckily I had my rifle out when I fell."

Spence caught his horse and led it into the gully and then took a look at George's leg. It was bleeding, and it looked like the shot had broken the bone in the upper leg. He took the bandanna off George's neck and then his own. Finding a couple of stout limbs he fashioned a make-shift splint for the leg and bound up the break and the wound.

"Here, keep your hand pressed on this hole and I'll see if I can find your horse." Spence took the rifle and checked to ensure a round was in the chamber. "Keep this handy just in case and I'll give a couple of hoots before I drop back down into this gully. Whoever shot you is probably still close."

Spence walked on down the dry streambed for a ways until he came to a thick growth of trees and underbrush. He moved out of the stream and into the brush. Moving slowly he approached the edge of the trees. Stopping he began to scan the area. Out of the corner of his eye he caught the reflection of metal. Turning his head he concentrated on the area that the reflection had come from.

Then he saw movement in the trees. It looked like three or four horses were moving through the trees. Then the lead horses came to a small sunlit opening. Spence did a double take when he saw what the rider was. Looking closely he examined the next rider to confirm what he had seen.

Indians. There were no known tribes of Indians in this area. The closest Indian tribes in this area were the Puyallup Indian tribe but they were in the far northwest. He watched them ride on out of sight then he went back to George.

"Got yourself shot up by a Indian," he said to the downed rider.

"There ain't been any Indians in this area for years. You must have been seeing things. What did they look like?" George asked.

Spence could tell that George was in a lot of pain. He was trying hard not to wince as he spoke but the pain still showed through.

"Couldn't get a good look at them from the distance and they were wrapped in furs. No noticeable paint, but I couldn't see their faces. They were riding range pinto ponies like you find in any camp or ranch corral. Here let's get you up and mounted on my horse. I think the quicker we're back with the rest of the riders the better."

Spence helped George get up and pushed him onto his horse. Taking the reins he led the horse out of the streambed and began to make his way back to the trail. About a hundred yards away they came across George's horse. Spence caught the reins and then looked the horse over. There was some dried blood on the side that George's leg had been. Looking Spence saw a hole through the leather in the stirrup and lifting it up he saw where the bullet had struck the metal fastener on the belly strap. It must not have had much energy left by the time it had gone through George's leg bone, the leather and hit the metal. The horse's only wound was a slight cut.

Spence mounted the horse and then leading his horse they continued back to the trail. When the other three riders saw them approaching they rode out to meet them.

"Where's the meat and why are have you two switched horses?" were the first questions asked.

Spence told them briefly of what had occurred. The other three were eager to ride out after the Indians but Spence cooled them down. They probably wouldn't be able to catch up with the Indians before dark, and he didn't want to face any armed individuals in the dark, especially if he didn't know where the individuals were.

They continued on and reached the range cabin. Approaching it cautiously they saw that no one had been around it for a while. They moved George inside to one of the bunks and began to build a fire. Two of the riders rode out to try to find some game and they paid special attention to their surroundings. They didn't want to be the next ones to fall prey to an ambush.

Spence put some water on to heat so he could clean up George's wound properly now. He took some old bedding and made some bandages and took an old lariat and unbraided part of it to help make a better splint. He went out and cut some straight limbs to use on the new splint. Coming back inside he had George take his pants off and he cut the leg of his long underwear off. He washed the wound and the leg and it started to bleed a little from the exit point.

The side where the bullet had entered was beginning to close but the exit wound was bigger and had some bone splinters in it.

Spence had George roll over and he cleaned the exit wound again and picked out as much bone as he could find. He then bandaged the wound with the main pressure point being on the exit point. He had Jess come over and help hold George when he got ready to pull the leg straight. Giving George a small limb off a bush he said, "Better chew down on this limb. This is going to hurt and it might help."

George placed the limb in his mouth and gripped it hard. Spence motioned to Jess, who took hold of George's shoulders and then Spence grabbed the lower leg and pulled sharply down and over. George moaned loudly and passed out from the pain.

Looking at him Spence said, "That's better for him anyway. Now we can finish and the pain won't effect him none."

By the time George came back around the other two riders had come in with a small deer and they had fried up some meat and corn pone. The first thing he asked for was a cup of hot coffee. His leg was already in the splint, and Spence had braced it so that George could move around a little without moving his leg.

They spent the night in the warm cozy cabin with their stomachs full and in good spirits. Spence still posted a guard though, as he didn't know which direction the Indians had finally gone. Checking the surrounding area and the horses he finally came back into the cabin and turned in, wrapping himself in his bedding.

CHAPTER FOURTEEN

Watching the five riders lead the Bar S's hired guns away the Colonel was pleased with the way things had gone. Maybe this situation had been settled with less death and confrontation then he had expected. Catching the gun hands away from the main ranch buildings had worked out very well.

Watching until the group of riders had ridden over the knoll he then turned and gestured for his group to start out. Hess rode up along side of him and asked, "Reckon we should leave a watch somewhere around here?"

"I had thought about that, but I don't think Wardlow has anyone else to send out. That bunch left down there are just cow punchers and I don't think they have any fight in them," the Colonel said. "But we will post some guards tonight just in case. Did we send any food with that group?"

"No, we didn't have any with us. I figured we all would be back in camp tonight so told the men just to take the bare essentials with them. No use being weighted down with stuff you don't need in a gunfight. Anyway I think Spence, George and Jess are pretty capable and can make do," Fester replied.

The Colonel nodded and rode on. He knew that his two men could make do with what they could find, and he had come to have respect for Spence's abilities also. He was glad that he could judge a man from an initial encounter and was glad that Spence had accepted his offer. The Colonel knew that with Spence having the upper range bordering the Triple Y ranch, then he would have a good neighbor protecting his own ranch.

They reached camp at the northern range cabin by mid-afternoon. The cook had seen them coming and had hot coffee and biscuits ready for them. He had a plate of fried meat and the cowboys had meat, biscuits and coffee to help keep them going until the evening meal. Having a good cook in camp was a morale builder and could keep cowboys going even in the worst of times.

Late that afternoon Hess sent two riders out to backtrack their trail to ensure no one had followed them. He told them to stay off the main trail and to head on back before it got dark. He watched them ride off, but had a funny feeling in his gut as he did so. As he walked around his men talking with them he continued to have a feeling that something was wrong. He shrugged the feeling off thinking that maybe he was just worried about Spence and that group being sent off without any supplies.

As night began to creep over the landscape, the cook rang his dinner bell. He had been busy all afternoon cooking up a stew, corn pone and was going to surprise the riders with some apple tarts. He had stuck in a bag of dried apples at the last moment, and now was glad he had. Having fried them up just before ringing the dinner bell he now had them covered up so the cowboys wouldn't see them as they got their stew and corn bread. He was going to pull them out later.

Hess moved down to the cook fire and was the last to get his food. He had expected his two riders back by now, but maybe they had ridden out farther then he had wanted. Eating his meal he kept watching the direction they should be riding in from. Even the cook's surprise dessert didn't help his feelings of ill omen.

Finally he called over Hank Moore and his helper and told them to ride back out over the trail to meet the two riders coming back in. He told Hank of his feelings that something didn't seem quite right and told him to be cautious and when he heard the riders, to make sure who they were before he presented himself.

Hank looked at Hess closely. It wasn't like the boss to be so skittish and he rode off with a feeling that he wasn't going to like what he found. He rode following the tree line so they wouldn't be silhouetted against the skyline. His helper must have picked up his feelings also, as there wasn't any talking as they rode along. His helper had his rifle out and lying across his saddle with a shell loaded but with the hammer not cocked.

Hank had them ride out for about two hours. They didn't see or hear anything. He stopped and just sat and listened for about ten minutes then turning his horse around he told his helper that they should ride on back in. Just as he was about to start his horse he heard something coming down the trail. He motioned his helper to move back into the trees just a little bit and stop.

As they sat and watched, they could make out the sound of a heavy animal coming down the trail. It was an elk, cow or horse, as it sounded too heavy to be less.

As the animal came in view Hank could tell that it was a horse wearing a saddle. Listening, he could not hear anything following the horse so he moved out and stopped the horse by grabbing its reins trailing in the dirt. He ran a hand down the flanks and could tell that it hadn't been running hard but he couldn't tell the brand by just feeling of it. He took out a match and cupping it close with his hands he lit it and saw that the horse had the Triple Y brand on it.

Maybe this was what Hess had been worrying about. His helper asked what they should do now. Hess replied, "Well, not knowing why this horse is by itself or where the two riders are and why they are separated, I think we need to go back to camp. Hess will probably get a search party together and ride back out here in the morning."

They took the horse and started back towards the camp. Hank didn't try to hurry and keep along the tree line. He didn't want to put them to any more risk since he didn't know what had happened to the riders. Coming back into sight of the camp he was stopped by a guard. Hank was glad to see that Hess wasn't taking any chances and asked the guard, "How many are out on guard?"

"Hess has three of us out, spread out and moving around to cover the area," the guard said.

They rode on into camp. As soon as Hess saw the rider-less horse he started over at a trot. He had halfway been expecting this. Coming up to the riders he asked, "What happened out there? Did you find Jim and Charlie?"

Hank got down off his horse and gave the reins to his helper, who rode off to take care of the three horses. Hank turned to Hess and told him what he had found out on the trail as they walked to the cook fire. "Any more of those apple tarts left, Cookie?" Hank asked.

He got a cup of coffee and took an apple tart from the cook, nodding his pleasure when the cook said that he had put some aside for the four riders.

"What you thinking of doing? I can lead a group back to where we found the horse, but I don't know how much farther Charlie and Jim might be," Hank said.

Hess told Hank to follow him on up to where the Colonel was set up. They filled their coffee cups. The Colonel knew something was wrong, but he respected the men's comfort enough to wait until they were ready to talk.

"Our two back trail riders hadn't come back in at supper time, so I sent Hank out to meet them coming back in. He didn't find them, but just a rider-less horse. I'm going to have a group on the trail by first light to go find out what happened."

"How many men you sending out?" the Colonel asked.

"I thought of sending ten along with Hank. That should be enough to handle most anything. And that will leave fifteen to come back with us along with Cookie."

"What do you think Hank? Want a few more?" the Colonel asked Hank. He was watching Hank's face to try to read his feelings.

"I think we need to send a few more. Send fifteen out with me and take ten with you. I'll need a couple of outriders on each side as well as the main body of men," Hank replied.

The Colonel looked over at Hess and then said, "Yes, I agree with that. Not knowing what to expect, I would have outriders also. Keep a loose group as you go out so an ambush won't be able to take a lot at one time. Keep your guns out and ready. Handle it sort of like you did at San de Pablo."

Hank nodded, remembering the last major Indian battle they had been in. With that he got up and went back over to the main camp to notify the men who would be going with him. He also went over to the cook to let him know that he needed an early meal, as he wanted to be moving before first light.

He had his men turn in, and then after a few last minutes of thinking about tomorrow, he also rolled up in his bedding and went to sleep.

The cook went around the next morning waking the sixteen men that would be leaving early. He had already cooked biscuits and fried meat with coffee. He had made up a travel pack for the men to take with them. As they came through for breakfast he had each man take enough for a dinner meal also. As Hank came through after all his men, the cook gave him a sack of the extra biscuits and meat. He also slipped him the last of the apple tarts.

Hank mounted and moved out from camp. The fifteen men going with him had already mounted and moved out after him. A couple of the last stragglers were still chewing their biscuits and meat. Hank went right onto the trail and was following it. He didn't want to waste the time following the tree line. He planned on being well down the path by the time the sun rose.

After a while Hank sent three outriders on each side to ride out and in front of the group. They were to look for signs of other riders and to give advance notice to the main group if they spotted anything. Hank then sent two riders out in front to ride about one hundred yards in front of the main group.

They came to where Hank had caught the rider-less horse about thirty minutes after full sunrise. Hank sent a rider up to tell the two lead riders to be more alert now and to signal to the outriders if they saw them. Riding for another mile Hank was beginning to wonder how far the two riders had gone. Suddenly two pistols shots sounded from the outriders on the left. It was the signal they had set up in case the outriders found anything.

Hearing no rifle shots or any other pistol shots he lead his group at a fast trot. The riders were about one half a mile up and out. He came upon them and they were on the ground holding their horses. Hank and his group rode up and he asked, "What did you find?"

Randolph, the oldest of the group pointed down toward some rocks. "Found Jim and Charlie. Both shot in the back."

Hank got off his horse and started walking toward the rocks. He dreaded times like this. Good men shot down in their prime. Good, hardworking men. Friends.

As he got closer he could see the two bodies. He looked and saw where they had been shot in the back. He took out his pistol and shot twice into the air. There wasn't any use in having his men separated. He walked around the bodies but the only tracks were from the two riders' horses.

Going back to the others, he told them to dismount but to keep watch on the ridge around them. Hank didn't want the others to be ambushed also. When the other riders came in Hank split them up into four groups and told them to ride out and to search for signs of where the shots had come from. He set three men digging a grave for the two men. It would take too long now to take the bodies back to the ranch and this warmer weather didn't aid much in preserving the bodies.

Before the graves could be finished, a rider came galloping in from the high ridge. He rode up to Hank and said, "We found the tracks of the ambushers. It was five unshod ponies. I would swear they were Indian ponies, but we haven't seen any Indians here in the valley in over four years."

Hank mounted and rode out with the rider to look over the tracks. Getting to the trail he dismounted and looked at the horse tracks. They did look like Indian pony tracks. They were the only people that he knew that did not shoe their horses. He told the other riders to split and to follow the tracks in both directions to see if they could find the spent shells or anything else that would help identify the ambushers. There had not been any trouble with Indians in over five years, and had not been any Indians in this area for over four years. Hank did not think that any tribe that would pass through the valley would endanger the peace treaties by ambushing ranch-hands.

Hank went on back to the gravesite and waited for his men to come back in. The other groups drifted in after about an hour and Hank briefed them on what had been found on the high ridge. The last group of riders came back in after about two hours. They had a handful of Winchester carbine .44-40 caliber shells. They had not found any other signs but had followed the tracks until they were well off the Triple Y ranch.

Giving a short benediction for the fallen riders, Hank then mounted his men and they started back to the range cabin. Hank didn't figure they should ride much past nightfall, and the range cabin would make a good camp again.

CHAPTER FIFTEEN

Arriving back at the ranch Fester, had his men gather around him in the barnyard. He went over the next day's work with them so he wouldn't need a meeting the next morning. This adventure had put his schedule for the spring round-up slightly behind his timetable. The men unsaddled their mounts and turn them loose in the near pasture. They would catch and ride their second string horses tomorrow.

The cook helpers had stayed behind to care for the ranch and they had started cooking when they saw the riders coming across the range. They figured these cowboys would be needing a good meal. They had caught some trout from the nearby stream and had fried up trout, red beans and corn pone. Using the last of the dried apples, they had made some apple pies to finish the meal. Not having enough trout to fill up every rider they had also fried some beef-steaks. The cowboys didn't linger long after they had eaten but went on over to the bunkhouse and most of them turned in.

Fester went on up to the main ranch house after briefing the cowboys on their chores. He and the Colonel discussed the trip over their supper and the Colonel told him to have Spence come directly to him whenever they rode in. Fester did not take the Colonel's offer of some brandy after supper but went on back to his cabin and turned in also. He thought to himself that he was getting too old for adventures like this, and more so, for sleeping on the ground.

The next morning saw the cowboys up and moving pretty early. They had hit the mess hall before the cooks were ready and some went back out to catch their mounts before breakfast. Eating didn't take long and the cooks were soon left by themselves. They started cooking the dinner meal, for now that the riders were preparing for the roundup, they would be eating their meals on the range.

The first cowboys had saddled horses from the corral and then they rode out and brought in the horse herd from the near pasture. The others roped and saddled horses from the herd and then roped another horse and put it in the corral to use as a second string mount for tomorrow. They rode out over the range in different directions to start preparing rough brush corrals and to gather firewood in areas to use as branding fires. As they rode across the range they made note of the small herds of cows so they could began to gather them up as they rode back in that afternoon.

The days passed fairly fast for the riders. The spring roundup was an exciting time as they got to use skills they normally didn't need. A few of the cowboys practiced roping tree stumps as they went about their business. They didn't want to be the first ones to miss roping a calf when the branding started. They had their pride to protect as they often split into teams and competed against each other for the number of calves roped, thrown down and tied. This was so the men on foot doing the branding wouldn't have to wait very long for another calf.

Coming back in off the range that evening they saw that the other riders with Hank Moore had returned. They unsaddled quickly, rubbed their horses down and turned them loose in the near pasture. They would rotate horses daily from now until after the roundup was over. Each rider was anxious to hear the news from Hank's riders but taking care of their mounts was engrained behavior in them.

The tale of the unshod horses and the .44-40 caliber shells were told over and over until the final riders had come in from the range. The mess hall was a noisy place that evening as most of the cowboys lingered over their coffee so they could hear the tale told again. With most of the cowboys being ex-Indian fighters, these tales brought back memories of Indian fights and they exchanged tales amongst themselves. The only thing that puzzled the cowboys was the fact that these Indians had Winchester .44-40 caliber rifles. These rifles were fairly new and were more expensive than the rifles the cowboys had.

Hank and Fester came in later and the cowboys gathered around them to hear the latest news and to see if the Colonel was figuring on doing anything about the two riders being shot and killed. Fester told them what he knew at the time and then went over the next day's work. He didn't want his boys to get into an uproar about the Indians, if that was who they were; he wanted to keep them focused on the work at hand. If the Colonel decided to take action it would take some planning first.

Hank went around asking the status of the cowboys' tack and

horses. He asked who the branders were going to be this year and told them of his new branding irons. He asked a couple of the riders to bring their horses up to the corral so he could check the shoes on the horses as he had noticed their horse prints had looked like the shoes were loosening up. Then he went on back to his shop to start getting things ready for the morning. He wanted some hot coals for his forge, so he built a fire in the shop and threw on some large logs that would burn all night.

Will Harris had seen lights on in the blacksmith shop and he wandered in. "Been looking over my plows, and I got some loose fittings. Would you mind looking them over in the next day or so?"

"No, just bring them on over. I'll look at them between horses tomorrow. You need new bolts on the plow or on the handles?" Hank asked him.

"On the plow itself. I replaced the handles last year and they're still in good shape. Was sharpening the plow blades and noticed they didn't fit together as tight as they should. Hit a couple large rocks and the blades will probably fall right off."

Hank asked, "Any other gear you want me to look at? If so just have your boy bring it on over. If fact I could use his help tomorrow as Jim is still out with Spence."

"Sure, I'll send him over right after breakfast. It would do him good to know a little about smithing. Might some in handy around the farm some day."

Will turned around and left. He was trying to get things together so he and his son could take the plows and some supplies out to the farm. He was wasting good plowing weather and he wanted to have the initial turn of the soil finished before it warmed up very much. The first plowing wouldn't be very deep, just enough to turn the surface over. After the ground warmed completely then he would be able to plow again and plow deeper turning the surface soil even farther down into the ground. This would help break up the ground and also put the decaying grass under as fertilizer.

Will went back over to his wagon and pulled the plows out from underneath the wagon. Then he took the plow reins out of the wagon and walked back over to his cabin. He went over the harness again and checked all the connections. His wife Francis brought over a cup of coffee and rubbed his aching arm.

"It won't be very long until you can start using those. The days are warming up now and even David Elliot is looking anxious to get started. I hope whatever they found out there doesn't delay us much longer. I don't know if I can put up with you two fidgety men around the house much longer," she said.

Will looked up at her and smiled. She always did know what he was thinking and what needed doing. He was constantly amazed at how he had been lucky enough to marry such a good woman.

The next few days followed the pattern of the first with the cowboys up early, eating and then heading out over the range. They came back in with tales of new calves, run-ins with ornery cows and the bulls had put a few back on their horses quickly. Even the young bulls were more aggressive in the spring and were quick to put a cowboy back on his horse.

When Spence and the others rode in with George on a make-shift pallet pulled behind his horse they all gathered around them. When the tale of the unshod horses and the ambush on George was told, then the cowboys had to tell their own tale of the ambush of the two riders. Fester maneuvered Spence out from the group and told them to go on up to the Colonel's house.

Fester and Spence had just climbed up onto the porch when the Colonel came outside. He shook Spence's hand and then led them back into the dining room. Pouring some brandy into three glasses he asked for Spence to tell him what had happened.

Spence glossed over the first part of the trip, just saying that the gun hands had been escorted over the mountains and they had watched the trail long enough to see that the gun hands weren't coming back. He went over the ambush in great detail and told the Colonel what he had found.

The Colonel listened intently and asked a few questions to clarify certain points. After Spence had finished the Colonel sat a few minutes thinking through what he had just heard. This had been the second attack on his men within a couple days of each other and on two sides of his ranch. He didn't think that it could be the same group of ambushers or Indians, as the distance was too great.

He looked over at Fester saying, "I think you should have every man arm himself when they ride out from here. It is going to slow down the preparations for the roundup some but I also want every rider to have a partner. No one will ride out by himself. Tomorrow night bring the group back up here and we will discuss what we need to do about this. Spence, I want you back up here also."

Fester and Spence left and went back to the mess hall. Getting tin cups and filling them with coffee they walked over to a table and sat down. A couple members of the original planning group soon joined them. Fester looked over and said, "The Colonel wants us all back up at the house tomorrow for supper. Plan on another long night and think about what we might have to do to clear this mess up once and for all."

They then discussed what was still left in preparing for the spring roundup. Spence sat quietly through this discussion and listened so he could catch up on what was happening at the ranch while he was gone. As the men updated Fester on events he would suggest alternative actions or comment his pleasure on what was being done. They completed their updates and then drifted out of the mess hall. Spence had refilled his coffee cup and was sitting by himself enjoying the strong brew.

Will Harris walked in and stated loudly, "Thought I might find you in here. How did the trip go? Heard you ran into some trouble also. You think this is going to affect my moving out to the cabin? Got to put those plows in the ground soon or I'll really be behind on planting."

Spence grinned at Will. It didn't seem that much of anything was going to deter the farmer from getting his ground plowed. He replied, "Run into some trouble. When you thinking of trying to start plowing?"

"Would have already been at it if'n I could. The burning of the cabin is sure gonna delay us. I was thinking of me and the boy hitching up and taking some of our stuff out there. Might try to plow some and try laying another roof in between. I wanna clear that brush out where that bushwhacker was laying. Don't want to give anyone else a chance like that again. Keep it cleared out farther than a rifle will reach anyway."

"Yea, that makes sense. Should be able to burn a lot of that brush out of there. But I think I would wait a bit. The Colonel is planning another campaign to try to clear up this mess. If it is Indians killing and shooting people around here then I think they have picked the wrong bunch to start messing with."

"When is he going to start?" asked the farmer.

"We have another planning meeting tomorrow night. It didn't take them long to go into action after the last meetings. These boys don't hesitate when something needs to be done," Spence stated.

"Well, I guess I can put off the plowing for a few more days then. I still have to get my plows worked over by Hank and some of the leather repaired. Let me know when you can about what's gonna happen."

Spence replied, "Will do. I think this time you should stay and get your stuff ready to move. It seems just a few Indians, and won't need as many men as before."

Spence was trying to protect the farmer from harm. The future of this area depended on men like Will Harris, and what he could bring to the economy of the area. It would be a shame to have him cut down before the first plow was in the ground.

Will nodded and seemed to agree with Spence. He was not an Indian fighter and these little skirmishes didn't seem to be his problem. That is why the US Cavalry was originally in the area to begin with, to protect settlers. Will was more than glad enough to let them do their job, even if it was soldiers that had already been mustered out of the service.

The next evening over supper the Colonel started the conversation with his group of planners. He talked with them about the spring roundup and asked their opinions of how many new calves they would have and the condition of the spring grass. He delayed talk of the reason the men were there until after supper. Then he moved into the study and brought out a bottle of whiskey. Pouring a shot for each man he said, "Now down to business. Have you each heard Hank's and Spence's findings?"

Each man nodded. Not only had they heard the original telling but they had heard it numerous times as the cowboys in the bunkhouse had retold it.

"Our purpose is to come up with a plan of action. First we must identify the riders of these unshod ponies and then decide what we should do. We also have to plan around the spring roundup. This should be planned so it affects the least amount of cowboys, and it should be done quick enough that Harris can start plowing his fields. I'm looking forward to a good harvest of grain this fall."

With that the talk started. Each man had ideas of who the ambushers were and actions that could be taken. As each idea was presented, it was discussed and dismissed or noted for later. Fester was writing on a sheet of paper as the ideas were presented to be discussed later. Once again, the meeting lasted well into the night. It had been decided that the initial action would be to scout around to try to find out who was riding the ponies and where they were camped. All other action would then be based around this information. Spence was designated to select a couple of ex-soldiers who had been in the Indians Wars to go with him on this first mission.

Spence was comfortable enough in this mission, as he had been a scout for his cavalry unit in the War and he had noted the actions of a couple of the cowboys on the last outing. He figured they should be able to locate the unshod pony riders within the week. Going back to the bunkhouse, he found himself actually looking forward to this mission.

The next morning he went to the mess hall and got his breakfast. He was waiting until Hess came so he could call out the two men he wanted to ride with him. He figured that it should come from Hess, as he was still just considered an outsider.

Hess did not come into the mess hall, and the cowboys were beginning to finish their breakfast and start to drift out to go to work. Spence, seeing that his two men were getting up to leave, finally walked over and said, "The Colonel has set me up for another mission and said that I should pick two good men to ride with me. Jess, I would like you to go back with me, and Charlie I would like you to be the second man. We're to scout around and try to figure out if those ambushers are Indians and where they are camped."

The two cowboys looked at each other and then Charlie Simson asked, "Well, when are we leaving?"

"Just as soon as I can get the cook to pack a bag of supplies and we get saddled up. We should be able to make the outer edge of the ranch before dark and stay in that far northwest cabin tonight. I figure we can use that as a central point and ride out each day from there until we hit any fresh sign," Spence replied. "I'll meet you out at the corral in an hour and we'll head out from there."

The two cowboys nodded and then left to go to the bunkhouse to start getting their gear together. They pulled out their bedrolls, rain gear and then took out their rifles for a quick cleaning before they packed their gear. Charlie had to go see Hank for a couple of boxes of shells for his rifle and Jess asked him to pick up a box for his.

Meanwhile Spence got with the cook and explained what the Colonel had him doing and how many days he expected to be gone. The cook set about filling small bags with coffee, cornmeal and other supplies for the three men. Turning to leave, Spence told him that he would pick up the supplies in just a little while. Spence then went to try to find Hess to inform him of whom he had selected to go on the mission with him.

Hess was not in his cabin and had not been in the mess hall, so Spence walked up to the main cabin. Knocking on the kitchen door he asked the Colonel's cook if Hess was up with the Colonel. Getting a nod he walked into the kitchen while the cook went out to the dining room to inform Hess that Spence was there to see him.

Coming back into the kitchen the cook said, "The Colonel wants you to go in and brief him on your selections."

Walking into the dining room the Colonel waved at a chair and as Spence sat down the cook poured him a cup of coffee and put an apple tart on a plate in front of him.

"You ready to leave?" the Colonel asked.

"Yes, I selected Jess and Charlie to go with me. I think those two are very capable men. I have the cook bagging up some supplies and we should be ready to leave within the hour," Spence replied.

"Where are you going to stage your operations from?" Hess asked.

"I figure from the northwest range cabin that got burnt down. That should give us the capability to make some long range scouting rides each day."

"Now I just want you to locate their camp and try to figure out who they are. I don't want you boys trying anything on your own. I've lost enough good men in the last month or so, and don't want you boys to even let them know you're around. Just get the information and get back here. I'm going to have the group ready to react on your information, and just adjust the size to take care of what you find," the Colonel stated.

"Yes sir. I have no intentions of getting caught up in a gunfight or anything. I still feel pretty bad about letting George get shot like he did. I won't let my guard down again."

The Colonel looked at Spence, and just now realized that Spence had taken the shooting personally. He said, "Now that wasn't your fault. Nobody could have known that we had ambushers on our range. Hess was in the same position when he sent out those two men to watch our back trail. It wasn't either of your fault and just part of a war and that is what this is turning out to be. Now just forget it, and take care of my boys and yourself, and let's take care of these ambushers."

Spence finished his apple tart and coffee. Then getting up he said, "Well I will be heading out then and expect to be back within the week. We will start on that last trail that Hank found, and work out from there."

Hess and the Colonel stood up and shook his hand and then watched as he walked out of the room.

The Colonel said to Hess, "That was a fine day when you ran

across that young man. He's going to make a fine neighbor when this mess is settled. Him and Harris' daughter will raise some good kids out there on the northwest range."

Hess looked over at the Colonel and was a little surprised that the Colonel had been able to see the interest Spence had in Emily Harris. But then over the years he had seen that the Colonel usually had a finger on nearly everything that happened with his men.

CHAPTER SIXTEEN

Riding out the morning of the second day at the northwest range cabin, Spence led the men toward the Bar S ranch. The first day ou,t they had tried to find the trail of the unshod pony riders that had ambushed Fester's two men. There had been too much rain, and the trail had been wiped out. Spence was going to ride over on the Bar S ranch and then ride from the foothills down toward the middle of the valley. With the three of them split out a little ways from each other, if there was any sign, then they should be able to find it.

They rode with their rifles ready, and alert to their surroundings. They did not want to be caught in an ambush, and Spence always had one rider on the highest part of the land. At night they only built a small fire on which to cook their supper and then put it out. They did not want a beacon burning to draw anyone's attention to their location.

Riding along, Spence kept scanning the horizon. He had noticed some dust arising back up the valley. It had looked like some horses running at a fast gallop. He moved up onto the ridge so he would have a better view. Motioning the other two men to come into where he was Spence continued to watch the valley and the dust. Eventually he could make out the horses and the riders on them.

When Jess and Charlie rode up he pointed out the riders coming down the valley towards them. Spence moved his horse down the ridge so they would not be highlighted and seen by the approaching riders.

"What do you make of that?" Spence asked the other two men.

"Looks like they are in a hurry to get some place fast," Jess stated.

"Looks like about twenty riders to me. They don't look like any cowboys either. A lot of buckskin on that bunch of riders," Charlie said.

"Yep, looks like Indians to me, and they sure are in a hurry to get somewhere. Looks like they are turning in this direction also. I think we had better move off this ridge and take some shelter back in that bunch of trees along the creek. I don't think we want to be caught here in the open," Spence told the other two men.

They split up a little so there would not be a bunch of tracks close together as they rode down toward the creek. Single tracks would be less likely to be noticed by anyone riding as fast as these riders were. Coming to the creek, they dismounted and led the horses down into the brush. They then moved back closer to the edge so they could watch the riders pass by.

It was about twenty minutes before the riders topped the ridge and started on across the valley. It looked like they were headed on toward the Triple Y ranch, and more specifically toward the northwest range cabin. Suddenly one rider reined in his pony and dismounted quickly. He knelt down and was looking at something on the ground. He called out to the others who stopped and rode back toward the Indian on the ground. He walked slowly and then pointed toward the trees and shouted out to the others.

Spence watched as the group of Indians all looked toward the trees where he was and he said to the other two, "Well, I think we have been found out. I suggest we take a quick ride unless you want to talk with that bunch out there."

About that time the group of Indians broke into a run toward the trees. Spence and the other two ran for their horses, mounted and dashed out the opposite side. Within minutes the Indians had made the trees, and hesitated just a few seconds before heading toward the creek.

Breaking out of the trees on the other side of the creek Spence headed toward the Triple Y ranch and the center of the valley. He figured that they should be able to outrun the Indians, as their horses were still fresh, while the Indian ponies had been at a hard gallop and were probably tiring.

Looking over his shoulder, he saw the Indians break out of the trees. The Indians saw them and a couple gave a loud yell and tried to force their ponies to a faster run. After a couple of minutes Spence could see that they were steadily drawing away from the Indians. Finally two of the Indians stopped their ponies and pulled out their rifles. Spence heard the sounds of the rifles firing, but they were out of range of an accurate shot.

Within another couple of minutes they were out of sight of the Indians. Spence eased up his horse a little, but still kept him moving at a fast trot. He didn't want to slow to a walk and have the Indians catch up. Coming to a high point where they could watch back over the trail, Spence stopped to give the horses a chance to rest.

"Looks like we lost them," Jess said. "Good thing their ponies were probably winded before they saw our tracks."

Charlie replied, "No, I don't think we lost them. I think they just eased back some to keep from killing their ponies. I figure they will stay on our trail figuring we will probably pull up and stop."

"I don't have much experience fighting Indians, but that's what I figure also. It looks like they were heading over to where we had made camp and now they don't have to go so far," Spence stated.

"Yea, I think we have found the ambushers that we were looking for. I think we need to head on back to the ranch, pulling in any riders we see on the range as we go," Charlie said.

Turning his horse around Spence replied, "Yea, I think that is a good idea, especially since they have just topped that ridge." Spence spurred his horse into a gallop and the other two having turned and looked behind them did the same.

Spence kept the same pace as they headed back toward the Triple Y ranch headquarters. He figured that if he kept to a slow gallop the Indians wouldn't be able to pull up with them unless they hit a fast run. If the Indians came in at a run then the cowboys' horses would still be fresh enough to outrun them again.

Then he thought of a plan that might end this, without having to bring the Colonel's plan into action.

He moved over so he was riding alongside Charlie. "If we can keep this bunch of Indians following us then I think as we can maybe end this thing. As we get closer to the ranch and hit some riders with fresh horses, then we will send a rider to alert the ranch and maybe ambush this group behind us."

"Yea, I think that might just work. We will need to slow up a little so they can spot us every ridge or so. If they think they are gaining on us then they'll keep coming," Charlie replied.

Spence slowed the group to a walk and they kept constant vigilance behind them. They wanted the Indians to catch up, but didn't want them to override them. Finally the Indians came over a ridge about one half-mile back behind them. That was a little too close for comfort, so Spence spurred his horse into a gallop. They still needed a little distance between them so the ranch would have time to react.

After about an hour, they saw a small herd of cows and three riders. Spence sent Jess out to inform the riders of the approaching Indians. Spence told him to have one rider take off to alert the ranch and the other two to rope three fresh horses and have them waiting. Jess took off at a fast gallop and Spence and Charlie continued their pace watching their back trail.

Getting to the herd Spence saw that the cowboys had pulled in three of their spare string of horses, and Jess had already switched his saddle over to a fresh mount. Coming up to the group Spence and Charlie quickly switched saddles to the fresh horses.

"These cows will be all right out here. They may wander a bit but won't get too far away until we can get back out here," Johnson, the Colonel's aide-de-camp ,stated.

Mounting up Spence asked if everyone was ready to ride. Most of them nodded and Johnson said, "Don't matter if we aren't ready to ride. Those Indians just topped the ridge."

They spurred their horses and Johnson spooked the other horses, driving them in front of the riders. This would keep the Indians from getting any fresh mounts. A rifle shot rang out, and a cow crumpled to the ground behind them. Another shot rang out with no noticeable results. They were well out of rifle range now and the Indians knew it.

The riders continued on toward the ranch, and ran across another group of three cowboys that joined their group after a couple quick shouts of explanation. A group of nine now would be a better opponent for the Indians but Spence wasn't about to engage the Indians in a gunfight.

They finally got into sight of the ranch houses. They could see four groups of three riders working various herds of cows. Spence sent a rider to tell each group of what was coming up behind them. Taking one more look over his shoulder he led the remaining cowboys on into the ranch.

Coming to the main ranch house he told Charlie to find Fester and inform him of the Indians and for the others to pass the word around the ranch to the other cowboys. He dismounted and started up the steps to the porch. As he stepped onto the porch the Colonel stepped outside.

"Found something have you?" the Colonel asked.

"Afraid so," Spence replied and then went on and told the Colonel what they had found and of the Indians that had chased them back to the ranch. He told the Colonel that he had sent Charlie down to inform Fester of the Indians.

"Fester has already mounted up as many riders as we have now here at the ranch and he should be about ready to go meet those

Indians. He had each man mount a fresh horse so we can run them down if we have to."

Saying that the Colonel turned around and went into the house to get his gear that he had already laid out. He also had a horse staked out in the back as he had put the ranch on alert for an immediate action such as this.

It was only about two minutes until Fester came up to the ranch house, leading twenty-four men. He had Charlie bring a fresh horse for Spence, who quickly saddled the fresh horse.

The Colonel came around the house mounted, and wearing his cavalry sword at his side. He didn't hesitate but spurred his horse to a fast gallop and led the men back down the trail that Spence had come in on. The Colonel expected to take the Indians by surprise.

Topping the first ridge past the ranch area, the Colonel motioned Spence and Charlie to ride up with him. He asked which direction had they come from. Spence pointed out the direction and then he called Jess and Johnson up also. He told the four to ride out, two on each side, and to stay well out in front of the main group. The Colonel didn't want to top a ridge into rifle fire from twenty opponents.

Spurring their mounts to a fast run, the four got quickly out in front of the main group. They separated about four hundreds yards between the two groups, each about two hundred yards on each side of the main group.

The Colonel led the men behind him on at a fast trot now that he had his scouts out front. They came upon a group of three more riders that had been coming back to the ranch, and Fester had them join the group, explaining what was happening as they rode on.

Spence and Charlie hit the next ridge before Jess and Johnson. As they topped the ridge Spence could see the group of Indians coming on up the valley. He reined in his horse and waved at Jess. Jess saw the wave and approached the ridge slowly, venturing just far enough to see the Indians riding their way.

Pulling back so they were not silhouetted against the skyline, both Spence and Jess started waving at the Colonel and the main group. Seeing the waves Fester pulled up to the Colonel and told him.

The Colonel stopped his group and issued some quick instructions to the group. His riders quickly recognized the cavalry tactics outlined by the Colonel. They formed a line abreast of each other and then started toward the ridge.

Being formed in a skirmish line abreast, they could meet the enemy head on and quickly surround them with their lines moving out and around the enemy. This movement gave them the advantage of squeezing the enemy force, yet gave themselves room to maneuver.

Charlie quickly told Spence that their action would be to move out and try to get behind the enemy group so they could kept any riders from breaking and escaping. Jess and Johnson had also noticed the skirmish line and were also ready to move behind the Indians. They had done this same maneuver many times over the years of the Indian Wars.

As the group of Indians broke over the ridge, the Colonel had his men in a full run. Within seconds the two groups met head on and the four outlying riders quickly moved to the rear of the action. With pistols to the ready, the cowboys were the first to engage and quickly downed six of the Indian riders. The Colonel met the lead Indian with his sword and took the Indian down with one swipe. The other Indians pulled up and started trying to get their rifles in position to fire. A couple of shots were fired but not having time to aim, the shots missed their targets. Two more Indians fell to pistol shots. A couple of Indians just pointed their rifles in the direction of the cowboys, and fired hitting two cowboys and one horse.

The Indians then tried to use the rifles as clubs, but the cowboys blocked their swings with their own rifles. It had become hand to hand fighting as the riders on both sides were knocked to the ground. Pistol shots rang out and a couple more Indians fell. One cowboy fell with a knife in his throat as the Colonel hit the Indian just a second too late.

Two Indians reined their ponies around to try to escape the fight and ran right into Spence and Charlie approaching from the rear. Spence took down the lead Indian and the other slipped to the side of his horse as Spence's shot went over his shoulder. But that put him on Charlie's side and two shots rang out and the Indian slid off his horse to the ground.

Jess and Johnson rode up just in time to take down another Indian breaking from the group. Jess continued on into the group of fighting men and kicked an Indian in the head as he was about to stab Fester in the back. Jumping off his horse Jess hit the Indian again to ensure that he stayed down.

Within fifteen minutes of intense fighting it was over. A couple of the Indians were surrounded and put down their weapons. Looking around, Spence could see the dead and wounded, cowboys and Indians. Five cowboys were dead and three were hurt pretty badly. Eight Indians were dead, ten were wounded badly and two had surrendered. These two were quickly tied with ropes and then the one Indian that had been kicked in the head was tied. The twelve wounded men of both sides were then treated.

The Colonel had all the Indian weapons gathered together. He saw that these rifles were the same caliber as the rifles that had shot George and killed the other two riders.

Bringing all his cowboys together he asked for anyone that could speak an Indian tongue to try to speak with these Indians. He didn't recognize their markings as being from any tribe he had encountered in the past. A few of the cowboys stepped forward and tried a few phrases in the language that they knew, but didn't not receive any indication from the Indians that they understood what was being said.

After the cowboys had stopped trying to speak to the Indians the Colonel said, "Might as well just line them up and shoot them right here. If we can't talk with them then they aren't any use to us."

Fester had a couple of the boys line the Indians that could still stand up into a line. The Colonel motioned for five riders to cock their rifles. As the cowboys took aim at the line of riders they heard a mutter from the group of Indians.

"If you have something to say step forward," the Colonel said.

An Indian from the back of the group stepped out and said, "Some of us understand your words. What do you want of us?"

"Where are you from and what do you call your people?" the Colonel asked him.

"We are from the land North of here that you call the Canadas. We have been brought down here by the man you call Wardlow to help fight a battle. He has promised us cows to take back with us to feed our families. He gave us new rifles we could use to hunt for fur and meat during our winter months. He promised us tools so that we can use to build better shelters for our families," the young Indian stated.

"And what *battle* are you suppose to fight?" the Colonel asked the young brave.

"We were told that you are trying to take his land and we were to help him drive you back off of his land. We were told that you had stolen his cows and his horses. For every ten cows we got back we were to be given two. For every ten horses we got back we were to be given four."

"How many more are there of you?" Fester asked. The range boss had been in too many Indian battles and figured there were a couple more bands of braves.

"There are two bands with eight and ten braves in them. They are elsewhere."

"Where were you educated?" the Colonel asked the brave as this Indian's English was better than some of his riders.

"I attended the Academy de Quebec where I learned to speak French as well as English. I have returned to my people to help them learn the skills to farm and raise animals to support their families," the young man stated.

"Is this the way you were taught? Is murder, cattle rustling and killing people what you learned at the Academy?" the Colonel asked the Indian brave.

"To right an injustice and to help protect a man's land and cattle for a fair price is what I was taught. Wardlow brought papers with him to show he was the true owner, and also a contract he signed with our chief stating the terms of our work and payment with him. This payment would enable my people to be self-sufficient without having to take handouts from the white man. We could raise our own cattle for meat and to sell. That is why we are here."

"How many cows and horses have you collected so far?" the Colonel asked the young man.

"We have not recovered any with the brand of Wardlow on them. We have taken twenty young cows with no brands and forty-two with the brand of the Triple Y. We have also been able to find eighteen ponies, four of which have the Triple Y brand and the rest have no markings."

"I have a new contract for you. Are you willing to consider another offer or should we just finish things here and now?" the Colonel asked.

"I do not think we have any choice. Let me speak with my elder first," the brave replied.

After about five minutes of intense exchange between the young Indian man and an older man the young man turned back to the Colonel, "We will listen."

"You return the animals that are marked with my brand of the Triple Y and you can keep the others. In addition I will give you twenty horses we have recovered from other battles. I will also give you two cows per brave, part from my own cows and part from Wardlow's cows. In return, you and your braves will go back to your tribe and return to this valley no more. You will cause no further trouble while you are here and will make your camp at my northwest cabin, that was burnt. You will stay there until we have your animals ready to travel. You will bring to me all your rifles but one which you may use to hunt for meat. The others I will return to you as you depart the valley, as I have no need for your rifles," the Colonel declared to the man and his elder.

The young Indian brave translated the Colonel's words to the elder Indian. After a brief discussion among the men of the tribe the elder spoke to the Colonel. The young man translated back to English.

"We have been beaten here in a fair fight. You owe us nothing. You are a generous and wise leader and we will accept your terms. However, if you take all of our weapons you must allow us to protect ourselves. Five rifles until we depart from this valley and one horse for each brave in addition to the cows, which should be three for each brave."

The Colonel looked over at Fester and Spence and smiled. He was more than willing to increase the number of animals and increasing the number of ponies was easy, as he would take them from the Bar S ranch.

"I agree. I want you to send out a rider to each of the other groups and inform them of our agreement. Tonight you stay here and we will feed you and treat your wounds and then tomorrow you will move to the range cabin. I will have the men that cannot ride moved in a wagon. I will shake your elder's hand and that will be our pact for this agreement," the Colonel replied.

The young brave spoke again with the elder. The older man stood up and walked over to the Colonel. He presented his hand and spoke to the Colonel as they grasp hands and shook solemnly three times.

The young man translated, "It is an honor to meet a man that is honest and is straight with his talk. We agree to your offering and will abide by our agreement faithfully. We will tell stories of this valley and the good man that is chief of the valley. Our children and our children's children will know of this valley."

The Colonel nodded to the elder and then turned to Fester to arrange for a cook and food to be brought out to this camp. He told Fester to have the cook pack enough for the Indians and ten of his riders for five days. That should be enough time to gather the promised animals and to see these men start on the long trail back to Canada.

CHAPTER SEVENTEEN

Spence had volunteered to be part of the riders that helped gather the promised animals for the Indian group. It had surprised him that the Colonel would have been so generous with the Indians. He could not think of anyone else that he had known over the years that would have been so forgiving and so generous.

The Indians were very helpful to the cowboys, and they picked up what needed to be done very quickly. The two other groups had already driven the sixty-two cows and eighteen horses to the range cabin. It didn't take them long to separate the Triple Y branded cows and horses from the herd, and two cowboys led them back toward the main ranch.

Jess and two men had brought twenty horses and twenty un-branded cows with them when the Indians had been moved out to the range cabin. He then organized a group of mixed cowboys and Indians to ride over to the Bar S ranch the next day to collect the remainder of the animals promised to the Indians. Having selected his riders and explaining their duties for the next morning, he had the men return to camp for food and rest. He was not going to be very selective, but was going to take the first seventy-four cows and twenty-two horses that they ran across.

Spence was leaving the entire roundup and herding to Jess. He had some experience with cows and directing men, but Jess was the expert here and knew cows and his own men a lot better than Spence would ever know them. So Spence just observed what was going on, and kept an eye on the Indians and the direction of the Bar S ranch.

The cook had recruited two of the Indians to help with the fire and with cooking the meals. They were attentive to what he was preparing and discussed the ingredients and methods among them-selves. The cook was sure that these Indians would be changing the way some of their food was cooked after returning home to their tribe.

The next morning Jess was surprised to be awakened by one of the braves he had selected for the roundup. It seems the Indians had been up and they were all ready to ride, while his cowboys were just beginning to stir. He looked over at the cook fire and coffee was ready and the two Indian helpers had some corn fritters already cooked and waiting on the men. The cook was still in his bedroll.

Getting up and putting his boots on, he went over and rolled the cook and told him he was needed no longer. The cook sat up and looked over and his fire and broke out in a wide grin. His helpers had really learned well.

The cowboys were hurrying to get ready and grab some chow. They were a little embarrassed to be the cause of the delay and to be outdone by the Indians. Most of them had lived around Indians for the past ten or twelve years and this really didn't surprise them. Most Indians liked to outdo the white man at his own game and they had let that little fact slip from their mind and had got caught with their pants down, literally.

Moving out onto the trail to the Bar S, the riders were all in good humor. The morning had got off to an amusing start and the cowboys had taken it in stride. They had already started planning to get back at the braves. It wasn't long before they were on the Bar S and had begun to hit stray groups of cows. They would run across groups of three to five and a couple of riders would move out to bring these into the main herd.

Jess figured that they would have the cows collected before the end of the day. He was more concerned with trying to get the horses, as he had never seen any stray horses the few times he had been across the ranch. He figured that the Colonel would have to make up the remaining horses from that bunch he had bought from the Mexican drivers a month or so ago. That would suit Jess as the Mexican ponies were still half-wild and needed to be broke in and trained more.

By mid-afternoon they had find and herded together sixty-seven head of cattle. It was a mixed group of cows, yearlings and older bulls. Part were branded but most was not as it seemed the Bar S ranch wasn't strong on marking their cows. Jess figured they didn't brand all of them so they could steal cattle from other ranches on down the valley.

Coming upon a little valley down close to the stream they found a herd of twenty-two cows and calves. This would put them over their total that they needed. Jess motioned for the Indians to pick out the cows that they wanted. He and the other cowboys sat back and watched the show and kept the other cows from wandering off.

The Indian ponies were not used to trying to cut cows and herd them, and the Indians constantly had to re-cut the same cow from the herd. It was a lot of hooting and hollering and good fun for both the Indians and the cowpunchers watching.

Looking up Jess saw four riders come through the trees and start over to where he and the other riders were sitting. Jess recognized the range boss from the Bar S. The riders were not approaching in a menacing way, and none had a weapon out. Jess watched them approach cautiously and had loosened his pistol. He noticed his other cowboys had done the same.

Bringing their horses to a stop about ten feet away from Jess, the Bar S range boss said, "You boys having fun? Looks like you taught those Injuns to herd pretty good."

"Yea, those boys learned pretty quick. They're just filling out their contract with your boss. Seven out of this bunch and that will be the last. How's your spring roundup going?" Jess asked the other man.

Jess didn't really know what to say to a man that was watching some other riders fixing to herd the man's cows off his ranch. He had a feeling that although this other range boss felt a responsibility for the cows, the way he was treated by his boss kept him from saying much.

"My name's Rudy McKeown. I've been on the Bar S for four years now. Seen a lot of strange things, but this just about takes the cake," the range boss replied.

"Jess, Jess McCoy's my name. This does beat all I've seen also. Whoever thought an Indian could cut cows?"

"Our roundup is getting started a little late this year. What with all the commotion the boss has been stirring up, we just now been able to start. Figured to round up the cows on this back side and work in towards the ranch. I guess we won't miss those seven cows. They must have strayed on off the ranch and got lost."

Jess looked over at Rudy. This had been one strange spring. Every time he thought he had got things sorted out, someone did something strange. Here sat a range boss that was letting a herd of cows just walk off his range. Things on the Bar S must be worse than he thought.

"They need a couple of horses to finish up. You run any wild ponies on your range?" Jess asked.

"Nah, the boss don't like ponies. We just got one spare horse for every rider and he likes to keep them close to the ranch. Every time those Mexicans come through with their ponies he runs them off. I had to talk real hard just to get him to run a second horse for each cowboy," Rudy said shaking his head as if he couldn't believe it either.

"Must get rough as the roundup gets started good. Some of the boys keep four horses on their string and still about run them down," Jess stated.

That confirmed the fact that the Colonel would have to let go of some of the Mexican ponies.

"Well, looks like they got their seven. We'll start back and won't be coming back this way. Gonna herd them Indians and their stock back through the pass and let them work their way back north over the high plains," Jess said as he was getting a little itchy to ride away from the Bar S ranch.

"Before you go, see that little gray bull with the long horns. Take him with you instead of that yeller heifer. I've been trying to get rid of him for a long while now as he's got a hold of a couple of the boys a time or two," Rudy said seeing his chance to rid himself of a problem cow. "Hell, just take it with you so you can get on your way."

Jess glanced over at the range boss and then yelled to the Indians as he pointed to the gray bull. A couple of them shook their heads. Jess didn't know if they knew they had their number of cows or if they just didn't want the gray bull. He yelled over to them again and pointed to the bull and three of the Indians broke away to try to cut out the bull.

"We're going to have a show now. Just watch that bull out maneuver those Indians. I'll bet a five dollar gold piece that they don't get him cut out," Rudy laughed as he watch the Indians work at cutting the gray bull out.

It didn't take long until all the cowboys were laughing so hard they could barely stay on their horses. The other Indian riders were also laughing at their comrades. That bull just wasn't going to leave the cows. Finally Jess told two of the cowboys to go rope the bull and pull him out of the herd.

It took almost ten minutes of hard work before the two cowpunchers finally got two ropes on the bull. It took all their horses' strength to pull the little bull out from the other cows and started toward the herd of seven. Suddenly he stopped pulling and charged one of the riders. The bull was stopped just short of the rider as the other cowboy jerked his horse in the opposite direction. The bull then turned and charged the second cowboy. The first cowboy had to jerk his horse in order to stop the little bull. It was a seesaw battle all the way to the herd.

The Indians had joined the watching cowboys in laughing at the show. The three that had tried to cut the bull were really enjoying this show.

"See what I mean. I don't think I have any rider that will miss that little bull. I guess he just got ornery to make up for his small stature," Rudy said.

"I hope he settles down some on the trail. He just might end up as trail meat if he keeps delaying us getting these Indians headed back where they belong," Jess replied.

"Well, good luck. I guess we'll take these others and head them back towards the ones we rounded up this morning. If'n you get back this way and see me around, come on down. I reckon we been neighbors long enough we should get to know each other. Some of the boys like to play a little cards on Saturday nights. Come bring your money and let's see how much we can take off of you," Rudy said to the Triple Y cowboys.

They nodded at him and turned their horses and started off after the Indians. The little gray bull was still giving them hell and Jess figured they would have to fight that little bull all the way back to Canada.

Topping the first ridge going back toward the Triple Y ranch they run upon Spence who was sitting on his horse smoking a cigarette with one leg thrown over the saddle horn and his rifle still out of the scabbard.

"Looks like them ol' boys have gotten right friendly now," Spence yelled over to Jess.

"Sorta surprised to see you here. Yep, they even invited us over to play cards," Jess replied. "How long you been sitting there?"

"As long as you've been sitting enjoy that Indian show. I reckon before long that little bull will be roasting over a fire."

"Yea, so do I. They will run out of patience with it before too long and put a bullet between his eyes. You know, that range boss didn't say a word about taking his cows. You don't reckon Wardlow has kicked the bucket do you? He even volunteered to give up that little gray bull on top of what we were taking, of course, we are taking part of his problems with us," Jess asked as he pondered the actions of Rudy McKeown.

"Might have. He didn't say anything, I assume?" Spence asked.

"No, he didn't. And then he freely invited the boys over to play cards on Saturday night. Said they do a little gambling and want to take our money."

"Maybe we need to pay them a little visit after we get these Indians on their way. Well now, look at that!" Spence declared.

The little gray bull had finally given up trying to turn around and had made its way up to the front of the herd. It had taken charge of leading the herd and the other cows had fallen in behind it and were causing less trouble now that they had a leader.

"I've seen that happen before where a cow would take the lead of a herd. Seems like our little gray bull is a natural leader. We'll just see what happens when we merge these cows into the main herd. See if he still wants to lead," Jess replied.

As they picked up the main herd the little gray bull continued to lead the herd. Seems he was ornery enough to keep the lead and none of the other cows wanted to challenge him. The other cows just fell in with the herd and the little bull sat a good pace and they were back onto the Triple Y ranch by late afternoon. They drove these cows over to the others and circled them a couple times to keep them in place and to stop them. They eased back from the herd and the cows began to graze so the group of men made their way back to the camp.

The cook had made some potato pancakes to go with the beefsteak and beans and had the meal ready to eat by the time the men rode into camp. They were all feeling well pleased with themselves as they had gathered all the cows they needed and Jess had explained to the elder that they would pick up the other horses as they went toward the pass. The group of men devoured the meal with the Indians eating as much of the potato pancakes and beans as the cowboys. They eagerly filled their cups with coffee afterwards and sat back talking amongst themselves.

Spence saw that men were men regardless of their race. A good satisfying meal put a smile on any man's face after a hard day of work. Jess went around picking out the men for the night ride out with the cattle. He had a cowboy and an Indian on each team. He had found that the Indians were eager to do their portion of the work. He felt very comfortable designating them for their duties, and knew that they were capable of handling the task of being a cowpuncher. They needed to know what to do anyway since they would be driving the cows up to Canada.

CHAPTER EIGHTEEN

Jess had sent a rider back to the ranch to inform Fester Hess of the lack of ponies on the Bar S ranch. As they drove the cattle herd toward the pass through the Coastal Del Rey Mountains, Fester had the remaining ponies waiting for them.

Jess joined these ponies with the others and they helped the Indians drive the herd through the pass and onto the other side. The little gray bull had assumed a natural leadership role for the herd, and he kept them moving at a good pace, knowing instinctually the easiest path to take. He had found the shallows of the river in the valley and had led the herd across the lowlands of the valley toward the pass. The Indians were now well pleased with the little bull.

The Colonel had sent a bill of sale out for the Indians and Jess had explained it to the elder using the young brave as an interpreter. This should keep the Indians from having any problems as they crossed the territory between the Coastal Del Rey Mountains and Canada.

Jess and Spence had the cowboys go a full day's ride after they went through the pass to help the Indians get a good start on the way back towards their homes. Then they helped the cook separate just enough food to get them back to the ranch and gave the rest to the Indians. As they departed that morning each Indian brave shook the hand of each cowboy and it was an eager, yet, sorrowful parting. Each man rode off feeling that the other group would have made good neighbors and friends.

Getting back through the pass, Jess had the group spend the night at the range cabin. Spence had some unease about this cabin now, as he had watched a man get murdered here and also had a good friend shot not far from here. He hoped that he did not have any further misadventures there.

The next morning dawned gray and rainy and it was a cold, wet ride on back to the ranch as it rained throughout the night and that day. The following day was cloudy and misted all day, keeping the cowboys and their gear wet. They were all glad to finally see the lights of the ranch.

Jess and Spence stopped at the ranch house to brief the Colonel of the trip with the Indians. The other cowboys headed for the bunk-house and then they went to the mess hall, where the other riders greeted them as semi-heroes. Having spent six days with the Indi-ans and taking cows off the Bar S ranch put them in an elite position, and they were the center of attention that evening as they told their stories over and over again.

When Jess and Spence came into the mess hall they had to tell their stories also. Spence transferred the spotlight onto Jess, though, saying that he had just been tagging along and Jess and the other cowboys were the real heroes.

Daily life quickly got back into the spring routine now that Fester had his full crew back and they could now concentrate on the spring roundup. The cook packed his gear onto a wagon and moved out to the range. The Colonel had purchased some canvas army tents and they put them up so the cowboys would have some protection from the spring rains at night.

It was up at daybreak, a quick breakfast and then onto horse-back. Some cowboys were dedicated to the branding of the year-lings. As the riders would drive in the unbranded cows, one cow-boy would fling a rope around the head while another roped the back feet of the cow. Then they would pull the cow off its feet and hold it while a cowboy would run over with a hot brand from a fire. A quick sizzle of the outer hide and the cow was ready to be sent back to the main herd.

The Colonel and Fester had also come up with a plan to dehorn some of the yearling bulls. They would be thrown to the ground and then their horns would be clipped so it would end in a blunt horn instead of the sharp tip. This prevented injury to the bulls as they fought amongst themselves. While they were down being de-horned most of the young bulls would be castrated into steers. Only the better breed bulls would be kept for future bloodlines, and the rest would be cut into steers. This kept the unwanted traits from increasing in the cattle.

As the cowboys were out on the range, Will Harris prepared to start moving his equipment out to his farm so that he could start plowing. Hank Moore had finished repairing his plows and had sharpened them also. The harness had been repaired, and one handle on a plow had been replaced. Will's arm had just about healed and now Will and his boy, Davie, were anxious to see what was under the soil. When he was ready to start moving equipment, Will rode out onto the range to where Spence was working cows.

"Looks like you have found your calling," Will called out as he burst out laughing at Spence.

Spence had just roped a yearling and was being dragged across the prairie. Just as the rope dropped around the calf's neck it had taken off running. Spence jerked on the rope and dug in his heels, but his left foot caught a loose rock and he had tripped and lost his footing. The young calf wasn't about to stopped just because he had some weight around his neck. Spence was being dragged across the prairie grass and into a thorn bush every now and then. That was when Will had ridden up. Will took out his lasso and roped the calf bringing it to a stop. Spence got to his feet, brushing the dust and stickers from his clothing with his hat.

Spence looked up at Will and said, "Thanks a lot for stopping that yearling. I might have ended up in the next range if you hadn't come along. This has turned into harder work than I would have expected."

"Yep, that's why I'm a farmer. The only ornery thing you have to put up with is the mule pulling the plow. Get one started, though, and you don't have much trouble after that."

"You look like you have something to say. You ready to start your plowing?" Spence asked.

"Yea, that's why I came out here to see you. I was wondering if you could give us a hand on the move. I've been thinking also that with the three of us, we could have those two cabins roofed again without too much trouble. Unless, of course, you would rather play around with these cows," Will answered.

"Well, now I have to know something about cows if I'm going to start that little spread just west and north of you. I figure if you learn the hard way then you tend not to forget it as quick."

Spence had tightened his rope by now. He was already too far from the fire and the branders so he was going to try to lead the calf back towards the herd and the branders. Finally he gave up and tossed his rope up to Will and said, "Drag him back to the fire there. We get this yearling branded we'll have a smoke and talk some more."

Will spurred his horse, which broke out in a trot, dragging the calf with it. When he got close to the fire one of the cowpunchers threw his lariat around the calf's back legs and pulled him to the ground. Another cowpuncher dropped his knee on the calf's neck to keep him down while a third cowboy branded him. These riders had worked together long enough that they were a good team and each knew what had to been done. They prided themselves in their speed at getting a calf down, branded and back to the herd.

Spence walked up right after the calf was let up and the ropes removed. They chuckled at him and one said, "Been on a trip? Saw you take out over the countryside while ago. Didn't know whether you was coming back or not."

This comment had them all chuckling and Spence took a bow and laughed with them.

"Let's have a smoke," he said to Will. "Reckon we do need to start on those roofs. I'm sure your wife is ready to have a cabin for herself and get her belongings unpacked from the wagon."

"Hear about it most every night. She wants to go ahead and move the entire bunch out there. I've been putting her off until we can clear the brush and get a roof up. She says she didn't have a roof for almost a year coming out here, why worry about it now."

"She's got a point there. I don't reckon it would hurt none if she were out there. Seems the Bar S has calmed down now, and ain't much else out there but that big cat your boy had a run in with," Spence replied.

"Well, if'n it don't bother you none, then we'll all pack up and move out. It is nice after plowing all day to get a good meal and not have to cook it yourself. When will you be in then, so I'll know when to be ready."

"When you are ready, I'll be in," Spence replied. "You know how much you have to pack and load up. I just have to get a few things from the bunk house."

"Well then we'll be ready day after tomorrow right after she cleans up from breakfast. Come on over to the cabin to eat and we'll leave from there," Will answered.

Spence could tell that the farmer was excited to be finally doing something.

"See you tomorrow night then," Will called out as he reined his horse around and spurred it. Now he was in a hurry, as he wanted to ensure that he was ready to go the day after tomorrow.

Spence chuckled as he watched him ride off. "Didn't get to have my cigarette. Should have waited until he got down and pulled his tobacco bag out."

Spence reached in and pulled his own tobacco out and rolled himself a cigarette. By the time he was finished he was feeling better and his banged-up knee felt like it would last the day out. Next time he would turn lose of the rope quicker.

Spence spent the rest of the day taking turns roping, dropping and branding the cows. The smell of burnt hide had been strong at first, but now none of the men even noticed it. At the end of the day they were all ready to ride into the range camp for whatever the cook would dish up that evening. It surprised Spence how good the food was out here. Of course the hard work and long days probably had a lot to do with it.

The herd was building as more small groups of cows were driven in from the outlying ranges. These cows sure could spread out when left on their own. There were more cows on the Triple Y than Spence had imagined. He could see now why the Colonel could afford the luxury of giving so many cows to those Indians.

With the evening meal finished and the roster of outriders set up, most of the cowboys rolled out their bedrolls and prepared to settle in. A few were sitting around the cook fire telling tales and Spence's ride across the range was told a couple times, getting a laugh with each telling. He laughed with the others, as it had gotten funnier with each telling also.

The next day was pretty much the same as the previous except for the unexpected trip. Spence made sure he didn't try to hold onto a running yearling if he lost his footing. He started out the morning branding the calves as they were brought in, and just had to rope and throw cows during the latter part of the afternoon. He had scorched his arm on a hot brand that morning as one yearling jerked and almost got up just as he was applying the hot iron to its hindquarters. The cowboy on the neck had moved a little and the calf was quick to take advantage of the lack of pressure on its neck. The cowboy pulled some ointment from his saddlebag though and doctored Spence's burn.

That evening at the cook fire Spence informed Fester that he would be riding in that evening to help Will Harris move on out to the cabin.

Fester replied, "Figured he would have already been gone, but Hank had to rework his plows. You boys don't get too busy out there that you don't keep us informed of your progress. Don't get too sweet on that gal now either."

Spence smiled over at Fester with the last remark. He didn't really know how he felt about her, except she was the nicest looking woman he had met since he'd left for the War. Being able to cook and help around the farm were great assets also. But Spence was one to take it slow around women. His experience with women was very limited, and he was usually too bashful to say much.

Spence gathered up his belongings and packed what he didn't need for his bedding. He didn't want to be fumbling around the next morning trying to get ready to leave. Fester had put him on an early outrider duty so he could sleep through the night. Riding around the cows in the quiet night gave him time to think. He remembered Fester's comment about the girl and decided that he might enjoy this trip more than he thought.

After he was relieved by the next rider, Spence went back to camp and settled into his blankets. Most of the cowboys were sleeping outside the tents as it hadn't rained in a while and it was cooler than inside. He gazed up at the stars and wondered what the next day would bring.

CHAPTER NINETEEN

After breakfast Spence roped his horse, saddled up and rode out for the ranch. It would be well after dark before he reached the ranch and he expected to leave his horse in the corral and head straight for the bunkhouse. He should have it almost all to himself, as most of the riders were staying out on the range. There would be a couple of riders that were working the lower ranges that would have come back to the ranch and a couple of men were busted up and couldn't do much work. These few men and a cook's helper were all the men at the ranch except for the Colonel and his own staff.

Arriving at the ranch Spence rode over to the corral and was unsaddling his horse when Will Harris walked up.

"Thought I heard someone ride in. Figured you'd be arriving somewhere about this time. Had your supper?" Will asked Spence.

"Had some the cook fixed up for me before I left the range camp. You want to see if there's a pot of coffee still on over at the mess hall?" Spence replied.

"Come on over to the cabin. The wife still has a pot on and she's got some corn muffins left from supper. Those with a little bit of honey are right tasty."

Spence finished unsaddling the horse and then turned him loose in the corral. The two men then walked back over to the cabin the farmer's family was staying in. Going in the door Spence could see that they had everything packed except for a few pots and pans and their bedding. The boy was asleep up in the loft but Emily Harris was still helping her mother with last-minute chores. They wanted to leave the cabin cleaner than when they first occupied it.

"Pour a couple cups of coffee for the men, Emily. Then take some of those muffins and pour honey over them. Spence is probable hungry from his ride in tonight," the Francis said to her daughter.

Emily Harris poured two tin cups of coffee and brought them over to the men. She smiled at her Pa and then glanced over at

Spence. With a twinkle in her eye she asked Spence, "Been roping any more calves lately?"

Spence blushed at her remark. It was all right for the cowboys to make fun of him but he didn't expect it from the girl. He looked over at her Pa and saw him grinning also.

"Just had to tell how you like to travel across the prairie behind a cow," Will chuckled.

Spence looked up at the girl saying, "Yea and if you want, I can teach you how to do it. It's real easy, just rope a yearling and then fall down. The calf will take it from there and you don't have to do a thing."

Emily laughed and went over to prepare the muffins. Her Ma smiled at her as she came closer to the fireplace saying, "Now don't go bothering Spence. He's got more important things on his mind than teaching a young woman how to drag along behind a cow. Speaking of cows, did you bring that old milk cow up this afternoon?"

"Yes ma'am, sure did. She's beginning to show real good now. We'll be having fresh milk before too long. Good thing Pa had her bred when we first got here."

Spence and Will had their coffee and muffins and then had a cigarette. They talked of the trip tomorrow and then Spence excused himself and left to go to the bunkhouse. Going inside, the other cowboys were sleeping but they had left one lantern burning. The wick was down low and was beginning to smoke. Spence gathered his few things together and put them in a bag so he could tie it on his horse tomorrow morning. He wiped down his guns and then blew the lantern out and went over to his bunk, whacking his knee on the edge of it as he did. Rolling over into his bedding he thought to himself that it was just his luck to be his banged-up knee that he hit on the bunk.

Coming out of the bunkhouse the next morning Spence could see his horse was already saddled along with Will's. The mules were hitched to the wagon and the milk cow tied to the back wagon wheel. The pigs and the chickens were in their coops ready to be loaded and Will and his boy was up inside the wagon doing last minute tie downs of gear.

Spence was walking over to his horse to tie the bag of gear on when Will called to him to bring it to the wagon.

"No use you having to fight with that bag all the way out there when it can ride real easy right here on the wagon. Now let me have it and then let's go on in and eat breakfast," the farmer said.

"Thanks for saddling my horse. That's twice now you've beat me to it," Spence said to the boy, rubbing his head as they walked to the cabin. Spence could smell the food cooking and his stomach gave a little rumble. "That food sure smells better when your Ma cooks it."

"That weren't my Ma. That was Sis cooking this morning while Ma finished packing the blankets and all. Probably won't be worth eating, burnt and such," Davie said of his sister.

"Now stop going on about your sister or Spence will be afraid to eat anything, get weak and then you'll have to do his work today," the farmer kidded with his son.

Going into the cabin, Emily saw them and started dishing up food onto tin plates. She filled a couple of tin cups with coffee and brought them over to the men.

Walking back to the fire she said, "Now you all eat fast and then get on out of here. We have too much work to finish up for you men to just be sitting around. There's more in the pans if you need more to eat, just don't make a mess." Then Emily went back to work packing the last of the dishes and pots.

They finished their food after having a second helping. It would be late getting to the range cabin this evening and they wouldn't stop to eat on the way. It would take longer pulling a wagon than just riding out on horseback. They would also have to detour down to the low water crossing in order to get across the river.

With the last of their gear packed and the milk cow and two extra horses tied to the back of the wagon, they started out. Will was driving the mule team pulling the wagon. Spence and the boy rode on out ahead of the wagon with the boy riding out to the side on scouting trips and then galloping back into where Spence was riding. He would tell Spence of what he had seen over the ridge and then turn and start out again.

Mid-day Spence and David Elliot stopped and let the wagon catch up with them.

"How you doing? Want to switch out so you can stretch some?" Spence asked the farmer. He didn't want to drive the mule team and didn't have much experience driving a team, but was being neighborly.

"Nah, doing all right here. These dang mules have got fat and lazy over the last couple of months. They are a little ornery and don't need to put you to the trouble," Will replied. He figured that

Spence was just being friendly and didn't really want to drive the mule team.

"Here, you two boys take some of this fried meat and hard bread before you take back off," the farmer's wife said to Spence and the boy. She handed them a couple pieces of the hard bread with the meat stuffed inside. "This will last you until we make camp to-night."

Seems Emily was cooking more than breakfast this morning, Spence thought. Spence hadn't seen very much of Emily since they had left the ranch. She spent most of the time inside the wagon canvas, but now she stuck her head out looking over at Spence.

"Need some fresh meat for camp tonight. Think you and Davie can do that? Some fresh rabbit meat or maybe some prairie hens would do if you think you can find any," Emily called over to Spence.

Davie looked over at his sister and made a face at her and then grinned at Spence saying, "Bet we can. We can get more meat than you can cook. Why we'll get both rabbit and prairie hens and you can cook both up. Why don't you do that stuffing thing that you did before with the hens? And a nice rabbit stew with corn bread."

"Ma, give him another piece of meat, he's drooling already just thinking about it," she replied as she dropped back into the wagon behind the canvas.

Spence hadn't been able to get a word in between the brother and sister's good natured kidding of each other. He just took another big bite of the meat and bread and spurred his horse so he could move on out from the wagon. He hadn't been raised in a family with all this laughing and joking around between family members. It disturbed him some as he enjoyed it, and missed being raised in a family like this one.

Spence kept out ahead of the wagon the rest of the afternoon. He hadn't seen a rabbit nor prairie hen, and when David rode back in from one of his jaunts he asked him if he had either.

"Ain't seen nothing out there. Maybe when we get closer to the river we'll run across something. Maybe a squirrel or two in the trees down there," the boy replied.

"Might be a skimpy supper if we don't find something soon. Keep your eyes open next trip you make out there."

They finally arrived at the river and Spence rode along the bank until he came to a place where they could get the wagon down and across the river. This was a natural shallows, and the cowboys had driven the cattle through here often enough to have broken the bank down into a fairly easy slope. The mules didn't have much trouble pulling the wagon across the river and back up the other side with some extra encouraging from Spence and the boy on each side of the mules.

It would only take a couple of more hours now to the range cabin. Emily was now riding behind her parents so she could see their new farm and home. Davie rode down the riverbank trying to find something for supper. He knew that his sister would kid him unmercifully if they weren't able to get something.

Finally he saw a couple of rabbits in the fresh young grass along the river edge. He needed both of them and got out an extra shell and put it in his teeth so he could shot and reload quickly and try for the second rabbit. Taking aim at the rabbit closest to the brush he fired and quickly ejected the shell and loading the second shell. He looked up just as the second rabbit entered the brush. Fast, but not fast enough he thought to himself.

He got down and got the rabbit and gutted it quickly, washing the carcass in the river. Mounting up he reined his horse into the brush and sure enough, the rabbit jumped out the other side of the brush. Aiming quickly at the running rabbit he followed through his swing as he pulled the trigger and watched the rabbit flew heels over head and lay still after hitting the ground. David got down and gutted this rabbit also. At least he wouldn't have to face his sister empty handed. He loaded the rifle again just in case he ran across another rabbit.

As he guided his horse down the riverbank the bank flattened out and the trees were much taller along here. He started watching the ground ahead in case there was more game. As he passed underneath a tree with some low hanging limbs, his horse reared up, neighing with fright. This caught Davie by surprise and he landed with a thump on the ground. His rifle flew from his arms and landed about five feet away. Then with a low growl a big mountain lion leaped from the tree, landing on the horse's back. The horse panicked and tried to buck the lion off his back.

With the saddle in his way, the lion couldn't get a firm grip on the horse, and with the second buck the lion fell to the side. The horse, feeling the lion falling, bucked once more and then took off running. The lion took a few running strides and made one swipe at the horse's flanks but wasn't a match for the horse's speed. The lion then turned and looked back at the boy.

David was still a little groggy from the fall, but when he saw the lion loosing interest in the horse he looked about for the rifle. He saw it about the same time the lion turned back around.

Easing his hand out slowly he reached for the gun. He was about three feet short of reaching the rifle. Easing himself a little toward the rifle he thought that maybe he could reach the gun before the lion decided what it was going to do. A little more movement toward the gun, another inch or two, maybe this was going to work.

The lion watched the small movements and then it turned and started toward the boy. The cat coiled itself for the final spring. Seeing the lion about to spring at him, David grabbed for the rifle, rolling as he went across it. He pulled the gun up, cocking the hammer as he did. There wasn't going to be time to aim as the cat had only three steps until it reached him. As he got the rifle barrel up, he pointed it at the big cat and pulled the trigger as the lion took the final sprang.

Spence rode down the riverbank just as the lion jumped at the boy. Drawing his pistols he fired at the cat as it soared in the air at the boy. The lion landed on Davie, and Spence couldn't tell if the cat was still alive or not as it was still moving. He couldn't tell how bad the boy was hurt either, as the boy was still yelling.

Finally throwing the weight of the cat off his body, David rolled down the bank. The cat was quite dead by now and was lying in a heap. Spence jumped down and ran over to the boy to see how bad he was hurt. There was blood all over the boy but Spence couldn't find but one set of claw gash wounds to go with the blood.

Finally he got all the blood washed off the boy and then he could tell the boy wasn't so much hurt as still shaking from fright. Spence couldn't fault the boy, as he would probably be the same way if he had a lion all over him, but he did start laughing.

"What's so dang funny? There's nothing funny here. Just stop your laughing," the boy yelled.

That just made Spence laugh harder. The boy then started smiling a little and then before long he was laughing also. He was laughing more from relief as from anything being funny.

Finally Spence got control of his laughter and walked over to the lion. Rolling it over he saw a big hole in the cat's chest where the boy had hit it. Looking back behind the cat's shoulder he found one hole where he had hit the cat, going in and into the heart. Either shot would have killed the lion.

"That's something to be proud of there," Spence told the boy as he pointed out the chest shot. "That cat never knew what hit him and was dead before he ever rolled onto you. Not many men can keep their nerve and shoot that well with a lion jumping at them. Here let's skin this cat and get on up to camp. Your Pa's probably wondering where we are."

It didn't take long for them to skin out and gut the cat. The boy was already planning on how he was going to dry the skin. He hadn't noticed the second bullet hole, and Spence didn't point it out either.

Spence mounted and then told David to jump up behind him. The boy started toward the horse and then said, "Wait just a minute. I've got two rabbits over where I fell." He went and retrieved his two rabbits and then jumped up on the horse behind Spence.

"Reckon where that horse went? Don't reckon he started back to the ranch do you?" the boy asked.

"No, saw him go out the other side. Figure he's out in the open there waiting somewhere. We'll get him on our way to the cabin."

They rode up the bank and it wasn't long before they found the horse grazing out in the open meadow. It was a little spooky, and it took almost five minutes before they could get close enough for David to grab the reins. Then mounting they broke out into a gallop towards the range cabin. Getting closer they could see a cook fire started, and Will was unloading some of the crates from the wagon.

Riding into camp brought all three of the others around them. David's Ma was concerned about all the blood on him, Davie's sister was asking about the meat for supper and David's Pa was remarking about the amount of work that had been lost because he hadn't come straight into camp. Spence looked over at the boy to see how he was taking all the commotion. The boy looked pleased with himself at being so loved by his family that they all had to make a fuss over him. He looked over at Spence and grinned his pleasure.

Holding up the lion's pelt he proclaimed, "I might not have killed a bear like Davie Crockett but I never heard of him taking a lion's pelt. I must be as good as Davie Crockett."

With that announcement the three then began to make more of a fuss over the boy. Spence just sat back and enjoyed the show. The boy deserved all the fuss, as he had put a shot into the cat that would have killed it, and most of all, he hadn't panicked and got himself all chewed up.

When the story was told, the boy's wounds cleaned and the lion's pelt checked for size, then the camp began to settle down. Emily took the two rabbits and began cooking, while the boy's Ma checked

the bags for some clean clothes for the boy. Will and Spence unsaddled the horses and hobbled them so they would not stray too
far from camp.

"Saw that other hole in that cat. Figure you must have been close
by," Will said.

"Close enough, I figure," Spence responded. That was all that
was ever said about the cat.

Coming back to the camp the two men moved over to Emily's
cook fire. She began to dish up their supper, and heaped a special
plate for her brother. As they ate their supper, she had David tell
his story again. The boy wasn't shy about talking and started his
tale, and it seemed to Spence that the danger, the closeness of the cat
and the killing shot had all increased. A few more times of being
told and this would be a great fable indeed.

After the supper dishes were cleaned up and the fire stroked up
some, Will's wife and daughter climbed up into the wagon and made
their bed. Will had set out the men's bedrolls and they rolled them
out close to the fire. It had been a long rough day for all of them,
and it wasn't long before Spence heard Will snoring and the boy
had dropped off to sleep almost as soon as he laid down.

Spence listened to the night sounds for a little while and not hearing anything that wasn't normal, he also rolled over and went to
sleep.

CHAPTER TWENTY

Spence woke up as the birds first started their morning chirping and as the sun was just beginning to lighten the skyline. The Coastal Del Rey Mountains kept the sun from coming right up, and it was light for almost an hour before the sun actually rose over the mountains. Spence watched the pink and orange reflections off the clouds against the deep blue of the sky. He thought there weren't many things prettier than a good sunrise.

He got on up and pushed aside the ash until he found some live embers and put some kindling on the fire. Using the embers he got the fire started and put a couple logs on so that there would be a lot of coals by the time the women were ready to start cooking. Grabbing the coffeepot and a bucket he started down towards the river.

The water was still cold from the spring run off coming from the snow in the mountains. He washed his face and took off his shirt and did a quick wash of his upper body. It was too cold to wash very long, and he quickly put his shirt back on. Moving upstream to an undisturbed hole of water right below where the water rushed over some rocks making a small waterfall, he filled the bucket and the coffeepot.

Walking into camp Spence placed the coffeepot on the fire and sat the bucket of water close to the grub box. Will had sat up and was scratching his beard. Spence could hear movement inside the wagon and figured the woman was readying herself to come out.

He rummaged in the grub box and came out with the coffee grounds. He threw a handful of grounds into the coffeepot and then took a green twig and placed it over the top of the pot. This would keep the coffee from boiling over the edge of the coffeepot. He looked around at how much Will had unloaded. It seems the farmer was concerned with getting his farming equipment unloaded first. There were two plows and the harness to go with them, a couple of hoes, shovels and a pitchfork with bent tines. Not many tools but enough to start farming with Spence figured.

Will had gotten up and wandered off to the river and came back with his hair still wet and his shirt damp in places. It looked like he had done the same as Spence had earlier. Spence took two tin cups and filled them, handing one to Will as he walked up.

"That water will sure wake you up in a hurry. Don't reckon there will be any bathing in it for another month or more," Will said sipping his coffee. "Woman, you two better get up and about. Time's a wasting. Davie, get up now and wash up some while your Ma is getting around."

The farmer moved over and started checking his plows and harness. Sitting his cup down, he carried the plow out from the camp a ways and stretched out the harness. He moved inside and pulled the plow a couple of feet until it fell over. Coming back to the wagon he picked up the other plow and moved it over close to the other and stretched out the harness on it also. Spence figured that he was getting them ready to put the mules into the harnesses.

Emily jumped down from the wagon and came over to the cook fire. "How about some hot biscuits this morning?" she asked Spence.

"Sound right fine to me," Spence replied. "A little ham and some white gravy would go well with them also."

"Well, you bring me some milk, and I'll fix your gravy. As it is I guess you'll have to settle for some beefsteak and corn mush to go with the biscuits," she joked back to Spence. "Didn't get my prairie hens yesterday either."

"You got every one we saw yesterday. Could have cut up those lion flanks and brought them in if you wanted," Spence laughed.

"No, I guess I'll settle for just those two rabbits. Still got some stew if you want it this morning."

"I'll settle for the hot biscuits," Spence stated.

With the last remark Will had walked up saying, "I'll settle for hot biscuits also. Put a big dab of butter on them and as the butter is melting, put a spoon of honey on it. Put three eggs next to the biscuits and a slab of bacon."

"You must be wanting this come fall. You ain't getting any butter, eggs or bacon until then," Emily laughed at her Pa as she kneaded the biscuit dough. She then greased a skillet and rolled the biscuits, placing them in the skillet. Taking the full skillet Emily put an iron cover on the skillet, placed it in the embers from the fire and covered the iron cover with hot embers also. She had created a campfire oven. Taking another skillet she cut up some beefsteaks and fried them as her biscuits were cooking and her corn mush was thickening.

David Elliot walked back into camp with his shirt and his pants damp and his hair dripping. He got right up close to the fire and was shivering a little.

"Not going to try that again for a while," he said. "That water must be almost freezing still."

"Most people feel of it before they go jumping into it," his Pa replied. "I thought you washed up in it yesterday after that cat jumped you."

"Did but didn't feel it at all yesterday. Must have been too excited to know the water was cold," the boy said.

"That or still scared," Emily responded. "Get back from my cooking, or you'll need another washing after I whoop your tail."

The boy moved quickly back from the fire some. He didn't know if she could or not any more but he didn't want to find out before breakfast.

Francis walked up then, looked at the cooking and seeming satisfied with the progress, she poured herself a cup of coffee.

"When you going to start on the roof?" she asked her husband. She knew the plowing was important but having a real home was important also.

"I'm going to start framing the roof while Will and the boy start their plowing. Whenever I need help then they will come in and help with the larger logs," Spence said to the woman.

She looked over at her husband saying, "You going to let him do the roof by himself?"

"When I finish your roof, Will and Davie is going to help me finish out my cabin. It was burnt out more than this one and I'll need help with it," Spence again replied.

The woman again looked at her husband but the explanation suited her so she then started getting the tin plates and utensils for breakfast. Emily started filling plates and as she handed them around she stuck the largest biscuit on Spence's plate. He looked up at her and she smiled back down at him. Spence quickly glanced down at his plate. This woman sure had an unsettling affect on him.

Breakfast was quickly consumed and the hot biscuits went quickly. The men went out and brought the mules into camp and harnessed them to the plows. Spence watched as the farmer and his boy handled the mules and the plows. Moving out to the start of the fields they kept the plows from digging into the ground. The plows just skimmed the surface of the ground. Getting out to the edge of where

Will wanted the first field he told the boy to wait until he laid out the first plow row.

Will started the mule and the plow dug into the ground. He laid the first row fairly straight and didn't hit very many rocks. He wasn't plowing very deep at this stage as after the entire field's surface was turned then they would plow it again deeper. He started on the west side of the first row and the boy started on the east side working themselves out from the center row.

Spence watched the first couple of rows being plowed, and then he went back to camp and got the axe. Walking into the trees bordering the river, he looked for some straight trees that would make the main beams for the roof. He came to a grove of ash trees, and every one of them was straight and tall. He selected a couple that were about the same diameter and notched them. Then he started working the first tree, cutting out some on one side and then moving around to the back. He worked steady until the first tree fell. He trimmed off the lower branches and while resting he realized he had not measured the length of the cabin so he didn't know how far up the tree to trim branches. After the next tree he figured he would trim it up a ways and then go get his horse to pull them back, taking a measurement of the cabin as he did so.

The second tree took a little longer to fall than the first. Spence hadn't worked hard labor in a while and his muscles weren't used to the action of the axe. He was glad when the second tree finally fell and he could rest a bit. Wiping sweat from his brow he moved over and trimmed branches up the first twenty feet of the tree.

Walking back up toward the cabin he stopped and watched the two farmers plowing. The boy hadn't just been bragging when he said he could work as hard as a man could. His Pa just had one-half of a row on the boy and the boy's rows were just as straight as his father's were.

Spence waved at Will and walked on up to the cabin. Emily saw him coming and started heating up the stew for his dinner with some corn bread made from the morning's mush. Spence went over to his gear and picked up his lariat and started walking out from camp.

"You want this dinner now or later?" Emily asked him as she dished up some of the stew. She was making it clear that he was going to eat it now regardless.

"I guess I had better eat it while it's hot," Spence replied. He was beginning to like being waited on like this.

Emily dished around for some of the meat from the rabbit and added it to his bowl. She cut some corn bread and then took it all over to Spence who had sat down close to the fire.

"You gonna have a bowl with me?" he asked.

"Not right now," she said. "I'll have mine after Pa and Davie get theirs. Plowing takes a lot from a man and they'll need all this and more. I'll fry them up a piece of meat also when they come in."

She sort of told Spence that chopping down trees wasn't the hardest work on a farm. He figured she was probably right, as he remembered some hard days from his youth working around the farms of his uncles.

Finishing his stew, he picked up his lariat again and went out to find his horse. Getting away from the cabin he saw the horse out in the meadow with the cow and the other two horses. He whistled and watched his horse jerk his head up to listen and look around. Waving his arms above his head he whistled again and the horse started trotting in to where he was standing. Spence wrapped his lariat around the horse's neck and then swinging up on the horse's back he rode into camp and stopped at his gear.

He put the halter on his horse and took out another rope to use to drag the trees. Moving over to the cabin he walked off the walls of the cabin trying to get a good measurement. Counting his steps he reached ten. Turning around he counted them again to make sure. He would count the trees at twelve steps so the beams would hang over the walls on each end. Emily had watched him as he walked the walls but she looked down to her dishes each time Spence looked over at her.

Mounting his horse he rode back out toward the ash grove. Going past the plowing men he shouted out that their dinner was ready and getting cold. The boy looked over at his Pa who motioned to finish the row first. Looking behind him right before he went into the trees Spence saw that the two men had stopped their mules and were walking in toward the camp.

Spence finished trimming the branches from the trees up to his twelve-step mark and then cut the trees at that spot. He moved the branches out of his way and then tied his rope to the first tree. Bringing his horse close to the end of the tree he looped the rope around the horses chest. He tried to get the horse pulling, but every time the rope tightened on the horse and it felt the weight of the tree it would balk and start fidgeting and sidestepping. Not having ever pulled a wagon or plow, the horse wasn't about to pull the log.

Spence spent about twenty minutes fussing with the horse and finally gave up. It was going to take the mules to pull the trees to the cabin. He tied his horse to some brush and then picked out another tree and started chopping at it.

Working all afternoon Spence had seven trees felled and trimmed and ready to pull to the cabin. Taking a look around he picked up the axe and walked over to his horse. Untying it from the bush Spence swung up onto the horse's back and rode out of the woods.

Coming back to the plowing he saw that the men had already stopped their plowing. Riding into camp he saw the two men brushing down the mules and feeding them a little grain. They couldn't afford to have the mules come up lame or weak so they were taking good care of them now. The trees would have to wait.

CHAPTER TWENTY-ONE

The next two weeks saw the completion of the roof on the Harris cabin. Spence, with Emily helping, was able to lay enough logs to cover the cabin. Working with the adobe mud found in the valley they layered the logs with mud, packing it into the spaces between the logs.

After Will and the boy finished plowing for the day, Will worked on framing the windows and the doorway. For now they used canvas to cover the openings until they could get glass for the windows and build a plank door. The Triple Y ranch had a saw that could be used to cut planks for the floor and the door and Will had plans on using it after his crops were planted.

Francis Harris had swept all the loose dirt from the cabin and had tramped down the floor until it was almost dust free. She figured this would do until she could get a real floor. Spence helped the two women move the rest of their belongings into the cabin. He then removed the canvas and bows from the wagon so it could be used to haul cargo now.

The evenings were cozier now inside the cabin. Spence took his meals inside with the family, but he kept his bed pitched outside under the stars. If it didn't rain, he preferred to sleep outside.

Having finished his work on the Harris cabin, he decided that he would ride back to the Triple Y and give a report to Hess Fester. It would also give him a chance to get away from Emily for a while. He had grown very close to her over the last two weeks, and he found himself waking early and longing to be in the cabin where he could watch her as she went about her morning chores.

Over breakfast that morning he said to Will, "I think I'll ride into the Triple Y this morning. Things are going quite well out here and the Colonel will probably be glad to hear that you are well on your way to getting the fields plowed and planted. Is there anything I can do for you while I'm in there?"

"Yes, there is. Hank had made new hinges for the Colonel's doors while we were there. See what he did with the old ones and what they'll take for them. We might get a door up on this cabin if we had the hinges. And I need to talk with Fester about the use of that saw, so when we get a chance we can start cutting some planks for a floor here. Eventually I have plans on replacing that roof with a real plank roof also. I can then build a loft for the boy to sleep in and store stuff," the farmer replied.

"Also talk with them and find out where they got their glass windows. If we have to order it and have it shipped in, then we might need to oil this canvas down so it'll last for a while," Francis stated.

Emily didn't say anything, but she seemed to have a disappointed look on her face. She had also enjoyed working with Spence the last two weeks. They had relaxed around each other and were constantly joking and talking. This was the closest she had come to being with a man since they had left their home and started out west.

Finishing breakfast, Will and Davie went to get the mules and Spence brought his horse in and began saddling it. As he mounted Emily came out from the cabin with a cloth-covered package.

"Here's something for you to eat for your dinner. I know that you won't reach the ranch in time and you might get hungry," she said. "And bring this cloth back with you, as it is mine."

"Why, you didn't have to do that. I would have been just fine. But I'm glad you did," Spence said as he reached down to get the food. Their fingers touched as the package was exchanged and Emily ran her fingers across the back of his hand.

The gesture caused a ripple along Spence's arm. It had been a long time since he had been given a caress of affection. Maybe this trip was needed more than he thought. Maybe the two of them had been spending too much time together, and things were progressing faster than it should.

Spence smiled at the woman then he tipped his hat and turned his horse and rode on out. Emily stood and watched him until he went into the trees by the river. Her Ma had watched the happenings from the cabin, and she watched Emily until the young woman turned and started back to the cabin. The farmer's wife was also pleased at the way their friendship was growing. She had been afraid that the trip out here would leave her daughter without a good man for a husband. She enjoyed Spence's presence and thought that he was good for both her daughter and her son.

The trip into the ranch did not take long, as Spence was becoming familiar with the land and now knew a couple of shorter routes to the ranch. Being by himself he could keep a better pace and his horse seemed to be enjoying the trip also instead of being force to drag logs.

As Spence rode along he noticed that the grass in the valley was greening up and it was actually quite thick in most places. He could see why the Colonel had settled here for his ranch. The grass could support more cattle per acre than most land that he had ridden across coming out here.

Spence didn't see any riders or any cattle on his way into the ranch. The spring roundup must be over and the cows were being moved down the valley to the summer ranges.

Riding into the ranch yard early that afternoon Spence saw that there wasn't anyone out working. He rode over to the blacksmith shop, but it was empty and the fires were out and cold. Turning, he rode over to the mess hall and went inside. There weren't any fires going, nor did he find any cooks.

Coming back outside he looked around and there weren't any hoof prints in the yard. It looked like there hadn't been anyone around since the last rain.

Spence mounted and rode up to the main ranch house. He got off his horse and tied it to the porch rail and went into the kitchen. There he did find the Colonel's cook.

"Where is everyone? I couldn't find anyone down at the main ranch buildings," Spence asked the cook.

"That's the way it is with the spring drive. The Colonel takes everyone with him. They drive the cows to the summer ranges and then take a couple wagons on into the city to stock up on supplies. Those that are busted up drive the wagons. They take turns with the cattle and everyone gets a couple days in town. A couple boys and me are left here to watch the ranch. I have no use any more for the city or what you find there, so I volunteer to stay here. The ride gets me in the back and the weather stiffens my bones," the cook answered.

"Where are the two riders? I didn't see anyone around the barns," Spence asked.

"They're laid up in the bunkhouse. One fell and busted his legs and the other was kicked silly by a cow he lost control of. I cook here and take the food down to them. They don't get out of the bunkhouse. Wasn't any use to the Colonel, so he left them here."

"How long have they been gone?"

"Only about three days now. You can catch up with them pretty easy, as they don't push the cows none. The Colonel lets them eat as they go to take advantage of the new grass and fatten them up some. He sells some to the city to help buy his supplies."

"How about packing me a grub sack then and I'll see if I can catch up with them," Spence said.

The cook pulled out an empty floor sack and began to put some stables into the sack; a little coffee, a little beans, a little corn meal and a small bag of sugar.

"Here, that should do you until you can catch up with the main group."

"How about a couple of small pots? I left my gear at the Harris's cabin. Didn't figure on having to make a camp on this trip," Spence said.

"Sure, but remember where they came from. I don't make a habit of lending cowboys my cooking pots," the cook replied.

Spence thanked the cook and then took the grub sack and tied it to his saddle. Mounting up he turned and started out of the ranch yard looking around the valley to get his orientation of the best way to hit the trail the herd had taken.

Looking back towards the pass, he saw dust coming from the trail. He couldn't make out what was causing it yet.

"Look up there," he said to the cook. "Looks like you have company coming in."

Spence and the cook watched the dust and eventually they saw a wagon being pulled by a team of four oxen. Then behind the first wagon, there were two oxen pulling another wagon and then a third pulled by two mules. Behind the wagons were four cows, two calves and a boy on a pony.

"Well what do you make of that? I reckon you are the official greeting party," the cook told Spence.

"Me? What do you want me to greet them with? Spence asked.

"Well, ride out there and extend your hospitality. See where they came from and where they expect to be going. Let them know that they are on the Triple Y ranch and see if you can be of any service. The Colonel always was friendly to any wagons coming through but he also made sure they knew this was not homesteading land either."

With those comments Spence rode out so he could intercept the wagons. He loosened his pistols in their holsters but didn't expect any trouble. Coming up to the first wagon he yelled out, "Hello the wagon. I'm Spence Pierce and this is the Triple Y Ranch."

Spence rode up to the first wagon. The driver was a bearded man in his early forties and a woman that looked like his wife. He had stopped his wagon and waited until Spence was within talking distance.

"I'm Jesse Goodman and this is my wife, Martha. Behind me are my two brothers, Joseph and Maxwell and their families. We're from Kentucky and heading for Santa Clara. Heard there was lots of land just north of there along the coast that farms real well," the man said.

The other two men walked up from behind the wagon. The older of the two was about six feet tall and broad while the younger man was smaller and shabbier. They both looked like they had spent considerable time behind a plow working hard but the younger man looked like life hadn't treated him very well. His wagon was also small and beat up and his mules were old and worn out.

"Where did you say we are?" the youngest of the two asked.

"The Triple Y Ranch. That's the main ranch house over there. You hit the ranch as you came out of the pass and most of this lower valley belongs to the Triple Y. The northern ranges belong to the Bar S ranch but they aren't very friendly."

"Yea, we've heard tales of the Bar S ranch. That last little town before the pass had a couple of rough looking men that said they had worked on the ranch but they sure didn't look like cowpunchers," Jesse Goodman stated.

"You here to run us off or turn us back?" the youngest man asked.

"Here now, Max, don't by so rude. This fellow hasn't said anything of the sort," Jesse stated.

"No, I'm just here to welcome you to the Triple Y and to see if you folks need anything. The Colonel likes to make folks welcome as they cross the ranch. He knows that it is folks like you that will help develop this part of the country," Spence replied.

"Now that's right neighborly of him. We don't need anything I can think of. We wintered in the valley across the mountains and fixed up most everything while we were there. Didn't have much else to do except work on our equipment. You can point out the easiest trail to get on down the valley though," Jesse said. Being the oldest he was the spokesman for the family.

"I was just about to leave going that way. I'll just ride along and help guide you through. We have about two more hours before dark and we can get a ways on down the valley," Spence stated.

"Think we should pay a courtesy call on the owner of the Triple Y since we are passing across his range?" Jesse asked pointing to the ranch headquarters.

"You'll meet up with him on the summer ranges as we go down the valley. Nobody up there now but the cook and a few hands minding the place," Spence said. He was beginning to want to get moving. He had the feeling that the farther he had these people from the ranch house the better it would be. He was going to push them until dark to get them a few miles from the ranch before they had to stop to make camp.

"Ready to move out? We still have a few hours until dark and we can get started down the valley and closer to water before time to make camp," Spence said to Jesse.

"We've been moving pretty steady the last few days. Maybe we should just make camp here," Max stated.

Spence had thought that might have been the man's intent when he first saw him. Max had the look of having spent time in a jail, and Spence figured it was probably for petty theft. He had no intention of camping within walking distance of the ranch.

"No, I think we better move on down the valley. The quicker I can get you hooked up with the Colonel the better. Jesse, you ready?" Spence asked.

Jesse looked down at his brothers saying, "Mount up. I think Mr. Pierce is right. We do want to get down the valley as soon as possible. The grass is probably better in the valley also, and these animals could use some good grazing."

The two men turned and started walking back towards their wagons. Jesse turned to Spence and said, "I apologize for the actions of my brother. He's a little rough and has lost his manners. I'm hoping that a new start in a new area will help him. Heavens knows his poor wife needs a new start also. But that's another story. Ready to go?"

Spence turned to led the way and Jesse started his oxen pulling his wagon right behind Spence. As the wagon started rolling Spence heard the chatter of a bunch of children coming from the canvas covered wagon. From the sound of the voices he figured that there were six or seven children in the wagon.

"All those yours?" Spence asked Jesse.

"No, just part of them. Joseph's kids come up here and ride with me at times. I've got the oldest boy riding back with the cows and three more, Joe's got three and Max has one. Since I've got the largest wagon and the most team animals, the four of them come up here. I get tired of the noise at times and make them all walk."

Spence kept the three wagons moving until he hit the river running down the valley. The grass was good here and there was plenty of firewood. And it was also out of walking distance of the ranch. Spence figured he could keep tabs of any animals moving so a man could not ride out to go to the ranch house area. He also had the feeling that Jesse had known why he wanted them to keep moving.

The three families were very efficient about making camp. The eight children were very helpful as they gathered wood and helped with the team animals. They uncrated chickens and piglets from the wagons and the kids feed and watered them. The three women started supper around one cook fire and it looked like a communal meal. They had pots on every part of the fire boiling and frying different items of food. Spence didn't know what all was cooking but it sure smelled good.

Helping Jesse unhitch the four oxen from the wagon and moving them out to graze on the fresh grass Spence also made note of where Joseph and Maxwell put their animals. The boy had brought his pony up and let it loose with his father's oxen.

Spence walked back to the camp with Jesse and the boy. Coming to the cook fire Jesse invited Spence to eat with the families. Spence accepted the offer and took a tin plate from Maxwell's wife. She had loaded it with a huge spoon of food from every pan. Before Jesse took his plate he called the group to prayer. Spence had just started to take a spoonful of food and quickly stopped and put the spoon down. Most of the family was holding hands in a circle around the fire and Jesse gave grace and then called the family to eat. Spence waited until Jesse had his plate and then picked up his spoon and started eating. The food was as good tasting as it had smelled while cooking.

The food was quickly consumed by the families, and the dishes were quickly cleaned by the women and the girls. Then the children ran out from camp and were playing chase out in the open meadow. Joseph and Maxwell came over to where Jesse and Spence were sitting, and Spence offered them his tobacco bag. The four men rolled themselves cigarettes and lit them with twigs taken out of the campfire.

"This sure is a lot of land for one man to own. Has the Colonel ever thought of selling any of it? This is prime farming land and a fellow could raise a good crop of wheat or oats here," Joseph said to

Spence. "When we see this here Colonel fellow, I think I just might ask him about it."

"What's on the other side of the ranch?" asked Jesse.

"I don't rightly know," Spence answered. "I just came over the pass this past winter and stayed on the ranch working around here until now. Had plans of just riding on down the valley like you folks."

"Changed your mind now?" Max asked.

"Yea, think I'll work for the Colonel for a while and get me a grubstake. Heard there was gold being found in the mountains of Northern California," Spence said. He wasn't about to tell these farmers about the deal the Colonel had offered him. It was up to the Colonel to tell these homesteaders if it was told at all.

"I heard that the gold finds had dwindled down now to hardly anything. Most people didn't find enough to pay for their tools, and most have left and wandered back home now," Joseph stated.

"Well that's just like my luck. I'm always a little late on time, or a little short on money," Spence said. The other three men laughed at that as they could identify with the bad luck.

"Need to buy you a little land and do a little farming. You'll never get rich but it'll keep you eating," Jesse said to Spence while looking at his youngest brother.

"It'll also keep you dirty and poor. You'll never be able to give your woman anything but hard labor and children," Maxwell stated.

Spence could tell that this was a discussion that the brothers had probably had many times over in the past. One brother was trying to convince another of the right path to take with his life and one not wanting any part of it.

Spence didn't want to get involved in a family matter, so he excused himself with the need to check around the camp before turning in for the night. He got up and walked out away from the camp and to where he had hobbled his horse. He didn't need to check on his horse, but this was in case anyone followed him.

Circling the camp he sat down next to a scrub tree back on the path toward the ranch house. If anyone was going to attempt to make the trip during the night he would hear them coming. He had sat there quietly for well over an hour before he heard what he had expected to hear, a mule making its way back down the path. He sat and watched as the mule drew closer with a small, thin rider.

As the mule was almost upon him he suddenly stood up and said loudly, "Going somewhere?"

The mule stopped suddenly and the rider was so startled he slipped off the side of the mule falling to the ground.

"No, no just taking a little ride to get away from that pack of kids and their noise," Maxwell stammered.

"Here let me help you with your mule. I figure this animal needs his rest after pulling that wagon of yours all day," Spence said as he grabbed the man by the arm and jerked him up.

Maxwell pulled his arm from Spence's grip and grabbed the mule's reins from his hand.

"Reckon I can take care of this mule by myself," the man stated.

"In that case I'll walk with you back to camp. Figure that bunch of younguns have bedded down by now and you won't be bothered by their noise," Spence said to the man.

They walked back to camp and Maxwell turned the mule loose before they walked into the camp. Jesse and Joseph were still sitting by the fire when they walked in. The two homesteaders looked at their brother and Spence but no one said a word. Spence walked over to his bedroll and spread it out.

"Reckon I'm finished for the night. Tomorrow is going to be another long day so I'm just going to turn in." With that remark he rolled up in his bedroll and turned away from the fire. He listened to the camp noises until the three men went to their wagons and the camp became quiet. He figured that Maxwell wouldn't make another attempt to ride out after being caught at it already.

CHAPTER TWENTY-TWO

Spence could see the cowherd well before they were close to it. The grass in this area was grazed over and stamped down by the cows. It was over an hour of travel after spotting the herd before they began to hear the bellowing of the cows and shouts of the cowboys. Spence was glad to hear the familiar calls of the cowboys. Three days on the trail with the three brothers and their families had been more than enough for Spence.

"I'll ride ahead and locate the cook's camp and then come back and guide you in," Spence said to Jesse. Jesse nodded and then Spence turned his horse and spurred it into a fast trot. Spence wanted to ride ahead and talk with Hess and the Colonel and give them an account on the families before they got there.

Coming into the cowherd Spence saw George just ahead. He rode on over and asked, "George, where is Hess or the Colonel?"

"The Colonel is in the city, but Hess should be somewhere around the camp. He isn't much to ride herd on the cows. The camp is off to the right on the high point going to the river. Less dust up there. You can't miss it," George shouted back.

Spence tipped his hat and rode off in the general direction of the camp. The grass in this area was lush and green and the cows would be kept in this area for a while. They would fatten up soon and would be close enough to the city where a drive would not take much fat off of them, bringing higher prices in the market.

Spence circled the herd so he wouldn't disturb it and soon saw the camp located on the high point of the valley. There were five canvas tents put up so the cowboys would have some protection from any spring rains and the heavy morning dew. Riding into the camp Spence saw a tent located a little ways off from the others and knew that was the Colonel's tent. He rode up close to the cook fire and dismounted. The cook was kneading bread dough and yelled for Spence to get himself a tin cup from the cook wagon and get himself a cup of coffee.

Spence filled his tin cup with coffee and walked over to the cook. "Know where Hess might be right now?" Spence asked.

"Saw him not too long ago going into the Colonel's tent. That's where he keeps his paperwork. Haven't seen him come out yet."

"Thanks. Is that sourdough biscuits you kneading up there?" Spence asked. He hadn't ever eaten sourdough biscuits until he had come to the Triple Y Ranch, and now he couldn't get enough of them. The cook didn't make them very often though, as it was hard to keep the starter dough going.

"Yep, Hess brought back a starter from a bake shop in the city and I've been making them nightly since we been out here. Want me to bake up a pan? I'll make some up and surprise the boys with sourdough biscuits for dinner," the cook said.

"Sure, and if you holler when they get done I'd appreciate a hot biscuit now," Spence replied.

Spence refilled his coffee cup and walked on over to the Colonel's tent. "You in there, Hess?" he asked through the canvas door.

"Yea, come on in here. Didn't expect to see you out here. How's the farming coming?" Hess asked.

"Plowing almost done and Will should be starting to plant his seeds by now. Him and that boy have really been working hard. Got the roof on their cabin and a few shelves up and some rough furniture made for them."

"Glad to hear they are getting settled and got a crop in the ground. I knew Will Harris would be a hard worker and he'll do well out there. The Colonel will have grain and crops to buy before he knows it," Hess stated. "What you doing out this way, tired of being a farmer already?"

"Got some homesteaders back up the trail a ways. They came over the pass about four days ago and hit the ranch about the time I had come in to check in with you. Figured it best if I brought them on across the ranch. It is three brothers and their families in three wagons. Two of the brothers seem to be hard working farmers, but the youngest one looks like he's just out for the simplest way of making money. I think he would have hit the ranch house if I hadn't been sitting in his way," Spence stated.

"Yea, we've seen quite a few come through like that. Too lazy to farm, too ignorant to ranch, and just looking for an easy way to make a dollar. Not enough honest farmers coming out here yet. Need more like Will Harris out in this part of the country," Hess said.

"The two older brothers seem quite honest. The older one looks like he did quite well farming before they started out here. The middle brother has a good team and a solid wagon so he must have been doing well also. The younger one looks like his rig is just barely staying together and all of his stuff is quite shabby."

"Well, bring them on in and park them down the ridge there. The Colonel should be back tomorrow and he'll want to talk with them before they get on with their trip."

"After dinner. They are still a couple hours back and I don't want to miss the cook's sourdough biscuits," Spence replied.

After Spence and Hess talked a little bit about the progress on the cabins and the layout of Harris's fields Spence walked on back to the cook fire. A couple of the cowboys had drifted in for their noon meal and Spence dished himself up some stew and a couple of the biscuits. They were still hot from coming straight from the fire and Spence ate one immediately and used the other to soak up some of the stew. Finishing his meal, he rinsed out his tin plate, got another biscuit and then mounted up to go guide the homesteaders in.

Clearing the cowherd Spence could see the wagons slowly making their way in. Jesse was guiding his little wagon train around the cows and waved when he saw Spence. Spence rode on up to the wagon and turned his horse to ride along side Jesse.

"The range boss says to bring your family wagons on into the camp and to set up just below the ridge where they are. There's plenty of grass for your animals and the Colonel will be in tomorrow. He wants to talk with you before you move on. I guess that is his way of keeping in touch with the east and to see what type of families are moving in this area," Spence told Jesse.

"Well, I guess it won't hurt to take a little break from the trail. The animals can use a day of rest and this grass sure looks good in this area. Might see if I can get those other two milk cows bred while we are around this herd. Can use the extra milk with all these children, and might have some butchering meat next year."

They rode along for the next hour and came to the ridge where Hess had said to pitch their camp. Spence led them on around the ridge a little bit to get them out of the path the cowboys used between the camp and the cowherd. It would be a little quieter and less dust for the families. Jesse had the wagons circle to create a center area for their camp. As they unhitched the animals the oldest boy moved them off to the upside meadow so the cows wouldn't try to join the Triple Y's herd. They hobbled the mules and the pony to keep them from wandering too far from the camp.

The children started their hunt for firewood and they went down to the woods along the river. Having dragged a pile of wood into camp they stated they needed one more load. The women started making camp, and the men started a common cook fire. They had brought in some stones to line the cook fire. After a while Jesse's wife looked around for the children, as they had been gone for a while. She asked Jesse to walk out and see if he could find them.

Jesse started out of camp and Spence fell in along side of him. They walked down to the woods along the river and could hear the children laughing and shouting to each other. Coming to the riverbank they could see the children playing in the shallow water. Then the oldest boy came swinging out of the trees on the other bank and swung out over a deep pool as he let go of the vine he had used. As the vine swung back to the bank, one of the girls grabbed it and she swung out over the water and dropped into the pool.

Jesse watched them for a little while and then shouted out to the children, "You kids come on out of there and dry off. If'n your Ma was to see you like this she would whup every one of you. Come on now."

The startled children quickly came out of the water and started wringing the water from their clothes. The ones swinging into the pool was totally soaked and the others had their pants and the bottom of their dresses wet. They put back on their socks and shoes and then came up to the two men.

Spence had started a small fire and the children gathered around it to dry their clothing before they went back to the camp. They knew their mothers would not be as understanding as Jesse was.

With the warm air and the fire, the children was soon dry enough to start back to camp. Jesse led the way but the children were soon running around the group chasing each other and picking up strange stones and other items they found on the ground. Spence watched Jesse watching the children and laughing at their childish acts.

This was a good man and a good father Spence thought. This country would be better off with men like this settling and making their homes around here. He meant to tell the Colonel his thoughts on this whenever he had a chance.

Coming back into camp, Spence could smell food cooking. The women saw them coming and began their last minute preparations. They went up to the cook fire and the women began dishing up food onto plates. Jesse's wife handed him a plate and then handed

Spence one also. Spence had just eaten earlier but the food smelled
so good that he couldn't resist eating again. And he wasn't wrong,
as the food tasted as good as it had every night on the trail.

After dinner Spence asked Jesse if he wanted to walk up the hill
and meet Hess. Jesse stated that he did and then told his two brothers to come with him and they started up the hill. Joseph, the middle
brother was talking about how good the soil was in this area and
about how easy it should be to plow. Jesse agreed with him and
they discussed the merits of different plowing techniques. The
youngest brother didn't talk at all, and Spence could tell that plowing just didn't interest him. Instead he had been looking around,
and tried to look inside each tent as they walked past them.

Coming to the cook fire Spence saw that Hess was sitting drinking a cup of coffee and talking with the cook. Spence led the three
men over and approaching the fire he said to Hess, "Hess, this here
is the men I told you about. Their families are camped down below.
This is Jesse, Joseph and Maxwell Goodman. They are farmers moving out here from Kentucky and they spent the winter in that little
town the other side of the pass."

Hess had stood up and he shook hands with each man looking
them over as he was introduced to them. He made a mental note,
and he agreed with Spence's evaluation of them. Hess had a good
knack for being able to judge a man quickly, and he was sure the
Colonel would find the two older brothers to be the type of family
men that he was trying to get to settle in the valley area.

"Welcome to the Triple Y gentlemen. I hope that you have had a
pleasant trip across our ranch and I hope that Spence has treated
you well. Have you had your dinner?" Hess asked. Then turning to
the cook he said, "Cooky, get a couple of cups from the wagon.
Gentlemen, won't you sit and drink some coffee with me?"

Not being given much choice the men sat down around the fire,
and the cook came back with cups and poured everyone some coffee. He filled his cup and sat down also between Spence and Hess.

"You folks set up O.K. for grub?" the cook asked Jesse. "I've got
some fresh beefsteaks hanging over there smoking. Just got some
sugar and molasses if you need any."

"Now that's right neighborly of you. We could use some meat
and the children would like some molasses. Sure you got plenty?
You've got a lot of hungry cowboys out here," Jesse replied.

"Yep, that's no problem. How many children you got down
there?" the cook asked standing up.

"We've got eight of them ranging in age from three to fourteen. They can be a handful at times, but wouldn't take a bag of gold for any one of them," Jesse replied.

The cook walked off and the five men sat and talked of the weather, the land, the soil, cattle and farming in general. The three told some of their trip across the country and what they had seen. Jesse talked a little about what they were looking for in a place to settle.

After a while Jesse stood up and looking at the sun said, "Well, about time to check on the animals and see about making the camp ready for night. You boys ready to mosey on back to camp?"

The three homesteaders got up and walked back down the hill to their camp and families. Hess and Spence were still sitting by the cook fire when the cook came back with a Dutch oven. He put the big black pot in the coals of the fire and with a small shovel put some more coals on top of the lid. Hess asked, "What's in the oven?"

"None of your business, that's what," the cook replied. He put a few more coals around the Dutch oven and walked back over to his wagon.

"Now I wonder what's gotten into him. He can get as ornery as a mule at times, especially concerning his cooking," Hess said.

"It might be something for those children. As soon as he found out how many there were, he walked over to his wagon and started making something," Spence replied.

"Might be. He always did have a soft spot for children, be they white folks, Indian or whatever," Hess stated.

He reached over with a small tree limb like he was going to open the top of the pot and look inside. The cook saw him and yelled over to Hess that the only way he would open that oven was under threat of a sound whipping and Hess put his tree limb into the fire.

"Don't reckon it is worth a fight to see what's in there," he said to Spence.

"Reckon I'll just wait and see what he pulls out of there when it is done," Spence replied, grinning at Hess.

About twenty minutes later the cook came over and scrapped the coals from his oven and sat it upon a rock. He carefully opened the top and the smell of apples and cinnamon spread over the camp. Inside the Dutch oven were the nicest looking cinnamon and apple rolls that Spence had ever seen.

Their mouths started watering just smelling them, but the cook looked up at them and said, "Don't you boys start fretting none over these sweet rolls. I baked these for those young'uns, down there and not even an extra one for myself. Just put your tongues back in your mouths now."

The cook wrapped a cloth around the handle on the Dutch oven and carried it over to his wagon where he picked up a bag of grub he had prepared for the families down the hill. He looked over at Spence and said, "Now don't be so lazy. Get over here and get that slab of meat and help carry it down the hill."

Spence looked over at Hess and shrugged his shoulders. "Don't reckon I have a choice in the matter," he said as he walked over to the wagon.

They carried the food down the hill and after handing over the food sack to the women the cook asked Jesse to call the children in. He made an instant hit with the children when he started dishing out the sweet rolls. Never having children of his own, he enjoyed doing things for the children of other people. The children were hesitant at first to eat their rolls, when they saw that none of the grown up folks was to get any but a word from Jesse and they ran out the camp laughing and eating their treats.

Cooky had made a hit with the three women also by treating their children. They gathered around him and were asking about his ingredients and how he had baked the rolls. Cooky was blushing but enjoying the commotion tremendously.

Spence smiled at the cook, enjoying the man's pleasure at being the center of attention of three women. Jesse and Joseph were enjoying it also but Maxwell soon went over and pulled his wife out and over to their wagon.

Jesse said, "Now that's a shame. There's not much pleasure in that woman's life as it is."

When the cook was finished talking with the women, he came back over to the men. Spence said to Jesse, "Well, the Colonel should be in tomorrow and when he arrives I'll come down and get you."

"Enjoy those beefsteaks tonight, and if you need more, just holler," the cook called back as he walked out of the camp with Spence.

CHAPTER TWENTY-THREE

"Come on in and have a chair Mr. Goodman. I just brought some brandy from the city. Would you care to have a little touch?" the Colonel asked Jesse Goodman as Spence escorted the settler into the Colonel's tent. "Spence, do you mind asking Hess in here to join Mr. Goodman and myself?"

Spence took the hint without the Colonel having to say more, so he turned and left the two men by themselves. Whatever business the Colonel had with the homesteader was of no concern of his. Spence wandered over to the cook fire and seeing Hess walking up, took two tin cups and poured coffee in each.

"Goodman in with the Colonel?" Hess asked as he took the cup of coffee from Spence.

"Yes, I just left them. The Colonel sent me to find you but I figured it was mainly just to leave them alone."

"Yea, I'll give them a while before I go up there. I told him what you and I had talked about concerning the three of them. I guess he wanted to talk with the oldest and get an opinion before he said anything to the other two," Hess said.

Hess finished his coffee and then slowly made his way up to the Colonel's tent. Coming to the door flap he pushed it aside and went on in.

Spence went out to where his horse was grazing, mounted and rode out to where George was tending the cattle. There wasn't much work to be done while they were on the lower ranges. The cowboys just had to keep the cows from spreading out too far, and to keep anyone coming out of the city from making some quick money off of someone else's cows.

Spence and George sat, smoked and talked for over an hour. Spence could still see the camp, and Jesse Goodman had not left the Colonel's tent. Whatever they were discussing must have been talked about in great detail.

A little while later George's relief rider came riding up and after talking a little bit, George and Spence rode back into camp. George invited Spence over to his tent, as there was a card game going on and he was told that his money was just as good as anyone's. Spence wasn't a gambler but he would occasionally sit in and play a few hands just for goodwill. He played until he had lost two dollars and then gave up his seat in the game. George sat down in Spence's vacated chair and pulled out a twenty-dollar gold piece. He stated that this was his last night's winning and he could afford to lose at least what he had won.

Spence watched for a while and joked around with the cowboys. After a few more riders came in from the range and started looking to sit in on the game, Spence walked out of the tent and looked around for Hank. He had some plans for his cabin and was going to ask the blacksmith if he could build some hinges for the windows Spence was thinking of putting into his cabin.

The blacksmith had his own wagon when the herd was moved down the valley so Spence walked over to the wagon. There was a fire going and three or four horseshoes were in the edge of the fire. Spence didn't see the horse they were going to be put on nor did he see Hank. He figured that the blacksmith had gone down to fetch the horse so he sat down to wait his return.

After about fifteen minutes and a cigarette, Hank came riding a horse into his area bareback. Sliding off, Hank shouted out to Spence, "Ain't seen you around for a while. Where you been hiding?"

"Well if you would come over to supper you would have seen me. What do you do, cook for yourself over here? I didn't even see you for breakfast," Spence replied.

"Well now that you mention it, I do cook better than ol' Cooky does. At least I can eat my own cooking," Hank said. "No, I was in town with the Colonel and we didn't get back until late. I slept right through breakfast and had to have Cooky fix me something. I must be getting old, as those long horse rides really tire me out these days."

"You been busy out here? I got a request from Will Harris' wife for some door hinges if you still got any around. They have that cabin ready now to frame the door and put it up and she wants some iron hinges for it instead of just some leather strappings."

"I still have those I took off the Colonel's house when I put those new hinges on his doors. Would she want those?"

"Those would do nicely. How hard would it be to make some window hinges and locks?"

"I've already got some of those also. The Colonel replaced all of his windows last year. I kept them around just in case," Hank replied. "Come by after we get back to the ranch and I'll fix you up."

Spence and Hank talked a little while longer and then Spence walked on back to the main camp. He had just reached the cook fire when the Colonel and Jesse Goodman walked out of the tent followed by Hess. Seeing Spence, the Colonel yelled at him to come over.

"Here meet your new neighbor. Jesse is going to buy some acreage just south of your land bordering the foothills to the west. I'm guaranteed the first crops and also garden vegetables," the Colonel said to Spence. Spence could tell that the Colonel was pleased with the way the talks had ended.

Sticking out his hand to Jesse, Spence stated, "Welcome, neighbor. Will that be your entire family or just you?"

Jesse looked over at the Colonel and said, "Well I haven't talked it over with the others yet and the Colonel here has yet to talk with my two brothers. I'll shake your hand on the friendship offered but haven't decided if I'll be your neighbor yet."

"Good enough. Now Spence, walked Mr. Goodman back to his camp and asked his brother Joseph up to talk. Mr. Goodman, you can tell them what I discussed with you or you can wait until each one has been made an offer. That will be up to you. I know you would not want to be separated very far from your kin. After I've expressed my offer to each then I expect a decision by noon tomorrow," the Colonel stated as he shook Jesse Goodman's hand.

Spence and Jesse walked off toward the homesteader's camp. Jesse was deep in thought and finally asked Spence, "Do you think that he will offer my brothers a piece of land also? He made a dang good deal for me, but wouldn't say what he would offer my brothers. We didn't come all this way just to be separated at the end of the trail. I don't think I'll say anything until they have both spoke with the Colonel. I wouldn't want them to get their hopes up and then not get offered anything."

"I think that is probably a good idea. I have no idea of how the Colonel thinks at all. I was surprised when I was offered the land that will be close to yours," Spence replied.

Coming into camp the three women and the two brothers were sitting around the central cook fire. The two men stood up as Jesse walked into camp.

"Well what did he want?" Maxwell asked his brother.

"We'll discuss it after Joe and you have talked with the Colonel,"

Jesse told his younger brother. Turning to his wife he said, "Martha, come with me to the wagon. I need to talk with you."

As Jesse and his wife walked off Spence turned to Joseph and said, "You ready to walk up the hill?"

Joseph got his hat, brushed it on his legs, brushed the dust off his pants and started walking over to Spence. Maxwell had watched his older brother walk off and now Spence and Joseph as they started up the hill.

"I'm coming too. No need for me to stay down here if I have to go up there also. If this colonel fellow can talk to one, he can talk with two."

Spence didn't say anything to the man but just continued walking up the hill with Joseph. They didn't slow down, and Maxwell had to run to catch up.

Getting up to the camp Spence turned to Maxwell and said, "Here take a seat at the fire. Pour yourself some coffee if you want. I'll be right back. Joseph, come with me."

Spence led Joseph to the Colonel's tent and spoke out that he was there with the middle brother. The Colonel asked Joseph inside and Spence walked back to the camp. He didn't like the duty of being host and having to sit with the younger brother for an hour did not appeal to him at all.

Fortunately, by the time Spence got back to the cook fire the riders were beginning to drift in for supper. Their good-natured ribbing of each other and jokes kept Spence from having much to do with Maxwell Goodman. The cowboys would look over at the young farmer occasionally but he wasn't the type of man to get much attention.

Finally Max got tired of waiting, and walked over to Spence saying, "I don't have to take this. If that man wants to talk with me then he can come down to the camp."

Maxwell turned to walk off and Spence watched him a couple of seconds and then thought that he should say something.

"I think it is probably in your best interest to stick around and talk with the Colonel. Here get yourself a tin plate and let's eat supper while we wait. Give yourself a break from the women's cooking."

Maxwell turned and looked at Spence as if he was going to say something but when he saw the cowboys watching he walked back over.

"I guess I could stand to have something different than stew and cornbread," he said.

That broke the whole camp into laughter, as they were all sitting there eating stew and cornbread. Maxwell thought at first they were laughing at him until Spence showed him his plate of stew and cornbread. Then Maxwell laughed also.

"Guess my luck is running true to form then," he said.

George called out, "In that case we have a card game going over in that tent, you want to join us?"

"I think I'll pass for now but might take you up on it later," Maxwell replied.

It wasn't fifteen minutes later that Joseph came out of the tent and walked over to Maxwell and Spence. He had a grin on his face, and Spence felt that Joseph had received some good news. Maxwell saw the grin also and said, "Does he want to see me now?"

"Actually no. He told me to tell you and Jesse that after we talk it over and if we agree and accept his offers, then he will talk with you," Joseph replied. "Come on now let's go down to the camp and talk."

Maxwell looked disappointed, but he sat his plate down and walked off with his brother. Spence had the feeling that if the brothers accepted the offers, then the Colonel wasn't going to offer Maxwell anything but was going to give him an ultimatum.

Watching them walk off George said, "I hope he doesn't come back up to play cards. I don't want to have to watch my gear behind my back."

Spence thought that remark probably summed up most of the cowboys' opinion of the youngest brother.

CHAPTER TWENTY-FOUR

Most of the riders were still sitting around finishing their break-fast when the three Goodman brothers walked up into camp the next morning. Hess saw them coming and motioned for them to come over to where he was sitting.

"You boys get yourselves a cup of coffee and have a seat."

"Well, we sorta wanted to go ahead and speak with the Colonel and get this settled," Jesse spoke up.

"Now there's nothing that won't wait a few more minutes. Have you had your breakfast yet?" Hess asked.

"Yes we have and had all the coffee we need also. Just take us up to the Colonel," Maxwell said to Hess.

"I suggest you have a seat and wait until I'm ready to take you up there young man," Hess growled back.

Jesse looked hard at his youngest brother and said to Hess, "You'll have to excuse our younger brother. He lost his manners some-where along the road. We'd like a cup of your coffee and one of those biscuits. The women had just got up and around when we left there. Maxwell, go get us three cups and bring them back here."

It was about twenty minutes later that the Colonel stepped out of his tent and gave his aid the breakfast dishes. Even on the range the Colonel liked to eat from china dishware. He had vowed after leav-ing the army that he would not live a life as he had while serving as a soldier.

Finishing his morning routine, the Colonel then gave a sign to Hess to bring the three brothers up to his tent. The Triple Y riders were pretty slow about going to their tasks this morning. They were just as curious about the Colonel's deal as Maxwell had been. Every one of them had a stake in the ranch and they wanted to make sure that this deal did not affect their future landholdings.

It was about fifteen minutes later that the pitch of voices increased coming from the tent. The riders could not make out what was be-ing said but they could tell that someone didn't like what was going on. Suddenly Maxwell stormed out of the tent, threw his hat on the ground and stomped it several times. Glancing up and noticing all the Triple Y cowboys looking at him, he picked up his hat, beat it against his pants legs and putting it back on his head, he turned and went back into the tent.

This caused the cowboys to break out in laughter. Then the voices increased again, Maxwell came storming back out of the tent, but this time Jesse was right behind him. Jesse grabbed his youngest brother by the shoulders, spun him around and shook him several times like a rag doll. Speaking sharply to him several minutes Jesse then pushed his brother back into the tent.

The cook then came over from his cook wagon and started slapping at cowboys with his dishtowel as he yelled at them, "Show's over boys, now get to your chores. Nothing more to see and you all know that the Colonel knows what he's doing. Now get up and get to work."

The riders moved out pretty quickly after that. They didn't want to make Cooky mad or they might end up with skimpy rations or something even worse. Spence didn't have any chores, so he started gathering together the cups and plates the cowboys had left scattered. The cook had two helpers that cleaned all the pots, pans and dishes, so Spence just stacked them on the tailgate of the wagon.

All was quiet in the tent and then about ten minutes later Hess came outside and motioned for Spence to come over. Coming within talking distance, Hess asked Spence to go get George and then both of them come into the tent.

Spence turned and went down to where the horses were and saw George just finishing saddling his mare. He yelled out to him, and George mounted and rode up to where Spence was standing. After telling him what they were to do Spence started walking back up the hill. George spoke to him, took one boot from the stirrup and offered his hand. Spence take George's hand and putting his foot in the stirrup swung up behind George. They then rode up to the tent and dismounted.

Seeing them walk in, the Colonel asked them to have a seat. He then started explaining what he wanted them to do. "These three boys have agreed to buy some of the land out close to you two. I've offered them five hundred acres apiece. One will neighbor you on the south, Spence, then George, your ranch will be between it and the next farm. Now then, the youngest brother has agreed to take the acres in that cutout valley just south where that wash comes down the mountains. George, I want you to ride out with Spence and these new neighbors of yours and mark out the boundaries so they can start getting settled in and put a plow into the ground. I'll have Hess ride into the city and get a surveyor to come out and lay out each of your boundary lines so every man will know exactly where his land lies."

Turning to Spence he said, "Spence I want you to guide these folks back out to their new farms and help George do the initial layout. Then inform Will Harris of the new families moving in and also that I'll have the surveyor lay out his farm also. Tell that wife of Will's that I have some real glass windows coming to her when we move back to the ranch as my home warming gift."

Looking at the group of men he then asked, "Any questions? Is every one satisfied with this deal?" The Colonel had looked at Maxwell when he asked the last question. Everyone nodded and stated their agreement. "Then let's shake hands on this and witness each others' agreement."

Everyone stood and shook hands among the six of them. Turning to leave, Spence told Jesse his pleasure at having him as his immediate neighbor.

Jesse looked at him and asked, "How did you know I was offered the place bordering your ranch?"

"Cause that is the best farm land of the three," Spence replied.

Spence and George helped the three men and their families pack up the items they had unloaded from the wagons. Gathering all the children into his wagon Jesse then turned his team of oxen and started back up the valley. Spence caught his horse and took him back up to the camp where his saddle and gear were. He saddled his horse and was tying his gear onto the back of the saddle when the Colonel walked up behind him.

"Thought you might prefer the oldest brother as your neighbor. With him and Will close to each other I foresee some good crops coming this fall."

Spence had turned around to face the Colonel. "Yes, I'm glad that it worked out that away. What are you going to do when that youngest abandons his farm and rides away?"

"Then the agreement has it that the land returns to my ownership. When the farms are paid for, then if they want to move out later, I have the first option on buying any farmland back. I don't think the two older brothers will be any problem but I might have that land around the draw back," the Colonel stated.

"Yea, you might be right about that. He paid the same price as the other two for his land?" Spence asked.

"No, couldn't rightly do that to the man. That draw land is about half the value of the other two, as only the lower half is good farmland. I figure that is more than he can cultivate anyway," the Colonel replied. "Well, have a good trip and come back into the ranch in about three weeks and have Harris bring his wagon."

"Will do. See you in three weeks then," Spence said as he swung up into his saddle. Then he spurred his horse in a gallop so he could catch up with the three wagons and George.

Jesse Goodman didn't let much delay them over the next three days. He had the families up early and moving so they could get to their new homes as fast as possible. He kept the wagons moving until almost dark, and the children had to hurry to find enough firewood for the cook fires before it would get dark. Spence and George were just along for the ride, as Jesse remembered the trail at least as far as the ranch. George did steer them more westerly, though, as they came out of the lower valley.

The fourth day saw the wagons arrive at the beginning of Maxwell's land. George led the wagons up the valley a little more and stopped them.

Maxwell, having guided his mules around Joseph's wagon, now brought it up even with Jesse's.

"This here's about where that youngest boy's land starts. The draw you all were talking about is over there in the lower part," George said. "I wouldn't pick out no house plot too close though, as the water really comes gushing down that when it rains."

"Thanks for the advice, but I think I know what water does to a house when it floods," Maxwell stated. That had been one reason the families had decided to leave their Kentucky homes. They had almost lost every thing they owned when the Green River coming down from Ohio had flooded their farms.

"You want to stay here and help him get located, or you want to keep moving?" George asked Jesse.

"We'll make camp here tonight, and help Max pick out a home site and then move on in the morning It'll be nice to know where to come looking for them when we come visiting."

Jesse and Joseph pulled their wagons into a 'L' shape and as their two wives began to make camp they walked along Maxwell's wagon as he started up onto the land George had pointed out. Jesse would walk along and occasionally pull up a clump of grass and check the soil round the roots.

"This will make some good oats or wheat here in this area. This soil will make a pretty good farm," Jesse yelled up to his brother.

Maxwell kept moving until they came to a grove of trees. The land was pretty level in this area and would make a good home site. He moved his wagon closer to the trees and then came to a stop and jumped down off the wagon. "This looks like where we will be making our home. It is protected some from the wind by the trees but still close enough to the fields. What do you think woman?"

"How long before you two will come back and help build the house?" she asked Jesse.

"It shouldn't be too long, Sarah. We will get some fields plowed and sowed and then we'll have time to start building the houses. We should have them all finished long before it's time to start the harvest," Jesse replied.

"Don't you worry none, Ma'am. As the boys come back to the ranch off the summer ranges we'll all come out and help you folks finish your homes. We build all these range cabins you saw and we've got fairly good at laying stone," George told her.

"Probably won't need your help," Maxwell said.

"Just being neighborly, neighbor. Won't do no more than I'd expect you to do," George replied stiffly.

"Don't pay no mind to him, George. He'll be more than grateful for your help after he's plowed a few fields and cut a few trees," Sarah replied. "I know Max too well and he don't mean what his mouth says most of the time."

Maxwell gave his wife a dirty look, but she smiled down at him and he looked down at the ground. He knew that she was right.

"Is there anything we can do for you before we go on back down?" Jesse asked Maxwell, but looked at Sarah.

They both shook their heads 'no' so the four men turned and started back to the other two wagons.

"They'll be all right after they get unloaded some and he starts plowing the fields. This turned out to be a better location with better soil than the impression I got from the Colonel's words. I think Max is surprised and pleased at his new farm," Joseph said. "George, when you start back to the herd why don't you just ride back by here and check. By then they might have found need of another hand to unload some of their stuff."

Those remarks surprised both George and Spence. They hadn't

heard Joseph say much of anything on the trip out to the new home-steads.

"Sure, I can do that. I'd be happy to check back with them," George said. After all, these two men here were bordering both sides of his ranch whenever he decided to claim it from the Colonel. He wanted to stay on their good side, as he would need help himself when he started his own house and barns.

Coming back to the camp, they found that the women had already cooked supper and were waiting for them to come before they served it. The four of them explained the layout of the home site that Maxwell had picked out and the fields and the draw. The women were curious, but knew they would have to wait until they could visit their sister-in-law later in the year.

The next day was a long ride, as it was across George's ranch. He had been with the Colonel a long time and was being rewarded with a large amount of land. It was evening and the sun was almost down before they got across it and onto the land that Joseph would own.

As they came to Joseph's land, the same story was repeated. This time, though, Jesse had Joseph lead the way and he brought his wagon along behind so they could camp together one last night before the two families were separated. Joseph also picked out a tree grove close to the center of his land and decided that would be a good place for the house. There was a small creek running through the tree grove and it would be centrally located to the fields he intended to cultivate.

The third day saw the last family approaching their land late in the afternoon.

Jesse stopped the group and said, "Let's make camp here. I want to see all of the land in the daylight before I decide where we will locate."

They stopped and made camp and Martha started cooking. She had her children collect the firewood, and her oldest girl started the dough for bread. Martha brought out some makings for pie that she had been saving for a moment like this. The meal wasn't much different from what they had been eating, except that Martha had baked loaf bread and fixed a pie. George and Spence were both surprised at how well her loaves turned out. Spence couldn't figure how she had baked bread without having an oven.

The next morning Spence was still in his bedroll when Jesse and his oldest boy came out from where they had bedded down. The two walked out from camp and into the meadow. Spence got up and filled the coffeepot with fresh water from the water barrel on the wagon and sat it on the cook fire that he had started from the coals left from the night fire. He pulled out his grub bag and found the coffee he had been given and put a couple handfuls of grounds into the water and put a fresh twig across the top of the pot.

George got out of his bed and rolled the blankets up and tied them together.

"Why do you put that twig on the pot? I've watched you do that near on a hundred times now and still can't figure why you do it," George said.

"To keep it from boiling over. If you had really been watching you'd have seen that I never have a coffeepot boil over and waste coffee," Spence replied.

"Well now I never do that, and I haven't boiled over any coffee. You just have to watch it and move it off the fire some when it gets to boiling," George retorted.

"My ma taught me not to be so lazy and to watch what I was doing," Martha stated as she walked up.

Both men laughed at her comments and watched as she moved the pot to a better place over the fire.

Martha started preparing to cook breakfast, but she would occasionally look in the direction that her husband and son had walked. Finally she saw them coming back in, so she put her pans on the fire and started the meal cooking. By the time Jesse and his boy walked back into camp, the food was done, and Martha dished up some food and took it over to Jesse as he was pouring himself a cup of coffee.

"Did you find a good place for the house? Does it have running water close by? Are there any trees?" Martha asked her husband.

"Now just slow down there. Yes to everything but you'll get a chance to see it in just a little while," Jesse replied.

The family finished cleaning up after eating, while Spence and George saddled their horses. Then they helped Jesse finish putting the last two oxen into their harness. Jesse led the way with Spence riding on one side and George the other. Jesse pointed out the good features of the land as they rode. It wasn't long until they topped a slight rise and everyone knew at a glance that this was the place.

Martha sighed and said, "It's perfect, just the way I knew it would look."

Jesse smiled at her and said, "Yep, as soon as we saw it we knew this was what we had been looking for."

Spence and George were also taken with the layout of the land below them. It had a slight rise for a house close to trees and a small brook ran along the tree line flowing down to where they knew the river was located. The house would be protected some from the northern winter winds and close to fresh water for the household. It was close enough to the river to harvest logs for the building of the house when Jesse started it.

"Welcome to our new home," Jesse said to the two men as he looked at his wife.

CHAPTER TWENTY-FIVE

Spence worked hard over the next few weeks on his own cabin. He had to clear out all the burnt wood and then clean the walls of the cabin. It was a shorter haul to bring logs to his cabin as the fir trees grew down the foothills of the mountains. They might not be as hard or as long lasting as the ash trees they used for the Harris cabin but they would last long enough for Spence.

Spence worked steady and finally he got so he could tell he was making some progress. He would cut and haul a few trees and rig them into place on the roof. Then he would spend the rest of the day washing the walls of the cabin. It was not as easy work doing his own cabin, because he lacked the help of Emily.

He had stopped by the Harris place after leaving Jesse Goodman and his family. He informed Will and his family of their new neighbors, and the approximate location of their home sites. After describing the women and children for Francis, he finally left for his own place. He had thought of asking Emily to come help, but did not have the courage.

At the end of the third week he decided that he had worked hard enough and had accomplished enough that he deserved a break and some decent cooking. Although he was a fair cook, he hadn't brought much out with him, and he had been eating beans and cornbread for the last three weeks. A meal cooked by Francis would certainly taste good now.

Mid afternoon Spence went down to the creek that flowed close by and washed himself and the clothes he had on. He changed into a fresh shirt and denims and saddled his horse. He was planning on arriving at the Harris farm in time for supper, and maybe could talk with Emily before Will and Davie came in from the fields.

Later that afternoon as he rode into the farmhouse yard, he saw Will up on the roof patching some holes where the sod had fallen through the logs. Will saw him coming and shouted a welcome from the roof. Hearing her father, Emily came to the door and watched as Spence rode up. She gave him a wave and then went back inside the cabin.

Jumping down from the roof, Will came over to where Spence was tying his horse. "Bout time you were making it back over this way. Thought you might have got out there and broke a leg or something."

"No, just got to missing Francis' cooking. Beans and cornbread gets old after a while, especially when you're cooking it yourself," Spence replied shaking Will's hand. "How's your seeding coming along?"

"Davie is plowing the last part of the last field today. He could finish it himself so I thought I would start doing some of the repairs around here. And Francis kept pestering me to fix that hole in the roof. Got to get some slabs before winter and replace that sod up there," Will stated. "How's your roof coming along?"

"Not as fast as we did this one. It turned out that Emily must have been doing more than I thought, as I'm pretty slow on my own."

"Well Davie can come over and help you when you start back. That boy has grown so he can just about lift those logs up there by himself. Speaking of which, here he comes now," Will said.

Looking up, Spence saw the boy coming in from the fields behind his mule. He was well-tanned and looked like he had filled out some from the constant labor. He had put on some weight and most of it looked like muscle. Spence thought that a person couldn't rightly call him a boy any longer.

"Looks like he's grown up and out since you folks moved out here," Spence remarked.

"Yea, most near a full man now. He sure puts in a man's day of work. Sure can't complain about him, but he sure complains now of my not being able to keep up."

Spence laughed and returned Davie's wave as the boy saw Spence with his Pa. He spoke to the mule to try to hurry it along some, but the mule didn't speed up any at all.

Will turned and started into the cabin. Spence followed him into the cabin and stopped at the door. This wasn't at all like he had left it. Not having entered the cabin when he had come with the news of the new neighbors, he hadn't seen the progress the two women had made inside the cabin. It looked almost like a home inside with the hand-built furniture and makeshift floor.

Francis and Emily both smiled at his surprise. Emily said, "See what a woman can do when she doesn't have a man to get in her way."

"Looks real nice in here. Makes a person feel truly at home and comfortable. Hope my cabin looks half this good when I finish," Spence commented to the two women.

"Sit down now and relax while the women finish up the meal. How's your cabin coming along anyway? What are you using for the roof?" Will asked.

As Spence sat down, Emily brought two cups of coffee and sat in front of the two men. Spence saw where Will had made two sturdy benches for the eating table. He sat down on the opposite side of the table from Will.

"Been using fir from the lower side of the mountain. It's a shorter haul than trying to find any ash or aspen trees. I cut and haul in the morning and then heave them up to the roof after lunch, and then spend the rest of the day washing all the soot from the walls. Just about got it finished now."

"The cleaning of the soot off the walls is the hardest part of the whole chore," Emily attested. "Get the walls clean and it's ready to move in."

"I agree to that. I would rather be cutting trees and hauling them than washing walls," Spence replied. "I haven't tried to put any furniture together yet. You did a real good job on this table and benches, Will."

"Just something my grandpa showed me when I was younger. If you want, I'll show you when you get ready to stop sitting on the floor," Will stated.

The door swung open and Davie walked in, still wet from washing in the river. He had begun to make an every day ritual of washing the day's work from his body. He walked over to Spence and shook his hand and then sat down next to him.

"When you want to borrow a plow and see if that patch of ground you got will grow anything?" Davie asked.

"Next year, maybe. I still have work to do for the Colonel before I can really start calling the place my own. You ready to take a break for a few days?" Spence asked the young man.

"Sure, just finished the sowing today. Had to move the old man out of the field and out of my way so I could get some work done. What do you have in mind?"

"The Colonel should be back from the spring trip to town and he has some things for your Ma. If your Pa agrees then we should take your wagon into the ranch and pick them up. Then your Pa can finish framing the windows and doorway before the rains start in again," Spence said.

"Sounds all right to me. He's been working hard enough and straight through the last few weeks. I guess a couple days rest wouldn't hurt him none. Davie, you know what kind of hinges I need from Mr. Moore, don't you?" Will asked his son.

"Not rightly, but between Spence and Mr. Moore we should be able to figure it out," Davie replied.

"Well, I know for sure what you need Pa. I think I should ride in with them and make sure they get what you need. It's only a day's ride in and another day back out, and Ma don't have anything for me to do right now," Emily stated.

The statements coming from his daughter surprised Will, and all he could do was to look at her. Then Francis said, "I think that is a good idea. I've been talking with Emily about how we should fix this place up and she did help you frame the door. She knows what you need to finish it, and I don't have anything at all for her to do around here."

"Well it ain't proper for a young woman to go riding around the countryside," was all Will could think of to say in reply.

"Pa, I've ridden clean across the country, and besides, Davie will be along and I'm sure Mr. Moore won't mind giving up his cabin for a night," Emily said.

"Well, you haven't asked Spence if he minds you tagging along and getting in his way. He'll have to watch over two of you, instead of just Davie."

Spence threw his hands up saying, "Whatever you say Will, goes for me. I don't mind the extra help when we start loading things. I've already seen that Emily can work as hard as I can. And maybe she can talk Cooky out of some of that special seasoning he bought in town." Then Spence told Francis of the cinnamon rolls Cooky had baked for the children back at the range camp.

As the conversation went on about food, Spence figured that the matter had been settled, and he would have Emily riding along with them in the morning. Spence figured that Will hadn't really objected to Emily riding along, but just had to make a show at being a strict parent.

After supper the three men went out to the wagon and unloaded the stuff left in it from chores around the place. Then Will and Davie took out the harness and made sure it was straight and ready for the mules tomorrow morning. Then Spence threw his bedroll up into the wagon and later Davie brought out some bedding and threw it in the wagon also. Seeing Spence look at it he said, "I'll sleep out here with you. Be nice to be out under the stars again as that cabin gets stuffy at night."

The next morning Davie was up early and brought the mules and his horse up to camp along with Spence's horse. He threw his old saddle on the horse and tied it to the wagon. Then he put the harness on the mules, but didn't put them in the braces yet.

Going in to breakfast Spence saw where Emily had already gathered together a traveling bag. He had expected eggs for breakfast, but Francis said that she had the hens sitting eggs and hoping to hatch some chicks soon. They needed to increase the size of the flock of chickens.

After eating Emily helped her Ma with the dishes while the men finished hitching up the mules to the wagon. Then Spence saddled his horse and tied it to the back of the wagon along side of Davie's. Then he drove the wagon up to the cabin. Emily came out and put a bag into the wagon and went back inside. Davie made himself a place in the back, and Emily came back outside with a basket covered with a cloth. She handed it up to Davie and then climbed the wheel up into the wagon and sat down next to Spence.

"You young'uns enjoy this trip. I got plenty of work for you to do when you get back. And don't forget the hinges," Will yelled out to them. "Be careful now, Spence, and tell the Colonel that he better get a grain barn ready for the fall as these fields are going to fill it up."

Spence started up the mules and guided the wagon out of the yard and headed toward the crossing on the river. As the wagon crossed the water and started up the opposite bank Davie untied his horse and swung into the saddle. Spence looked back at him and Davie said, "Been in back of those two mules' behinds long enough. I'm going to ride in the open air for a while."

The boy dug his heels into the sides of the horse and galloped off. The horse had been idle for a couple of months and was also ready for a run. It wasn't long before they topped the ridge and were out of sight.

As they rode along Spence and Emily talked of the land, the trip out across the country and their past lives. They had a lot of time and no interruptions and found that they were relaxed with each other and could talk freely. Spence found out that after Emily had heard about the children with the new settlers and she had been thinking of starting up a school. With eight children and Davie, she would have enough students to justify a schoolhouse. This was one of the reasons she had wanted to come along, as she had plans of bringing up the subject to the Colonel. She wanted a schoolhouse central enough to all the children so they could ride in for lessons. The schoolhouse could also be used for a church on Sundays for the families to get together to worship.

Spence agreed with her idea, and then told her of the Colonel's plans of eventually having a small town somewhere on the western side of his ranch. The schoolhouse/church would be a good start.

About noon Davie came riding back to the wagon. He asked Emily if it was time to open the grub sack for dinner. Having got used to his Ma fixing a big dinner each day while they were plowing, his stomach needed food. Spence stopped the wagon and helped Emily down with the sack of food. She spread out a cloth and laid out the food she had prepared. It didn't take long for the two men to finish their meal and help Emily pack the grub sack with what little remained.

Davie rode along side the wagon for the remainder of the trip and they arrived at the ranch house late afternoon. Pulling into the main yard by the barns, Hank Moore saw them and came out of the blacksmith shop. He was a little surprised to see Emily riding with Spence and Davie but recovered in time to welcome them.

"Why hello, Miss Emily. You out visiting us for a couple of days?"

"Yes I am, Mr. Moore. I had got used to seeing all your faces around and thought I'd ride in with Mr. Spence and tell you all hello. I hate to impose on you Mr. Moore, but I do need a place to sleep for the night and wondered if I could fix a bed in the tool room there?" Emily said. She didn't figure Hank would actually let her sleep in the tool room and she was right.

"No need for that. I can bunk with the cowboys for a night or so and you and your brother can stay in my cabin again. I think you know your way around it well enough."

"Now that's mighty kind of you, Mr. Moore, and I do appreciate it very much. Pa told me not to impose on you but I can't turn down such a generous offer," Emily replied with a winning smile for Hank.

Spence stepped down from the wagon and asked Davie to pull it over next to the barn. Emily took the reins and told her brother just to follow as she could handle the mules as well as he.

As Spence and Hank watched her guide the mules and the wagon up next to the barn Spence said, "Just came in for those hinges we talked about before. Is Hess and the Colonel back in yet?"

"Yea, we all got back to the ranch about four days ago. Took half the crew to get the wagons back here and unload supplies. The Colonel really brought back a haul this time. Those windows are in the barn for Mrs. Harris, and he even bought two for your cabin. He bought a new saw for the ranch, and said to send the old one back with you whenever you came in. It's only a few years old and works real well. Don't know why he wanted to replace it except to have the old one help out with the new settlers," Hank replied. "Speaking of which, have you seen them lately?"

"No, I haven't. Been meaning to ride over that way but been roofing my cabin and haven't made the time. Thought I might get over their way later on," Spence said.

Turning back toward his blacksmith shop Hank said, "Well come on then, let's start getting your things together. I've got those hinges you wanted in the back room somewhere. Haven't had time to look for them since we got back."

The two men were going through the iron and junk that accumulates in a working shop when Emily stuck her head inside.

"Here, let me help also," she said as she plowed into the midst of the piles of iron.

Finding the first of the hinges, Hank held it up and Emily took it from him and measured it against her fingers and wrist. "This will work perfectly. It is just long enough for the doorframe Pa put up," she said.

Hank pulled the rest of them from the stack along with the window hinges he had replaced on the Colonel's house. Turning to Emily he asked, "Did you see those windows in the barn yet?"

"Yes, are those the ones the Colonel is sending out to Ma?"

"Yep, as a house-warming gift to your mother. He also had Cooky buy some extra cloth to send to your Ma so she could make a couple of curtains. Hope she likes what Cooky picked out, as he makes a good cook but sometimes his taste in material is like an army issue," Hank said.

Emily laughed saying, "Well I'm sure my Ma will be pleased to have it anyway."

They finished up in the storeroom and carried the hinges out to the wagon. Spence walked into the barn to look at the windows and to see the two that was to go to him. He picked them up and was trying to visualize how he was going to try to frame them into the window gaps in his cabin.

"Don't worry about the fit. Pa can make anything fit into a house. He was a carpenter as well as a farmer back home. Ma expects a real frame home before too long, and that cabin can be turned over to Davie to live in. Pa built regular mansions for the rich folks, with upstairs and kitchens and columns out front," Emily said to him.

"Looking at Mr. Moore's work, him and Pa could build just about anything," she finished.

"Now that's kind of you to say," Hank stated as he walked into the barn. "Hess just rode in and asked your whereabouts."

"I'll move my bag into the cabin while you take care of your business. Then Davie and I will start loading these windows," Emily said to Spence.

Spence and Hank walked out and over to the mess hall as they saw Hess's horse tied out front. Spence gave Hess a report on the progress of the work on his cabin and the fields having been sown on the Harris place. Having caught up on the news on both sides, Spence then asked about any work that needed to done before he took the Harris wagon back out to their place with the supplies.

Hess told him that he wouldn't be needed back on the ranch until fall when they started moving the cattle back onto the winter ranges. His range riders could care for the herds of cattle through the summer, as they just watched them for cow thieves and wild animals. After the spring roundup, branding and dehorning, there wasn't much work to be done until the fall.

"Been out to the Goodman's place lately? George said that by the time he got back to that youngest brother's place the kid had already started plowing and had a tent pitched for his wife" Hess asked.

"No, but will do that before too long. I imagine they all have lots of work to get done due to their late start on plowing their fields. Emily, Harris's daughter wants to speak with you before she leaves," Spence was saying as the door opened and Davie and Emily walk in.

They walked over to the table and Emily remarked, "I can finish now, Mr. Spence. Mr. Fester, I was thinking about all those children with the new settlers and how they needed a schoolhouse and someone to teach them their lessons. Now I can teach, but I will need somewhere close enough to all the children so that they can come in for their lessons. If you can get a schoolhouse built, it could serve as a church on Sundays also. Your cowboys would be more than welcome, as Pa has been wanting to do a little preaching again."

Hess looked over at Spence and Hank. He didn't know what to say at first.

Davie said, "You might as well agree, as she won't stop pestering you until she gets her way."

The three men laughed at the boy's comment and Hess said, "Well, are you willing to go up and talk with the Colonel about this?"

Emily smiled at him and said, "Tell me when I should," and the door opened, stopping the girl in mid-sentence.

"Talk with me about what? I thought I saw you boys ride in, Spence how you doing? Davie, it's been a while, got your crops planted? Young lady, what is it you want to talk with me about?" the Colonel spoke as he walked over to the table.

Spence and Davie shook the Colonel's hand and Emily composed herself.

"I wanted to talk to you about a schoolhouse for the new children. It's probably been a while since they had a chance to learn any lessons, and a schoolhouse is the first thing a new town needs."

"Now wait a minute, Missy. We don't have a town around here yet," the Colonel said as he began to tease the young woman.

"Not yet, but with four families now in the area and with your men wanting to bring their families out and settle in, then a schoolhouse that can be used as a church would be a good start," Emily replied, ignoring the Colonel's teasing.

"Well, even with a schoolhouse we would need a schoolmarm. Don't know if we could get an educated young woman to come all the way out here just to teach a few children their ABCs."

The Colonel knew that Emily had attended teacher's college after talking with her Pa. He had been thinking the same thing and was pleased that Emily had ridden in just to talk about a schoolhouse.

"Can't spare but a couple of men off the range to build a schoolhouse, and don't have any that knows much about building. Any thoughts on that, young lady?"

"With a couple of men and a good saw, my Pa could build a house in just a little while. All we need is a good place that you will let them build it," Emily replied.

"And church? Didn't I hear you say something about a church?" the Colonel asked.

"The schoolhouse could be used for a church on Sundays. With the benches for the people and Pa doing the preaching, we could have services for the new people and your cowboys in the same building," Emily said.

"You still haven't answered the question of where we would get a schoolmarm."

Emily smiled and said sweetly, "I think you already know that answer Colonel. My Pa told me that you had talked about me when you offered him his farm. I would be that schoolmarm as you call her and would even be willing to give any of your cowboys lessons in reading and writing."

The Colonel smiled back at her. He could see that she had the spirit to handle a bunch of children. He said to her, "All right I guess we can do that. The school will be called the 'Sacrifice School'. That is what I'm going to name the town as it grows around the school and church. Now are we going to have to build you a house also?"

"No, I can ride in from Pa's place. If the children will have to come in each day, then I can also. That will take away an excuse why they can't attend daily," Emily stated.

"See, she's always planning," Davie chipped in. "Why, she even wants *me* to go to the school."

The men laughed and Emily blushed a little at her younger brother's remarks.

"Well, consider it done. I will have Hess ride out later and pick out a spot and then send some help out to your pa. We should be able to get something up so the children can start lessons after the fall harvest."

The Colonel stood up and said, "Spence come with me now. Miss Emily it was nice to see you and Davie again. Give my regards to your folks and tell your Ma I'll ride out and see her new windows and curtains later. Tell your Pa if he needs anything, to come in and see me. I have an vested interest in his farm and making sure he has what he needs."

Turning he walked out with Spence following. The others spoke a few minutes about the school and then Emily and Davie went back to the barn to finish loading the windows.

They worked hard all that day getting the saw loaded and the supplies from the blacksmith and the spices and supplies from the cook. Emily was surprised at how generous the cook had been buying supplies for her family. They now had things she hadn't seen since leaving their home in the east. Her Ma would be well pleased when they started unloading the wagon at home.

CHAPTER TWENTY-SIX

Having the saw, Will Harris helped Spence cut slats for shelves and a table with benches so that he wouldn't have to use logs for seats. They cut enough wood to build a little overhang over the doorway and Will told Spence how to slope the roof so the rain run off would be to the sides of the door instead of the front of the cabin. Will framed the two windows to fit and helped build a door. Spence told Will that after all the other work was done that he would cut planks for the floor.

Having finished cutting enough wood for his cabin, Spence went back helped Will start cutting logs into boards. Will has going to frame the new windows the Colonel had sent out and to build a real door for the cabin.

Having finished for now, Spence decided to make the rounds of the Goodman's farms before he returned to his place with the newly-cut wood. Will, hearing of his plans said that he too, would like to go meet their neighbors. Francis and Emily stated that they would make the trip also. Will told Davie that they would be gone for a few days and for him to take care of the place and the animals.

The next morning Spence and Will loaded supplies and bedding into the wagon for ten days on the trail. They climbed into the wagon and started out for Jesse and Martha Goodman's place. Will had fashioned a bench for the back of the wagon so they could all ride together. Spence had tied his horse onto the back and brought it, as he didn't know when he might have to ride off on some errand.

The four people enjoyed the ride across the land and finally came in sight of the valley where Jesse had moved his family. Topping the final hill they came to a plowed field and could see a large tent and the wagon close to the trees on the far side. Will turned the mules and went out around the field and as they turned back toward the tent they could see the Goodman family gathering and watching their arrival.

"Hello the camp," Will called out.

"Hello the wagon, come on in folks," Jesse yelled back. The children started running out to meet the wagon. They had recognized Spence in the wagon. As the children ran up to the wagon, Will stopped and let the children climb on. They hadn't seen anyone since they had moved onto the land, and they were all chattering and asking questions.

Emily smiled and took the youngest into her lap, and tried to answer as many questions as she could. They reached the tent and Jesse yelled up to his children to come down and leave the good folks alone.

Will climbed down and extended his hand, "I'm Will Harris, and that is my wife Francis and daughter Emily. We have the farm just north and east of you here."

"I'm Jesse Goodman and my wife Martha and those are my children, Katherine, Georgia, and Edward. Keith is my oldest boy but he's out hunting supper right now."

Spence climbed down and helped Francis and Emily from the wagon. He then shook Jesse's hand and spoke to Martha. Martha had come over and took Francis and Emily and led them into the tent with the children following.

"How's your planting coming along? I saw that top field and it's beginning to show shoots coming up," Will said.

"Yes, that was the first field I plowed and planted. I hope the growing season is good here as I just finished the second field and have plans for a third. My boy and I have been working steady at it, but Martha keeps talking about starting a shelter of some kind," Jesse replied.

"That's part of the reason I came along with Spence to meet you. We just finished fixing up our cabin some with the saw the Colonel sent out to us. I wanted to see how far along you were before we plan on coming over to help raise a house for you," Will said.

"Well ain't that neighborly of you. I take it that you have your fields sown then?"

"Yea, we got a earlier start than you did. I don't know if you know it, but this will be my first planting out here also. We came across the mountains early winter and Spence here helped us on into the Colonel's ranch where we rode out the last snow storms of the season."

"The Colonel did mention that you were out here. We spent the winter in that little town just over the Coastal Del Rey Mountains. Was told we had come too late to make it through the pass, so we hunkered down and spent the winter there," Jesse remarked.

"What was the name of that town, Lost Hope or something like that?" Will asked.

"Something like that, and Lost Hope sure describes the place," Jesse laughed.

The men walked on out into the field and Will had to check the soil. Then they walked on to the other field Jesse had plowed and planted. They checked the third that Jesse had laid out and Will commented on how well planned they were and the good quality of the soil.

They heard a shot fired in the woods on up the creek and Jesse commented, "Sounds like the boy. He takes my Long Fowler to hunt with. It's a black powder charged shotgun and he says he gets better range on these prairie hens with it. I bought a Savage Combination gun before I left Kentucky but it is a 20-gauge shotgun and a .22 caliber rifle. That Long Fowler is a 14 gauge and really reaches out with its 39 inch barrel."

Spence had heard of the combinations guns where a hunter could quickly change from a smooth-bore shotgun to a rifle in just moments but had not seen one. He had seen some of the muzzle loading shotguns called Long Fowlers though. A couple soldiers had still been carrying them at the start of the War.

They walked on to the creek to check the flow of water and as they came back up the bank the boy walked out of the woods on up the creek. They waited until he had walked on down to where they were.

"Got enough for four extra people for supper?" Jesse asked his son.

"Do if they like squirrel and sage hen," the boy replied, holding up four squirrels and three hens tied together by leather strips. The game had been field dressed already by the boy.

They took the game back to the camp and cleaned them before giving them to the women to cook. Francis had Will unload some of the grub sacks she had brought so they could put in their share of the food. Will went ahead and unloaded the bedding and placed it underneath the wagon while he was at the wagon.

Sitting around the fire later eating supper, Martha told Jesse the plans for the schoolhouse to be built and the Sunday use as a church.

"Joseph will sure like to hear that. He is a certified preacher and enjoys doing that more than he does farming, and he does like to farm. He would hold small revival meetings as we came across the country and was offered more than once, a church in different communities," Jesse said.

"That's what we need out here. I do a little preaching myself but haven't done it full time. I was a deacon in our church and preached a little when the minister couldn't do it," Jesse told the group.

"What with Emily being a teacher and Joseph being a minister, we have the makings of a good community here," Francis said. "Spence, you just need to go push the Colonel a little and get the help out here to put up the school building."

"Sounds like a community project. Let my two brothers know about this and after the plantings are done, then maybe we can have a barn raising, but in this case, a schoolhouse raising," Jesse retorted.

The group laughed and the children gathered around Emily asking questions about books, slate boards and lessons. She quickly took them aside and started telling them her plans about starting lessons. The oldest boy, Keith, didn't participate and he acted like he didn't need any more schooling.

Seeing his expression, Jesse stated, "Come winter when the harvest is in, you'll be attending that class also. You haven't got all the schooling you need yet."

"We have a fourteen year old boy also that will be attending his sister's classes. His name is Davie and he thought he was too old for lessons but he'll be right there sitting with you," Will stated.

The next morning was spent with the women exchanging recipes for cooking game and Francis measuring out some of the seasoning that Cooky had sent her. She had brought enough for the three women and was generous in her allotments. Just having another woman to talk with was worth giving away her seasonings. The men discussed where the house was to be built and Will told Jesse that he should start cutting down some trees and hauling them close by. The wood would age as it dried out and would make better planks that wouldn't shrivel and warp later when they were sawed.

They finally left after the noon meal and started on to Joseph Goodman's farm. They had to cross George's ranch so would spend the night on the open range. Having seen the children and their need for an education had Emily talking about the new schoolhouse for quite a while. Francis and Will enjoyed having their daughter excited about teaching again. Spence just enjoyed watching her face as she talked.

Over the last few months he had grown quite fond of her and

really enjoyed being around her. At first he had not thought much about Will coming with him, but now he was glad it had turned out like this. When he had heard that Joseph was a *bona fide* minister, the thought had come to him that he would now have a preacher to marry them. That thought had shocked him at first, but he had grown into liking it very well now.

They arrived at Joseph and Helen's farm late the second day. Joseph had placed their tent on a slight hill, and they saw the approaching wagon while it was still a long distance away. Joseph and his wife and three children were waiting at the camp when Will drove his wagon up close.

"Get down and make yourself at home. You folks look like you can use a cool drink and a good supper," Joseph said.

Will got down and helped Francis from the wagon while Spence helped Emily down.

"Haven't seen you for a while, Spence. I don't remember you telling us you had a wife," Joseph said.

"Don't," Spence replied. "This is Will Harris and his wife Francis, and this is their daughter Emily."

"I'm Joseph and my wife Helen, and these are Jonathan, William and Elizabeth," Joseph stated pointing out his children.

"I've heard so much about you from Spence and your brother Jesse, it seems I almost know you," Will told the man as he shook his hand.

"You been by Jesse's?" Joseph asked. "How are they doing? Has he got a crop sown yet?"

Once again the women went into the tent and the men walked out to the fields. Will told Joseph how his brother was doing and informed him of his own farm and crops. Joseph was trying to farm by himself, as his oldest boy couldn't quite handle an ox for plowing yet. His two boys had planted the field after their father had got it ready and they had one field with some oats coming up. The two boys had shoveled up a small garden plot and had vegetables growing with some rows of corn.

The stay with Joseph was much like the stay with his brother, as the families exchanged information and Emily told about the school and church that was to be built. Joseph lit up when told about the church and asked more questions than could be answered about it. He told Spence to let him know just as soon as they started and he would come on down and help.

Joseph had already started cutting down trees and trimming the logs to start their first house. He had thought that he would have to build a log cabin for the first winter, and was pleased to hear that they would have a saw available to cut planks.

The next morning the family wished them well and said to extend their greetings to the youngest brother and his wife. Will started them off down the trail with the family waving and the two older boys running along side the wagon for a ways.

Francis was pleased, as she had taken a liking to Helen immediately and asked Will to stop back by on their way home. Will and Joseph had taken up a discussion on religion and the lack of it in this area so he was more than willing to come back by this farm. As the two boys stopped running with them, Will turned and yelled to them to tell their folks that they would see them again soon.

Spence thought that they would arrive at the youngest brother's place by late afternoon, but the draw had washed out and they had to go down it for a ways until they could find a place to cross it again. They camped out on the other side for the night. Francis made known the point that she had packed extra grub just in case of events like this. Those months on the trail had given her a good feel of how planning cannot always plan for everything.

Reaching the Maxwell Goodman farm mid morning the next day, they rode up to the tent without anyone coming out. Getting down Spence checked the cook fire and it was still warm from the morning's cooking.

"They must be out in one of the fields," he stated.

Francis and Emily got down and asked Will to unload their grub sacks. If both of the people were out plowing, then the women intended to have a good dinner cooked for them.

Will and Spence walked out of the camp, following the trail of the mules. They came to a small field in an open meadow and saw that it already had a crop coming up. It must have been the first field Maxwell had plowed. Looking around they saw another field through the tree line and walked on over that way. Coming out on the other side they saw a larger field being plowed. It was three times the size of the first field and Will remarked, "Someone is really ambitious here. I don't think I would have taken on a field this size."

Walking out into the field they finally saw Maxwell and his wife following the two mules on the far end. They walked out that way and meet the two as they were plowing back their way. Maxwell had their baby strapped onto his back so both of them could plow.

"Spence, is that you?" Maxwell yelled out. "Who you got with you?"

"Yea it's me. This is Will Harris, the man I told you about with the farm over by me. He and his wife and daughter came to visit," Spence called back.

Coming up to the team, Will extended his hand to Maxwell and tipped his hat to the woman.

"This is my wife Sarah," Maxwell told Will.

"My wife Francis and daughter Emily is back in your camp. They're cooking your dinner for you. Here, let me finish out this row for you," Will said taking the reins from Sarah. "You go on back to camp and meet with the women."

Sarah looked over at her husband who nodded. "Much obliged, Mr. Harris." Maxwell gave her the baby from his back.

"Now don't start that, my name's Will. Now go on and get and let me see how this mule handles," Will said as he started the mule on down the row.

Maxwell and Spence watched him for a few seconds. "Just came by your brothers' places. They both send their regards. Wanted me to ask how you're doing and if you need anything," Spence said.

"Just another hand on the mule. Sarah's got spunk but she tires out before mid-afternoon. The baby takes some out of her also as it still stays up most of the night."

"You still have almost as much plowed as Jesse and more than Joseph. That first field is coming up pretty nice," Spence told him.

That comment made Maxwell smile. To hear that he had more farming in than one of his brothers was good to hear. "You're just not joshing with me are you? Joseph doesn't have all his fields plowed yet?"

Maxwell started his mule again and said to Spence that they would stop for dinner after reaching the far end. Spence stepped back and let Maxwell go by with the mule. The man could handle a mule pretty good. Occasionally he would hit a rock and Max would stop and pitch it out of the way and then continue on down the row. He caught up with Will as he was turning the mule to come back down. Max told him just to unhitch the mule and tie it in the shade of the trees and they would go in to eat.

As the men walked back to camp Maxwell told them of his plans for his farm. He had taken to this land and told Spence that he wouldn't trade it for land in the middle of the valley now. Spence thought that maybe the Colonel wouldn't have to worry about buying this farm back.

Dinner was waiting for them, and Sarah had washed the dirt from her face and arms. Her dress still had dirt stains from the plowing, but she did look better now. Having two more women around probably helped. She was about the same age as Emily and the two young women were getting along like they had known each other for years.

Walking up, Maxwell noticed Emily right off. The glow of the young woman was hard to miss, and Spence felt a twinge of jealousy as he saw Maxwell looking at her. He walked up and put his arm around her, turned her and introduced her to Maxwell, while still holding her.

Emily noticed Spence's arm around her and moved into it more. She had noticed the look from Maxwell and was using it to her advantage now.

Serving the meal, Francis brought out some biscuits she had baked to go with the meal. Sarah walked off and came back with a bowl of fresh butter. This really made the meal, as none of them had had fresh butter since last fall. It wasn't long before the biscuits and butter were gone. Spence requested the same for supper and the three women laughed at him.

After dinner Maxwell told the men that he was finished plowing for the day and would visit with them, since they hadn't had any company since George had ridden back through. Spence and Will walked back out with him to gather in the mules.

"These two can probably use the rest any ways," Max said as he turned them loose into the meadow. The mules looked like they didn't know what to make of being loose so early in the day. They finally walked off and started grazing on the thick grass.

"Not going to plow this meadow. The grass is really good in it and will try to use it for hay," Max told them. They walked on and came to the draw. The sides of the draw had been shoveled out some and Maxwell said, "Going to dig this wash out and try to make a pond on this side. If I can get the water to channel into this low place, I might be able to make a small lake here."

"Now that's quite smart. I hadn't thought of trying to channel run off water," Will stated.

"As long as I have this draw through the place, might as well try to make good use of it. Of course the water might get to running too fast and deep and wash my whole plans out, but going to try it anyway."

They made the round of the farm and heard Maxwell's plans and Will told him how his brothers were doing. Will told him of his own farm and the river running along the edge, and they talked of Will putting in a small dam to create some deeper water along the river. Maxwell had heard of how some farmers were using irrigation on their farms instead of having to trust to the weather to water their crops. He hadn't seen it in action but he had his own thoughts about how to do it.

The afternoon was spent talking and eating. Sarah wasn't the best cook, and she was getting tips from Francis on how to prepare some of the food that was available in this area. Francis cooked the evening meal, and even cooked a pie to serve after supper with coffee. Maxwell ate his share plus some, and then invited Francis to stay a few more days.

Spence knew what Maxwell was talking about, as he did enjoy Francis's cooking also. When told about the school and church, these two weren't as enthused as the other families. Their baby was only three years old, and they weren't as religious as the older families. They were also a farther ride from where the school would be built, and it would be an overnight trip for them.

Francis didn't leave as much of her seasonings with Sarah as she had the other two women, as Sarah wasn't into cooking and would not use it. She did leave the rest of her cured ham that she had brought. Sarah gave her some fresh butter as their milk cow was still giving milk and they had plenty of milk. Sarah also gave them some fresh cream she had been saving to churn as she had more butter than she could use now.

The trip back was taken in reverse so they could pass news of the families to the others. Both Joseph and Jesse were surprised at how well Maxwell was doing with his farm. They were more surprised when told that Max had more land plowed than Joseph. Francis left the rest of her seasonings with Helen and the rest of her supplies with Martha, who had more children.

Overall the four were please at the way the trip had turned out and were anxious to get the church built so they would be able to gather together more often.

CHAPTER TWENTY-SEVEN

Spence didn't see much of the farmers during the next couple of weeks. He was hard at working trying to learn how to handle the saw and make slats from logs. He finally got enough straight boards cut to finish the roof on his cabin. He framed the windows and door and he even put together a rough table with two benches and a bed frame. Finishing the shelves and a rough cupboard, Spence decided that he had done enough carpentry work and it was time to see what was happening with his neighbors.

Spence loaded up the wagon with the saw and the extra slats that he had cut and then went down to the stream to wash up. As the spring had turned into summer the stream had started drying up and was now just a trickle. Spence figured that within the week it would dry up and stop running completely. After the snows had melted from the mountains there wasn't any other feeder water into this stream.

Arriving back at the cabin, Spence built a small fire and started his supper. He was cooking outside because it was too warm inside the cabin with a fire burning in the firepit. Finishing his meal, he put the coffee pot on to boil over the coals and went out and brought in his horse to pull the wagon back in the morning to Will's farm. His mount didn't like being in the harness and pulling, but Spence had finally got him to tolerate the wagon being behind him for a short pull.

The next morning Spence got on the trail early so he would arrive by dinner. He was looking forward to a good meal cooked by Will's wife and daughter. He was planning on spending a couple of weeks with the Harris family as he helped Will replace the sod roof on the cabin with wood slats. He felt he was competent enough now with the saw to cut some fairly straight boards.

Topping the final ridge above the Harris farm gave Spence a start at first. The area around the cabin had been transformed into an actual farm. All of the fields were covered with plants, and were growing quite well. If he had not known this was the first planting, Spence would have thought this farm had been here for years. Looking again Spence noticed that Will and his boy had also started building a pole barn back behind the cabin. Will was putting up the supports for the wall and roof and would use boards to finish the sides and roof.

He clicked to his horse to try to get it to move a little faster, but the horse was as stubborn as a mule when it came to pulling the wagon. It refused to go faster than a walk, so Spence didn't try to push it.

Will had seen the dust and wagon approaching so he and Davie were waiting in the yard when Spence finally pulled in. Will must have yelled into the cabin to his wife also because Francis and Emily came out as soon as Spence had stopped.

"Get on down, you're just in time for dinner. How you been? You beginning to look like a farmer with that sunburn on your neck. Did you get any logs sawn with that thing? You hungry?"

Spence didn't try to answer any of Will's questions. He knew that if he answered one, then Will would have ten more to ask so he just got down from the wagon and shook hands with Will and the boy and waved to the two women.

"Hungry enough to eat that old horse. Been looking forward to Francis's biscuits. Hope she cooked enough for one more," Spence said.

"Sure, saw you coming from the ridge out there. She had time to cook for an army before that horse of yours got that wagon down here. Come on inside."

Davie took the reins from Spence and stated that he would unharness the horse and turn him loose before he came in to dinner. Spence smiled his appreciation to the boy and ruffed his hair. The boy tried to act like he didn't like it, but Spence knew better.

As they sat down to eat, Spence inquired of the crops and if the recent rain had been enough for the plants. He could still remember his uncles complaining of the lack of rain, and then when it did rain they complained of having too much or having it too late.

"Rained just about right around here so far. I've noticed that the river isn't running quite as full as it has been though. Guess the snow runoff has about finished," Will replied.

"Well, we don't need any rain for a week or so until you men get the new roof on the house. I think we will move everything outside so Emily and I don't have to clean it all again," Francis stated.

"I figure we'll push all the sod off the back side of the house where the run off has washed out some gullies. We'll just build up around the walls and taper it off toward the river. Those logs might be a little damp at first to start cutting but they'll dry out as we go. The internal wood should be aged by now," Will said.

They finished off the meal, discussing the merits of different means of taking the old roof off and preparing it for a real roof made of boards. Will talked some of grooving the slats and using a tongue to groove installation but Spence couldn't see how that old saw could cut grooves into the edge of the boards. He figured they would end up doing like he did, cut them as straight as possible, lining them up and then filling in the gaps with tar to keep it from leaking.

Davie had come in during the middle of the conversation, but he didn't contribute much to the discussion. He knew that his father was an expert carpenter and whatever was decided would work well.

After the noon meal the men took the saw from the wagon and set it up. Will's mules would work better on the turnstile than Spence's horse had. The horse had been cramped and would stop quite often. The mules would have more room and with three men working, one could keep the mule moving. This would result in cleaner cuts than Spence had been able to get.

Looking at the contraption, Will had told of seeing a wheat harvester back in North Dakota that held three mules on a treadmill up on the harvester. The treadmill turned the combines. He said that it took twenty or more mules to drag it across the field, but it was faster than ten men with two mules apiece pulling a cutter, a raker and a combine.

Spence didn't believe the tale but Davie backed up his father's tale. He said that they must have spent a couple of hours, just watching the harvester being pulled across the fields.

"What won't they think of next?" was all Spence could reply.

As they emptied the furniture and goods from the cabin, Will placed the things that rain would damage under the wagon canvas that he had staked up like a tent. He expected to be able to roof his house before the next rain, but Francis wasn't going to take a chance on the weather.

They worked all afternoon and by early evening the cabin was empty except for the beds. The women cooked a quick meal and afterwards Spence threw his bedroll down outside by the tent. David went inside and came out with his and throw it down by Spence stating, "Got to do this in the morning anyway so might as well start tonight."

The boy had rather been sleeping outside but his Ma wasn't letting him 'as long as they had a decent roof over their heads.' He knew she wouldn't say anything now that Spence was here sleeping outside.

As the two men sat looking at the stars and David asking questions of how Spence had handle the logs and the saw by himself, Emily came out with two plates of blackberry cobbler and two cups of coffee. She handed Spence a plate and a cup and gave David the other plate. She sat down on the log close to Spence with the other cup of coffee.

"Yes, I would like to know how you handled those without me being there to keep you straight," she said as she sipped her coffee.

Spence grinned over at her saying, "Well, now every time I got into a jam I said to myself, self, what would that nosey woman say now, and then I would do the opposite and it would work real well."

"That's because your initial thought would be a man's thought and doing the opposite would be what a woman would have thought of first."

Spence choked a little on his cobbler with that remark, and didn't have a quick comeback. It was obvious that Emily could hold her own.

"If it wasn't for women then we wouldn't have to go to all that trouble anyway," David spoke up in Spence's defense.

"That's the problem with the world today, not enough women riding herd on you men and keeping you straight," Emily replied. "Anyway, go on telling us how you sawed your logs."

Spence gave a quick outline of how he had handled the logs going through the saw and how the most trouble came from trying to keep his horse walking on the treadmill to power the saw. The other two laughed at his tales and they kidded Spence about his lack of knowledge of milling and his learning experiences. Spence laughed along with them, as now, he could see the humor in the situation.

After a while Emily took the dishes and returned to the cabin. Spence watched her walk off until David said, "You're not getting soft on my sister, are you Spence?"

"Turn over there and get to sleep. I'm going to work you hard tomorrow and you need your rest," he replied, embarrassed that he had let the boy see his interest in the young woman. The comments didn't faze David as he just chuckled and watched Spence watch his sister. Spence reached over and pulled the boy's hat down over his eyes and then he pushed him over onto his bedding. This brought on a short wrestling match between the two until Spence was finally able to pin Davie's shoulders to the ground.

"Had enough? Say uncle."

"Uncle, uncle but if you don't let me up, I'm going to tell Sis you were watching her walk back to the cabin," the boy warned Spence.

"You tell her anything and I'll pin your ears back instead of just your shoulders," Spence replied good-naturedly to the boy.

They moved over to the bedding and lay down. Both of them were thinking of the young woman. Spence was having thoughts of trying to develop a relationship and Davie was already thinking of having a brother-in-law.

The next morning the two women already had breakfast ready before Spence and Davie got up. Francis was going to ensure she got her roof finished as soon as possible. The two women moved all the food outside to the table and benches so the men could begin working as soon as they had eaten. Spence wasn't going to get his special meals until the roof was well on its way to being finished, but the food was still better than what he had been cooking for himself.

After breakfast Will and Spence climbed up onto the roof while David went to get one of the mules for the saw. He didn't figure they would need the saw for a couple of days but it would be better if the mule was close in just in case.

Removing the sod from the roof turned into more work than either man had anticipated. The grass had rooted through the soil and some of it had roots in the outer bark on the logs. It had to be sliced into chunks, thrown off and the remainder had to be scrapped from the logs.

David had returned with the mule and was now helping on the roof. It wasn't long before the three of them had mud all over their clothes, hands and faces. As the sun rose and the morning progressed, they had sweat running over their faces and smearing the mud even more. They would wipe the sweat with their mud stained shirtsleeves and put more mud on their faces.

Coming off the roof for dinner, the two women broke in laughter looking at the three men. They then looked at each other and couldn't help but laugh also. They had been too involved in their work before to notice the mud on each other faces.

"Looks like we need a walk down to the river to wash up before dinner," Will stated.

"No, I brought up two buckets a while ago just for this. I thought that you might be needing it as the longer you all worked, the darker you got," Emily joked with her Pa.

The afternoon was even hotter than the morning, but they were able to finish removing the sod before mid afternoon. Then they began to roll the logs off the backside of the cabin. They had all the logs removed before early evening and were more than ready to stop and go wash up in the river. Spence removed his trousers and shirt and washed the mud from the clothing. He hadn't counted on getting so dirty so quick and had not brought but one other change of clothing with him.

He hung his clothes on the brush along the river while he washed his body and his hair. He had been wearing a hat but had still managed to get mud in his hair. Davie had just jumped into the water; clothes, shoes and all. He washed at his clothing while wearing it but wasn't really concerned with cleaning it, as he knew Emily or his Ma would do it later. He was just enjoying the cool water.

Will removed his shirt and washed his upper body, face and hair, and then removed his shoes and washed his feet. He then sat back on the back and watched the other two cut up in the water for a while. He then called to them to come on out as supper was getting cold and those two women would skin them alive if they didn't come on.

Dressing, Spence told the other two to go on and he would be there in a minute. He wrung a little more water from his clothing and then dressed again. He left his trouser leg bottoms hanging outside his boots so he wouldn't get his boots too wet.

Coming into the yard he walked over to the cook fire that the two women had started so his clothing would dry a little more quickly. Now that the sun had gone down, the night air through the wet clothing was a little cooler than Spence liked. Will and David came out from the tent after having changed into other clothing and they all sat down at the table while Emily served the food.

The two women were still cleaning the supper dishes and pots when the three men rolled out their bedding and turned in for the night. The day's work had proved harder than they had thought it would be and they were ready for sleep. Finishing the dishes Francis looked over at her husband and son and then walked over and pulled the blanket up over the boy. She ran her fingers along her husband's cheek and then went to her own bed in the tent. Emily had watched her Ma's signs of affection, and yearned to be able to do the same with Spence. She was attracted to the man but was frustrated at his lack of action. She made up her mind then to help push him some. She took one more look at the sleeping man and then went into the tent with her Ma.

It took six hard days of work and they had still not got enough boards for the roof. They had twice as many boards cut and laying on the ground as they needed, but the boards had not met Will's standards. Will wasn't concerned though, as he knew he could use the boards for the barn. David was used to his Pa cutting three times more boards than most men would need, so the extra labor hadn't bothered him.

Spence had watched as board after board was cut from the logs and just pitched aside. He had started getting frustrated with Will's desire for quality and finally Emily had came over and told Spence that she had fixed a picnic lunch for the two of them. She wanted him to take her over to the river for a cool dinner. Spence was startled at the request but with the urging of Will and David Elliot, Spence finally accepted.

Will had noticed the impatience rising in the younger man and was glad his daughter had seen it also. Good carpentry work was something most men didn't have the patience for and he found no fault in a man that did not have it. He had learned from his grandfather that wood was something you had to take your time with and he had practiced being patient for many years as he developed his skills. He was glad to see that his son had also started developing his level of patience for fine woodwork.

Spence had taken the wicker basket of food and he walked off toward the river with Emily. There was a grassy meadow right by a deep pool that would make a good, shady, cool spot to eat their lunch.

As they walked Emily was bubbly with small talk. She spoke of the work, the wood, her father's skills at carpentry, the growing fields, the birds around this area and anything else she could think of. Now that she had made the first move, she was nervous at her daring act. Spence did not think much about the picnic request now that the initial shock of being asked was over. He had begun to think that Emily has seen the need for him to have a break from the wood sawing and that was the only reason for the picnic.

Coming to the river, Spence continued down through the trees along the riverbank. He remembered the pool from when he was cutting logs from these woods. He had sat for a smoke a few times in the meadow but it had seemed closer to the cabin than now. They walked a little further and Emily finally asked, "You taking me over to the next valley? This is a nice spot. Why don't we have lunch here?"

"I think the meadow is just right around the next bend there. I don't think I was cutting logs much farther than this," Spence replied.

The walk was making them both more nervous as they went along. Emily was nervous about finally being alone with the man she was planning to make her husband, and Spence was getting agitated at not being able to find the meadow he had wanted to show Emily.

Finally, at the turn in the river, Spence saw the water was darker and slower indicating a deep pool of water. He knew then that they were almost to his meadow. "Here we are now. Isn't this just about the prettiest place you ever saw?" he asked Emily as they rounded the last bit of brush.

Emily stopped and looked at the meadow. The trees were taller here, and the lowest branches were twelve feet or more above the meadow floor. The grass was thick and green and the wind blowing across the water was cool. There was the chattering of squirrels in the trees, and occasionally a songbird would trill into the air. She had never seen such a lovely place.

Spence was relieved that they had finally found the meadow. He moved over to the shade of some trees growing closer to the water and sat the basket down. The meadow was not as pretty as he had remembered it to be, as the spring flowers had been in full bloom back then. But it was still a pretty meadow, with a cool breeze blowing across the river. He was now beginning to notice that Emily had on a good dress and bonnet and that her hair was down and shining from a recent brushing.

He watched as she took a cloth from the basket and spread it out over the grass. Taking off her bonnet she brushed a few strands of hair from her face and then opened the basket once more. She had spent all morning preparing fresh loaves of bread and soaking the brine from some ham. She had picked some fresh vegetables from her Ma's garden and had baked some small fruit cobblers. She was glad that blackberries were some of the first berries to ripen and that there were plenty of wild vines along the river.

Laying the food out, she gestured for Spence to take a seat on one side of the cloth. Then kneeling down on the other side, she prepared two plates of food and gave one to Spence. She poured two cups of fresh buttermilk she had brought along in a small crock jar.

Seeing the milk Spence stated, "I didn't know your cow had birthed. Will didn't mention that."

"I guess what with everything else happening around the place, it slipped his mind. Davie is supposed to be milking her every morning, but you all have been keeping him so busy that I have been milking just enough for the baking. I was beginning to think that this milk would clabber and you would churn it into butter before we finally reached this meadow."

The last remark threw Spence off again. Every time she would make a remark like that he would have to look into her face to see if she was joking. This time she was laughing and then he chuckled a couple times also. It seems she had a quick wit and a sense of humor that was quick to surface.

As they eat the picnic lunch they exchanged banner back and forth. Spence was now remembering how it was when they had first been working on her Pa's roof. He now picked up on her comments and could returned one almost as fast. He found that he really enjoyed being with Emily, and could picture himself being with her every day.

The food was gone quickly, or so it seemed to Spence. Then he looked up at the sun and saw that time had also passed quickly.

"Geez, your Pa will probably think I have run off with you. We've been out here for a couple of hours now. Here, let me help you pack this stuff up."

"Now don't get in too much of a rush. I don't want to have to be running back to the house. Ma knows where we are and she can handle Pa, but he knows you needed a break from the sawing also," Emily said in a matter of fact tone. She brushed Spence's hands away from the picnic leavings, and packed her basket as careful as she had packed that morning.

Finally, having folded up the picnic cloth and put it into the basket, she put on her bonnet and announced, "Now, I'm ready. And don't take off like some barn horse."

"Barn horse?" Spence asked.

"Yea, you know, like a horse that every time you take him out, the first thing he wants to do is run back to the barn," Emily explained.

Spence laughed at her comments, which brought a slight tint of red in her upper cheeks. That just made her looked even prettier to Spence.

They walked back to the farmyard with Spence swinging the basket as they walked. He was totally relaxed now with Emily like he had never been with any other woman in his life. He was beginning to realize that he missed having a woman in his life, and that to settle down with a wife and to raise children was what he really wanted.

Coming back to the yard in front of the cabin, Emily got in one last comment to Spence saying, "Pa's gonna figure that by now he'll be needing his shotgun so as to protect my honor."

She grabbed the basket from Spence's hand and turned as she ran toward the tent to see the blush that had redden his face. The last he saw of her was her laughter as she went under the tent flaps.

He walked over to where Will and Davie was just placing a new log into the saw groove. "Here, need some help with that?" he asked.

Will looked up and saw the red still in Spence's face. "That girl get the best of you again?"

Spence looked over at Davie. "You been telling tales on me again?"

"Nope, just been telling Pa that I had to come to your rescue a couple of times the other evening when Sis put your accomplishments down," Davie said as he smiled up at Spence.

Spence decided to drop it, as he was beginning to have problems keeping up with anyone of them, much less the three together. He grabbed the log and shoved it into the saw grove and pushed it down to the start of the blade. Will and Davie were both still chuckling as Davie started the mule up on the treadmill to turn the saw blade.

They worked steady the rest of the afternoon and finally, Will announced that they had enough straight boards for the roof. Davie looked as relieved as Spence did as he stopped the mule and started unhitching it from the saw's treadmill. Spence picked up the last stack of straight boards and carried them over to the cabin. Davie having turned the mule loose, ran over and climbed up on the roof so they could finish the last boards before dark. Spence started handing the boards up and Davie moved them over to the last gaps in the roof.

Will took his time by going over and having a long drink of water from the bucket. He then climbed onto the roof and started placing the last boards into place and nailing them down. Finishing the last board, he stood up, stretched and then grinned down to Spence.

Climbing down from the roof, the three men gathered up the remaining boards and carried them out to the pile they had started by the barn. Coming back to the cabin they saw that the two women had already started moving things back into the house.

"Did you want a floor laid before you moved that stuff back in?" Will asked his wife.

"You can lay the floor around the stuff in the house, as you can. Right now that storm coming over the mountains isn't going to wait for your floor," Francis yelled back to him.

Looking up, the three men noticed the layers of black clouds rolling over the mountaintops. They had been so involved in the roof that they had not noticed the storm moving in. They ran over to the tent and quickly started moving items into the cabin, placing the stuff just wherever they found an open spot. They emptied the tent first and then started on the furniture sitting outside. Davie grabbed all the bedding and rolled it together and moved it inside. The rain and hail hit before they had everything inside and they were soaked before they finished.

"Looks like one of those hail stones caught you a good one," Will said to Spence, looking at a red welt on Spence's temple.

"Yea, lucky it didn't lay me out. Came right up under my hat and whacked me one," Spence replied.

"Make a fire over in the fireplace and let's get you men dried out," Emily said.

"This is going to be a good test for your roof, Will. We should know real quick if it's gonna leak or not," Spence stated.

As they gathered around the fire to dry their clothing, they watched the roof, but there wasn't a leak anywhere. Spence changed his attitude about Will's sawing and gained more respect for the man's carpentry skills.

CHAPTER TWENTY-EIGHT

Having finished the Harris' roof, Spence and Will talked about moving the saw on over to the next farm and help them raise a roof. Each of the other families had lots of children and they needed a solid home before the winter began to sit in.

Will sat down with Davie and laid out a list of chores that needed to be taken care of while Will was gone. The main chore was to tend to the crops and weed the seed crops to ensure the prairie grass didn't try to take over the fields again. The vegetable garden was to be watered by bringing buckets of water from the river. The slats by the barn were to be nailed to the sides and Will would lay the roof when he returned. The barn would need a watertight roof also to protect the grain seed after it was harvested and through the winter until next spring.

Francis packed a sack of food for the two men to take with them and she and Emily cooked a special supper that evening. The last of the ham was cooked with dumplings, fresh beans from the garden and also cucumbers, onions and tomatoes. A blackberry cobbler was served with fresh butter melting on top and hot coffee. Spence ate his fill and had to loosen his belt before he finished. He really enjoyed his stays at the Harris farm. Later he unrolled his bedroll in a corner as it was still raining outside and the wind had blown the tent down.

Davie had climbed into the makeshift loft with his bedding and was already asleep. Will and Francis moved their bed back into its position and as soon as Francis had made it up, Will turned in. Spence laid and watched Emily finish washing up the supper pots and pans. He liked to watch her while she was busy and didn't know she was being watched. Her movements were brisk and efficient, and every so often she would toss her head to get the loose strings of hair hanging over her forehead, out of her eyes.

Finishing a pot, she turned for the drying towel and looked over at Spence. She saw him watching her and smiled at him. Offering the towel out, she waited to see if he was going to get up and help.

Having been caught watching her, Spence figured he didn't have a choice other than to get up and help dry the pots and pans. He grinned at Emily, slipped his boots back on and got up and reached for the towel.

Pulling it back she said, "Not until you wash your hands. I don't want you getting my clean dishes dirty again."

Spence washed his hands and helped finish the dishes. Emily then poured two cups of coffee and sat them on the table as she sat down on a bench. Spence sat down opposite her and took a sip of coffee.

"You watch my Pa out there and don't let him work himself down. Once he gets started, he don't quit. You have to just pick him up and make him take a break," Emily said.

"I've noticed that. He does tend to get a little hard headed at times."

"If Ma or me is not around, he'll work until he falls down. I expect you to return him home in the same shape as he is today," Emily stated.

"I'll try my best. I'm not one to try to tell a man how to run his life," Spence replied.

"How do you expect him to hold that shotgun on you if he's laid up in bed?" Emily joked.

Spence was caught by surprise again at Emily's humor and had to look up into her eyes before he saw the laughter in her.

He smiled at her remark then and took a big sip of coffee to hide his lack of having a comeback remark. She smiled at his slight embarrassment. Taking his coffee cup from his hands she said, "Now get on to bed so you'll be ready to travel tomorrow."

Spence sat down on his bedding, removed his boots and laid down again so he could watch her as she finished putting up the pans and turned down the lanterns. He could hear her movements as she prepared for bed and finally lay down. He went to sleep thinking of the pretty young woman.

The next morning saw the sun rise in a sharp, brisk, clear sky. The storm of the night before had washed the earth clean and the sky was blue and clear.

Even the mules acted like they were glad to be pulling the wagon loaded with the saw and men. They moved out briskly and sat a good steady pace as Will turned them toward his neighbor's farm.

The rain had been good for the crops, and the plants looked like they had grown overnight and were even greener. The hail that had been in the storm hadn't damaged the plants much and they were strong enough to have resisted the wind.

Will was pleased with his fields and was looking forward to a good harvest in the fall. For the first year of plowing, the fields had produced extremely well.

They followed the river for a while and then turned upland towards the Goodman's farm. They expected to pull into the farm right after dinner as they had got an early start that morning. They ate their lunch while traveling and drank water from their canteens.

Spence watched a small herd of antelope off in the distance and then asked Will, "Reckon they need some fresh meat?"

"No, don't reckon so. Remember that gun that boy had the last time we visited. I reckon he has kept them in meat. I doubt if you could hit one of those antelopes from here anyway," Will replied.

"Stop the wagon," Spence said. Will brought the mules to a stop while Spence dug out his rifle scabbard. Unsheathing the rifle he sat the sights up for long distance. Resting the rifle on his outer leg, Spence took aim and squeezed the trigger. A burst of smoke filled the air with the bang of the rifle and Will and Spence both stood up to look. The antelopes had looked up at the sound of the rifle but none had fallen.

"I don't believe I missed," Spence said, checking his sights.

"Don't get in too big of a hurry. Look at that one that just laid down. Yep, there he goes," Will laughed as the young pronghorn buck laid over on its side and then laid its head down. "I think you hit him and he just didn't know it for a while."

Looking up as the animal finally laid over, Spence felt better. He knew he had been fairly accurate at that range numerous times before, but he hadn't had to shoot for his meals in a while.

Spence got on his horse and told Will to keep going and after he field dressed the antelope he would catch up with him. Spence rode off over the plains to where the animal was still laying. The others had watched Spence start towards them and then had run off over the ridgeline. Coming up to the animal, Spence saw the bullet entry point right behind the front shoulder. This pleased Spence as a good hit in this area saved more meat from being damaged by the bullet.

Spence field-dressed the animal, being careful not to burst the stomach, intestines or other organs that would spoil the meat. After it had stopped leaking blood, Spence threw it up behind his saddle and then took off in a fast trot. He wanted to catch up with Will before he got to the farmer's yard. The antelope flopped around behind him but his horse was used to it ignored the dead animal.

Finally, pulling up along side the wagon, Spence flipped the antelope into the wagon and then got into the wagon and tied his horse back on the tailgate.

"That should make some tender eating," Spence said to Will as he sat down on the wagon seat.

"Help us pay for our stay with them. Jesse seemed real friendly, but it always helps to bring your own grub into a camp," Will stated.

"They just might be tired of rabbit and squirrels anyway. Of course those prairie hens sure were tasty that the boy had brought in. I could go for a dish of them again," Spence replied.

As they were talking, they came over the last small hill and could see Jesse Goodman's farm below. He had his fields finished and they were as green as Will's fields. This land seemed to be perfect for farming. Having an older boy and two teams of oxen had enabled Jesse to plow and plant some large fields of grain.

As they rode down past the fields, Will looked them over pretty good. He had checked how straight the rows were and how clean the grain was of weeds and grass. He had to admit that Jesse was a pretty decent farmer, and was glad that he had a neighbor that knew what he was doing.

Spence had been watching Will, and saw the admiration in the man's face. He figured that Jesse had met with Will's approval.

Coming closer to the farm, Spence saw that the entire family had come out and was waiting for the wagon as they approached. Will stood up and waved his hat at the family and every one waved back at him. Then the children broke into a run out to the wagon. Jesse, his wife Martha and the older boy stood waiting.

As the children got close to the wagon, Will stopped and let them climb into the wagon. They all made a fuss over the dead antelope, and then stood right behind the wagon seat and started asking hundreds of questions. They all remembered Will and Spence because they had not had any visitors since they and the two women had left the farm a couple of months previously.

Spence just let them jabber on but Will tried to answer as many questions as he could. He enjoyed children and often wished that he and his wife could have had three or four more.

Finally pulling into the farmyard, Will yelled out to Jesse and his wife. Spence spoke and tilted his hat to Jesse's wife. The couple both yelled for the two men to dismount and come into the shade. As they got down from the wagon, they helped the children down also. Then as they walked over to the couple, the children grabbed their hands and walked with them.

Shaking Jesse's hand and then the oldest boy's, Will and Spence looked around the yard. There was a large stack of logs on the edge of the clearing and an area that had been cleaned of vegetation and leveled off. Spence figured that is where Jesse was planning on building his house.

"Saw the saw in the wagon. You two finished with it already?" Jesse asked Will.

"Yep, and we're here ready to start on yours. That saw may be old but it still cuts a straight board if you can keep your mule moving," Will replied.

"Well, I have some logs that have aged for a while now and should be ready to cut up. Got plans on framing a single level house this summer but braced for a second storey later on. I reckon we can put up with each other through one winter and then build separate bedrooms later on," Jesse stated.

"Well, let's look over your plans, and maybe we can get that second floor built at the same time. That way you only have to put in one water-tight roof on the house," Will replied.

This remark surprised Jesse. Then Spence spoke up, "Don't settle when you don't have to, as you're speaking to a master carpenter here."

Will redden a little and then said, "Well, maybe not a master, but I've done a few houses in my time."

These remarks really pleased Jesse. He had help build some rough homes in the past but he wanted a real house out here for his wife. If he could get the entire house build the first time, it would make life easier for her and his family.

Martha had been listening to the conversation and then spoke up, "Here, you children go on and play. You men come on over and have a cool drink. Jesse, pull out those papers you've been sketching on and let Mr. Harris have a look at them."

The three men all noticed the use of the title Mister. The children had also and they quickly moved out of the way. Jesse led the two over to the table and benches he had built and had them sit down while he went into the tent to fetch his drawings.

Will took the papers and looked them over. Taking Jesse's pencil, he began to make changes on the drawings; erasing here, adding there and looking them over again. Finally he laid the pencil aside, looked at the drawings one more time and passed them over to Jesse.

"Look at these now. If there's anything you don't like, just speak up and we'll change them."

Jesse looked them over carefully and then got up and took them over to Martha. She looked at them and then ran over and grabbed Will around the shoulders, hugging him.

"Mr. Harris, these are perfect. This is just exactly what I've been trying to explain to Jesse." Turning to her husband she exclaimed, "This is going to make me the happiest woman in the valley."

Jesse reached over and shook Will's hand. "She kept talking at me, but I just couldn't picture what she was getting at. Now, Will, you're going to have to build this or we both are in trouble."

Will smiled at the couple. He knew that actually what he had drawn was a standard house plan, and was a lot easier to build than what Jesse had put on paper.

"I reckon we better start sawing those logs then so we can make the little lady happy," Will said.

"Now, have you two had your dinner? I don't want you starting on an empty stomach," Martha said.

"Oh, that reminds me. I have a young pronghorn buck laying out there in the wagon. It needs hung up in the cool shade and finished dressed out," Spence said.

"I'll get it, Pa," the boy said and started over to the wagon.

"Yes, we've had our dinner. We can at least get the saw out and set up. I'm going to have to adjust the blade to saw the supports before we start on the planks. How's your oxen if'n they're hook on a tread, Jesse?" Will asked.

"I've never tried them, but they're pretty solid pullers. I'll try the old one first as he's more steady," Jesse replied. "I'll go bring him in."

While Jesse went out to the fields to bring in the oxen, Will and Spence moved the wagon around to where they wanted the saw and then unloaded the saw. While Will was leveling the saw and then starting to adjust the cutting blade, Spence moved the wagon out of the way and unhitched the team of mules. He hobbled them and then turned them loose. He didn't want them to wander very far from the house. He then unsaddled his horse and hobbled it also as he turned it loose with the mules.

Jesse had come up with an ox and tied it up close to the saw. Will looked up from adjusting the cutting guide and said, "We're about ready to try the first log. You two go bring in the first log and we'll see what we have here. I want to cut the supports first, then cut the framing boards and then the slats last."

Jesse untied the ox and he and Spence moved over to the pile of logs. They tied a rope around a log and hooked the rope up to the harness on the ox. He started off and didn't seem to even notice the weight of the log.

"Here help me get this log up on the saw. I've just about got it ready now. As soon as we can get an ox onto the tread and get this saw going, then we can start. I figure we can cut a couple of supports this afternoon," Will said to Spence.

"Not if you're as picky as you were when we were cutting your boards," Spence replied.

"These aren't going to have to be as straight to start off with. As long as they are fairly straight and will hold a floor, then it will be just fine," Will stated.

Getting the log over next to the saw, the three men wrestled the log onto the grooves on the saw. Jesse maneuvered the ox onto the tread and started it walking.

As the blade turned, Will guided the log into the saw blade and started his cut. Each log was going to require five cuts, four to square it and then one to cut it into two pieces. These would be the primary supports for the house. Will figured that he would need thirty-one of this size and then he could saw the other logs and get four out of each log.

The ox was steady on the treadmill and Jesse had brought up another ox to pull logs so they could keep Will going steady. The older boy pulled the logs over while Jesse and Spence loaded them. Will did the guiding and blade adjustment and the work went pretty smoothly. They had to yell to the other children a couple of times to stay out of the way but Martha came out and took the children. She didn't want anything to interfere with her new house.

As evening fell, Will let the last log finish and then he stopped the ox. As the saw spun to a stop, the other three looked over at Will.

"Reckon that's enough for today. We did real good and got a better start than I would have imagined," Will said.

Jesse turned the ox loose and they started walking back up to the tent and cook fire. Keith, the oldest boy had butchered the antelope earlier and Martha was frying up some breaded steaks with biscuits and milk gravy. Spence felt his mouth start watering as he smelled the food cooking.

"I figure I can put a little extra effort into my cooking for the men building my house," Martha said.

"Seems the pay is more than adequate if you keep cooking like this," Will replied.

Martha smiled at the compliment and went back to her cooking. Katherine, the oldest girl, started sitting out plates, utensils and cups. These were a little better quality than Spence and Will were used to using. Will remarked to Spence that it seems Jesse had been doing quite well back in Kentucky before they came out west.

The three men walked over and washed up from some wash pans of water Martha had sat up for them. Drying their hands, they really began to smell the meal that was being spread out on the tables. It looked like a feast to Spence. Fried prairie chicken, ham and dumplings, antelope steak, hot biscuits, fresh green beans, tomatoes, okra and radishes were sitting on the table. Jesse gathered his family and said grace.

Turning around he said, "Dig in boys. Martha doesn't like for her food to get cold. Just make yourselves at home now."

It didn't take two invites for Spence and Will to start serving themselves. They knew that no one else would start until they had filled their plates, so they heaped the food on their plates and then got out of the way.

"You know, Will, if we keep eating like this, it might take longer than expected to finish this house," Spence said as Martha walked over with two cups of coffee. Martha took the compliment and smiled at Spence.

"It'll be worth every hour spent over the cook fire if that house turns out half of what it looks like on paper," she replied.

As Jesse sat down with his plate of food, Will looked over at him and asked, "Who's going to lay in the fireplace? I'm not the greatest at laying rocks, but I can do some of it. I never seem to be able to get the draft just right though."

"My youngest brother has some training at laying rocks. He used to work it some back home. Might try to get him over and work his farm for him while he's doing it," Jesse replied.

"I wonder who laid the rocks for the fireplaces in our cabins?" Spence asked Will. "They draw really well and I've never had a back draft on mine. I noticed that even during that wind storm the other night, yours just kept on burning."

"Didn't think of that. I bet we could get the Colonel to let the Triple Y rider come out and lay all three of the Goodman's fireplaces. Whoever it was sure, knew what he was doing and then, it wouldn't interfere with any farming. Those cowpunchers are just laying around right now anyway," Will stated.

Spence didn't figure the riders were just lying around, but he was sure that Hess would be able to cut the rider loose for a while to lay the fireplaces.

"When we finish here and you start over to Joseph's place, I'll ride over to the ranch and see if we can borrow the rider. If he's so good then he might want to lay rocks instead of punch cows for a while," Spence said.

Martha had walked up with coffee for her husband and had heard the conversation. "That would be the best thing to do. I've seen different fireplaces and I've got a few ideas of how the kitchen fireplace should be. The fireplace to heat the house can be the standard layout though."

"Now Martha, don't start making plans. We don't even know if the man wants to do the work yet and if we have to use Maxwell, then you'll probably just get a fireplace that'll draw well," Jesse stated.

"Won't hurt to check none though," Spence said.

The men continued to cut up lumber for the house until Will thought they had enough to get a good start on the frames. He didn't want to have to stop and cut more while in the middle of putting up a wall. At the end of the third day he told the other two men that they would start working on the house in the morning.

Jesse and his boy had been moving the cut lumber over next to the house site while Spence and Will ran the saw. Jesse still had a few more trees sitting on the ground next to the saw. He had been planning on having to build a log cabin at first so he and his boy had cut and hauled in quite a few logs. Will told him that they would probably all be used before the interior walls were completed.

Early the next morning Spence rose and looked around. Will was already out of his bedding and was walking around the level area where the house was to be built. Spence rolled out of his bedding and out from under the wagon where he and Will had been sleeping. Walking over to Will he asked, "What's bothering you? It's not like you to fret and worry about anything."

"I was just thinking that the first framed house built out here should have been Francis's. I feel that I have let her down by being over here fixing to frame a house for someone else."

"I don't think Francis would think like that at all. You have re-done that cabin into a very comfortable place, and you know that Francis would want her neighbors, especially if they have children, to have a warm and dry place for them."

"I guess you're right. She is a kind and generous woman. But I swear here and now that right after the harvest is finished, I'm going to start on her a house that will put this one to shame."

With that the two men walked over to the cook fire where Martha was just beginning to build a fire.

"Here, let me do that for you," Will said. Handing the coffee pot to Spence he said, "Go get some fresh water in this thing. Times a wasting and the sun is rising."

After breakfast the three men and boy started laying out the frame for the sides of the house. After they were in place, Will and Jesse would hammer as Spence and Keith held the lumber in place. By mid morning they had two sides ready to go into place. Jesse called Martha and Katherine, the oldest girl, over to help hold the frames in place. It took the four men to lift the side frame and get it set in place. Then Keith, his Ma and sister held it while the three men lifted the side frame upright and slid it over up against the front frame. Will nailed supports to both frames and then nailed the two frames together.

Working until dinner saw the other side frame ready to go up. Will urged them along and they got it into place before they broke for lunch. As everyone sat around the cook fire eating dinner, they all watched the frame of the house. The younger children chattered on about the work being done.

By mid afternoon the back frame was together and ready to be put into place. Once again Jesse called for Martha and Katherine to help. This frame had to be lifted up and over as it was on the low side of the house's level area. The men got the frame upright and were beginning to move it over to start lifting it up to the level house plat.

"Be careful now, we all have to go up at the same time," Will cautioned the group.

"Ready, heave!" Will called out.

The frame started up into the air. Spence and Keith were on the lower end with Will and Martha on the other end. Jesse and Katherine had the middle supports.

"Careful now. That's right. Easy, easy," Will keep up a steady chant.

Suddenly the middle support board groaned, cracked and then split totally. The frame bowed in the middle and then started going over backwards. Everybody hung on and tried to counter the frame's backward progress but it was too heavy and awkward at that point. The frame suddenly was too top heavy for the men to hold and it came crashing down.

"Everyone OK?" Will shouted but suddenly he saw Katherine under the middle supports. Running over, he threw the wood out of the way and picked up the limp body of Katherine and moved her over away from the frame. She had blood running from a cut on her forehead.

Martha saw her daughter's limp body being moved by Will and she ran over and took her from Will and laid her on the ground. Jesse was right behind her.

Spence ran over to the water bucket and doused his handkerchief into the water and came back over and handed it to Martha. As she was cleaning the blood off the young girl's forehead, Katherine opened her eyes and asked, "Did we save the frame from falling?"

They didn't know whether to laugh or cry with relief. Martha hugged her daughter and started laugh-crying and the others smiled down at the poor girl. Jesse picked her up and she cried out in pain as her arm fell from her mother's lap. The upper arm had been broken by the falling frame. Jesse steadied her arm and carried her over to the tent where he put her on her bed. Martha stayed with her to tend the wound on Katherine's forehead and Spence came into the tent.

"I treated some of these during the war. Let me see what I can do," Spence stated. He felt very carefully along the arm and detected the area of the break. "Get me some clean cloth while I get some wood slats to use as splints."

Spence and Jesse walked back up to the broken frame and Jesse stated, "I don't know if it would have been worth while."

The others knew what he meant. Spence picked out some straight slats and went back over to the tent. Will moved over and started accessing the damage. "Keith, go over and get two more planks like this one and let's see if we can't brace this a little more in the middle."

The next two weeks passed fairly quickly with the four men up working early morning until late evening. The cutting of the wood was going quickly and the pile of logs was finished before Will had enough slats cut. Spence and Jesse had to start cutting down more trees and hauling them in until Will was satisfied that he had enough wood to start the house. The green logs were cut into slats and were to be used as the floors on the two levels. Then as the wood dried out, it would not affect the rest of the house. This wood was laid out in the sun to try to cure some before it was to be used in the house.

Jesse was a decent carpenter's helper, and Spence was learning fast. Between the three men and the oldest boy, the house started to take shape quickly. Will even planned out a covered porch for the front of the house. He was putting aside ideas for his own house that he was planning on building next summer. He wanted to cut the wood and age it in his barn before he started his own home. The cabin that they had would make do this first winter in this valley and by next spring he would have a list of material and items to send with the Colonel during the spring buying trip.

The middle of the third week found Will nailing in the last boards on the porch. Getting up he looked over at Jesse saying, "This porch might start leaking some when those boards dry out and warp a little. Some good coal tar will take care of that though. I guess that just about does it for the house though."

The house still didn't have any doors, windows or fireplaces but the structure itself was finished. Inside there wasn't any slats on the walls, railing for the stairs or internal doors for the rooms, but it was livable for now.

Martha walked over and stood beside her husband. "Can I go inside now and look?" she asked.

Jesse had been keeping his wife away from the house while it as being built. He wanted as much of it as possible to be a surprise to her.

Picking her up in his arms Jesse said to his wife, "Tradition is that a husband carries his wife over the threshold of their first home. Even with four children, this is your first new home and I'm going to carry you over it."

Jesse started up the steps and across the porch with his wife wiggling in his arms and surrounded by his children, giggling as they went. He walked across the threshold and into the first room making a circle with his wife as he went. Then he put Martha down so she could see her new home.

"You told me that eventually we would have a home like this after we got out here, but I sure didn't expect one for five or six years. Jesse, I'm glad that you made me come out here with you.

This is the best we've done for ourselves since we've been married."

Jesse smiled at his wife. He hadn't expected a house to be built for five years either. The best thing he had ever done was to get off the main trail to California and end up in this valley. He had a great debt of gratitude to pay the Colonel and to Will Harris and Spence. He walked back outside and over to the two men that were waiting for him. He reached out and shook Will's hand and then grabbed him around the shoulders and gave him a hug. Turning to Spence he did the same.

"I'll never be able to repay the kindness and the work you two have done for us. We had expected to live in a log cabin for the next four or five years, as we tried to get settled into a new place and raise the first crops. I will be indebted to your kindness for the rest of my life."

"Nah, now you just hush up talking like that. This is what neighbors are for, and I'll be expecting your help when I raise my own house. I figure Spence will also be building soon and will require your help. We'll just let the debt be until the coming year and forget this lifelong debt nonsense," Will told Jesse.

"You have my promise. Just holler, and me and the boy will come running when you are ready, crops in or not."

Spence felt a warm glow of satisfaction on how the house had turned out and how these good people felt. He knew that if any of them needed his help again, he would offer gladly and freely. Being able to help your friends was one of the pleasures of life, and Spence saw that Will Harris had learned this lesson a long time ago and practiced it whenever he could.

CHAPTER TWENTY-NINE

As Spence and Will rode across the range toward Joseph Goodman's farm, Will was quieter than normal. Spence had got used to him talking a mile a minute and for the man to be quiet was strange.

"You did yourself proud back there for Jesse and Martha. That is a really nice house and should stand up very well to the weather in these parts," Spence said.

"Yep, it is. I got caught up in my work and actually did more than I intended to do. It's been a while since I got to work on a house like that. Makes my cabin look pretty shabby now. What was I thinking, having Francis living in a rock and mud cabin, when I should have built her the first home out on this range."

"Now Will, do you really begrudge those nice folks the house that you just built?" Spence asked.

"No, no I don't. I just feel I've let Francis down some. I just hadn't planned on building anything until after the first harvest is put away, and we know that we can make it out here."

"Is there any doubt that your farm won't support you and a half dozen more?" Spence asked.

"No, I'm quite pleased with the land, and I have no doubt that Davie will be farming that land well after I'm gone. It is fertile enough to support two or three families with grain to sell. I'm going to draw up some plans, and you better be planning on working on a house come this fall. I might even put white columns on the front porch like I seen in a picture of those plantations houses around the South."

Spence could tell that just talking and thinking about the house he was going to build Francis had cheered up Will. Will talked for the next two miles about how he was going to build that house.

About that time Keith rode up from behind them. "Pa sent me to go with you to help out. He figured now he could mind the chores and an extra hand would come in handy putting up the walls."

"Well he's right and you make a dang good extra hand. Now just tie that horse to the rear of the wagon and join us up here," Will told the boy.

Jesse Goodman had sent his oldest son with Spence and Will Harris as they traveled over to his two brother's farms. With summer coming on he had figured that the more help with the work, then the quicker his brothers could build their houses. The other two brothers wanted single level houses, and both had enough logs already cut and drying to build their houses. It didn't take Spence and Will but eight and then seven days to build the other two.

Spence had made a side trip over to the Triple Y ranch and had inquired about the rock mason that had built the fireplaces in the line cabins. Hess had told him that it was a rider named Addison Robinson who was out on the southwest range with the summer cowherd. He had informed Spence that he would send a rider to replace Addison and send him out to build the farmer's fireplaces for them.

Spence had told the other two brothers of the rock mason coming to help build the fireplaces. Maxwell had at first declined, until Will had started telling him of Martha's plans on having her kitchen fireplace laid out with those special features, and Sarah had quickly changed his mind.

While at the farm with Maxwell, Spence asked him about the pond he had been trying to dam up. Maxwell walked the men out and showed them his lake. He had been able to channel the ravine into the natural low lying area and the last rains had helped fill the little lake. He showed them signs of the fish that had washed down from the streams and into his lake. Will walked all around the lake and then into the ravine, noting how Maxwell had channeled the water. He was beginning to have thoughts of his own about creating deeper pools of water on the river close to his own farm.

As they were beginning to prepare to leave Maxwell and Sarah's farm, Sarah took Jesse's boy aside and told him to inform his mother that she was now due with child. Martha had helped her with the first child and she wanted Martha to be ready again.

Hearing the comments, Will shook Maxwell's hand and said that it called for a round of smokes. Will pulled his bag of tobacco out and offered it to Maxwell, then to Spence and then he rolled a cigarette for himself. The three men smoked to the good health and well being of the new child and to the first baby to be born in the valley.

Sarah laughed at this comment saying, "It's not birthed yet, let's not get too far ahead of ourselves."

"I'll pass that onto the Colonel also," Spence told Maxwell. "He'll be glad to know that his plans to civilize this valley is now well on its way."

"When is the schoolhouse going to be started?" Sarah asked. "Now with the second one on its way, I've got to start thinking about things like that."

"I've been thinking that after we all have our crops in and we've readied for the winter, then we should all have a gathering and a visit before the first snows. The rising of the school house would be a good reason enough but the families getting together would be a better reason," Will replied.

"I talked with the ranch hands that are planning on bringing their families out soon and they would like to participate. I think this coming year will see three or four new families as the riders complete their commitment to the Colonel. They want to help so their children will have a school and their wives will have a church," Spence said.

"I think that would be really nice. Max, you'll be able to meet our neighbors as I think you said we were bordered by ranchers on three sides of us," Sarah replied.

Maxwell stated, "Yep, that's true. I just hope that our neighbors are as kind and helpful as Will and Spence. By the way Spence, when are you and Emily getting married? That will be another good reason for a gathering."

Spence stuttered and Will laughed, and Sarah and Maxwell looked at each other wondering.

"Spence doesn't know he's getting married soon. You'll have to ask Emily that question and she'll let you know. This boy acts like he's lost around her most of the time and then watches her when he thinks no one is noticing. Just like a love struck calf he is, and doesn't know it," Will told them.

"Now hang on a minute. I think I should have some say in the matter, and I haven't even thought about it enough to even be thinking about it yet," Spence stated.

"We'll let you know on that also. I think Emily has been wanting to get back over here, as she enjoyed her stay with you folks. She said something about you having some books to start the children's schooling with or something. I'll let her know you were asking," Will replied.

Spence and Will climbed up on the wagon with Jesse's boy. Say-

ing their last good-byes, Will turned the mule team around and they
started out toward the trail. Spence and the boy turned to wave one
last goodbye and saw that Sarah and her husband were still standing, watching them leave. Sarah waved until they were almost out
of sight. Spence thought how lonely the young woman looked, and
wondered if Emily would look the same way if they were married
and didn't see folks very often.

It surprised him how quick and easy it was to think of his being
married to Emily. He had never let himself think about it before,
but the last conversation with the couple they had just left, made it
seem natural to think in those terms. He was surprised that Will
was so accepting of the marriage between him and Emily. Will had
never let on that he had noticed any feelings between his daughter
and Spence.

It was a quiet ride back to Joseph and Helen's farm. The three
spent the night there and got an early start the next morning back to
Jesse and Martha's place. Coming into the farmyard, which did
look like a farmyard now with the new house up and the tents taken
down, Spence noticed a large pile of rocks at both ends of the house.
It seemed that Jesse was going to be ready for the rock mason whenever he came.

As the wagon pulled up close to the house Martha came out onto
the porch. Smiling she yelled to the men, "Get down and come on
inside. It sure is good to be able to say those words."

Will smiled at her and asked, "Where's Jesse? I just wanted to
tell him how much help this here boy had been to us. I swear I could
almost let him go and he could lay out a house by himself."

The boy laughed at Will's comments and then ran and hugged
his mother. She hugged him back and then kissed his forehead.
That made him blush and he wiped it and ran into the house to
greet his brother and sisters.

"Jesse and Addison are still out gathering some more rocks.
Addison wanted some large flat rocks for the hearth and we didn't
have any here close to the house," Martha said.

"I didn't expect him to get out here so soon. Hess must have sent
out a rider that same day," Spence said.

"He's been here a few days now. Jesse had just started talking
about gathering rocks for the chimney and all when the man rode
in. Told Jesse that he was glad that he hadn't started as most folks
gather the wrong stones and then get mad when he doesn't use

them."

"Well, even Maxwell is looking forward to Addison showing up. After I told Sarah of your plans, she wasn't going to let Maxwell build their fireplace either," Will stated. "I think that boy of yours has some news from Sarah she said to pass on."

Will and Spence got down and walked across the porch. Will was checking the slats to see if they had started to warp any as they dried out. He seemed satisfied at them and walked on into the house. He stood in the center of the room and twirled in one slow circle checking the walls and ceiling. Seeming satisfied at his work he went on into the kitchen where Martha and Spence had gone. Spence was drinking water from a cup and Martha handed Will one also. The men were used to tin cups and this glass cup with flowers painted on the sides was something special.

"Here, don't waste your good dishes on us. We'll just use those tin cups over there," Will said.

Spence was about to tell Will to forget about protesting, when Martha started in on Will. Spence leaned back against the table and just enjoyed it as Martha let Will know that she was now living in a civilized house and that she would use her fine dishes for whom-ever she wanted and that the tin cups were now for children and not for guests that had helped put her into a house.

Martha was finishing her reply to Will when she looked over and saw Spence smiling at her. Then she stopped and smiled at both men. "I guess I got carried away a little there."

Will was still standing there with his hat in his hands. "I guess you did a little, but we both probably deserved it. You go on now and finish getting it out of your system."

"Here you two sit down there at the table. I've got some hot cobbler fresh from the fire and some cool milk to go with it. Have a seat and eat your pie."

Spence and Will sat down at the table while Martha dished up the hot cobbler and poured the milk. They finished the dish off quickly as the cobbler was the first sweets they had eaten since leav-ing Will's farm. As Will was scrapping the last tidbits from his dish Jesse and Addison rode up in the wagon. It was full of flat stones in the bed with some of them being as much as two men could lift. Jesse brought the wagon around to the south end of the house where the kitchen hearth and fireplace was being built.

Walking outside Spence yelled out, "Need any help with those stones?"

"I guess we could use a little. Here you two grab those two stones over there and move them. Mind now you don't drop and break them. Those are going to be Martha's hearth stones," Jesse called back.

Spence and Will grabbed the first of the large stones while Jesse and Addison took two tin cups from Martha full of water. It was all the two men could do to lift it from the wagon and they stumbled over to the house with it and sat it gently on the ground. Going back to the wagon they grabbed the second stone and found that it was just as heavy. They didn't get it quite over to the wall before they had to sit it on the ground.

"Looks like you two boys had a day's work here. I didn't know there were any stones this large around here," Will stated.

"Had to travel over to the foot hills and check all those ravines before we finally found those two big ones," Jesse replied.

"Figured there might be some over there. I've been able to find enough to build the fireplaces for the range cabins by checking ravines. The rain run-off washes the dirt from around them and makes them easier to find," Addison added.

"I guess I need to find some of those for my cabin. It still has just a hole in the wall for a cook fire," stated Spence.

"Yea, been meaning to go out there and finish that place up but got busy and things never slowed down. That range cabin was the last to be built and it wasn't very long before you came over the pass. You know how it's been since then," Addison said.

"Yep, been a little busy. I can see how you never found the time to get back out there. And then after it was burnt, there wasn't much use to go out there for a while," Spence replied.

The four men finished unloading the wagon. Addison directed the placement of the rocks so that he could get to some of them first as he started the chimney. Martha called them in to supper before they had finished but they continued until the wagon was empty. They then went and washed up before going into the house for supper.

The conversation was lively as the family and visitors ate their meal. Addison was to have the farm next to Maxwell and he was trying to get his family out from St. Louis before winter. He had plans on having his wife, two sons and daughter ride a train into San Francisco and them coming north from there. He had made an agreement with Hank Moore to use his cabin until Addison could build a dwelling for his family. Hank was always quick to give up his cabin to a family as Will had experience during his stay on the Triple Y ranch.

After coffee and cobbler was served and eaten, the men moved outside for a smoke. They discussed the weather, crops, farming and Addison's plans for his ranch. Spence and Will then stated they were going to try to get an early start back home the next morning and rolled out their bedding. Addison brought his over and stretched it out close by. It wasn't long before the three men were sleeping and the full moon rose in the night sky without any observers.

CHAPTER THIRTY

The rest of the summer passed quickly, with the farmers weeding their crops, tending their vegetable gardens and building their sheds and pens for their animals. The valley got enough rain to keep the grain crops growing and Maxwell's lake was filling up with the run off water from his ravine. Joseph had ridden over twice during the summer to check on Sarah's pregnancy, and he and Maxwell had discussed possible ways to irrigate crops from the lake.

During the latter part of the summer, the Colonel and Hess had ridden out to visit with the farmers. The two men were very impressed with the progress of the home steads and the growth of the crops. The Colonel was quick to praise the farmers for their abilities and was glad he had made the decision to offer land to the farmers. He was surprised with the farm and lake that Maxwell had created as he had figured the young man would have decided to move on by now.

Seeing that Sarah was carrying a baby that was to be the first child born in the valley, the Colonel offered Maxwell an additional hundred acres of land in honor of the baby. This would bring his total holdings up to five hundred acres, which was what his two brothers had bought. Maxwell and Sarah were surprised by the offer, and Maxwell at first declined. But, with a little urging from Hess, they accepted the land on condition they could use the Colonel's name for the baby. Both sides were pleased with the deal.

While at Will Harris's farm, the Colonel was shown the fields that Will and David had planted just for the Triple Y ranch. David had called it their money crop, and explained his plans for future plantings. The Colonel noted that he would have to be careful in future dealings with this young man, as the boy had a good head for business.

Eating supper the last evening of their visit, the Colonel turned to Emily and asked if she was still planning on teaching the valley's children. Emily took this opportunity to lay out her plans for the schoolhouse and how it would be used for a church. She told the Colonel how Joseph Goodman was an ordained preacher and how the schoolhouse could quickly be turned into a church. Emily went on and told him that the books that Sarah had brought, with her added to her own, would be enough to start teaching the children, but eventually more would have to be bought during one of his trips into the city.

After Emily had finished, the Colonel told her that he was planning on having his riders construct the school with a house nearby for the schoolmarm. He stated that Hank Moore had been making plans on opening a general store and blacksmith shop, and those would be the first buildings in his new town.

Everyone around the table was surprised by the Colonel's statement. Will and Francis was pleased that Emily would finally get her school. Emily was flustered and began to quickly think of all the things that must be done before she would be ready for students. Davie was dreading when the harvest would be over and he would have to sit in a building and study lessons. Spence could only think of one thing though, and that was he would be losing Emily before she was ever his.

Everyone began to talk at once, with Emily having a dozen questions for the Colonel and Francis and Will added their thoughts to the conversation. The only person that noted Spence leaving was Hess and the range boss figured he knew the reason. He got up and pulled out his tobacco bag and swung it around as he walked out the door.

"Thought I might find you out here," Hess said to Spence who was leaning up against the end of the cabin. "Here, have a smoke."

Spence nodded and took the bag from Hess and rolled a cigarette.

"You didn't say anything about the Colonel's new plans."

"Well, they sort of caught me by surprise. I hadn't figured on a school being built until this fall," Spence replied.

"You know how the Colonel operates. When he gets an idea, he pushes through with it and don't wait around. The riders are in a lull period right now and the Colonel wanted it done before the fall roundup starts. After that it would be snowing before he had the riders again."

"Yea, I know how that goes. Emily was taken by the idea of having her school built now. She's talked about that school every since the two of them had that conversation back last spring," Spence said.

"I think that is what got the Colonel started. When he saw Emily had already been thinking of the children's need for studies, he started planning his little town and talked with Hank about his plans. Hank can do a lot of his work over there and just bring the repaired items back to the ranch. There won't be much need for a general store at first but as more families move into the valley then it would start growing," Hess stated.

"How many men are staking their claim to their land and bringing their families out?" Spence asked.

"Let's see, there is George, Addison, Charlie Simson and about three more. George and Charlie both plan on leaving after the fall roundup and coming back in the spring with their families. I think Addison has his family coming this fall and the others are planning for next summer," Hess replied.

"I guess the Colonel is doing this at the right time then," Spence said.

"He has had this dream ever since we rode over the Coastal Del Rey Mountains. The ranch was just a venture to help settle this valley some and to give the men an investment worth staying in the valley for. Of course it turned out that the valley created a lot of wealth for those willing to stay with the Triple Y, so it turned out well for all of us," Hess stated.

"Now what was that look of distress that I saw on your face when the Colonel announced his plans?" Hess asked Spence.

Stuttering a little Spence replied, "I didn't think anyone noticed."

"I don't think they did. I think I was the only one that saw you walk out," Hess said.

"No, you weren't the only one," a voice said from behind them.

Turning, the two men saw Davie standing behind them.

"I was distressed at first about having to start lessons again from my sister but I saw you both leave. I do have a question for Spence though," David said.

"And what is that?" Spence asked the young man.

"When are you going to do the right thing by my sister and quit fooling around? She might get living over there next to Hank and I'll end up with that smithy as my brother-in-law."

Hess broke out into a laugh and said, "I hadn't thought about that. Maybe Hank had more plans than I or the Colonel thought he had."

Spence looked even more distressed as he thought about Emily and Hank living alone on the prairie together in the start of the new town.

Looking at Spence, David and Hess both broke out into more laughter. Seeing him looking at them so strangely made them laugh even more.

"What's so dad burn funny out here?" Will asked as he walked around the corner of the cabin.

David and Hess were laughing so much they couldn't talk and Spence wouldn't say anything. Will looked at the three of them and then chuckled a little, as the laughter was catching. He could tell that the other two were laughing at Spence but he couldn't tell why.

Finally Hess got control of his laughter and said, "Spence looked like a coon hound that got caught swiping the bacon off the table. Ever see a hound's face that was getting a good scolding?"

"Yep, but who was scolding Spence. What did he do?" Will asked.

"Now Pa, think about what was going on in the cabin," David said. "Here the Colonel has Emily moving out to the new school house and Hank moving out to his new store, and Spence is stuck out on his place all by himself."

Will thought about that a few seconds and then took Spence by the shoulders saying, "Well now son, it looks like you're going to have to take some action real soon now or I just might have a black-smith as a son-in-law."

With that comment Hess and David started laughing again and Will joined in. Spence even laughed this time and said, "It seems to be the general consensus then that I need to talk with Emily, and probably need to do it right soon now."

"Talk with me about what?" a voice asked around the corner.

The laughter died suddenly as the men realized that Emily had walked up and probably heard part of the conversation.

"Anyway, Ma says for you men to come back in the house as she has a pie ready to be cut and some hot coffee made," Emily said as if she had not heard a thing.

The men quickly shuffled around the corner of the house and being careful not to look Emily in the eye they went into the house and took their seats again as Francis started serving the hot pie. Emily came in and got out the cups and the coffee pot, filling the cups and passing them around.

"Will, Francis has shown me the plans you have drawn for the house you plan to start building in the autumn after the harvest. Is there anything you need from the city that I can pick up for you?"

the Colonel asked.

Will started running through a list of items that he had thought about. Spence was glad the conversation had turned to other topics other than his need to talk with Emily. He glanced at her occasionally and quickly turned away when she would look over at him. Now that the need for him to start thinking about his plans for a life with this young woman was forced upon him, he found that he wasn't quite ready for the commitment. He wanted the young woman for his wife, but was now hesitant to act on it.

Emily had heard the conversation, and was now wondering if Spence would follow through on the need to talk with her. She had spoken with her parents about her feelings for Spence, and what she should do if Spence ever did ask her to marry him. Her parents were both pleased that the two were attracted to each other, and felt it would be a good marriage. All three of them though, felt that Spence would need some pushing before he would ask Emily to be his wife. Francis and Emily had spoken of ways to influence Spence and how to push him along.

The only person that felt he could talk to was Davie and the boy now thought that he would talk to Spence every chance that he had. Maybe with the new school and a new husband, Emily would forget about his need for lessons.

The Colonel and Hess left the next morning with berry turnovers that Francis had cooked for their trip. The Colonel promised Emily that he would let her know when the riders would start on the school-house and he turned to Will and asked about the construction of a grainery.

As Will walked off beside the Colonel's horse giving an explanation of how to construct a grain storage bin, the other three turned and looked at Spence, Emily with a big question on her face.

CHAPTER THIRTY-ONE

Spence was sitting beside his campfire at his cabin reflecting on his actions two days before. After the Colonel and Hess had started to leave, with Will walking along explaining a grain bin to the Colonel, Spence had suddenly turned and walked off towards his horse, saddled, mounted and rode off.

Spence was not usually so rude to people he was staying with and partaking of their food, but the night before had not gone so well. He was confused and had wanted the quiet of the ride across the prairie to help settle his mind. Of course the ride did not help, as he had ridden along side the fields that Will and David had planted.

He knew that he had left Emily confused also and probably Francis and Davie. They had all been looking at him as he turned and walked away. If he intended to ask Emily to be his wife, he had to decide now and quit his hesitation. He needed a commitment before she moved out to the new schoolhouse.

Spence knew that he really wanted Emily to be his wife, and that she would make a great wife and mother to their children. He liked her parents and her brother and felt closer to them then he had ever felt for anyone.

Getting up, he threw the rest of his coffee onto the fire, threw some dirt on it and went to get his horse. "Might as well get this over with so I can get on with our lives," he told his horse. Swinging up into the saddle Spence heeled the horse, which sprang away in surprise and anticipation. It wasn't often his rider wanted a full run to start off with.

After about ten minutes of letting the horse have his head, Spence reined him down into a trot. He was now anxious to see Emily, but he didn't want to run his horse down.

Coming over the ridge above the Harris farm, Spence could see the two men out in the fields hoeing out weeds. Francis was in the back of the cabin hanging newly washed clothes on a make-shift clothes line that Will had strung up for her. As he approached closer the three people saw him and stopped what they were doing and watched him ride into the farmyard.

"Good morning, Mrs. Harris. I have some formal business with your family this morning. Is Emily around?" Spence asked as he looked around the farmyard for the young woman.

"No, Mr. Spence. She rode out day before yesterday heading towards Sarah Goodman's place to see about the books that Sarah has. She was quite confused and said that the trip would help ease her mind some. Seems some young man can not make up his mind about something and she is confused about her feelings," Francis scolded at Spence.

"Well, I deserve that, but now I know what I want and who I want, and have come to make amends. I would like to ask yours and Will's permission to marry your daughter. I think we should have a ceremony quite soon but of course that would be up to Emily and yourself," Spence responded.

"Spence, you know that you have Will and my full blessing to marry Emily, even Davie'if that helps sets your mind to rest. We've just been wondering what has been taking you so long to see what the rest of us have known for a while," Francis stated.

Spence reddened a little around the ears. "I guess I've just been too dense to see what was before my eyes."

Will and David had walked up and they both added their comments to those of Francis. Spence was beginning to wonder what kind of fool he had been if everyone had known he and Emily had fallen for each other, but he hadn't seen it.

"I think I will ride out and try to catch Emily then, and finalize this proposal. If you two don't mind, we can inform the Goodman families of our intended date on the way past each farm," Spence said.

"That will be fine, Spence. You and Emily talk about it before you leave Sarah and Maxwell Goodman's place and we will finalize the preparations after you get back here," Francis stated.

Spence nodded and turning his horse he heeled him again into a run. He let the horse run until he was over the hill heading toward Jesse's farm.

Watching him ride off, Will commented, "We should have prodded him earlier I guess."

"Sure should have Pa. I was hitting him up every chance I could but it wasn't enough," David replied.

Finally getting to the Goodman farm Spence reined into the yard and looked for Martha. He was hoping that Emily had stopped with either Martha or Helen Goodman and was at either farm.

"Martha, have you seen Emily lately?" Spence called out to the woman just as soon as he saw her.

"Yes, she came by day before yesterday and just stopped long enough for a brief chat. She was in a hurry to get over to Sarah's to see about some books for the new school. Isn't it wonderful that the Colonel is going to build the school now instead of waiting?" Martha said.

"Yes it is. Excuse me now, but I must be on my way," Spence told her.

"Can you wait until Jesse comes down and have a cup of water or something before you go?" Martha asked.

"Thank you kindly ma'am but I do need to go. I will stop on my way back and we will have a visit, just you and Emily, Jesse and myself," Spence replied.

Spence turned his horse and heeled the horse again into a run. The horse wasn't quite as surprised this time and broke into a gallop.

"Now that was the strangest visit I ever did have," Martha mused to herself.

As Spence rode into the farmyard of Joseph and Helen Goodman he looked around for the Harris wagon but did not see it. He figured he was right behind Emily, but had missed her here.

Joseph came out of the house and his children were right behind him.

"Well now, two visitors in two days. We must be getting pretty popular around these parts. Get down and have a cup of coffee. Helen still has food on the table and she can fix you a plate," Joseph called out.

"That's mighty neighborly of you, Joseph, but I don't have the time for a visit right now. How long has Emily been gone from here?" Spence asked.

"She was through here about this time, day before yesterday. She stopped for a brief visit with Helen, but said she was on her way to Sarah's to get some books for the children to start lessons out of. Told me to oil down my preaching duds and to limber up my voice, as we were to have a school and church build real soon now."

"She's right. The Colonel decided to get it built before the fall roundup starts. Gives his riders something to keep them busy with right now. Well, I've got to be on my way, we'll stop by for a longer visit on our way home," Spence yelled out as he turned his horse out of the yard.

Breaking into a gallop Spence didn't see Joseph and the children waving good-bye to him.

"Right odd behavior for Spence. Seems he is highly distracted by something. I wouldn't have thought anything could jitter that man," Joseph thought out loud.

As Spence rode across the prairie between Joseph and Maxwell's farms, he notice that the sky was beginning to darken over the mountains. He turned and checked to make sure that, in his haste, he had put his rain gear into his saddle bags. Seeing his gear he was glad that his instincts had kicked in as he was preparing to leave his cabin.

The storm continued to build and Spence could see lightening flashes in the dark storm clouds. He was trying to remember if there were any ravines in this part of the range. The only one he could remember was close by Maxwell's farm so he wasn't concern with getting caught in a flash flood, as the rainwater came gushing down from the mountains.

As the storm came over the mountain Spence could now hear the thunder to go with the lightning flashes. He figured it would be just a matter of minutes before the first raindrops began to fall. Spence pulled out his rain gear and put it on and pulling his hat down a little tighter on his head, he continued to ride toward Maxwell's farm.

The first drops started falling and within ten minutes it was a full storm. It wasn't long before Spence was drenched, as the wind blew his gear up and around and the rain quickly drenched his clothing. His horse kept trying to turn its tail to the storm and Spence had to fight to keep the horse moving.

Finally seeing a group of trees, Spence let the horse move under the branches to try to break the force of the wind and rain some. The lightening had quit so Spence wasn't afraid of the trees being hit.

These summer storms were quick to build and just as quick to blow over. Spence figured that he would be able to be on his way in about thirty minutes. He hunched his shoulders to keep the rain from running down his neck and waited.

After twenty minutes of heavy rain it suddenly quit and just a slight sprinkled was falling. Within minutes the sun was shining and you could hardly tell a storm had just moved through the area, except for the rain puddles still on the ground.

Spence reined his horse and started back on the trail toward the younger Goodman's farm. The earth looked renewed and birds were singing in the brushes as Spence rode by. He was beginning to feel pretty good about his life and thought this after-storm feeling was the way his life was beginning to look like new.

Emily had been watching the storm build over the mountains and was wondering if she would be able to make it to Sarah's house before the storm hit. It had been quite a while since her parents, Spence and her had made this trip, and she could not quite remember how much farther the house was. She was not looking forward to being caught out in the open when the storm finally reached her.

Emily was looking around for possible shelter from the rain as the wagon moved slowly across the countryside. She had wished a hundred times that she had just ridden a horse instead of taking the wagon and a mule. The mule was never in a hurry even when her father was driving, and it sure wasn't going to pull faster for her.

As the lightning started flashing in the storm clouds Emily climbed over the wagon seat and started gathering her rain gear from her bag. She had put it in as a last thought and was now glad that she had. She laid it up on the seat with her and then climbed back over and took up the reins.

The storms back home were entirely different from the storms in this valley. Back home, clouds would move in and it would slowly rain for a couple of days. Here in the valley, the rain would suddenly start falling and would flood everything within minutes, but it would only last a short while. Emily preferred the rain from back home.

As the storm moved down the mountains, Emily put on her rain jacket and poncho. She figured that no matter what she did, she would get wet anyway. Suddenly she saw a gully ahead that looked like it might offer some relief from the wind and rain. She guided the mule over in that direction and had him pull the wagon beneath some overhanging branches with the mule's back to the storm. This way the rain wouldn't be blowing in her face either.

Emily got down from the wagon and laced the mule's reins underneath the wagon. She intended to wait out the storm beneath the wagon and maybe she could stay a little drier that way.

The storm hit with great intensity. Water was whipped around the wagon and Emily had to get almost in the center to keep from getting wet. The mule just lowered his head and waited patiently.

Looking around, Emily noticed that the water was forming a small stream as it ran down the gully. She didn't pay it any attention as she thought it was just the water running off the side of the gully into the dry streambed.

The rain and wind kept hammering at the wagon and mule for about twenty minutes. Emily had to move from the center of the wagon as the small stream had grown in size. She thought to herself that if the rain didn't stop soon then she might have to move out under the branches to stay out of the water.

Just as quick as it had started the rain stopped. "It's about time. I just hate these rain storms," Emily said to the mule. "Now let's see if we can get this wagon out of this gully."

Emily climbed back onto the wagon. She hadn't taken off her rain gear as the wagon seat was still wet and she didn't want to get her dress any wetter than it now was.

Looking back and around her, Emily looked for a break in the gully wall that the mule could pull the wagon out and over. "Looks like we might have to go down this stream bed a ways. I don't think you can back this wagon up now, can you, mule?" Emily didn't usually talk to herself but the stream in the middle of the gully was larger than before and it was a little unsettling.

"Hey, get up now mule!" Emily shouted to the mule. The mule jerked into the harness and the wagon moved a little and then stopped.

"Hey, mule, giddup!" Emily shouted again to the mule. The mule jerked into the harness again and the wagon moved out into the steam of water. The mule pricked up his ears and listened back behind him. The mule didn't know what the sound was, but he started pulling harder on the harness.

"That's the way mule!" Emily shouted out. She didn't know what had caused the mule to start pulling harder but she didn't care at this point, as long as they were moving forward. Emily started scanning the gully walls in front of her looking for a break in the walls.

Spence suddenly started. Was that a shout he had heard? He looked at his horse's ears and saw that they were up and turned forward. His horse had heard it also.

Another shout. It had sounded like Emily's voice. Was he that close to her? She must have pulled over for the storm just as he had.

Another shout. Yes, that definitely was Emily's voice and it sounded like she was yelling at her mule.

Spence chucked to his horse and it broke into a trot. The voice had sounded muffled like something was between himself and the girl. Suddenly Spencer's stomach turned. He had spotted the gully and had the feeling that Emily and the wagon were down in the gully. With that storm just passing the gully would flash flood at anytime. All that water usually ran off into a central stream and combined into a flood down the few ravines.

Spence heeled his horse into a full run. He could now hear the flood rushing down the ravine. He had to get to the gully before the water hit the wagon and Emily. He spurred his horse now into a full run. It was going to be close, as the water sounded like a freight train now as it gushed through the small gully.

Emily now heard the noise behind her that the mule had heard earlier. She didn't know what the sound was but she didn't like it. She whipped her reins out to the mule and the mule instantly starting a slow run. The weight of the wagon in the mud of the new streambed was almost more than he could pull.

Now Emily was beginning to be frightened. If the mule was straining to run she knew it didn't like what was coming down the streambed either. She flicked the reins again at the mule and it put a little more effort into his pull. The mule was at top speed though, which was little more than a fast walk.

Emily stood up in order to see the gully walls better. She still couldn't see any type of break in the wall. Why had she pulled into the gully, she now wondered? The sound behind her was getting louder. It sounded like water rushing down a narrow streambed.

Emily almost collapsed on the wagon seat when the reality of her situation suddenly hit her. She had heard of flash floods before, but had never seen one. She now remembered the stories of whole wagons being washed downstream in these torrid gushes of water. Oh what a fool she had been.

The mule was straining more now as he thrust into the harness. It was scared now and just wanted to get this wagon out of the water.

Emily looked at the sides of the gully. Maybe she could climb out, leaving the wagon. Seeing a lower bank she moved over to the side of the wagon. Reaching the bank she jumped. Her foot slipped on the wet wood and she plunged into the side of the mud bank. Recovering, she started scrambling up the side. No use. The mud was more slippery than the few hand holds she was able to get.

Sliding down to the bottom Emily got to her feet and ran after the wagon. The mule had never stopped pulling. Climbing into the wagon again Emily looked for another break in the gully wall.

Spence saw the point that the wagon had entered the gully. He turned his horse to ride along the side of the gully. It would not be any use to be in the gully also when the flash flood waters hit.

The sound of the water was getting louder now and the water was rising in the streambed. Spence turned and he saw the headwaters of the flood approaching. He spurred his horse trying to get a little more speed.

There she was, just climbing back into the wagon. Mud was all over her clothes and her hair was plastered to her head. The mule was straining in the harness.

"Emily, get out of there! Emily, get out!" Spence shouted.

She couldn't hear him. Spence reached down and loosened his lariat. He was now glad of all the practice he had done during the roundup. Emily's life might depend on his ability to rope.

"Emily, get out! Emily!" Spence shouted again.

What was that? It sounded like someone shouting at her. Grabbing onto the back of the wagon seat, Emily turned and looked behind her.

Fear grabbed her. All she could see was a wall of water rushing down the gully towards her.

Her knees weakened and she sat down in the wagon. It was the most frightening sight Emily had ever seen.

The water was already up to the middle of the wagon wheels and the mule was beginning to struggle just to maintain its footing. The wagon had begun to slow.

The wall of water was beginning to move even faster as it was fed more floodwater from the small ravines emptying into it.

Suddenly Emily heard the shouting again. Looking up on the top of the ravine, Emily saw Spence approaching on his horse. The horse was at a dead run and Spence was looping a rope and began twirling it around his head.

"Spence! Spence! Get me out of here!"

Emily moved over to the side of the wagon nearest the bank Spence was approaching on.

Suddenly the back of the wagon gave a lurch up into the air. The head of the floodwaters had reached the wagon and hit it, causing it to float up. Emily stumbled and fell into the wagon bed. Getting up quickly she grabbed the seat back again and looked toward Spence.

The rope swung out and towards her. Emily made a grab towards the rope.

Spence saw Emily stand up and look towards him. Yes, she sees him. He heard Emily call out to him and then the first of the water hit the wagon. Spence saw Emily fall but quickly stand back up.

Spence knew he would only have one chance to rope Emily and try to pull her to safety. He swung the rope out and let it fly towards the girl. Emily saw the rope coming and reached out towards it.

Spence thought, 'yes, she has it'. Just as Emily reached for the rope the brunt force of the water hit the wagon. It quickly pushed the wagon aside and knocked the girl out and down. The mule was wrenched out of the harness and the wagon crumbled under the weight of the water.

Within a fraction of a second the wagon and everything on it was gone. All that was left was a bank full of water as the floodwaters filled the ravine. Spence was stunned. His rope was still in his hands, but the only pull on it was from the water. Looking down, he saw that his horse was knee deep in brown, muddy floodwater.

Where was the wagon? Emily had surely been roped. Spence pulled his rope in and as it came up from the water, all he had was his small loop above the knot.

It was all Spence could do to keep from falling off his horse into the water. The shock of seeing Emily suddenly disappear beneath the water had stunned him. He had never seen anything so horrible, even during the worst battles of the war.

Suddenly he sat up. Maybe there was a chance that she had came up and washed upon the bank. Spence heeled his horse and took off down the gully bank. He didn't try to get too close to the ravine banks though, as he couldn't see it through the muddy water.

CHAPTER THIRTY-TWO

It was all Spence could do to sit through the memorial service for Emily. They had not been able to recover Emily's body, despite Spence being in the saddle for days looking. Joseph conducted the service to help comfort Will and Francis in this time of grief. All of the farmers and their families gathered at the Harris farm. Spence could not bear to face Will or look at Francis. He had told them his story and of his effort to save Emily. But the hard part was to tell them of his failure to save their daughter's life.

As the service was ending, Spence began to walk off. Hess walked over and put his arm around Spence's shoulder.

"I know how you must feel. Don't blame yourself. There wasn't much you could do Spence," Hess said to the sadden man, trying to show his sympathy.

"I just wasn't fast enough. If I had just been a second sooner I would have had her," Spence said.

"That might not have saved her either. The flood could have pulled you into the water also and we would have lost both of you," Hess replied.

The man's words made sense, but they didn't help the way Spence was feeling. It was as if he had been given a new life and suddenly had it all washed away.

"I'm leaving in the morning. There's no reason to stay here now. Even if I did stay, I would constantly be reminded of Emily. I couldn't face having to see Will and Francis and Davie either," Spence told Hess.

"Why don't you take a little time and think it over before you make a hasty decision like that. I know this hurts real bad right now, but time will heal your wound," Hess replied.

"No, I've already made up my mind. Let the Colonel know my decision and thank him for all his has done for me. I just have to get out of this valley right now," Spence said.

"You know that your cabin and land will be waiting for you whenever you decide to return. The Colonel never backs off on any deal, and will hold it for your return," Hess stated.

"Thank him for his kindness and if I decide to return, I'll ride in and let him know."

Spence and Hess watched the group slowly break up. The women had brought food and cooked more at the Harris cabin and they were guiding Will and Francis back towards the cabin. The families would camp around the farmhouse for a few days, giving the family comfort and support for their grief. Martha and Helen had both lost a child over the years and they knew how Francis was feeling. They kept their children from bothering Will and Francis and fed Davie Elliot more than he wanted.

The Goodman brothers tended Will's fields for him and Hank went around checking equipment and repairing what he could. The Colonel had Hank bring over another mule to replace the one lost in the flood. Everyone did what little they could, but knew it would never be enough to replace Emily.

Francis had clung to Sarah throughout the ordeal. Sarah thought that it was because she was almost the same age as Emily had been. She kept with Francis, and helped as she could, but couldn't do much due to her pregnancy.

"Leaving without saying anything to the Harris family?" Hess asked.

"Said my good-byes as I was apologizing for not being able to save their daughter. I see Emily's face every time I look at Francis. The look of relief that had come over Emily when she saw I was there, and then the look of terror as the water washed over her. I will remember that as long as I live," Spence said.

Will turned and looked over at Spence and Hess. He was still stunned at the suddenly lost of his daughter, and knew that Spence was feeling equally as bad. He wanted to comfort the young man, but he didn't know how. All he could feel was his own grief. He couldn't even comfort his wife right now. Turning, he gave a short wave to Spence and then continued on to his cabin.

Davie had walked up and now stood with the two men.

"Leaving soon? I don't blame you. It is going to be bad around here for a while. I miss her already, and I know my folks are feeling real bad," Davie said.

Spence reached out and pulled Davie next to him. "I know how you feel. I think the bottom has fallen out. I hope your folks understand why I must ride away from this valley," Spence said.

"Maybe not right away, but eventually, when the pain subsides some. Pa probably already knows but don't know what to say to you. For Ma, it'll take a while longer. Just be sure to come back this way before too long," Davie said as he took Spence's hand and shook it before he walked down towards his Pa.

"Quite an intelligent young man. He's a credit to the valley," Hess remarked.

Spence turned, took a couple steps and then turned back to Hess, "Tell George and the boys good bye for me and encourage them to bring their families as soon as possible. Life is too short not to have your family around you."

Hess watched Spence walk away and thought about the man's last words. *Too bad that he had found out too late how precious a family can be,* thought Hess.

The next morning found Spence already riding down the valley. He did not know where he was going, but he knew it would be out of this valley in the Coastal Del Rey Mountains.

Welcome to the world of Domhan Books! Domhan, pronounced DOW-ann, is the Irish word for universe. Our vision is to provide readers with high-quality hardcover, paperback and electronic books in a variety of genres from writers all over the world.

ORDERING INFORMATION
All Domhan paper books may be ordered from Barnes and Noble, barnesandnoble.com, Amazon, Borders, and other fine booksellers using the ISBN. They are distributed worldwide by Ingram Book Group, 1 Ingram Blvd., La Vergne, Tennessee 37086 (615) 793-5000. Most titles are also available electronically in a variety of formats through Galaxy Library at www.galaxylibrary.com. Rocket *eBook*™ editions are available on-line at barnesand noble.com, Powell's, and other booksellers. Please visit our website for previews, reviews, and further details on our titles: www.domhanbooks.com. Domhan Books, 9511 Shore Road, Suite 514, Brooklyn, New York 11209 U.S.A.

ACTION AND ADVENTURE
Paladin - Barry Nugent 1-58345-365-2 192 pp. $12.95
Princess Yasmin must go on a quest for a mythical crown, the only thing that can prevent civil war erupting in the exotic land of Primera. Along the way she meets her favorite adventure author Barnaby Jackson, and the sparks really start to fly. This is a taut action novel reminiscent of the Indiana Jones series of films.

Yala - Don Clark 1-58345-561-2 180 pp. $12.95
In the no man's land between the U.S. and Mexico in 1896, a Chinese clan stakes a claim to a new territory. Two Texas Rangers decide to end their law officer careers and go to New China in order to raise the bankroll needed to start a ranch. Hank and his younger sidekick, Luke, soon meet Yala, a condemned and notorious Chinese criminal: a female assassin.

MYSTERY
St. John's Baptism - William Babula 1-58345-496-9 260 pp. $12.95
In this first of the Jeremiah St. John series, the hero is summoned to a meeting by Rick Silverman, one of San Francisco's most prominent drug attorneys. St. John knows Silverman's unsavory clientele and so does not think anything of the invitation—that is until he finds Silverman dead.

According to St. John - William Babula 1-58345-521-9 240 pp. $12.95
In this second St. John adventure, St. John's friend Denise is supposed to be in Frisco appearing in a new production of *Macbeth* with legendary

actress Amanda Cole. They arrive at the theater only to discover that Amanda has been murdered and Denise is the prime suspect. St. John soon learns that everyone involved is playing a role. By the time they track down the killer, St. John and his intrepid colleagues uncover some horrifying secrets from the past, and the mind-boggling motive.

St. John and the Seven Veils - William Babula   1-58345-506-X 208 pp. $12.95

In this third mystery in the popular series, St John and his two partners Mickey and Chief Moses are hired to track down a serial killer by a woman claiming to be the killer's mother! Three men have been brutally murdered, but they are without any apparent connection until St. John stumbles across one through a seemingly unrelated case. From the Seven Veils Brothel in Reno to a hideout in Northern California, St John is hot on the trail, crossing paths with a famous televangelist, prominent military man, high-powered doctor, and a complete madman.

St. John's Bestiary - William Babula 1-58345-511-6 264 pp. $12.95

St. John should never have taken this fourth case. But he just couldn't help it — Professor Krift's story of his eight stolen cats strikes a sympathetic chord. After rescuing the victims from a ruthless gang of animal rights activists, the CFAF, he is caught catnapping as the CFAF kidnap the professor's daughter. Suddenly the morgue is filling up, and not just with strangers. St. John's new love Ollie is killed, and he determines to stop at nothing until her murder is avenged. The tangled case drags him through every racket going: money laundering, dope pushing, porno, prostitution, and very nearly drags him six foot under.

St. John's Bread - William Babula 1-58345-516-7 hardcover 180 pp. $18.95;
1-58345-516-7 paper $12.95

In this fifth volume of the series, St. John and his two intrepid partners get caught up in a tangle of missing children's cases after he and Mickey rescue a baby about to be kidnapped in a public park. Mickey tries to tell him that he needs the "bread" to pay for his brand new Victorian stately home which houses him and their detective agency, but this case comes with a higher price tag than any of them are willing to pay.

THRILLERS
The Delaney Escape - Brent Kroetch 1-58345-021-1 264 pp. $12.95

Ex-CIA agent turned IRA man Noel Delaney plans to escape from Leavenworth prison.

Guy Morgan, an ex-agent trained by Delaney, is determined to track his old mentor down. He teams up with his long-time love, Karly Widman of British Intelligence, to trace Delaney's movements to Ireland. But the trap springs. Who is the hunter, and who the prey?

WESTERNS

West of Appomattox - Harley Duncan 1-58345-404-7 212 pp. $12.95

After the Civil War, a group of rugged and disgruntled soldiers seek their fame and fortune west of Appomattox in the new Mexican territory, with explosive results. This is a fine new novel sure to please devotees of the western genre.

Blow-Up at Three Springs - Colby Wolford 1-58345-541-8 148 pp. $10

The town took away Frank Gilman's badge, called him a killer, and treated him like dirt when he refused to turn tail and run, and started a stagecoach line with his brother Todd. Frank knew that Deejohn was behind his troubles. The town's biggest rancher, he was arrogant enough to believe he could bend the law any way he liked. Then one day Martha Lexter arrives at the railhead to threaten Deejohn and his empire. Deejohn will stop at nothing to get rid of her. Frank is faced with a choice: ignore Martha, or sell her a seat on his stage, an act which will certainly unleash Deejohn's pack of hired killers, and split Three Springs right down its seams!

The Guns of Witchwater - Colby Wolford 1-58345-525-6 248 pp. $12.95

Winter Santrell is a young peddler who tries to stay out of trouble. But unable to resist a damsel in distress, he comes to the aid of Vivian Kern, desperate for money to save her ranch after her father's death. The whole town of Witchwater is paralyzed with fear as a pack of renegades led by Baird Stark ride rough-shod over them. Santell decides to stand up for the people of the town, even though a few of them are mighty tempted to take up the thousand dollar reward that Stark puts on his corpse!

The Iron Corral - Colby Wolford 1-58345-533-7 160 pp. $10

When drifter Dan Allard takes the Sheriff's badge in La Mancha, he and his deputy Owen Fielding lock horns with Harlan Younger and his tough gang, who are determined to drive the lawmen out of town.

Soon the banker, Jabe Miller, is murdered, and Owen is framed for the crime. Even his own friends and family turn against Dan as he struggles to bring Harlan to justice and clear Owen's name.

Stranger in the Land - Colby Wolford 1-58345-529-9 160 pp. $10

Derek Langton, ex-English cavalry officer, is a stranger in a strange land when he heads out west at the close of the Civil War. He has come to claim his inheritance, the Tower Ranch and fertile Strip with its wild, unbranded cattle. But others covet the Strip, especially Delphine Judson and her gun-toting crew. Derek must fight for his very survival to make a home for himself in his new-found land.

Green Grown the Rushes - Shirley and Nelson Wolford 1-58345-522-3 244 pp. $12.95

Lieutenant Boyd Regan is unjustly despised by his fellow soldiers and hated by the Mexicans of Alta Lowa. He is scorned by the woman he loves, half-Mexican beauty Catrina MacLeod, and her blonde sister Jennie. He is unfairly accused, tried and convicted for treating the Mexican peasants cruelly.

Yet if Mexican general Santa Anna obtains artillery, he will destroy Mexico City and all the American troops in it. Only Boyd stands in the way of complete annihilation of the entire city, even Mexico itself....

The Southern Blade - Shirley and Nelson Wolford 1-58345-537-X 168 pp. $10.00

Seven rebel prisoners on a desperate flight for freedom....

The Civil War is in its last days, but these prisoners only know they want their freedom. They are willing to risk hostile Indians and the even more dangerous climate of New Mexico. Lieutenant Sawling leads the motley group on their journey, pursued by the relentless Union captain who has sworn to retake and hang them. The only thing standing between them and the gallows is a beautiful young woman they have taken as hostage....

The Whispering Cannon - Shirley and Nelson Wolford 1-58345-545-0 184 pp. $10.95

Craig Dixon attracted trouble. A war correspondent, he was banned from the battlefield after criticizing Zachary Taylor's 1847 campaign against the Mexicans. But Dixon simply had to be where the news was being made. So he enlists as an officer in the Texas Volunteers, and is chosen as a messenger to get vital information to Taylor. The Mexicans will wipe Taylor's men out unless Dixon can get to him in time and persuade Taylor he is telling the truth.

ORDERING INFORMATION

All Domhan paper books may be ordered from Barnes and Noble, barnesandnoble.com, Amazon, Borders, and other fine booksellers using the ISBN. They are distributed worldwide by Ingram Book Group, 1 Ingram Blvd., La Vergne, TN 37086, 615 793-5000.

Most titles are also available electronically in a variety of formats through Galaxy Library at www.galaxylibrary.com. Rocket eBook editions are available on-line at barnesandnoble.com, Powell's, and other fine booksellers. Please visit our website for previews, reviews, and further details on our titles: www.domhanbooks.com

Domhan Books, 9511 Shore Road, Suite 514, Brooklyn, NY 11209